By day, **Maggie Wells** i  she pens tales of intrigue
She has a weakness for h
the product of a charmi
you only have to scratch the surface of this mild-mannered
married lady to find a naughty streak a mile wide.

Addison Fox is a lifelong romance reader, addicted to
happily-ever-afters. After discovering she found as much
joy writing about romance as she did reading it, she's
never looked back. Addison lives in New York with an
apartment full of books, a laptop that's rarely out of sight
and a wily beagle who keeps her running. You can find
her at her home on the web at addisonfox.com or on
Facebook at Facebook.com/addisonfoxauthor and Twitter
@addisonfox.

Discover more at millsandboon.co.uk

OZARKS WITNESS PROTECTION

MAGGIE WELLS

UNDER COLTON'S WATCH

ADDISON FOX

MILLS & BOON

First Published in Great Britain 2023
by Mills & Boon, an imprint of HarperCollins*Publishers* Ltd
1 London Bridge Street, London, SE1 9GF

www.harpercollins.co.uk

HarperCollins*Publishers*
Macken House, 39/40 Mayor Street Upper,
Dublin 1, D01 C9W8, Ireland

Ozarks Witness Protection © 2023 Margaret Ethridge
Under Colton's Watch © 2023 Harlequin Enterprises ULC.

Special thanks and acknowledgement are given to Addison Fox for her contribution to *The Coltons of New York* series.

ISBN: 978-0-263-30730-6

0623

OZARKS WITNESS PROTECTION

MAGGIE WELLS

For Julie. You are everything light, bright and beautiful, and I am thrilled to call you my friend.
Team Awesome rules!

Chapter One

Kayla Powers never imagined there would be a day when she'd consider a half-mile walk down her driveway to be meditative, but then again, her life was full of surprises these days. Some good, some horrifically bad. Some simply…surprising. She pressed her hand to her stomach and drew in a deep breath of fresh air.

Sobriety made a person look at things in a different light.

Before now, she would have never labeled herself an alcoholic. She'd been a rebellious drinker in high school, a party girl in her undergrad days and an I-earned-this tippler all through law school. After she'd entered the workforce, she'd slid effortlessly into the postwork-drinks crowd, and later into the wives-gathered-in-the-kitchen-swilling-wine set. But until she'd watched the footage captured by the security cameras the weekend her husband and his son were murdered, she'd never considered her drinking an issue.

Talk about a wake-up call. And only the first of many.

She bent to pick up a particularly vivid leaf from a red maple and twirled it by its stem. Nearly two months had come and gone. Time was flying and moving at a snail's pace all at once. Due to the nature of Tyrone's murder and the subsequent ongoing investigation, she hadn't been able to submerge herself in the details of death—the suitable black dress, the music selections for the memorial service, what food they'd provide for her fellow mourners. Looking back on it now, it felt like she'd gone from the discovery of their bodies into the deep end of the ocean.

Only the presence of her right-hand woman and newly minted best friend, Michelle Fraser, kept her grounded. But the thought that woke her early in the morning wasn't one she'd dared speak aloud. Not even to Michelle, who was not only her friend, but also Kayla's personal attorney and therefore bound by attorney-client privilege to keep her secrets. She couldn't. Not until she was certain.

Michelle was an undercover federal agent and attorney who'd embedded herself in the fabric of Powers, Powers & Walton. Even after her investigation had revealed the financial crime of the law firm's elder statesman, Harold Dennis, and cast dark shadows over the Powers name, she'd stayed on to help.

Michelle took over the running of the firm Tyrone had left to Kayla, allowing her the quiet month she'd spent "processing" his death at a treatment facility known for their discretion. In truth, her friend had driven her right to the front door of the facility and left her there with a promise to return in thirty days.

Like clockwork, Michelle showed up at Briarwood when the month was over and greeted Kayla with an anger-meltingly warm hug and an enormous peanut-butter-cup, ice-cream blender from the nearest dairy bar.

Kayla had been forced to admit her friend had been right on a number of levels before Michelle agreed to hand over the treat. And nothing had ever felt—or tasted—so good to her.

Since she'd found her husband murdered, Kayla had taken to eating her feelings. Her sweet tooth had been nearly insatiable. She'd put on ten pounds and was reduced to selecting the day's outfit from the section of her closet comprised of Lycra-enhanced ensembles, but she couldn't quite bring herself to care too much about her appearance.

She felt good.

Healthy.

Grounded.

Her newfound peace of mind also came with a side order of survivor's guilt, but she had a therapist to help her work through those issues.

She was alive and well, working herself up to taking over the empire the man she'd loved had entrusted to her. She didn't have time to worry about a few extra pounds.

Michelle even had the nerve to tell her she looked better with the extra weight. But she didn't have her friend's beautifully rounded curves, nor had she been so fashionably thin the gains weren't noticeable.

Therefore, she walked the half-mile to the end of the drive and back again each day. Pumping her arms slightly faster, she vowed to make the mostly uphill trek back at the same pace. The house had a home gym, but she liked being outdoors. Walking the driveway and wandering the sprawling house counted as cardio as far as Kayla was concerned. And, since she was never going back to the house where her husband was killed, the lake house would be her home base until she got her legs under her.

Continuing to twirl the stem of the leaf between her thumb and middle finger, she rounded the bend in the road leading to the gate. The heavy old wrought iron stood stalwart between her and the outside world. The mailbox was built into one of the brick pillars that supported the ostentatious gate with its stylized *P* worked into its curlicues.

The walk was an exercise in futility on top of being exercise for the body. There was rarely anything but junk mail in the box. The need to have mail delivered to their remote lake house was a relic from the days when Tyrone's father refused to leave town without every available means of communication.

In the years since she'd married Ty, Kayla never thought to check the box. The caretaker who came by once a week to do routine maintenance gathered anything of importance and forwarded it all to the PP&W offices. But the day Michelle had driven her back here, she'd spotted the mailbox as they waited for the gate to open and decided the walk down the drive and back daily would do her some good.

A few yards from the gate, she stopped, reached into a neatly trimmed boxwood hedge and lifted the cover on a concealed keypad. When Tyrone first showed her the hidden control panel, she'd laughed. It seemed like one of those ridiculous, rich-people things to do—hiding an unsightly keypad in a hedge. Now each time she reached into the shrub, she heard his voice reciting the code and repeating it over and over.

"Eight-six-three-seven," she whispered to his memory.

Kayla had never considered herself a particularly spiritual person. She didn't get all woo-woo about being in touch with her late husband. She missed talking to him. The scent of him. Sharing her thoughts with a man who appreciated her mind as well as her body.

But he was gone, and in the past month she'd done her best to come to terms with that distasteful fact. If her stint in rehab had taught her anything, it was how to live in the here and now.

Stepping back, she smirked as the iron gate began its slow swing on creaking hinges. This was all part of the routine. And routines were important these days. Routines kept her tethered.

With the gate standing wide open, she walked around to the other side of the column and pulled the latch on the metal box. She stuck her hand in to be sure she'd gathered everything. An office-supply company was pushing a special on copy paper and there was a notice from the marina where Tyrone had the family's boats serviced and stored for the winter.

She hadn't thought much about boats lately. She certainly hadn't thought about going out on the lake. Tyrone's son, Trey, had been under indictment when they were killed. He'd been awaiting trial in the death of a young woman who'd either fallen or been pushed overboard while riding on Trey's boat.

Another unsolved death.

Michelle had been defending Trey on behalf of Powers, Powers & Walton, the firm Ty's father had founded. Kayla was relieved Michelle had agreed to act as her counselor after the murders, and grateful when she agreed to take leave from the FBI in order to stay on and keep the firm on an even keel until Kayla could come back at full strength.

The time had come.

Kayla expected to step into the role of managing partner at Powers, Powers & Walton. She also planned to do her level best to convince Michelle to give up her work with the Bureau and stay on at PP&W.

She was fairly certain she might be able to recruit Lieutenant Ethan Scott, the detective assigned to investigate the deaths of her husband and stepson, as an ally in her campaign to convince Michelle to stay. There was something going on between them, even if her friend had remained frustratingly reticent about the relationship under her cross-examination.

Kayla stooped to check the box one last time to make sure she'd gathered every last circular. As she straightened, she heard a loud pop behind her. She spun around as a hot gust of wind whooshed by her and a sharp searing pain ripped through her left arm.

"What the—"

She looked down and saw the sleeve of her shirt was torn. Blood seeped through the fabric. Pressing the hand holding the sale flyers over the hole, she scanned the area on the opposite side of the lake road.

But she saw no movement.

Not surprising. The whole area was heavily wooded. A good chunk of the land was owned by the Powers Family Trust, but a number of acres were leased out to hunting clubs. It wouldn't be unheard of for a bullet to go astray in these woods, but she was fairly sure the noise she heard had not come from a rifle. No. A handgun. Someone had fired a handgun out here. At her.

She dropped the junk mail, then held her injured arm as she ran back through the gate.

She grimaced as she poked at the control panel concealed in the hedge with fingers trembling and smeared with her own blood.

"Come on," she whispered, her voice shaking nearly as much as her hand.

She felt a trickle of blood run down her arm, and she jabbed at the button again.

"Come on, come on, come on," she repeated through clenched teeth as the ancient gate finally swung into motion. Then, realizing the rusty iron bars would provide no cover, she wedged herself into the neatly trimmed boxwood hedge, hoping it might conceal her as well as it did the control panel for the gate.

Her mind whirred while she waited to hear the solid *ka-thunk* of the gate latch falling into place.

She'd been foolish to refuse the offer of having a police

officer on scene. With Tyrone and Trey's murderer still at large, both the Arkansas State Police and the Carroll County Sheriff's Department had offered protection. But she'd turned them down, thinking she'd be safe at the lake house. Who would come all the way out here to take a shot at her?

"Someone who doesn't want me coming back to Bentonville," she muttered under her breath.

She leaned out of the hedge, impervious to the sharp pokes and jabs from the shrub.

She heard a motor start and prayed the damn gate would latch already.

Tempted to run out and shove it closed, she froze when an engine revved. She hadn't even had time to sink back into the shrub when a pickup truck roared up the road, slowing as it passed the gate.

Biting her lip to keep from making a noise, she stared hard at the vehicle and tried to take in as much as she could. New. An import. No rusted-out Chevy or Ford for this hunter. She squinted, trying to get a look at the driver. But the sun glinted off the windshield, and all she could make out was the shadow of a man.

Something about him was breathtakingly familiar. This was a man she knew. But from where?

And why would he shoot at her?

Try as she might, Kayla couldn't get her brain to engage.

The gate finally clanged to a close, and the sound seemed to startle the driver into action. He cut the wheel hard to the left and peeled away from the driveway, sending up a spray of loose gravel when he caught the shoulder of the county road. She ran back to the gate and craned her neck but could not get a clear view of the license plate.

The vehicle was either a dusty black or dark gray. Dual rear tires. These details might help make it easier to spot here, where the locals would disparage anything not made by an American car company.

The moment the sound of the truck's engine faded away she took off and started up the drive. She kept her head low and stuck close to the tree line until she knew she was around the bend. The gate would stop a car, but it would prove no deterrent if her assailant decided to pull over and hoof it through the woods. She needed to get to the house.

Who was he?

Recognition niggled at her, but she didn't take time to puzzle it out. The parcel of the lakefront real estate the first Tyrone Powers had snatched up not long after the US Army Corps of Engineers dammed the White River was massive and largely unfenced. And the waterfront was entirely unprotected. Table Rock Lake's many inlets and hidden coves could provide the perfect access point for anyone who wanted to get to the house.

The house she'd left completely unlocked.

What had she been thinking?

Kayla trotted along the edge of the drive, thankful the property sloped down toward the waterfront. She slowed to a fast walk when she caught sight of the turreted roofline of the pseudo castle Tyrone Powers Senior had built as a testament to his wealth. Feeling slightly safer away from the road, she patted the side pocket of her yoga pants, then grimaced.

No phone.

A glance down at the bloody streaks she'd left on the fabric added insult to injury. She gritted her teeth and allowed herself a soft hiss as she covered the wound with her hand again. Steeling herself against the pain, she flexed the fingers of her left hand to confirm the arm was still in working order despite the fire radiating from her bicep.

When she entered treatment, she'd willingly handed over

her cell phone, knowing Michelle or Lieutenant Scott could get ahold of her whenever necessary. In the three days since she checked herself out, Kayla had almost forgotten what it was like to check her phone constantly, and now made a conscious effort to move about in the world without it.

In the weeks she'd been away, she'd become accustomed to going without her phone. Life without a constant source of communication proved to be refreshing,

Following the arrest of Harold Dennis they'd been inundated by both local and national media. Harold was believed to be the mastermind behind a Ponzi scheme dedicated to funneling money into a political-action committee used to fund Senator William Powers's campaigns. With charges of fraud and money laundering pending, and proof Harold had a private jet at his disposal, the attorney who'd once been her husband's mentor was being held in the Benton County Correctional Facility while various government agencies battled it out to see which one would get to charge him first.

The ties to Senator William Powers and allegations of possible campaign-finance violations were chum to the media frenzy. The arrest compounded the notoriety gained by an unsolved double homicide and the possible murder—or at best negligent homicide—of a local young woman, Mallory Murray.

All in all, the Powers family had become lightning rods for news stories guaranteed to make readers say "No way!" as they gobbled up the details.

The stress of being left in charge of the family firm, her grief over the loss of her husband and the trauma of being the one to find his body had nearly broken her. Nearly, but not quite, thanks to her best friend. Within a week, she was downing more than a bottle of wine a night. Barely ten days after Harold's arrest, Michelle and the ever-present Ethan Scott staged a sort of intervention.

Thank goodness.

But she regretted her insistence on staying isolated and disconnected at the moment.

Hustling up the lane, she focused on the front door. She couldn't think too hard about the pain in her arm or possible blood loss.

"Fool, fool, fool," she murmured.

What made her think she was safe here when Tyrone hadn't been safe in their own home in the middle of town? Someone could have walked right in while she was out strolling along picking up leaves. She might as well have left a pie baking on the windowsill and rolled out a red carpet for a welcome mat.

Still, instinct told her inside was better than outside. Besides, she needed to call for help.

"Get inside, get inside," she whispered to herself.

Kayla stumbled over the threshold and made a beeline for the back of the house. Her cell would be in her purse, but she wouldn't bother trying to locate it now. Instead, she headed for the ancient phone mounted on the kitchen wall.

She'd teased Tyrone for insisting on keeping a landline connected, but cellular service could be sporadic in the area. Aside from the wall-mounted handset in the kitchen, there was a multiline speakerphone in Ty's former office. It was another relic of his father's days at the helm, but Ty could never bring himself to cut the cord.

Chest heaving, she snatched the kitchen phone from its cradle and fumbled it with fingers sticky with drying blood. She managed to press the numbers 911, then raised the receiver to her ear. The call didn't go through right away and the silence on the other end shot a fresh burst of panic through her. What if the person who'd shot her had cut the phone lines?

Gripping the receiver, she lunged for her handbag. But to her relief, the call connected at last and the line began to ring.

"Carroll County emergency," a woman with a thick drawl answered. "Police, fire or medical emergency?"

"Uh…" Kayla hesitated, her brain freezing. The only thing she could rule out for certain was fire. "Not fire," she blurted.

"Police or medical?" the dispatcher repeated.

"Both," Kayla said, her voice a hoarse whisper.

She gritted her teeth as her breaths came short and fast. Her vision blurred around the edges. She blinked and tried to lock in on something solid. Immovable. But everything was getting fuzzy, and she couldn't force her gaze to light on any one item.

"I need help," she said weakly "I've been—"

Her knees turned to jelly, and she grabbed the side of the kitchen island in a vain attempt to stay upright. But it was no good. She'd reached out with her left arm and a fresh lightning bolt of pain brought her to her knees.

"What kind of help, ma'am?" the dispatcher replied. "Ma'am?"

Kayla tried to form words, but the only ones that sprang to mind were so incomprehensible to her she couldn't make them come out.

"Ma'am?" the dispatcher said sharply, and Kayla let out a soft moan. "Ma'am? Stay with me," the dispatcher implored. "What can I do for you?"

"I've been—" Kayla tried to take a deep breath, but her chest felt like a cartoon coyote had dropped an anvil on it and blackness narrowed her blurry vision to pinpoints.

"Shot," she said at last. "I've been shot."

As the darkness closed in, she thought of the pregnancy

tests she'd planned to purchase when she went into Eureka Springs. "Please, please," she whispered, her hand moving to cover her stomach as consciousness slipped out of her grasp.

Chapter Two

Kayla woke up in a room so preternaturally white, for a moment she thought it might be heaven. This antiseptic, blinding room was not painted one of the many shades of white the decorator had used in the sumptuous living room of her Bentonville house.

A beautiful house she'd never live in again.

This was not the house where Ty had been killed. The thought gave her a modicum of relief. But where was she now?

An overhead light glared down at her. She squeezed her eyes shut against the pain, but the brightness seared through to the inside of her eyelids, turning them a glowing orange. For a second, she wondered if she'd passed out at the dentist's office, but then she heard the blip of a machine and felt the squeeze of a blood-pressure cuff on her right arm.

"She's coming around," a brisk female voice said from somewhere behind her.

Coming around. Kayla wondered what the words were supposed to mean. She hadn't agreed to any of this. She closed her eyes again, wishing herself back into the oblivion, but then another voice broke through.

"Mrs. Powers?"

She flinched but didn't open her eyes. Kayla didn't recognize this woman's voice, either, and she wasn't entirely certain she wanted to give up her identity so readily. Something prickled at the back of her mind.

Danger.

Crack.

Shot.

At last, her eyes flew open. She found a blond woman with a stethoscope draped around her neck peering down at her, her own eyes narrowed with focus.

"Mrs. Powers?" she asked again, but the use of her name was more statement than inquisition.

Kayla returned her stare. "Who are you?"

"I'm Dr. Michaelson. You're in Emergency at Eureka Springs Hospital. Do you remember how you came to be here?"

"Nine-one-one," Kayla croaked as a flood of memory washed over her.

Shot.

Crack.

Danger.

Was this woman going to help her? She gave her head a shake to clear it, but a sharp lancing pain raced from the back of her scalp down to her neck and radiated through her body. The doctor placed a gentle hand on her arm to still her.

Kayla grimaced. "What happened?"

"We think you hit your head when you passed out. The EMT said it looked like you might have banged it against the corner of a cabinet."

"Passed out," Kayla repeated. Had she been drunk? No. Not drunk. No drinking. Hurt. She closed her eyes. "Hurts."

"Yes," the doctor confirmed. "You were injured. Do you remember calling emergency?"

She made a noise she hoped passed for an affirmative, because speaking and nodding were proving to be equally disagreeable. Bile churned in her stomach as flashes of the trek back up her driveway played through her mind.

Shot.

The conclusion ricocheted around in her head like her assailant had pulled the trigger on it. She'd been shot in the arm. But she couldn't feel her arm. Had they taken it off? She wanted to open her eyes to check, but the second she tried to move her head, the pain came rushing back on a wave of nausea. She squeezed her eyes shut and managed a whispered reply. "Shot."

"Yes." She could hear Dr. Michaelson moving about the small space. "It appears you were shot in the left arm. Do you know how it happened?"

"Mail," Kayla replied, grimacing at the discomfort the single word unleashed.

"A male shot you?" the doctor asked, moving closer again.

Kayla chanced a peek through slit eyelids. "Yes. No," she corrected. "Can someone turn off the light?"

She heard a *click*, and the searing orange glow behind her eyelids dimmed. She exhaled but couldn't bring herself to open her eyes quite yet.

"I was getting the mail, but the person who shot at me was male. M-a-l-e," she added for clarity. The moment the letters left her lips, she began to doubt she'd selected the correct homonym. "As in male man." She gritted her teeth again as her word choice registered. "Male as in a human male," she corrected. "Not a mailman."

"I see."

Kayla cracked an eyelid and saw the doctor glancing up at someone on the other side of the room. She wanted to turn her head, but the pain stopped her. She sucked in a sharp breath, then asked breathlessly, "Who's over there?"

"Deputy Forester, ma'am." The response came from a nervous-sounding young man. "Carroll County Sheriff's Department. I responded to your call along with the EMTs from the Beaver Township Volunteer Fire Department."

"I see," Kayla said softly. "Thank you."

He shifted uncomfortably, then responded. "My pleasure to help, ma'am. Now, so I'm clear, the person who shot at you was a man, but not a mailman. Am I correct, ma'am?" he asked in his soft drawl.

"Correct."

"Deputy, if you don't mind waiting a few more minutes to interview Mrs. Powers, I'd like to go through a few routine tests with her and maybe help her get a little more comfortable," Dr. Michaelson interjected.

"Of course." The young man sounded abashed. "I'll step outside?"

The doctor nodded. "Yes, please. And I know the drill—none of the good pain meds until you've taken her statement."

"Thank you, ma'am, um, I mean, doctor," he corrected.

"A nurse will be out to get you as soon as we're finished in here."

Kayla let her eyes slide shut again as the metal rings holding the curtain surrounding them rang out. She took three long, careful breaths, releasing each one as gently as she could. Doing her utmost to avoid moving too much.

"Mrs. Powers?" Dr. Michaelson said gently.

"I'm awake," Kayla responded. "But can I keep my eyes shut for now? My head is killing me."

The doctor murmured something to her nurse. "We can give you some analgesics if you think you can keep them down."

"Yes. Thank you."

The doctor adjusted the blood-pressure cuff on her arm.

Kayla felt the cool press of a stethoscope in the crook of her arm. "I'm going take your vitals, but then I'm afraid I'll need you to open your eyes when we do the cognitive exam, okay?"

"Okay," Kayla replied.

Wincing, she submitted to the thermometer under her tongue and the squeezing of her arm from the inflating cuff. She assumed the steady *beep-beep-beep* of the machine behind her was driven by the pulse monitor clipped to her index finger. She focused on keeping her breaths as even as she could while they noted her readings, but she couldn't help dreading the moment they asked her to open her eyes again. She'd been shot in the arm, not the head. How hard did she fall?

"Okay, then," the doctor said as the pressure from the cuff released and the stethoscope was removed. "You can keep them closed for a minute more. Marcy's going to get you an ice pack and some ibuprofen."

"God bless Marcy," Kayla whispered.

She could hear the smile in the doctor's voice when she responded. "I say the exact same thing several times a day."

"Come on now. Y'all are going to make me blush," the efficient nurse replied. "Back in a sec."

Kayla chanced opening an eyelid and allowed herself a soft groan. The woman standing on the other side of her bed was short, unsmiling. She wasn't plump so much as perfectly rounded. Some women had the good fortune to have all their body weight distributed evenly. Like her friend Michelle, the stranger in the pale blue scrubs looked like a cartoon pinup girl.

A cartoon pinup girl who not only had a license to practice law, but also a badge and a gun to go with it. She needed to call Michelle.

"I need to make a call," she said.

"Sure. In a minute," the doctor said distractedly.

Kayla was mustering the energy to push, when the curtain parted and a nurse she assumed was Marcy reappeared. She gulped the pills given to her in a plastic cup, swallowing them without water, but took a grateful sip when offered. She blinked once, twice, then sighed as Marcy gingerly slid the gel pack she'd activated to the base of Kayla's skull.

"Marry me," Kayla said with a tight half-smile.

"I doubt your husband would appreciate you dumping him for a girl with a cold pack," the nurse said with a teasing smile.

"My husband is dead," Kayla said, letting her eyes fall shut again.

A heavy blanket of awkwardness fell over the room. Kayla didn't need to open her eyes to know she'd wiped the sassy smile right off the other woman's face. But Marcy was no pushover for emotion, and she obviously wasn't the kind of woman who let embarrassment overtake good manners. "I am sorry to hear."

"He was killed," Kayla said in a voice as rough as sandpaper.

She opened her eyes again in time to see Marcy draw in on a sharp intake of breath, even though she was wearing a mask. Sugarcoating the truth wouldn't help. She had to make these women aware that she—and they, by association—might be in peril.

Kayla forced herself to look up directly into the doctor's concerned gaze. "He was shot. In our home. In Bentonville."

"I see," Dr. Michaelson said quietly.

"Do you want me to ask the deputy to come back in?" Marcy asked without missing a beat.

Kayla wanted to shake her head, but she couldn't work

up the strength. "No. Not yet. I need my phone. There's a lieutenant with the Arkansas State Police who's working the case," she informed them. "Ethan Scott."

"I'll give the deputy Lieutenant Scott's name," Marcy promised. "As for your phone, let me go check to see what the EMTs brought in with you. They would have looked for ID. They may have grabbed your whole purse."

The curtain swished shut behind her, and Kayla allowed her eyelids to slide shut again. "You may want to ask the deputy to stay nearby," she said, knowing the doctor hadn't moved one millimeter from where she'd been a moment before.

"I have no doubt Marcy has already given Deputy Forester more instructions than any man could want," she replied evenly.

"How bad is my arm?" Kayla asked, her voice shaky.

"Not bad at all."

"I can't feel it," she noted.

"The magic of a local anesthetic. I sewed you up as best I could, but it's a gouge of a flesh wound. Like a deep scrape, which can hurt like the devil."

"Like getting a bad paper cut. Might as well lop the whole hand off," Kayla said quietly.

"Exactly. Sometimes the nonfatal wounds hurt the most."

Kayla needed this dark oblivion a few minutes longer. "Pretty profound, Doctor," she said quietly.

The other woman placed a hand on her shoulder. "Rest for a few minutes. I'll speak to the deputy. Maybe he can reach out to your lieutenant, and you can answer all their questions at once."

Kayla felt one corner of her mouth twitch up involuntarily. "He's not my lieutenant," she said with a rueful little smile.

"But his and my best friend Michelle Fraser's numbers should both be programmed into my phone."

"Any family we should contact?"

Kayla's throat ran dry. She licked her lips, hoping she could force out the sad syllable trapped there. "No. Michelle can handle everything."

The doctor gave her wrist a squeeze, then stepped away from the exam table. "I hear that. As long as you've got a best girlfriend, you've got everything you need to get through this."

"Not only is she my emergency contact, but she's also my attorney."

"I've already made a note of her name," the other woman assured her. "Rest for a few minutes if you can."

When she woke, Kayla couldn't say whether minutes or hours had passed. The moment she'd been left alone, she'd fallen into a deep sleep. The kind too thick for dreams. Thank God. She awoke to find herself peering into the concerned blue eyes of her best friend.

"Hey," she croaked.

"Hey," Michelle responded. "Guess who's not allowed to go to the lake house by herself anymore?" she said in a voice tremulous with emotion.

"I'm going to go out on a limb and say it's me," Kayla rasped.

"Bingo."

"Is Ethan with you?"

"Of course. I sent him to get us coffee. You were pretty zonked out, and the poor deputy out there is drooping."

"Someone shot me."

Michelle gripped the rail on the side of the bed. "I heard a rumor."

"The thing is, I can't be exactly sure, but I can't help thinking the person I saw in the truck reminded me of someone I know."

"Have you been able to piece it together?" Michelle asked, cutting to the chase.

"I want to say it was Del," Michelle said in a strangled whisper. "Actually, I don't want to say it was, but my gut is telling me I saw Del."

Her husband's nephew. Senator William Powers's son. A man she'd once considered a friend. But that was before she'd inherited the law firm his family founded.

"Did you get a good look at him?"

"No. The sunlight was glinting off the windshield. I couldn't swear to it. It's…"

"Okay." Michelle nodded once in simple acceptance.

Kayla looked over at her friend, for a moment marveling how easy the relationship between them was. She'd told Michelle nothing but the unvarnished truth from the day she walked into the house and found Tyrone and Trey dead on the sofa, and Michelle believed her.

"Do I tell Ethan?" Kayla asked, looking her friend directly in the eye.

"Why wouldn't you?" Michelle answered.

Kayla huffed a laugh. "Lawyers. Always answering a question with a question."

Michelle leaned in. "Seriously, why wouldn't you tell Ethan?"

"I didn't see his face. I can't swear to it in court. As far as I know, Del doesn't own a vehicle like the truck I saw. I have no reason to say it's him other than my gut."

She pressed her hand low on her belly, suddenly remembering she'd never taken a pregnancy test. She'd need to talk to Dr. Michaelson. Perhaps she could have her hunch confirmed before she was discharged.

"Gut instinct hasn't steered us wrong yet," Michelle reminded her. "But if it is Del, we're going to have to be careful not to tip our hand. It's bad enough a prominent lawyer and good friend of Senator Powers has been arrested for financial crimes. It's another thing entirely if we go around accusing his only son of attempted homicide without something solid."

"I know. I'm asking you. Do we tell Ethan?"

Michelle nodded. "Yes, but maybe let it sit a bit until you feel more certain. You're shaken up now, and he'll want to go after Del. He won't do anything rash, but things are precarious at the moment."

"One way of putting it," Kayla muttered.

Her friend's eyes twinkled, but her smile was small and reassuring. "When you feel sure you can trust him."

"If you say so, then I do."

Michelle reached over and grasped the hand Kayla had pressed to her belly. Squeezing it hard, she said, "In the meantime, we want to get you some protection. We need to get you away from here." Kayla started to protest, but Michelle only squeezed her hand harder. "Don't argue with me. You know I'm right. Until we can figure out who killed Tyrone and Trey, you're not going to be safe."

"I won't be driven away."

"Your hubris is showing," Michelle said harshly. "Someone shot at you today."

"I know. I was there," Kayla replied. "But I was oblivious. Thought I was impervious. Now I know I'm a target." She met her friend's gaze and held it. "I won't let my guard down again."

"No. And even if you do, I'm making sure someone has your back."

"Michelle—"

Ethan Scott of the Arkansas State Police Criminal Investigation Division chose that moment to make his entrance.

"Knock, knock," he called from the other side of the curtain.

Michelle's face instantly lit, and Kayla found herself so enraptured by the happiness shining from her usually stoic friend's bright eyes that she failed to respond.

"Come in," Michelle said, her smile widening when he extended one of the coffee cups to her. Deputy Forester entered behind them, surreptitiously taking a sip from his own cup, then turned in a tight circle as he looked for a surface to place it on. At last, he settled for placing it on the floor.

"Mrs. Powers, are you up to making a statement now?" he asked, his expression eager as he pulled a phone from his belt.

"Are you going to record it?" Michelle stepped in, always a lawyer first.

"Since Mrs. Powers can't come in to make a statement, it's easier for me to capture everything I need for my report on audio, ma'am. If you prefer, I can type notes." He turned back to Kayla and shrugged. "I'm happy to do whatever works for you."

Kayla and Michelle shared a glance, but Kayla wasn't worried about saying anything wrong. She'd walked to her mailbox and gotten shot. If he pressed about the truck or its driver, she could give a description without naming names.

"I'm okay with recording," she replied. "Easier to do it all at once."

Ethan pulled out his phone, too, and set it beside the deputy's on a small rolling table, but he let the younger man take the lead in gathering her statement. Kayla recounted her walk to the mailbox and the routine she'd fallen into over the course of the week, but not the reasons behind it. She explained the gate setup, and what she'd found in the mailbox.

Closing her eyes, she relived those moments of pain and confusion. And when the deputy asked her for any description she could give for her assailant, she gave him exactly what she remembered seeing.

When she finished, Deputy Forester thanked her for her time, wished her a speedy recovery and left with a promise to stay in touch with her and with the state police.

Michelle stepped over to the curtain, presumably to be sure they would be alone for at least a few minutes. Kayla took the opportunity to close her eyes again, but whatever rest she thought she might get was quickly preempted by Ethan Scott.

"Don't go back to sleep," he ordered in a tone so commanding she couldn't have kept her eyes shut with superglue.

She glared up at him. "I was only resting my eyes. I don't know if anyone told you this, Lieutenant Scott, but I have a mild concussion."

He smirked at her officious tone. They'd moved way past formalities. "Hard to believe someone so hardheaded can be concussed."

"A thick skull makes the brain sloshing more damaging," Michelle said, letting the curtain fall back into place. "She thinks she can go back to the lake house."

Ethan's eyebrows rose as Michelle joined him at her bedside. They stared down at her like disapproving parents. It was enough to get her hackles up. "I know I can go back to the lake house. It's mine and I am not being detained for any legal reason."

"Only logical ones," Ethan said gruffly.

"You have a concussion. You can't be left alone," Michelle began.

"You're welcome to join me for the night," Kayla responded magnanimously. "After you're done updating me on P, P and W, we can play board games and watch movies."

Rather than prickle, Michelle smiled. "An excellent plan. But we need to formulate one that extends beyond tonight."

Ethan spoke quietly. "We need to think about our next steps carefully, but I don't think we can do so without making sure you have security on you 24/7."

"I don't know if I can handle being under surveillance."

"I don't know if you have a choice," Michelle interjected.

"There's always a choice," Ethan replied smoothly. "We are asking you to make the smart one."

"I don't want a deputy parked outside my door all the time."

"I think we're beyond a patrol car as a deterrent," he said gravely. "Someone came after you, Kayla. You don't need a marked car parked outside to scare people off. You need personal protection."

"Like a bodyguard," she stated flatly.

He nodded. "Sort of. I have a friend also with the Arkansas State Police based out of Little Rock who specializes in protective services. I'm going to see if we can get him up here. Given how high-profile these cases have become, I doubt I'll get any pushback."

Gnawing her bottom lip, Kayla sighed and lowered her gaze. "Who is this friend?"

"His name is Special Agent Ryan Hastings. He used to be CID at Little Rock. Now he's a sergeant in the Executive Protection Division."

She sniffed, shifting him a peevish look. "Only a sergeant? Shouldn't I get someone who's at least officer-grade?"

Ethan smirked. "Different division, different rankings, but trust me, you want this guy on your side. He's protected presidents, celebrities, foreign dignitaries…even your brother-in-law."

Kayla and Michelle's gazes met and held at the mention of

Bill Powers. She knew she had to tell Ethan about her suspicions regarding Del.

"I gave Deputy Forester my description of the guy in the truck, but what I didn't say is, I think—" she paused and held up the finger with the pulse oximeter attached for emphasis "—*think*, the person driving it might have been Del Powers."

To his credit, Ethan didn't flinch.

"Did you see him clearly enough to testify?"

"No."

"This is nothing more than an impression?"

"My gut feeling. At first, I couldn't place him. Couldn't figure out what was familiar, but when I woke up, his name popped into my head."

"Noted," Ethan said with a brisk nod. "I'm going to step out and make a couple of calls." He turned to Michelle. "Try to talk her into coming back into town. The lake house is too isolated and not at all secure."

"We can argue later?" She turned to Michelle. "Would you send Dr. Michaelson back in? I need to speak to her about my follow-up care."

The minute they'd left, she ran her hand over her still-flat belly, wondering but afraid to hope her suspicions would play out. And she figured she couldn't ask for a better time or place to get answers. If she was indeed pregnant, she would have to give in to some of Michelle and Ethan's demands.

She sighed as Marcy poked her head in. "Dr. Michaelson is with another patient. Did you need something, hon?"

Wetting her lips, Kayla nodded, then beckoned the nurse to come closer. In a voice so low she was certain it wouldn't carry, she whispered, "Is there a way you can run a pregnancy test for me?"

The nurse blinked, gripping the rail on the side of the bed as she reared back. "A pregnancy test?" she repeated. "Oh, honey, we do that as a matter of routine when we have an unconscious female." Her brow crinkled. "Did you not know?"

Kayla shook her head, a hot prickle of tears stinging her eyes and clogging her throat. "No," she croaked.

"Well, sugar, you are indeed pregnant." She consulted the tablet she held, tilting her head as she looked for the information. "Do you have an idea of possible conception date?"

Kayla shook her head, this time impervious to the pain. She searched her memory, trying to remember exactly how long it had been since she and Ty last made love. A week before his death? Two?

"Months," she said at last. "More than two."

Nurse Marcy looked up sharply. "Oh," she said softly, her mouth rounding with the shape of the sound. "I see."

"My husband has been gone nearly two months," Kayla said, allowing the tears to fall. "Maybe a couple weeks before he was—" She couldn't finish the sentence.

"You'll need to see your ob-gyn as soon as you get back to town, then. They'll probably want to do an ultrasound, too."

Kayla let go, letting the sobs rack her body as her mind whirled. How much wine had she drunk in those months? Her doctor had given her a sedative the night she found Ty and Trey. Would it hurt the baby? Had she somehow managed to mess this up already?

Marcy was handing over the tissue box when Michelle reappeared with a jangle of curtain rings. "Okay, I'm going— What is it? What happened?" she demanded, dividing her piercing blue glare between Kayla and poor Marcy. "What's wrong?"

"My head," Kayla gasped before the nurse could say a word.

She and Marcy shared a long look before she shifted her attention back to her friend. Kayla wasn't ready to tell anyone yet. She needed more time to process. A chance to plan. She'd tell Michelle and Ethan soon, but for this moment, she wanted to hold this knowledge close to her heart. At least until a doctor could tell her everything was okay.

"My arm hurts, too. I got shot, remember?" she said, focusing on Michelle again.

"I'll go process your discharge paperwork," Nurse Marcy murmured, and with a swish of the curtain, she was gone.

Chapter Three

Ryan Hastings wasn't particularly thrilled by the prospect of babysitting a socialite, but these days he'd do about anything to get out of the office. When he'd been a special agent for the Criminal Investigation Division, he was always on the go. But then the opportunity to transfer to Executive Protection Division came up, and it seemed like a great opportunity. In a lot of ways, it was. But the job also came with a ton of downtime.

Arkansas wasn't exactly a hot destination for visiting celebrities and dignitaries.

Now, he'd torn his ACL while protecting the head football coach from a particularly exuberant scrum of students and players following a stunning victory. He didn't blame them for storming the field. Nor did he resent being injured in the line of duty. He'd done his level best to protect the state's highest paid public employee, he thought with a smirk. He simply hated being desk-bound.

As he drove the long stretch of interstate west out of Little Rock, he wondered if most people in the United States realized their highest-paid public officials weren't governors or senators, or any of the people who made the laws who govern their land, but rather the men who led their collegiate teams into battle each week.

He winced as he drew up his left leg and planted his foot on the floorboard. Sitting for a three-hour car trip was never pleasant, but flexing and straightening his leg periodically helped. He'd switched off the radio an hour outside of Little Rock, tired of searching for something he found palatable. With nothing left to do, he activated the voice command and placed a call to his old friend, Lieutenant Ethan Scott.

"You on your way?" Ethan asked by way of greeting.

"Yep. Still a couple hours out," Ryan responded. "Give me the skinny on this whole thing again."

"Ah, you're bored," Ethan replied.

"Radio wasteland." He stretched his neck. "Entertain me."

He'd done his homework, of course. Aside from the official case filings on the charges pending against Trey Powers at the time of his murder, and the ongoing investigation into who had shot both Trey and his father, Tyrone, he's also done a deep dive into the media coverage.

The story was sensational. National news outlets had picked it up and couldn't seem to let it go. Mostly they seemed to be amazed anyone outside of New York or Los Angeles had any kind of real money, power or influence. Those metropolitan worlds were so insular they couldn't imagine the scheming going on beneath the seemingly bucolic settings of America's small towns and rural cities.

"Once upon a time there was a man named Tyrone Delray Powers. Old Tyrone bought up a good chunk of hill country in northwest Arkansas," Ethan began.

"Seems like a dubious investment," Ryan replied dryly. "Must have had some insider information."

"Seems he probably did, doesn't it? Only a couple years later, the US Army Corps of Engineers came in and dammed up the White River, flooded the valleys and created the lakes we now know as Bull Shoals, Beaver Lake and Table Rock Lake."

"Three of my favorite places on earth," Ryan interjected.

"Same. Anyhow, old Tyrone had amassed a fairly substantial fortune in real-estate speculation. He made some friends who turned out to be successful, too. One who started a massive chain of discount stores you may have seen scattered around."

"Birds of a feather," Ryan said.

"They do indeed flock together. Our friend Tyrone was the industrious type. Aside from all his real-estate wheeling and dealing, he put himself through law school and opened one of the area's most prestigious law firms, setting himself up to be the guy all those birds came to when they pooped on the wrong person."

"Okay, spare me the bird jokes," Ryan interrupted.

"Anyhow, Tyrone sent his two boys back east to law school so they could rub shoulders with more—sorry—feathered friends, then bring those connections back to their sweet little setup in a mountain town they helped put on the map."

"Those two boys would be Tyrone Junior and Senator Bill Powers," Ryan concluded.

"Bingo. Daddy also helped one of his good buddies by letting him buy his favorite nephew a partnership in the firm."

"And the nephew would be the Walton in Powers, Powers and Walton."

"Yes. Some might have called him a poor relation, but not anymore," Ethan said with a chuckle. "Like all these guys, he managed to make his way up in the world."

"He's a judge now, right?" Ryan said, lining up players in his mind.

"Correct."

"If he's a judge, doesn't partnership in a law firm create some kind of conflict of interest?"

"Well, it might seem fishy to an outside observer, but let's not forget we're dealing with what was a fairly small community up until the last decade or two. When he took the bench, he withdrew his partnership in the firm."

"Ah, America. The land of a chicken in every pot and a finger in every pie," Ryan said wryly.

"Exactly."

"And folks around there didn't mind?"

"Are you kidding me? Folks around here love these people. Up until a few months ago, they wanted them to come to every event, kiss their babies and toss hundred-dollar bills into the air when they left." Ethan hesitated for a second. "We think we see the haves versus the have-nots down in Little Rock, but I promise you the dividing line up here's a whole lot more...marked."

Ryan thrummed his fingers on the steering wheel as the tires hummed below him. "We don't think there's any chance whoever did this was simply somebody who is tired of not getting their slice of the pie?"

"It's possible," Ethan said fairly. "We haven't ruled it out, but there aren't any other suspects. P, P and W did not specialize in the sort of law that puts people in regular contact with the more troubled parts of the local society. At least, not the way we think of as troubled. I'm sure these people have their own set of worries, but they mainly deal with corporate law. White-collar stuff. As they say in the legal community, a white-shoe law firm."

"What's that supposed to mean?"

"I don't actually know, but I'm assuming it means something to do with wearing shoes so clean and white they wouldn't dare trek through the muck."

"Gotcha." Ryan immediately formed a picture in his mind of a bunch of white-suited, white-shoed Gatsby types tiptoe-ing their way across a plush lawn, croquet mallets in hand. "And the widow Powers?"

"Kayla?" Ethan chuckled. "I think you're going to be pleasantly surprised."

"How so?"

"She wasn't exactly what I expected when I came into town. I imagine she won't be what you have in mind, either," Ethan said cryptically.

"How do you know what I have in mind?" Ryan chal-lenged.

"I think we all pretty much have the same image in our heads when we imagine the much-younger second wife of a rich man."

"A Hollywood stereotype," Ryan said, a dark edge creep-ing into his voice.

Ethan didn't know—couldn't have known—Ryan's own mother had been the second wife of a wealthy man. But his past wasn't relevant to this case.

"How is she going to surprise me?"

"Kayla is bright. Sharp. She was an attorney at the firm when she married Tyrone."

"Gold digger?" Ryan asked, his tone flat.

"Some people say so, of course, but I don't think so. She got there on her own and doesn't seem to want what's been left to her. I think they had an actual relationship. A real mar-riage with all the ups and downs. She's shockingly forthcom-ing, so I'm sure she'll tell you herself that their relationship was in a bit of a rocky patch at the time of Tyrone's death."

"What kind of rocky patch?"

"Nothing dramatic. She said some of the newness had worn off and he didn't seem as interested in her as he had once been. He had his own set of problems with the son, Trey, and the charges against him."

"I read the news stories. This family sounds like a bit of a mess," Ryan commented, knowing he was greatly understating the dynamics at play.

"Aren't all families?"

"Maybe," Ryan conceded. His certainly was.

"I like Kayla," Ethan admitted gruffly. "She's a straight shooter." Then, as if realizing what he said, he rushed to clarify. "Not an actual shooter, but I mean—"

"I get it. She doesn't bother with a lot of filler," Ryan concluded for him.

"Exactly. She's an attorney. Thinks like one. Strategic, factual, logical..."

Ethan paused, and Ryan wondered what was hanging up his old friend when it came to describing this woman.

"Cold fish?" he said, hazarding a guess.

"No," Ethan answered. "Definitely not."

Ryan sensed a hesitation. "But?"

"I know she won't mind me telling you, because it's probably going to be the first topic she brings up, but she recently came out of a thirty-day treatment program."

Ryan spotted a sign for the exit that would take him north over the Boston Mountains and into the Ozarks. He signaled a lane change then settled in, his gaze fixed on the exit in the distance. The road would take him closer to this straight-shooting woman with addiction problems, a big, fat pile of money and someone taking shots at her.

"Pills?"

"Booze," Ethan corrected. "Wine, actually."

"Any other issues I need to be aware of? Disruptive behavior? Violent tendencies?"

"Nothing along those lines," Ethan assured him. "I would

assess her more as a woman with too much time on her hands and not enough attention from her husband. She's an introvert. Tends to hole up. Maybe a strong desire to numb herself comes along with the urge to hide."

"Because she needs to be insulated from all the money and power she married into?" Ryan asked, a note of snark entering his tone as he coasted onto the exit ramp.

"More like she needed to blunt the edges of the slings and arrows aimed at the replacement wife," Ethan replied evenly.

Ryan's shoulders dropped and he exhaled, the sound soft and low. He knew exactly the kind of treatment Kayla Powers had likely endured as the newer, younger model. He'd watched his own mother try to navigate those treacherous waters. Watched it whittle her away to a sharp stick of a woman so afraid of making a misstep, she'd stood frozen by her husband's side, simply absorbing the vitriol so casually flung at her.

Through his teenage years, he'd watched as the loving mother he'd known cloaked all of her soft spots in armor plating. He couldn't help wondering if she missed being married to his dad. Jerry Hastings had been a moderately successful insurance agent. A middling handsome guy with dark red hair and a friendly smile. He'd been Ryan's Little League coach and helped him construct cars for soapbox derbies and ships for cardboard regattas.

He'd been killed by a drunk driver when Ryan was only thirteen years old.

For three years, Ryan had done his best to protect his mother, assuming the mantle of man of the house and taking care of her the best any teen boy could. But then, his mother had met Richard Stephenson and married him after a whirlwind courtship. Suddenly, he found himself with a stepfather he barely knew, and Ryan's services as head of the family were no longer needed.

"I'll keep an open mind," Ryan assured his old friend.

"Thank you. I didn't want you coming into this thinking anyone was trying to hide her circumstances from you."

"I appreciate the information. The more I know about what she's dealing with, the better I can plan."

"Yeah, I know." Ethan paused for a moment. "She needs someone with an objective eye. Needs you."

Ryan winced as the other man inadvertently pressed the hottest of his many hot buttons. He could never resist helping someone who needed him.

"Listen, we're going to meet you at her lake house. I'll send you a pin drop for the GPS."

"A pin drop? Is it far off the beaten path?"

"It's over on Table Rock in a remote and fairly isolated area." Ethan's response was terse. "Michelle and I have been trying to convince her to move somewhere closer to town. We're hoping hearing it from you will convince her we aren't being overprotective."

"Didn't you say the lake house was where she was shot?" he asked, incredulous.

"Yes. I told you, she's stubborn. We need backup on this, and we're counting on you to give it to us."

Ryan's phone dinged and the dash display showed the message with the GPS coordinates. He grunted and jabbed at the screen until the system rerouted him to his intended destination. "ETA—one hour, fifty-two minutes."

"Ten-four," Ethan responded. "See you soon. And thanks," he added before ending the call.

Ryan readjusted his grip on the steering wheel and his expectations of the woman he was meant to protect. From the sound of things, he wouldn't find a cowering widow waiting for him at this remote lake house. With Ethan's insider information in mind, he formulated a new strategy for how he'd approach Kayla Powers.

The drive passed quickly. Ethan hadn't been exaggerating when he said a pin drop was easier. The place was out in the middle of nowhere. He hadn't been impressed by the lack of fencing adjacent to the ancient iron gate. A gate without perimeter deterrent was a moot point. The lackluster security was a disappointment. But the lake house itself was something to see.

And the moment he stepped into the room he could tell the widow with the formidable stubborn streak was not what he expected.

He'd seen photos of her in the news coverage of the Powers family's trials and tragedies. There were her photos in the official state-police files, and dozens more polished images taken at fundraisers and parties popped up with a simple internet query. He'd read enough about her background to combine all of those snapshots with the snippets of information to form a composite of the woman he thought he was meeting.

The reality of her made far more of an impact.

He took a minute to catalog the differences as Ethan made the introductions. He recognized the woman who'd been seated beside Kayla on the sofa as the defense attorney who'd represented both Trey Powers and Kayla.

Michelle Fraser. He repeated her name to himself before he turned to make a closer inspection of his charge.

Mrs. Powers's dark blonde hair was still streaked with lighter strands, but it seemed to be a bit more subdued than in some of the photos. Her cheeks were no longer gaunt, but her eyes appeared haunted. She had on the kind of stretchy pants women wore to run errands rather than do any actual running. The oversize sweatshirt she wore was silk-screened with the University of Arkansas Razorback hog mascot.

They shook hands. "Did you go to the U of A?" he asked, even though he knew the answer from the dossier Ethan had sent to him.

"Yes. For my undergrad. I attended Yale Law for my postgrad."

Coming from most people, the last might have sounded like a boast, but Kayla Powers spoke in such a direct manner he knew instinctively she was doing nothing more than stating the facts.

He smiled and took a seat in the armchair she'd waved him toward. "Are you from Arkansas originally?"

"Yes. Born and raised outside Altus," she replied, shooting Ethan a sidelong glance. "Don't tell me you didn't direct him to the Kayla Powers Cyberpedia page."

Ethan had taken the seat on Michelle Fraser's opposite side, Ryan noted. In an instant, he realized they were together. Everything about their body language screamed intimacy. There wasn't any overtly physical contact between them, but there was definitely a charge in the air.

"I prefer to ask questions. As I get to know you, I'm able to form a strategy for protection I hope would suit you, rather than other people's impressions of you."

"Funny, your friend here," she said, gesturing to Ethan, "wanted me to tell my story rather than answer questions."

"We all have different styles," he replied with what he hoped appeared to be an easy smile. "Ethan's a big-picture guy. I like the nitty-gritty data."

His statement earned him a blooming smile from Michelle. "I keep telling him data will set us free," she said, pinning Ethan with a mock glare. "He only wants me to boil everything down to the salient points for him."

"Okay, okay," Ethan said, waving them both off. "Ry, what are your thoughts on staying here at the lake house as part of your protection plan?"

Kayla Powers rolled her eyes and stuffed her hands into the pockets of her sweatshirt as she dropped back into the plush sofa cushions. "Wow. Way to serve up the softball, Lieutenant."

"I'm pretty sure I'm not going to say anything surprising, Mrs. Powers," Ryan said, meeting the woman's gaze directly. "This house is too remote. There's only one road in and out of the area. There is a gate, but the surrounding property isn't secured. I'm assuming the shoreline isn't, either."

"Correct," Kayla Powers responded, holding his gaze.

"I'm sure you have a decent security system here, but unless you plan to stay barricaded inside the house for the unforeseen future, it would be extremely difficult to be certain you'd be safe here."

"I don't relish the idea of being terrorized into making life choices," she said coolly.

"I'd say this is more of a life-or-death choice, given the circumstances surrounding your husband's murder and what happened to you yesterday."

Her chin came up a notch and her jaw stiffened, but she didn't look away. This woman was nobody's pushover.

"Sergeant Hastings—" she began.

"Ryan," he interrupted.

"Sergeant," she repeated, cocking an eyebrow at him.

He had to smile. Ethan hadn't been wrong about the stubborn streak. "Yes, Mrs. Powers?"

She huffed softly, then gave her head a rueful shake. "Ethan and Michelle have had a full day to work on me prior to your arrival. I'm not an unreasonable woman. I'm not digging in out of sheer stubbornness," she said, sliding Ethan a narrowed side-eye. "But where do you propose I go?"

Ryan opened his hands to show her he was open to any number of options. "You could go back to Bentonville. You could go to Little Rock. Or you could leave this area entirely."

"I have a law firm to run," Kayla said briskly.

"You know I would take care of things as long as you needed me to," Michelle interjected.

"I do, but the point is, I don't need you to," Kayla argued.

"Let's not get into semantics," Michelle said, raising a hand in surrender. "I know you don't need me to run the firm, but I would be happy to help you with it if it meant we could get you someplace I know you'll be safe. As much as we would all like to believe Harold Dennis had something to do with Tyrone and Trey's deaths, we have no proof. And given what happened yesterday, I think it's safe to say there's still somebody out there who wants to harm you."

Ryan watched as Mrs. Powers took in everything her friend said. It was clear she didn't like the crux of the message. He saw her shift her jaw, her teeth clearly on edge as she bit back whatever she wanted to say. The two women stared at one another, seemingly communicating without a word being spoken. Starting to feel a little left out, he glanced over at Ethan only to see his old friend give a helpless shake of his head.

"They've got this mind-meld thing going on," he drawled in a soft undertone.

Michelle didn't bother sparing him a glance. "We're sitting right here. We can hear you."

"I'm never sure how deep it goes when you're doing the telepathy thing," Ethan answered, his grin spreading wide.

Always a man of action, Ryan decided to jump in with both feet again. "Don't you own a house in town, Mrs. Powers?"

"I'm not going there," Kayla said, tearing her gaze away from Michelle and turning to face him again.

Only then did it occur to him the house she owned in Bentonville was likely the scene of her husband's murder.

"Okay. Perhaps we can find a rental? Something clean but modest. Unassuming," he said, casting another meaningful glance around the over-the-top surroundings. "A place no one would expect you to go."

"I wasn't born with a silver spoon in my mouth, Sergeant," she said quietly.

"No, ma'am, but you have one now. No one is going to expect you to be living in anything less than the style to which you have become accustomed. We can use preconceived notions to our advantage."

"Maybe we should rent a log cabin in the woods," she suggested with an edge of snark in her tone.

One corner of his mouth kicked up. Ethan was right in his assessment. Ryan liked her spirit. "Perhaps we should. How do you feel about mounted trophies and stuffed fish?"

"You think you're going to scare me off, but I grew up around avid sportsmen and married one as well. I'm not cowed by threats of taxidermy."

"Good to know. Here's what I suggest," he said, leaning forward and planting his elbows on his knees. "A series of short-term rentals. They can all be here in the area if you want to be in the office, but we'd spread them out between Fayetteville, Rogers, Springdale and Bentonville. I know the commute can get to be a bear if you have to go at rush hour, but since you own the firm, I'm assuming you can set your own hours if you want to be a presence in the office."

She gave him a wry smirk. "Yes, I can set my own hours."

"We'll rent houses through one of those vacation services. Rent for a week, maybe two at a time. We can pick a couple of places in town, then shift out to one of the lakes for another week or two, whatever it takes."

"How long do you think this is going to take?"

"A question for the lieutenant," he said, glancing pointedly at Ethan. "His job is to solve your husband and stepson's murders. My job would be to keep you safe until we know we have the culprit in custody."

"A bodyguard," she said dryly.

Ryan shook his head. "A common misnomer. A bodyguard is one of those big burly boys you see pushing people through crowds of paparazzi. My job is different, ma'am. I would do it if it were necessary," he added with a shrug. "But my service here is about protection. I find strategic ways to keep you safe and out of harm's way."

"And are you good at your job?" she asked coolly.

"I believe I am," he replied. "If you'd like some references, I can provide a few for you."

Again, she lifted a single eyebrow. "Can you?"

"I can't give you their contact information outright, since all of these assignments are completed in the course of my duty as an officer of the state police, but if you're a Razorback football fan, you'll recognize the name of one of them. Heck, living so close to Fayetteville, I'd bet you've probably had dinner with the man."

Sure enough, he didn't have to name names. "You would be correct. I have had dinner with him and his wife," she confirmed. "They're lovely."

"I've also worked on details for your brother-in-law," he told her, figuring he'd better put it all out there so there'd be no surprises later.

"Have you?" She cast a glance at over Michelle and Ethan, then turned back to him. "What if he recognizes you?"

Ryan chuckled. "Mrs. Powers, a man learns to stand out in this particular job by knowing how to blend in. I'd bet my badge Senator Powers couldn't pick me out of a lineup."

Chapter Four

The first house Sergeant Ryan Hastings procured was a typical suburban three-bedroom house in the depths of a subdivision on the north edge of Fayetteville. It was furnished comfortably enough, even if there were a few too many signs proclaiming it a happy place and making declarations about putting family first.

When Ty had been taken from her, she believed she had no family. Now she was starting to reframe the concept. Though their friendship was still new, she felt a deep connection to Michelle. A kind of kinship she imagined she might have felt if she'd had a sister. And though Kayla had a somewhat more contentious connection with Ethan, she could see him in the role of annoyingly bossy older brother. As an only child, she used to envy the kids who complained about their siblings. Now she felt close to becoming an honorary member of the club.

Her stomach muscles clenched as a rush of hot tears threatened. Instinctively, she covered her belly with her palm, and stared out the kitchen window at the wooden play set in the fenced backyard. If she kept collecting people at this rate, she'd have more family than she knew how to handle.

"This okay?"

Ryan's voice was deep, slightly breathless and held a

note of warning that tempted her to push back. To insist she couldn't stay here in this bland oasis he'd booked for them. How would he react if she refused?

"This is fine." The words were out of her mouth before she'd finished her internal debate, surprising them both.

He moved to the sliding doors off the little breakfast nook and peered out as well. Was he scoping the swing set to be sure no bad guys were lurking there?

"I know it's not what you're used to, but I made sure we were within range for food-delivery services. We won't starve," he said offhandedly.

Something about his reassuring tone rubbed her the wrong way. Did he think she was so spoiled she couldn't fry an egg?

"I grew up in a house a lot like this one," she informed him.

He turned to look at her, his expression blank, but his tone gave away his surprise. "Did you?"

She nodded. "My dad sold farm equipment, and my mom was our dentist's office manager. We didn't have live-in help." She added the last part so dryly the words practically crackled.

"I see."

"I can cook. I also clean up after myself," she informed him, turning to face him head-on. "I'm fully housebroken."

He smirked at the last bit and her stomach coiled again. Sergeant Hastings was a handsome man. She didn't blame herself for the tiny tug of attraction she felt whenever a corner of his mouth lifted, but she was no fool. She was reasonably attractive and a soon-to-be wealthy woman, if Tyrone's will stood up to the challenges brought by his family. She was a target in at least a half dozen ways, but the one she could guard herself against was getting caught up in Ryan Hastings's gravitational pull.

"Good to know." The half-smile was gone as quickly as it had appeared, and he was back to being all business. "If you'll make a list of anything you want or need, I'll add it to mine and we'll get the essentials stocked," he said briskly.

"I can do my own shopping," she insisted.

He sighed with the gusto of a man dealing with a particularly recalcitrant two-year-old. She didn't appreciate the sigh, nor did she like the look of implacable patience he wore as he heaved it.

"I won't be held prisoner—"

But he cut her protest off with a raised hand. "You are not a prisoner, but I do think it would be nice if we tried to get at least one night's stay under our belts before we run the risk of a sighting," he said gruffly.

"No one I know comes to Fayetteville outside of football or basketball season," she insisted.

"No one? Not one person from your undergrad years hung around after the ceremony. None of your fellow alumni went on to work for the university? Maybe they stayed in town and work for other companies that were on a hiring spree at the time of your graduation?"

He asked his questions with such patent disbelief she knew instinctively he might be better equipped with an answer to his questions than she was. "Okay, maybe, but the people who know me from after—"

"We all know what a small town this entire state is," he insisted. "You're free to hit up the megacenter if you want, but don't be surprised when word of your whereabouts gets out and we find ourselves moving." He paused, fixing her with an insultingly patient gaze. "The Powers family name has featured prominently in local or national news the past couple of months. Didn't you make the cover of a tabloid? I could've sworn I saw you in the checkout line," he persisted.

"No, wait, it was here." He pulled out his phone and held it up to show a headline that read "Has the Black Widow Met Her Match?"

"What the—"

She reached for the phone, her jaw dropping as she gazed at the web page in disbelief. This was no tabloid. She was staring at the front page of Little Rock's biggest newspaper. Granted, it was the digital edition, but lack of print coverage was of little consolation. The news outlet had ceased running daily print editions years before.

"I'm giving it a C minus on the truth scale. They did say you'd been unarmed when injured, but there was definitely a tone in the reporting," he said with a dismissive shrug.

"What kind of a tone?" she asked, baffled.

"The kind that says, 'It's possible she killed her husband and stepson, so maybe whoever is taking potshots might be doing the population at large a favor?'"

She tossed his phone back at him. "Disgusting."

He caught it against his chest. "Their job is to get clicks these days. And the internet lives forever. Makes you yearn for the good old days when people would line birdcages with old newspapers."

She inhaled deeply, then let out a long and loud exhale, through her nose. "Fine. I'll make a list."

"Going to the office will make keeping your whereabouts unknown tough enough. Are you sure I can't talk you out of it?"

Typical man, she thought. He tried to take a mile when she gave an inch.

Truth be told, she wasn't sure. She, Ethan and Michelle had decided she would take another few days. Del hadn't come to the office in the weeks since Harold Dennis was arrested, but the Powers men had team players all over the firm. Both Senator Powers and his son would know the minute she stepped over the threshold at PP&W, and if Del had been the one…

Kayla bit her lip as she turned away from the yard and stalked back into the main living area of the open-concept home. With every passing hour, her gut-level suspicion of Del Powers wavered a little more. She'd learned in counseling to recognize that pervasive self-doubt often rode sidecar with addiction, but she hadn't quite mastered the art of squashing it. She chose to deflect her doubts and his worries in one quick pivot.

"How many bedrooms are there?"

"Three. The main suite is on the west side. You're welcome to take it, but I have to say I'd prefer it if we could both sleep in the same part of the house. The bedrooms on the east side aren't as large, but they look comfortable enough, and I'd keep out of your way as much as possible."

The tightness in his promise pricked holes in the thin skin of her indignation. He was here to do a job, and like it or not, it was a legitimate one. She sighed, her shoulders sagging as she moved to pull one of the tall stools out from the breakfast bar.

She couldn't blame Ryan for eying her warily as she climbed onto it and planted her chin in her palm. She cringed, then ran her hand over the bandage on her upper arm, hoping he would attribute some of her foul mood to pain from her injury, not her being a pain in the rear.

"Sorry," she said, though it rang false even to her own ears.

"I understand this isn't easy," he said, meeting her gaze directly. "If it helps any, I'm every bit as uncomfortable as you are."

Oddly enough, it did make her feel better. "You are?"

He nodded. "Of course. You and I met yesterday," he

said with a laugh. "I don't usually move in with a woman so quickly."

"Ha ha," she said dryly. Then it occurred to her she knew almost nothing about this man. For all she knew he was married or had a girlfriend waiting for him back in Little Rock.

"I'm sorry," she said again. "It occurred to me I don't know anything about you. Are you married?"

He shook his head. "Divorced. A long time ago."

She chuckled. "Couldn't have been too long ago. What are you, thirty-three? Thirty-four?"

It was his turn to laugh. "I'm thirty-eight, but thanks. I got married at eighteen. Divorced a year later."

Her eyebrows shot up. "Wow. You were both so young."

"Yes. And neither of us were equipped to do much more than to play house for a few months," he said with a sad half-smile. "In the end, we actually parted on fairly good terms. My ex is remarried. Has two little boys. I ran into them at a baseball game last summer."

"Oh, wow," she said softly.

"Her husband seems like a nice enough guy. In the end, I think we all made the right choices."

"And your choice was to remain single?" she asked.

"My choice was to focus on my work as much as possible."

"To the exclusion of everything else?" she persisted.

"I'm content with my life. There aren't many people who can say the same, so I count myself as lucky." He drew out the other stool and pulled it a couple feet away to leave a good amount of space between them before taking the seat. "I should say I *was* content." He gave his left knee a hard pat. "I've been sidelined with an injury for a while. Desk jockeying is not my favorite thing."

"When Ethan called to see if you'd be interested in taking this assignment, you..."

"Packed a bag and hit the road."

Turning her head, she looked at him squarely. "Surely there has to be some kind of protocol. It sounds like there's no pecking order in the state-police organization if he can call and ask you to come up here. I mean, I have to assume you have superiors and ongoing assignments. You couldn't have simply packed a bag and hit the road," she said, tossing his words back at him.

"Mrs. Powers, you have to know by now the case involving the deaths of your husband and his son are the criminal investigation division's number-one priority at this time. If Ethan Scott told the higher-ups he needed a purple unicorn with a polka-dotted mane in order to close this case, they'd be out spray-painting a horse as we speak."

She chuckled. "There's a visual image for you. I'm never going to be able to stop picturing Ethan riding around on a purple horse with a horn stuck to its head."

He chuckled, but quickly sobered. "The fact of the matter is, you are a priority within the state-police hierarchy. Your safety is of the utmost concern to everyone involved."

"Doesn't ring true if they sent a guy with a bum knee instead of an entire SWAT team," she said with a teasing smile.

"Budgetary constraints," he returned, his tone desert-dry.

She laughed out loud. "Fair enough."

She pulled her cell phone from her hip pocket, opened her note application and started typing with her thumbs. "Are you a breakfast person?"

"I'm a breakfast, lunch and dinner person," he replied without missing a beat. "But you don't have to worry about my meals. Make a list of the things you want for yourself."

"I like to cook. It relaxes me." She looked over at him. "Easier to cook for two than for one."

"I can cook, too," he assured her.

"Good. Then we can take turns." She tapped out another entry. "I didn't use to be a breakfast person," she said, continuing to type. "But now I'm embracing the whole most-important-meal-of-the-day thing. I think part of it is a rebellion against diet culture. I feel like I've been obsessed with the scale for too much of my life."

"I think people worry too much about weight and not enough about what they're putting into their bodies," he said gruffly.

She tipped her head to the side to let him know she was listening. "How do you mean?"

"Preservatives, too many chemicals, that sort of thing."

She looked up from her phone and eyeballed him with growing curiosity. "Are you a health-food guy?"

"Not necessarily. I'm more of a real-food guy," he said, shrugging off the label.

"You mean stuff like cracking an actual egg versus pouring egg substitute from a carton?"

"Pretty much. I don't go particularly out of my way to eat organic, but I do tend to try to pick foods that haven't been all radically altered from their original state."

"Makes sense. I pretty much try to do the same thing." She typed a couple more items into the list. "But I do have some weaknesses."

"Don't we all?"

She looked up, meeting his gaze directly. "I'm thirty-seven days sober. If alcohol is one of your weaknesses, I'm going to have to ask you not to bring it into the house."

"Mrs. Powers, I'm here to protect you. Even if I were one to imbibe, I could hardly do my job if I were impaired."

"And you take your job seriously," Kayla stated, still holding his gaze.

"Very."

"My name is Kayla," she said, dragging her attention back to the phone in her hands. "If we're going to be spending time together, there's no sense standing on formality. May I call you Ryan?"

"Of course," he replied easily.

She nodded, satisfied with the exchange, but not entirely at ease. She felt strange sharing a house with a man who was not Tyrone. Almost as if she was cheating, though she knew the notion was unfounded. Trying to shake herself out of confusing thoughts involving her late husband and the man seated nearby, she zoomed in on her shopping list again.

"Yeah, well, if you have other weaknesses you want to indulge, shout them out now, because I'm putting mine on the list."

"Let me guess," he said sarcastically. "Chocolate?"

"A stereotype." She tapped a few more keys, then turned the screen to face him. "I tend to gravitate toward the salty snacks rather than the sweet."

His eyes widened as he took in the extensive list of items she was requesting from the chip aisle. "Wow. Okay. I stand corrected."

She turned the phone back and tapped out a few last items. Then, she pulled up the contact information he'd insisted they exchange immediately following the meeting with Michelle and Ethan and shared her shopping list with him.

His phone chimed a moment later. She watched his face as he scrolled through the wish list, but saw no sign of judgment, only mild bemusement. He glanced up and caught her staring. "Sorry," she murmured, then busied herself with a response to a text from Michelle.

Del was still boycotting the office, but according to her tech-savvy friend, he'd been logging into the firm's server daily.

You'd think he'd have figured out you know the computer stuff, Kayla texted.

The dots indicating an incoming message appeared. Kayla did her best to keep her eyes glued to her own phone but couldn't help sneaking peeks at the man beside her as he typed on his own screen. At last, Michelle's response appeared.

I'm not sure he knows enough computer stuff to worry about how much computer stuff I know.

I love it when you talk nerdy to me, Kayla teased.

Michelle didn't miss a beat. I could tell you how to rig a thingamajig with a doohickey, but then I'd lose my mystique. What are you and Sergeant Smokin' Hot up to today?

Kayla tried to tell herself the glance in Ryan's direction was reflex, but she never could master self-deception. Rather than attempting to fool her friend, she tried for something breezy and casual with a side of snark.

Settling in at our new nest. Making a shared shopping list. Global thermonuclear war. Trying not to think about the killer on the loose. You know, the usual, she responded, hoping a dose of flippancy would be enough to mask exactly how uncomfortable she was with this entire "personal-protection" situation.

Always the same old...

How's my law firm?

Still standing. There was a pause and the ellipses disappeared. She was about to set aside the phone when the dots popped up again. My friend at the Bureau is telling me Del signed in from another IP address today. He's been on the move lately.

Kayla pursed her lips, doing her best to ignore the creeping feeling that was crawling up the back of her neck. As far as she knew, Ty's nephew was a homebody, of sorts. He wasn't a social creature, like his cousin Trey had been. He didn't party, like Trey and the other young attorneys at the firm did. He was quiet. Happy to fade into the background. More difficult to know, and therefore to read. All things she'd once considered attributes. Now, his habits—or lack of them— came across as something more menacing.

He is a homebody. The fact he's moving around is making me nervous, she admitted, finding it easier to be open via text than talking.

I hear you. But at the moment, the more important thing is to be sure you aren't a sitting duck.

You've been spending too much time with Lieutenant Looker.

You should have heard my snort, Michelle responded. I'll be using your pet name for him later.

TMI.

Kayla must have cringed as she typed out the letters, because Ryan's gruff inquiry startled her so much the phone almost squirted out of her hand.

"What's wrong?"

"Oh. Nothing," she said, reflexively closing her phone screen when she looked up and found him watching her.

"You had a look on your face just now," he insisted, gesturing to his own face.

"I was… My friend was making a bad joke."

"Okay." He resumed typing. Without looking up, he asked, "Any sign of Del Powers?"

"He isn't coming into the office," she reported.

Her brow furrowed when she realized he hadn't asked if the friend she referred to was Michelle. "Hey, how did you know I was texting Michelle?"

"Hmm?" He looked up at last, his forehead furrowed.

"How did you know it was Michelle I was texting?" she repeated, waggling her phone at him.

His eyebrows shot up, and a slow, sheepish smile tugged at the corner of his mouth. Ryan set his phone on the counter as hers vibrated with an alert. "It's my job to pay attention to you." He hesitated for a moment. "I'm not trying to invade your privacy, it's—"

His explanation was cut off by his own phone. Kayla saw Ethan Scott's name flash on the screen before Ryan swiped it away to accept the call. "Hey. Got anything?"

She glanced down at the notification on her own screen. Apparently, he was done updating their combined shopping list. Her thumb hovered over the icon to open the app even as she chastised herself for being too curious to see what he'd added. But then Ryan gave a low grunt. She glanced up to see him scowling fiercely as he listened to whatever Ethan was relaying on the other end.

"What? What is it?" she asked in an urgent whisper.

He gave his head a slight shake, then signaled he was still getting information. At last, his scowl faded into a grim line as he nodded. "Okay. We'll hang tight," he said into the phone. "Check in with you later."

"What? What happened?" she demanded as he ended the call.

"Nothing happened," he assured her. "But it looks like we need to pare the list down to where we can stay nimble and be ready to move," he said, regret tingeing his tone.

"Why? How can anyone possibly know where we are?"

He nodded to her phone. "Maybe he's more tech-savvy than we thought." Sighing, he ran a hand over his face. "Anyway, he hasn't been returning calls from the police, so Ethan finally got the search warrant for Del's place."

"Did they find anything?"

Ryan shook his head, his expression grave. "More about what they didn't find. His work clothes and car are still there. The cleaner he had coming in weekly showed up at near the same time Ethan and his team did. She said the place looked like he hadn't slept there for a couple of days or more, but he hadn't informed the cleaning service he'd be going out of town, which was unusual for him."

"I can't even begin to guess what is usual for Del," she murmured. "He's definitely not the guy I thought I knew." The wound in her arm ached. She reached up to cover it with her hand, hoping the pressure would ease the pain away. "But he didn't pack anything?"

"He didn't pack any suits," Ryan corrected. "According to the cleaning woman, nothing appeared to be missing except the outdoors gear he kept in the garage. Said he had a whole other wardrobe in a cabinet out there. Didn't like his suits smelling like fish, I guess."

"I take it the cabinet was empty."

"Yes." He drummed his fingers on the countertop. "He also took a kayak, his fishing gear and left the gun safe unlocked."

"And empty," she concluded.

"Yes."

"And they think it all means…" She trailed off meaningfully.

"We think it means Del Powers has gone to ground."

Chapter Five

"Again, I've gotta say I think this is a bad idea," Ryan grumbled as he followed her through the front door of Powers, Powers & Walton the following morning.

"Your objections have been noted for the record, but overruled," Kayla replied without glancing back at him. As she made a beeline for the midcentury command console helmed by a young blonde receptionist, Kayla searched her memory for the young woman's name. Brittney? Brianna?

"Mrs. Powers." The receptionist blurted her name in a half-shout as she shot to her feet, her headset hooked over one ear. "You're here."

"I'm here. How are you... Bailey?" The name came to her in a flash of pain-laced memory. Tyrone had once joked the young woman was so effusive, he wouldn't dare offer her a cup of coffee much less the Irish coffee better suited to her name. It was one of those silly things he liked to say. A prototypically groan-worthy dad joke, and Kayla had loved laughing at them with him.

"I'm fine, ma'am." The younger woman tilted her head. "I didn't expect... I mean... It's nice to see you," she said at last.

"Thank you." She offered her warmest smile.

"We didn't expect you to come in today."

She glanced over at Ryan Hastings, who was taking in

every inch of the reception-area decor. He couldn't have looked more like a cop if she had dressed him in uniform and handed him a baton. "This is Sergeant Hastings from the Arkansas State Police," she said, seeing no point in concealing her companion's identity. "I stopped by to speak to Ms. Fraser."

"Ms. Fraser is in her office. Would you like me to buzz up there?"

Kayla shook her head. "Don't bother. If she's busy I'll wait," she answered breezily. "Come in, Sergeant, I'll show you around. Play your cards right and I'll let you score a cup of coffee from the world's fanciest coffee machine," she said as she blew past the reception desk, her gaze set on the open-riser staircase leading to the firm's upper floor.

"I don't need any coffee," Ryan grumbled as he lengthened his strides to catch up with her. "Isn't there a back door we could've come in through?"

Kayla hiked her handbag into the crook of her arm, tilted up her chin and sent him a quelling look. "This is my firm. I'm not coming in through the back door."

"You realize this defeats the whole keeping-a-low-profile plan," he huffed as they made their way up the stairs.

Kayla kept her gaze fixed straight ahead, all too aware of the murmurs and stares coming from the attorneys and assistants who worked in the bullpen on the first floor. "It's important for them to see me," she said softly. "It's important for everyone to see me."

She switched her handbag to her right arm as they turned the corner on the landing. Her left still ached like the devil, but she was loathe to show any weakness in front of Ryan. He'd add her injury to his long list of reasons why she shouldn't do whatever she wanted to do.

"Listen, I understand you think it's important to put face

time in the office," he said . "But surely you know somebody here is likely in touch with Del Powers or his father. Somebody is going to let them know you came in today."

As Kayla reached the top of the stairs, she stopped and turned to face him. "I'm counting on it."

"This is a dangerous game," he warned, pitching his voice low.

"It's not a game, it's my life. I'll play it safe as much as I can, but I'm not about to let someone else dictate how I live it." She leaned in, holding his gaze steady. "I make the rules."

He nodded, then twisted to look around. "Give me the lay of the land." He gestured to the closed doors surrounding them. "Looks like no one is here."

"This is the executive level. Michelle is working out of Tyrone's old office these days." She gestured toward one of the doors leading into a corner office. She shuddered when she thought of Michelle's old office on the first floor and the frosted pane of glass shattered into a million tiny pieces by a bullet fired by an unknown intruder. "The one she was using downstairs needed some repairs."

Someone took a shot at her friend. Had it been Del? A shiver raced down her spine. Shaking it off, she pointed to the opposite corner. "Bill's office. Senator Powers," she corrected. "Obviously, he's not practicing law here, but Tyrone wanted to keep it for him to use when he came to town."

"Does he?" Ryan asked, quirking an eyebrow.

"He used to," she replied. "Like Del, I don't think he's been here since the will was probated."

Ryan pressed his lips together, nodding as he digested the information. "Are they contesting it?"

"They've made threats, but as of yet, I don't believe anything has been filed."

"They won't."

Startled by the confidence in his assertion, she glanced over at him. "What makes you so sure?"

"If they were serious about wanting the place, they'd have started the process. Plus, if they wanted the firm so badly, Del Powers would be here all day, every day, hanging on to the place even if his father can't."

She frowned as she parsed through his logic. "They said they wouldn't come in as long as I was in charge."

"And if they had a legal way of removing you as the boss, no one would need to take shots at you when you go out for a walk."

Pivoting, she met his gaze directly, resisting the urge to cover her aching bicep with a protective hand. "You think Del was trying to shoot to kill?"

To her relief, he gave a quick shake of his head. "I think he was shooting to scare. But I also think they won't hesitate to raise the stakes. They have a lot on the line, and you're an obstacle no one banked on needing to hurdle."

"Sergeant, I'm not an obstacle, I'm an immovable object," she replied tartly.

She turned on her heel, leaving the truth bomb she dropped in her wake. *Immovable* was her new keyword. Ryan had given her a half-dozen good reasons not to come into the office, and she'd ignored every one of them. She spotted people darting away from the bottom of the staircase when she turned and had little doubt they were hurrying to spread the word of her arrival.

This visit would be nothing more than a flyby. A bit of showboating to let them know she wasn't scared. Or, at least, to make them think she wasn't. Truthfully, Del's disappearance left her more unsettled than she wanted to admit.

The man she knew was a creature of habit. A person who liked numbers, order and routine. The idea of him deviating from the image she had of him in her mind was disconcerting. Of all the people in the Powers sphere of influence, Del was the last she would have expected to go rogue.

She caught the sound of Ryan Hastings's heavy footfalls right behind her and forced herself to breathe evenly. The last time she'd been in this office, the gun someone had used to murder her husband had fallen out of Tyrone's wall safe and landed with its muzzle pointed directly at her.

She wasn't ready to do more than make an appearance, but by the same token, she wasn't ready to concede this space to William and Del Powers's acolytes. Tyrone had left the firm in her care, and he had compelling reasons for his decision.

Ryan must have sensed her faltering. "Are you okay?" he asked, his voice quiet and compelling.

"I'm fine. This won't take long," she assured him.

Her steps slowed when she saw Tyrone's longtime assistant, Nancy Ayers, rising from her desk, a look of concerned confusion furrowing her forehead.

"What are you doing here?" the older woman blurted. Then, as if the impertinent question was a starter's pistol, she shot out from behind her desk. "I mean to say, Ms. Fraser had me thinking you wouldn't be coming back to the office for some time now."

"I'm only here for a moment," Kayla replied, wincing only a little as Nancy pulled her into a hard, fast hug.

"Well, you know we're keeping everything running as tight as we can around here," Nancy assured her. "You take all the time you need, bless your heart."

Kayla straightened with a smile, wondering exactly which variation of the multipurpose Southernism Ty's secretary was employing. Pity? Sympathy? Annoyance? Or was it honeyed condescension?

"Is she busy? With someone?"

"Lieutenant Scott came in earlier, but I think she's reviewing case files at the moment." She made a show of peering over Kayla's shoulder at Ryan. "Do you want me to buzz her and tell her you and your, uh, friend are here?"

Kayla smiled. Nancy Ayers was *über*competent in all fields except subtlety. "Nancy, this is Sergeant Hastings from the Arkansas State Police. He works with Lieutenant Scott," she added with a cordial nod. "Sergeant Hastings, this is Nancy Ayers, the woman who truly runs P, P and W."

Nancy ducked her head but didn't bother trying to deny the assertion. "I see. Nice to meet you."

"It's a pleasure, ma'am," Ryan said, extending his hand.

Nancy took it, her warm smile unfurling at the polite greeting. "Call me Nancy, please."

Ready to continue her mission, Kayla gestured toward the door to Ty's old office. "No need to buzz, I'll give her a knock before I burst in."

The office door swung inward, and Michelle stood framed in the opening. "No need. Someone forgot to remove me from the office early warning system when I moved up here." She stared hard at Nancy. "And don't you tip them off. I like knowing my presence instills unrest."

Kayla rolled her eyes and started toward her friend. "The FBI should have given you the title 'Special Agent of Chaos' when they planted you here." She waved Ryan in the direction of the office. "This will only take a minute."

"Early warning system?" he asked Michelle as she stepped aside to allow them to pass.

"A group text the associates use to alert one another one of the partners is on site," she explained, closing the door behind them. The minute the latch clicked, she turned on Kayla. "Is this your idea of keeping a low profile? If so, you're bad at it."

"Maybe, but I'm awesome at playing Whac-A-Mole," Kayla said, dropping her handbag into one of the guest chairs.

"Is this what this is?" Ryan asked, his back pressed against the closed door. "Are you popping your head out?"

"Perhaps a bit," she admitted.

"What's going on?" Michelle asked, her innate lawyer's caution creeping through in her tone.

"Ryan didn't want me to come into the office, but I thought it was important to show my face," Kayla explained.

"Okay, so you agreed to disagree," Michelle responded with a diplomatic nod. "What prompted this unexpected, yet delightful, drop-in? It wouldn't have anything to do with Del Powers going on an unannounced vacation, would it?"

Ryan shrugged. "Mrs. Powers thought it was important to be seen in the office."

As if on cue, Michelle's phone dinged. She glanced over at the device lying on its charging station. "I'm betting confirmation of the sighting has hit the wires."

"See?" Pleased with herself, Kayla plucked her handbag from the chair and looped it over her arm as she cast a pointed glance in Ryan's direction. "I told you we wouldn't be here long."

"And I told you it wasn't a good idea to come anywhere near this place. How do you know we won't be followed when we leave?"

"Oh, but I'm hoping we are. We're making a public exit right now," she announced. She crossed to her friend and gave Michelle a one-armed squeeze. "You should be able to access the lobby camera on Tyrone's desktop," she murmured.

"I'm already binge-watching the show," Michelle assured her. "Go. Get out of here, you troublemaker. I'll call you later."

"Talk to you later," Kayla confirmed, then headed straight

to the door. Ryan stood in her path, tall and unmoving. "Come on, Sergeant, we need to get a move on if we're going to get any snitches to scurry."

He blinked as if needing a moment to process her meaning, then grasped the door handle and pulled it open. "After you, ma'am."

"Don't *ma'am* me," she murmured as she swept past him.

She could hear the smile in his voice without turning to look back at him.

Kayla made a beeline for the stairs, blowing kisses at Nancy Ayers and quelling the older woman's sputters of protest with promises to call her soon. Her heels clattered on the steps, alerting everyone below of her imminent arrival.

By the time they reached the bottom, most of the employees in the warren of cubicles had their heads down and their fingers moving furiously across keyboards. She wondered how much gibberish was being generated for show. Still, she didn't break stride as she lifted a hand to wave to the few brave souls who looked up from their pseudo work.

By the time they hit reception, Bailey was seated at her desk with her hands folded neatly on the work surface and her eyes fixed on the doorway.

The girl jumped when they blew past her. "Mrs. Powers," she chirped. "Are you leaving already?"

"Yes. I only needed to pass something along to Michelle," Kayla said briskly.

"Nice to see you again," Bailey called as Kayla marched through to the vestibule.

Ryan nodded an acknowledgment as Kayla held the door open for him. He shot her a stern glare as he passed, then pushed open the outer door. He made a point of checking the foot traffic in both directions before allowing her out into the glaring afternoon sunlight.

Within minutes, they were ensconced in his bland, state-issued SUV, and headed away from downtown Bentonville.

"I'm still not exactly sure what you are hoping to gain," he said after three minutes of tense silence passed between them.

Kayla sighed heavily, then pulled her phone from her bag. When he slowed to a stop at an intersection, she held it up to show him the screen filling with message bubbles from Michelle.

"I gained the names of two people who left the office hot on our heels."

He cast her a sidelong glance as the light turned green and he accelerated. "What do you think that proves?"

"I'm pretty sure it's going to lead to someone alerting Del to our presence."

"I thought you said he wasn't one to hang out with the office crowd," he reminded her.

"He wasn't. At least, not to my knowledge. But that didn't mean he was a loner. He had friends. Or at least people who would act like friends to get close to a senator's son."

"And the names are?"

"Chet Barrow and Joshua Potter."

"Who are they?" Ryan prompted.

"Two of Trey Powers's closest friends. They were on Trey's boat the night Mallory Murray went missing."

"I thought you said Trey and Del didn't socialize with one another outside of family functions. He wasn't out on the boat with them, was he?"

"No, but Trey is gone now, and you know how nature abhors a vacuum," she said with an airy wave of her hand. "With me out of the office, Del would be the most likely candidate for these two sycophants to suck up to, wouldn't he?"

He made a grunting sound she assumed to be agreement.

"I'm assuming Michelle has already fed information to Ethan Scott?" he asked without inflection.

"No doubt," Kayla answered.

She dropped her phone back into her bag and let her head fall against the seat rest, sighing as she rolled her neck back and forth. She stopped when she was facing him. "I know you didn't like this plan, but we can't sit in some hidey-hole and do nothing. Listen, you gave me this, so I'll promise to lay low for a few days. Deal?"

"Is this how it's going to be? Are we bartering for your safety?"

"No, but I'm also not going to be stashed away because it's the easier option. At some point this has to come to an end. I need it to happen sooner rather than later."

He draped a hand over the top of the steering wheel and glanced over at her. "Listen, I understand you're under a lot of pressure, and you're eager to get your life back on track, but you can't put a timeline on these things. Sometimes they have to run their natural course."

Kayla sighed, closed her eyes for a moment, then whispered, "I have to put a time line on it. I need this to be over once and for all."

"I understand—"

"No, you don't understand anything," she said, interrupting him before he could feed her another line of platitudes. After drawing a deep breath, she let the truth go on an explosive exhale. "I have to know it's safe for me to bring Ty's baby into this world, and I can't do that if the people responsible for his death are the ones making the rules."

Ryan's head whipped around, and he hooked a sharp right into the driveway of a semi-occupied strip mall. Instinctively, Kayla reached for the handle above the door to brace herself. When the SUV jerked to a stop with a sharp squeal of brakes, she stared back at his shocked expression impassively.

"You're pregnant?" he asked, incredulous.

Kayla's answering smile was small, but genuine in its pleasure. She nodded, blinking back tears as she tried not to imagine all the ways she might have broken the happy news to Tyrone himself.

"Surprise," she whispered, then pressed a knuckle to her lips in time to suppress a hiccup of a sob.

Chapter Six

He'd done his best not to pry after she dropped her pregnancy bombshell on him, and she hadn't offered anything but the barest facts. She was pregnant, Tyrone Powers was the father and no one else knew. Not even Michelle and Ethan. And she didn't want them to know yet.

The last part bothered him the most. Why had she told him when she hadn't even told her friends? But it didn't take long for him to work out the reason why. The child she was carrying would be Tyrone's heir. A fact that made her even more of a target.

Kayla was true to her word. After their brief appearance at PP&W, she'd stuck to the rental house in Fayetteville. As far as Ryan could tell, she spent her days reading, attending to bits of firm business Michelle sent over and avoiding him. Other than conversations about grocery lists or food-delivery orders, they'd hardly done more than exchange polite pleasantries for three days.

Now they were moving locations.

She'd been quiet as she watched the scenery around them change from strip malls to subdivisions to sprawling suburban spreads. He chanced a glance at her as he turned onto the county highway that would take them to their next location, and saw the slight lift of one pale eyebrow.

But still, she said nothing.

Unable to contain himself any longer, Ryan broke the silence. "I got us a cabin."

She turned to look at him, and he saw both eyebrows lift a millimeter more. "A cabin?"

"A nice one," he quickly added, but immediately regretted it. This woman was accustomed to luxury homes. A cabin rated exceptional on the Staycation site might look nice to him, but it would more likely resemble a hovel to her. "Well, you know. Clean. Comfortable."

She pursed her lips, but he was fairly sure he caught the beginnings of smile before he turned his attention back to the road.

"Clean and comfortable are nice," she said in a tone of exaggerated encouragement.

He chuckled. "Well, it's on Beaver Lake, so maybe that will add to the appeal."

Apparently, he'd said the magic words, because Kayla sat up, angling to look at him. "You rented a cabin on Beaver Lake?"

"I thought it would be good to get out of town, and you said you liked staying at your place on the lake…" He trailed off, wishing he hadn't even hinted at a comparison between the cabin he'd booked online and the massive castle on Table Rock Lake she'd inherited from her late husband. "I thought the water would be nice," he finished sheepishly.

"It will," she reassured him with gratifying speed.

"I could only get it for two nights, so it won't be long." Ryan wondered if he was trying to reassure her or temper expectations.

"That's fine."

"And, you know, it's not one of those luxury cabins—"

"I told you I didn't grow up with money. Why do you keep acting like I'm some pampered princess who's going to throw a fit if my sheets aren't silk?"

The image of Kayla Powers's blonde wavy hair trailing across a slinky white pillowcase flared in his mind, but he quickly squelched it.

Heat crept up his neck and set the tips of his ears on fire. Inwardly, he cursed his ancestors for blessing him with his red hair and the complexion that went with it. Groping for something to say, he fell back on offense as the best defense for his wayward thoughts.

"Bet it didn't take you long to get used to it," he muttered. He could feel her gaze on his profile, but he didn't dare look at her.

"Some parts of it were easier than others," she said at last.

Grateful for the conversational gambit she lobbed his way, he dove in. "I can take a guess at which parts were easier, but what was harder for you?" he asked, genuinely curious.

She was quiet so long he was afraid she wouldn't answer, but at last she spoke. "Most people think getting rich is the hard part. They don't realize all the work that goes into staying rich."

He chanced a peek at her. "How do you mean?"

She shrugged. "Most of those people are born with some sort of cushion. I had your average middle-class childhood, but even the poorest of Ty's friends would have thought my parents were paupers."

"I see," he conceded as he signaled a right turn.

"I don't think you can," she said dryly. "There are strata within the social stratum. Layers as thin and transparent as puff pastry, but as strong and pungent as an onion."

"Way to nail those analogies," he said, matching her tone. "But I do have some clue. My mother's husband has money."

She turned in her seat again, her interest piqued. "Your stepfather?"

He gave her a lopsided smirk. "He was no more my stepfather than Trey Powers your stepson."

Kayla inclined her head. "Point taken."

"Anyhow, back to what was harder," he reminded her.

She chuckled. "You're a dogged one, aren't you?"

"I'm curious. You went to Yale Law, so you had to have some clue what it was like to move among the moneyed."

"Yeah, I did." She paused as if needing time for reflection. "I guess the hardest part to master was taking it all as seriously as they do. You'd think with all that money and all that power, people would be satisfied, but they never are, are they?"

He shook his head, but kept his mouth shut, wanting to hear her take on the phenomenon.

"Even Ty. As comfortable as he was with his life, he hated the thought of someone having more influence or control than he did. His need to be the master of his universe was what drove him to suspect Harold Dennis was making some kind of move."

"Oh?" He tapped the brakes to slow the car as the pavement gave way to a gravel road, but hoped she'd keep talking.

"Of course, he would have said he was protecting the firm from any possible repercussions if one of Hal's shady real-estate deals went south, but honestly? I think he was more afraid one of them would succeed spectacularly. Hal may have been his mentor in many ways, but he was still Ty's father's hired hand."

"Do you think your husband was playing both ends against the middle?"

She stared straight through the windshield, not even sparing him a glance when she answered. "I think my husband was doing what he was raised to do—protect the status quo."

"And you had a hard time doing the same?"

"Let's say I needed some training wheels when it came to walking the party line."

Ryan had to tamp down a surge of guilt. He'd always thought his mother was being weak when she went along with her new husband's wishes. He never considered the possibility she was feeling her way through her new life. A typical teenager, he was more focused on how the change in her relationship status impacted him, not how hard it had to be for her.

"Must have been difficult," he said, trying to keep his tone neutral.

Kayla sighed. "Some of it was tricky. The keeping up with who had what and trying to make sure people thought we were more than one step ahead of them." She paused and drummed her fingertips on her leg. "Hard to pretend you care about the approval of people who clearly don't care about you as a person." He glanced over and she wrinkled her nose. "I probably didn't make any sense there."

"It made perfect sense," he assured her as the rutted road opened into a clearing and the modern log cabin came into view. A slice of the blue lake sparkled beyond the wraparound porch.

"Oh."

He wasn't sure how to read Kayla's soft exhale. Was it one of surprised delight or dread? "Is that a good *oh*, or a bad one?"

"Good," she said, a self-conscious laugh burbling from her. "Definitely good. This looks lovely. Being on the water always relaxes me."

"Alright, then. I'm glad." Gravel crunched under the tires

as he slowed to a halt. "I brought most of the stuff we had at the house and replenished the perishables," he informed her as they opened the car doors.

She walked to the corner of the porch and stopped, peering around the house at the lake as if she was using the cabin as cover. Concerned, Ryan opened the liftgate, but abandoned the contents of the SUV in favor of finding out what was eating at his client.

"What's wrong?" he asked, drawing to a halt about a foot behind her and scanning the area for possible threats.

Kayla hugged herself tightly for a moment, then blew out a breath as she let her arms fall, her shoulder visibly dropping. "Absolutely nothing." This time, she gave him a smile that reached up and lit her eyes. "I'm happy to have the lake view, even if it is only for a couple of days."

"I'll keep that in mind. In the meantime, we should get our stuff and get inside," he said gruffly.

"Hopefully, you won't have to search out too many lake properties for me." Kayla brushed past him on the way back to the SUV. "But I guess I'm going to have to learn to pack lighter if we're going to keep moving so often," she commented as she pulled a designer suitcase she'd stowed in the back of the vehicle. She set it on the ground at her feet with a huff then blew her hair out of her face.

"If I offer to carry your bag for you, am I being helpful or sexist?" he asked with a tight half-smile.

"Depends on whether or not you believe I can handle my own suitcase," she replied.

"I'm prepared to believe you can handle anything life throws at you." He glanced and pointed at her left arm, then met her gaze again. "I know it's healing, but it still has to hurt to strain your muscles."

"I'm secure enough in my power to allow you to carry my

bag, as long as you understand my muscles are unquestionably up to the task," she drawled.

"I have no doubt," he said as he lifted the heavy suitcase with ease then grabbed his own nylon duffel from the cargo hold and swung the strap over his shoulder. "Go on ahead," he urged her. "The code for the door lock is three-seven-nine-one," he told her.

She started up the path toward the front door. "You've already memorized it?"

"The owner used the last four of my phone number," he explained. "I hate it when they do that. Don't they know how vulnerable it makes both their tenants and the properties?"

"I'm sure you'll point it out to them in your review." Kayla reached the front door, punched in the code and swung the glass pane door inward. "Cozy."

It was a nice cabin. Possibly the nicest cabin he'd ever seen—and growing up in Arkansas, he'd seen quite a few. Once over the threshold, the rustic exterior gave way to a modern, comfortable interior with an open-concept floor plan and towering ceilings. He noted a ladder to a sleeping loft to his left, but rolled her suitcase into one of the two bedrooms off the hallway leading from the living area. Once again, he left her belongings in the main room with its en suite bathroom, then dropped his own duffel in the room opposite. When he turned, he found Kayla standing in the short hall glancing from her room to his, her bottom lip caught between her teeth.

"If you want, I can sleep up in the loft, but I'd prefer not to," he said with a grimace. "I'm not sure how my knee will do with the ladder."

Kayla waved off the suggestion and then gave a sharp shake of her head. "Don't be silly. There's plenty of room for both of us." She turned around to face the open living area again, with its wide wall of windows that showcased the shimmering lake.

"This is beautiful," she said quietly.

"Not as impressive as your house on Table Rock, but, yes, this is nice."

Kayla rolled her eyes then strolled into the living room, trailing her fingers over the fabrics of the sofa cushions and throws artfully tossed over stuffed armchairs that faced a stone fireplace. "You mean not as obnoxious as the house on Table Rock." When he said nothing, she gave a short laugh. "Don't worry, I am aware the house is both ostentatious and beautiful," she said with a twinkle in her eye. "I have an attachment to it, but I can admit it isn't exactly to my taste."

"I would think a place so impressive would be to anybody's taste."

"Don't get me wrong, I'm not complaining. It's simply not what I would have chosen for a lake house. Too over-the-top. Then again, I'm told Ty's father had a massive ego, so the size and style of the house probably suited him."

This place suited her. The thought popped into his head unbidden, but true. The decor was soft and welcoming. Bright and airy, but still plush. Almost sumptuous.

Needing to rein in his thoughts before his assessment got out of hand, Ryan pointed to the front door. "I'm gonna go grab the groceries. I'll be right back." He strode out the door, making a beeline for the SUV.

He didn't need to be having thoughts about how perfect she'd looked in the comfortably luxurious cabin he'd chosen. Didn't want to think too hard about how it pleased him to please her. If he stayed in the house with her, soon his brain would be waxing poetics about the way her face lit every time she turned her gaze toward the water. And distracted thinking like that got people hurt.

Leaning into the cargo area, he snagged the handles of multiple grocery bags and hefted them with a grunt. He turned and straightened abruptly when he nearly stepped on Kayla's foot. "Ow!" he howled when he hit his head on the open liftgate. "Ugh."

"Sorry. I thought you knew I'd be right behind you," she said in a rush. "Here, let me carry some of those."

He surrendered the bags from his left hand and automatically reached up to rub the soreness from his scalp. "I can get the rest."

"I'm not helpless, and you're not here to fetch and carry for me," she countered, turning on her heel.

He huffed as he reached into the SUV to get the remainder of the groceries. When they had everything inside, he locked the door and put the chain on out of habit. He turned to find her watching him, her expression dark.

"What?"

"Did you bring me to the lake to lock me in?"

"Huh? Oh!" He glanced back at the door and felt his ears heat with a blush. "No. Sorry, I… Habit."

She tipped her head to the side as she unloaded one of the shopping bags. "Occupational hazard?"

"Occupational safeguard," he corrected.

They worked together swiftly and efficiently, and in a matter of minutes, they had their provisions stored. When the last bag was stowed under the sink, Kayla turned to him, her expression open and hopeful. "Can I go down to the lake?"

He nodded. "Of course, we can."

"You'll come, too?"

"I will need to stay reasonably nearby, but I'll do my best to give you whatever space you need," he assured her.

To his surprise, Kayla shook her head adamantly. "Not

what I meant. I... I want to go down to the dock. Do you want to come, too?"

"Sure. Let's go check it out," he replied.

He saw no reason to tell her he'd already been out to the property to inspect the area. The floating slip was tucked in a small cove, but was bracketed by docks belonging to the neighbors on either side. The area at the front of the cabin was wooded, but the shoreline had been cleared and tamed. A few oaks and maples provided shade, but the rest was the work of a landscaper rather than Mother Nature.

He followed Kayla down the flagstone steps that led to a small dock. He wasn't about to miss this opportunity to get her to talk more. Choosing a lakefront property had been a good idea. She was more relaxed here than she'd been in the tidy house in the nondescript subdivision.

She might not be completely on board with the plan for her protection, but whether she realized it or not, Kayla was beginning to open up.

Not that he was going to point it out. She said being on the water relaxed her. Perhaps he could get her to talk some about her pregnancy.

He understood the need for secrecy. The birth of this child would certainly not be cause for celebration for the remainder of the Powers family. But was she happy about it? Was she excited to have a child by the man she clearly had loved, or would the baby be a painful reminder of all she'd lost?

Regardless, this pregnancy put her in even more danger than anyone anticipated, and he was going to do his best to protect her and her child.

She walked out to the end of the dock and kicked off her sandals before sitting down on the edge of the weather-resistant resin planks. Though the seasons were turning, the afternoon sun was warm. The sky was bright blue and cloudless. Kayla tipped up her chin to the bright rays. With her eyes shut, she spoke softly. "I have to tell you something."

"What?" he asked, instantly on high alert.

"I had a text from Bill Powers this morning."

He tensed, but kept his mouth shut. Now he had an explanation for why she hadn't resisted the move. But it ticked him off she'd held on to this information for more than two minutes. Worse, he could tell by her glance she knew it would make him worry and did it, anyway. He bit his tongue, refusing to rise to the bait.

"Your basic, how-are-you-doing, we're-all-thinking-about-you text," she said, pulling her phone from the front pocket of her jeans.

He remained stubbornly silent while she unlocked the device and opened the message, holding it out for him to see.

Hope U got the rest you needed at Briarwood. Hope 2 have this mess with Ty's estate straightened out asap. Plz call.

While he frowned at the message, Kayla peered over his arm. "I always find it weird when people use text abbreviations, but throw in all the appropriate punctuation. I mean, are you being lazy or not?"

His eyebrows jumped at the snide edge in her tone, but he let it go. "Did you call him?"

She scoffed. "Of course not."

"Did you tell them you were going to Briarwood?"

"No."

"Probably not hard for them to figure it out, though. Do they know what you were being treated for?"

"Michelle and I figured we'd go with grief, exhaustion and general depression if anyone dared to ask."

"Did they try to contact you while you were at the facility?"

"I didn't have my phone for the time I was in treatment, but Bill did try to talk to Michelle while I was there."

"What can you tell me about his relationship with his son?"

Kayla eyed him as if it was a trick question. "There are worse relationships," she said cautiously. "Del was his son from his first marriage. It's my understanding Bill's divorce from his ex-wife was contentious. He remarried and had two more children with his current wife. Del's mother passed away before he went off to college. Ty said their relationship improved after she was gone."

"Would you say they are close?" Ryan probed.

She paused as if selecting each word carefully. "I would say Del would like to secure his place in his father's world."

Kayla met his gaze directly, so he asked a direct question. "Do you think in his mind that entails clearing the way for his father's ambitions?"

Kayla shrugged. "I don't know. Truthfully, I didn't know either of them well enough to have any depth of knowledge concerning their motivations. Mostly I saw superficial stuff. In public, the Powers family always presented a united front."

"Do you think it's possible Del is in contact with his father now?"

"Possible?" She raised an eyebrow. "Of course. But I don't believe he is acting with his father's blessing, if you're thinking Bill was part of it."

"What makes you say so?"

"Tyrone and Bill were brothers. They were close when they were younger. Trey was his nephew. He may have grown up to be a spoiled jerk, but I assume he was once a cute kid like any other. Aside from any familial affection, Bill is a politician. It's his nature to avoid anything that might blow back on him. He has presidential ambitions. He's not going to do anything that could cause long-term damage to his reputation."

"A son who may or may not be a loose cannon can be an enormous liability."

"Del is not the son Bill trots out into the spotlight," she reminded him, her voice soft. "If there's anything the Powers men excel at, it's controlling the optics of the situation. Tyrone was no different."

Ryan was surprised by the implied criticism of her late husband. He wanted to believe a tragic death meant a person should be canonized a saint, but he was thrown off by Kayla's offhanded acknowledgment of her husband's flaws. Undoubtedly, her stay at Briarwood had included at least a session or two of grief counselling. And her training as an attorney had taught her not to volunteer information unless asked a direct question.

Keeping that in mind, he charged straight into the topic.

"We haven't talked about your pregnancy—"

"I'm not ready to," she said without a beat of hesitation.

"But you told me—" he began, hoping to draw at least a little more information from her before she froze him out again.

"Because knowing I am pregnant is germane to your mission here," she replied. "My feelings on my pregnancy are not."

He was still formulating his rebuttal to this logic when the crack of a gunshot echoed across the lake. Ryan's arm shot out, and they hit the water with a splash.

Chapter Seven

Water went straight up her nose. She swallowed a good gulp of it, too. Thankfully, she'd been taking a breath in preparation for putting Sergeant Hastings in his place with regard to her personal life when he'd toppled them both into the surprisingly chilly water. He held her tight against his torso, his arm a steel band around her waist as he propelled them to the surface.

Kayla burst from the water, sputtering and gasping. "What—" He tightened his grip on her and tugged, using one arm to push them back until they were both sheltered beneath the dock.

"Gunshots," he whispered in a low urgent voice. "Shout at me later. Voices carry across the water."

She opened then shut her mouth again, gazing at him in disbelief. Then a volley of gunshots rang out across the water of the lake.

"Oh, my God." Wriggling in his grasp, she turned to look him straight in the eye. "Those *are* gunshots," she whispered, her eyes wide.

He braced one hand against the underside of the dock, but did not ease his hold on her. He tilted his head to one side, clearly listening for more. Her own breathing sounded like a rush of wind in the silence between them.

She picked up the distant hum of a boat motor. Water slapped against the dock's pilings. Birdsong. Birds tweeted and trilled all around them. How could birds be singing when someone was shooting at her again?

Sure enough, another barrage of gunfire jolted her from her reverie. Kayla went stiff against Ryan's chest, her hands digging into his broad shoulders as she anchored herself to him.

"Six rounds," he whispered to her. "I don't think someone is shooting at us, but I can't get a good bead on which direction it's coming from. Water messes with the sound."

To her horror, her teeth began to chatter. Ryan shifted slightly, bringing her chest flush against his.

"Hang in a couple minutes. I know you're already cold. We won't stay in here too long."

He pushed off the underside of the dock, moving them closer to the ladder attached to the side, but keeping them sheltered beneath it.

"I'm going up to make sure the area is clear." He physically removed one of her hands from where she'd embedded it on his shoulder and wrapped her chilled fingers around the handle of the ladder. "Stay right here. I'll let you know when it's okay to come up."

Kayla nodded mutely as she watched him clamber up the ladder, water sluicing from his sodden clothes. Squeezing her eyes shut, she listened to his heavy footballs as he strode the length of the dock. He stopped the moment the report of a bullet being fired split the air. Five more shots followed in rapid succession. Clamping her chattering teeth together, she gripped the sides of the ladder with both hands and hauled herself up a few inches so the top of her head brushed the bottom of the dock. She felt trapped between the cold pull of the water and the echo of gunfire across its surface.

Ryan's footsteps shook the planks. The toes of his shoes appeared over the edge, water dripping down onto the top rung of the ladder.

"You can come up. It sounds like it's coming from the east. I'm pretty sure it's somebody out target shooting."

Kayla moved hand over hand to the outside of the ladder and planted her foot on the bottom rung to hoist herself out of the chilled water.

"Sometimes I hate living in a gun-happy state," she said through chattering teeth.

With her torso out of the water, Ryan offered both of his hands to help her up.

"It can feel like we're still living in the Wild West some days," he said dryly. "Come on, let's get inside and get changed. I think we're both going to need a hot shower."

Her sodden jeans and long-sleeve shirt clung to her as they made their way up the shore incline toward the cabin. They were approaching the sliding door when whoever was shooting let loose with another barrage.

Her back stiff, she walked past Ryan into the open kitchen she'd so admired a short time before—now, all she could see was how exposed the back half of the cabin was to anyone who was looking.

"D-Do you think we're o-okay here?" she stammered as she hugged herself tightly.

"Shower first. Get into some warm, dry clothes. We'll talk later," he said, planting his hand on the small of her back and propelling her toward the narrow hallway. "I'll make sure the house is secured and will wait to shower once you're finished."

"But you have to be freezing, too," she protested, glancing back over her shoulder.

"I'll grab a towel and dry off. It'll be okay," he said firmly.

As she stripped out of her cold, wet clothing, she couldn't help but wonder at the strange direction this new chapter of her life was taking.

Murder.

Mayhem.

She was being hunted by a man she thought she knew fairly well, but entrusting her life, and her most precious secrets, to a man she'd met barely a week ago.

Turning her face into the warm spray, she marveled at how quickly she'd grown accustomed to Ryan's quiet, competent company. She'd had no doubt he'd figure out where the shots were coming from and whether she was actually in danger. When he gave the all-clear, she didn't hesitate for a moment. Not even when second-guessing would be second nature to any rational human.

It was a novelty.

Before Tyrone, she'd only had one relationship that lasted beyond six months. All through college and law school, she'd kept her eyes fixed firmly on the future. Once she'd joined PP&W, she'd been buried too deep in the workload of an associate to find much time to socialize. Then she and Ty had hit it off, and before she knew it, they were married.

And though they'd lived together as husband and wife for a number of years, they'd never melded their lives. Ty was older, had an established group of friends whose wives were more his contemporaries than hers. And she couldn't hang around her former PP&W colleagues without draping whatever festivities they had planned with a giant wet blanket monogrammed with "the boss's wife."

She sighed as the hot water chased the cold from her bones, but she was all too aware of Ryan waiting for her to finish. After shutting off the water, she quickly dried off, then wrapped the towel snugly around her body.

As she pulled a pair of yoga pants and a sweatshirt from her suitcase, her mind whirred, trying to slot the events of the past week into some sort of order. But she couldn't. The past few months had been extraordinary, and not in the best way. As she pulled on the clothes, she considered talking to her counsellor about possible PTSD.

It was so odd to even consider talking to a stranger about such personal subjects. She'd grown up in a small town, where any gossip that even hinted at illness—physical or mental—carried the taint of stigma.

A thump from the other room jolted her from her ruminations. She pulled on her clothes, all the while thinking about how she could answer Ryan's questions about her pregnancy. She didn't know exactly how she felt beyond the most basic surges of happiness and fear. How was she supposed to express the jumble of emotions roiling inside her each time she let her mind wander in that direction?

She wasn't good at sharing. Ty had been one of the few people she'd let in. She'd thought she was a part of the Powers family, but Bill and Del were making it abundantly clear she'd been accepted only as a part of her husband's life, not on her own merit. Michelle and Ethan were the first people she'd taken into her confidence in years. And now, apparently, Ryan was a part of her circle. After all, she'd entrusted this near stranger with the most vital bit of information she'd ever shared with another living soul.

She opened the bedroom door and saw his door open at the opposite end of the hall. "I'm out of the shower. You can get in and get warm now."

Her heart rate shot up again when she caught a glimpse of Ryan as he exited his bedroom wearing nothing more than a towel wrapped around his waist. She blinked when it registered that the man had more than his fair share of muscles. She jumped when his deep voice came right back to her.

"Great. I'm getting in now. Do me a favor and stay in this part of the house? I don't want you to go near the windows until I've had a chance to give the area a more thorough check."

Backing away from her door, Kayla bumped up against the bed. Her knees bent automatically, and she dropped onto the firm mattress with her jaw agape.

"Kayla? Did you hear me?"

Was he coming this way? Dressed only in a towel?

"I heard you," she blurted as if the confirmation might ward him off. At the same time, her curiosity tugged her head to the side. Her cheeks flamed and she forced herself to straighten. She shouldn't be hoping for another glimpse of her protection agent in a towel.

She jumped up and paced the small area between the bed and the door. If she closed it now, would it be too obvious? Had he even noticed her door was open? She pressed the heel of her hand to the center of her forehead and forced herself to turn back to the suitcase she'd left open on the bed. The sound of water rushing through the pipes spurred her into action.

She'd unpack what she'd need for the next couple of days, then sort through the rest in an effort to pare down what she was carrying. Every place they were renting had laundry facilities, and it wasn't as if she needed an extensive wardrobe to hide out in Staycation homes. Her stubborn insistence on packing clothes she could wear into the office, or even out and about in Bentonville, now seemed as ridiculous to her as it must have been to Ryan. She'd sort it out and arrange for Michelle to collect the excess.

Ryan's shower took less than five minutes. She'd heard the water shut off, but stubbornly kept her back to the door.

She didn't even allow herself to break from her task when she heard the click of his bedroom door. By the time she'd separated her clothing into piles of what to keep and what could go, she could hear him moving around the main room of the cabin.

She'd started to comb through her toiletries case when a soft beep indicated the disengagement of the lock. The cabin door opened and closed, and another beep assured her he'd secured the door. No doubt off to check the perimeter of the property.

She abandoned her task the moment she heard him reenter.

Peeking around the corner, she found him dressed in his everyday uniform of worn jeans and a dark T-shirt. He'd gone into the water wearing his brown shoes with the thick soles. Now he had on what she knew to be fairly pricey running shoes.

Was he a runner before his knee injury, or was he simply into having the best of everything, as Ty's son, Trey, had been? Ryan didn't strike her as the type of man to be overly concerned about impressing others, but who knew? People were hard to read sometimes.

Suddenly, she found herself intensely curious about him.

"Is everything okay?"

He nodded. "I contacted our host, and he informed me there's a gun club about a quarter mile down the road." Ryan tipped his head to the side, presumably indicating the direction of the property in question. "I checked the surrounding area. We're safe here."

"As safe as someone can be with live ammunition flying all over the place."

"I could find another place for us to go," he offered.

"No." The answer popped out of Kayla's mouth before her brain caught up.

This time at the lake, any lake, was what her heart and soul needed. A refuge away from the heartbreak mixed in with the shambles of her life in Bentonville. "No," she said, gentling her tone. "I want to stay here." She gave him a tremulous smile. "Please don't stuff me in some soulless subdivision in Springdale. At least not for a couple days," she added with a wry smile.

Ryan gave a slow nod. "O-o-okay," he said, drawing the word out. "I may need to rethink our next location."

Kayla laughed then shook her head. She didn't want to cause this man any more work than she absolutely had to. "I was kidding. I can deal with subdivisions," she assured him.

"Good to know," he exhaled. "But for future reference, I'll do my best to keep us away from town, if you prefer. When we first spoke, you wanted to be close to the office, remember?"

She nodded. "I remember," she said definitively. "At the time I thought I'd be going into the office and making some sort of difference there. It's clear Michelle has everything under control, and given the fact Bill reached out to me after we made our appearance there, I suspect his informants were on the ball."

"Can you think of anyone other than the two you mentioned who may be close to Del?"

Kayla shook her head. "I've been racking my brain, but I wasn't there much over the past few years. My relationship with Del was friendly and cordial, but we didn't interact often until I married Ty."

"Understood."

Needing something to do, she gestured to the kitchen. "I'm hungry. How about you?"

He nodded slowly. "I could eat."

She opened the fridge and began to pull packages of sandwich fixings from it. "Let's talk about something else for a while," she suggested.

Ryan joined her in the small kitchen area. As he reached into a cabinet to pull down plates, he gave an agreeable nod. "Lady's choice."

"You grew up in Little Rock?"

"Didn't we cover this?" he asked, shooting her a sidelong glance.

"I'm rusty at making conversation that doesn't revolve around the Powers family," she replied stiffly. She could feel him watching her, but she kept her focus on arranging slices of bread on the plates. A long beat of silence passed, and for a moment, Kayla thought he was going to leave her dangling.

To her relief, he picked up the jar of mayonnaise and uncapped it as he spoke. "Did I tell you how I got into protective detail?"

"No." Cocking her head to the side, she eyed him curiously. "Is there a story?"

Ryan nodded. "I had a stepsister," he said gruffly.

His use of the past tense did not escape her notice. Kayla's shoulders tensed, but she forced herself to continue spreading thin layers of mayonnaise over each slice of bread. "A stepsister?" she asked, keeping her tone carefully neutral.

"Yes."

He reached for the package of ham and pulled it closer to him, then handed the sliced turkey to her. It didn't escape Kayla's notice that in a matter of days they'd already learned each other's preferences and habits.

"Talia," he said quietly. "Her name was Talia, but she went by Lia."

Kayla fought to keep her hands steady as she peeled off the thin slices of turkey breast and layered them onto the bread. "Pretty name."

"Yes. She was pretty, too."

She watched as he slapped half of the package of ham onto his own bread in a giant slab. She reached for the Swiss cheese and took out a thin slice, then handed it to him. "She must have been quite a bit younger than you," she observed. "Didn't you say you were in high school when your mother remarried?"

"Good memory," he said gruffly, accepting the package from her.

Tiring of the game of cat and mouse, Kayla turned to face him. "What happened to her?"

He placed two slices of cheese atop the pile of ham, then carefully zipped the package closed before tossing it aside. Instinctively, Kayla gripped the edge of the counter, bracing herself for whatever would come next in what she knew in her gut was the sad story. "What couldn't you protect her from?"

He didn't try to evade her amateur psychoanalysis, but he did not meet her gaze as he answered, "Herself."

"Oh, no." Her words came out in a hushed rush. "Did she hurt herself?"

She could tell by the way he held himself still that her deductions were close, if not precisely on the money. He shook his head. "Not exactly."

They stood frozen in place. The silence stretched so long Kayla wondered if she was going to have to cross-examine him to get the full story.

Beside her, Ryan heaved a full-body sigh then flipped the top piece of bread onto his sandwich, pressing down to meld his creation together. "She met some guy online," he said, picking up the plate and moving to one of the seats at the breakfast bar. "When my mother and her husband found out she was talking to the stranger on social media, they completely lost it. They tried to shut down all of her accounts, take away her phone, restrict about everything you could restrict in a fourteen-year-old's life."

"Fourteen," Kayla exhaled.

"Yeah." He cleared his throat then lifted one shoulder in a helpless shrug. "She lived with her dad most of the time, and she was pretty spoiled. Her mom wasn't particularly interested in being a full-time mother, and my mom...she was good at the mom thing."

"You seem to have turned out okay," Kayla teased with a small smile.

His lips quirked in response. "Lia didn't make it easy on her. When they did something she didn't like, she'd call me from the house phone and tattle on them." His gaze fixed on the lake beyond the windows. "I guess I was supposed to be her ally. Supposed to agree with her side of things. When they cut off her contact with the guy, she called them everything from monsters to fascists. I don't think she even knew what a fascist was other than it was something you weren't supposed to call somebody," he said wryly.

Needing to cut to the chase, she asked the direct question. "What happened to her?"

He kept his gaze fixed on the glistening lake. "She took off to meet him, of course."

From the deep timbre of his voice, she knew Lia's disappearance wasn't the end of the story. "He hurt her?"

Ryan nodded, his Adam's apple bobbing. "They found her body in the woods behind a rest stop on the interstate."

Kayla didn't ask for details about what had happened to her. She didn't need them. A young girl had been used and discarded. She reached over and gave his forearm a squeeze. "I am sorry," she said quietly.

He nodded in acknowledgment of her sympathy, then tore

his gaze from the water. "I tried to work in cybercrimes for a while, but it hit too close to home. I couldn't be objective."

"You chose to protect people in other ways."

She moved to take the seat beside him, embarrassingly relieved to not have to look him in the eye.

"Yes." He was quiet for a moment, then picked up his sandwich but put it right back on the plate. "He'll have to go through me to get to you, Kayla."

"Thank you, but I don't want anyone to get to anybody," she countered.

"One way or another, this will come to a head," he warned her.

"Yes, it will."

He turned and eyed her warily. "You sound as if you're hoping it does."

"I am," she answered honestly. "I want Del caught and questioned. I want to know why he shot me. I need to know if he had anything to do with Ty and Trey's deaths." She held his stormy gray gaze. "I hope to one day get back to living my life, whatever that means."

"I know you want answers—"

"No, I'll have answers," she interrupted. "I told you before and I'll tell you again, I won't hide forever. You and Ethan need to come up with a plan to flush Del out of the underbrush, or I will."

"Sounds like a threat," he growled.

"Not a threat," she said without the slightest hint of rancor. "A promise."

Chapter Eight

Ryan met with Ethan Scott a few hours after they moved into a town house in nearby Springdale. Kayla had mocked him mercilessly for the selection of the nondescript subdivision, but when he pointed out the relative anonymity provided by the identical units, she grudgingly admitted his plan was good. No one would look for her there.

The dairy bar not far from the Benton County Sheriff's Department was bustling. The roots of a scraggly tree had turned the asphalt driveway into chunks, but it provided a modicum of shade for customers waiting on their orders. He found Ethan leaning up against the side of his state-issued vehicle drawing deeply on a straw protruding from a foam cup.

"Hey," he said as he approached.

Ethan stopped sucking on his drink long enough to return the greeting and a jerk of his head. "Hey."

"How are things?" Ryan asked, falling in beside the other man.

Ethan shot him a look from under lowered eyebrows, took another pull on his straw, then muttered, "Quiet. Things are quiet."

Ryan nodded his understanding.

For most people quiet was good. Quiet was peaceful. Quiet meant all was well.

For a cop working an investigation where the brass continued to breathe fire, but the trail had gone cold, it was misery.

"I take it nothing came of Senator Powers's attempt to contact Mrs. Powers?" Ryan asked.

This time, Ethan didn't even remove the straw from his mouth when he shook his head.

"Man, you're gulping that thing down like it has all the answers," Ryan commented, amused by the other man's single-minded determination to drain whatever was in the cup.

"Pineapple milkshake," Ethan said from around the straw. He took another draw, then let it go with a sigh. "I thought it sounded gross at first, but Michelle's got me hooked on the darn things."

Ryan smirked. "Personally, I like the banana-cream ones."

Ethan nodded. "A respectable choice."

"No sightings of Del, I assume?" Ryan stated flatly.

Ethan returned to his milkshake lifeline. "You assume correctly."

"Does Michelle believe he's in contact with somebody at the firm?"

"Yes."

"Any suspects other than the two she named the day we went in there?"

Ethan shrugged. "No. I had a little informal chat with the two of them, but they're not giving anything up." He sighed and lowered the cup to his side. "I'm hanging on to the knowledge that I've never known a person to go underground and stay underground successfully. Certainly not one of these office types. You always have the paranoid paramilitary types who know how to go off the grid and live off in a lean-to in the woods, but they can never resist showing themselves eventually." He shrugged. "For all I know, Del Powers was one of those all along. Maybe he couched his survivalist tendencies in the safe I-like-to-fish-but-I'm-not-much-of-a-hunter kind of camouflage."

"We're pretty sure he is hunting Kayla, though," Ryan said grimly.

"My instincts tell me he hasn't gone away." Ethan turned and scanned the area beyond the razor wire fence that encircled the detention center attached to the sheriff's office. "Problem is there's too many places to hide in the hills."

"From what Kayla tells me, he's the patient sort. Who knows how long he'll wait?" Ryan mused grimly. He crossed his arms over his chest and joined Ethan in his perusal of the horizon beyond the secured facility. "Thoughts on using his father to flush him out?"

Ethan shot him a sidelong glance. "You want to be the one to suggest using a senator for bait?"

Ryan chuckled and shook his head. "No, sir."

"He's the one who's keeping the heat on the higher-ups. When I spoke to him about Kayla's impressions of the shooter, he dismissed the notion of it as ridiculous. Claims he's been in contact with Del, who has simply gone off on what the senator called 'one of his rambles' to get away from the discord over Tyrone Powers's will."

"If they've been in contact, then surely he has no opposition to telling Del we want to talk to him," Ryan countered.

"Senator Powers claims he's already informed Del of our interest in a conversation, and his son has assured him he will be in touch with us as soon as he returns from his trip." Ethan shot him a pointed glance. "Of course, neither of them could say when exactly that would be."

"And, in the meantime, the senator and his family have decamped to DC," Ryan said dryly.

Ethan heaved a sigh, then raised the cup to his mouth again. "Well, the man does have a job there, doesn't he?"

"That he does." Ryan ran a frustrated hand through his hair. "We moved again."

Ethan looked at him with interest. "Oh, yeah? How's it going?"

Ryan tipped his head to the side as if weighing his answer, but in the end, decided to admit he needed help. "She's restless. Anxious to get this resolved. Not only Del, but also the murders of her husband and stepson."

"I don't doubt it."

"I was wondering if maybe you and Michelle wanted to come to the place we're staying tonight. We could order in some food or I could cook. I think she's getting antsy."

"Tired of your company?" Ethan asked with a smirk.

"My company is scintillating," Ryan replied, deadpan. "But she's restless, and maybe between the four of us we can come up with some thoughts on how to draw Del out of the woods."

Ethan took a long pull on the straw that ended in a gurgle and a slurp. Heaving a disappointed sigh, he gave the now-empty cup a look as if it had betrayed him by not being bottomless. He then pushed away from the car. "Sounds good to me. Send me the details and let me know when you want us."

"Oh, and Kayla wanted me to ask about Harold Dennis," Ryan said before Ethan could get away.

Ethan let his head fall back and scrubbed a hand over his face. "Ah, Dennis," he sighed. "As somebody who was a lawyer, I can tell you there's nothing more miserable than having a lawyer in custody. Not only do they have a phalanx of other lawyers surrounding them at all times, but also it's hard to know exactly what to charge him with from one moment to the next. It's a veritable smorgasbord of choices."

"Isn't he the FBI's problem?" Ryan asked, straightening

away from the vehicle and shoving his hands into the pockets of his jeans.

"Yes, which is why Michelle can probably give you better intel on him than me. He was her collar."

Ryan inclined his head in acknowledgment. "I forget she's a Fed." He shook his head. "What a mixed-up little world we have going on up here."

Ethan slapped him on the shoulder with a laugh. "Welcome to life in the Ozarks," he said sarcastically. "You thought Little Rock was a small town. Everybody is intertwined up here in one way or another, whether they're native or not." Ethan smirked and let his hand fall away as he started toward the door of the sheriff's department. He raised the hand in farewell.

Ryan stood watching as the other man trudged back into the building. It was clear the weight of the unsolved homicides weighed heavily on Ethan. The combination of pressure from within the ranks of the state police, the expectations of the public at large and the fact he was involved on a personal level had to make it all much more difficult.

Heading back to his car, Ryan thought that he would make every attempt to steal himself against the pull of Kayla Powers. The last thing he needed was to get any more enmeshed with these people than he already was. He had no intention of doing anything but finishing up his detail, and proving he was ready to come off desk duty back in Little Rock.

The town house they were staying in all week actually had more square footage than the cabin, but its vertical layout meant the space was narrow and deep rather than sprawling and spacious. The only way to avoid living on top of one another was to literally go upstairs to one of the bedrooms and spend their free hours cooped up there. Their companionable stay in the cabin had brought them together enough that it seemed churlish to take refuge on the second floor of the house.

Kayla had obviously decided she no longer felt the need to claim her own separate space. When he arrived back at the town house, he found her lounging on the living-room sofa flipping through options on the television. The temptation to join her was strong enough to force him to claim work responsibilities and head up to his room. After speaking with his superior and updating his assignment notes, he now had no choice but to shower, change for dinner and come downstairs to join her.

When he returned, he saw she'd changed into jeans and a pretty top with silver-gold thread running through the fabric. He assumed the change in wardrobe was for the sake of their company, not him, but he could appreciate it, nonetheless.

She sat perched on one of the stools at the kitchen island, a laptop open in front of her. She gave him a distracted hello as he came down the stairs. His brow furrowed as he approached the kitchen. "Hey," he returned. "Michelle and Ethan should be here soon."

She frowned at the screen. "I think Harold Dennis knows Del is somehow involved in Ty and Trey's deaths." She tapped the end of the stylus she was holding against her lips. A pucker formed between her eyebrows as she read whatever was on the screen.

"What makes you think he is?"

"Huh?" Then, as if realizing she'd actually spoken out loud to another human being, she jolted and slammed the lid of the laptop shut. "Oh. No reason… A gut feeling."

Ryan laughed and then circled the island to face her. "You're a terrible liar for a lawyer," he commented mildly.

She opened her mouth to protest, then snapped it shut. Pink spots appeared on her cheeks and she lowered her gaze for a moment, but then a bashful smile stretched her mouth. "I'm out of practice."

"What makes you say Harold Dennis suspected Del had something to do with your husband's death?"

"I'm not sure," she confessed.

He nodded. As a cop, he never discounted intuition. "Do you know what's giving you this feeling?" he persisted.

"No, it's—" She heaved a sigh then pried open the lid of the laptop again. When she turned it to face him, he could see she'd been marking up a document that looked like a transcript.

"What are you reading?"

The color on her cheeks deepened another shade. "Something I'm not supposed to."

He stared at her for a moment, weighing how he was supposed to respond to such a confession. "Do I want to know about it?" he asked cautiously, averting his gaze to the floor before he could register any of the verbiage on the screen.

"Maybe not at this point," she said quietly. "If I come across something concrete, I'll pass it along to Ethan and Michelle, but for your purposes, it's not need-to-know. I don't want to risk you crossing any ethical lines."

Ryan nodded then turned his gaze to the sliding door that led to the town house's minuscule patio, acting like he wasn't tempted to stare too hard at her or her ill-gotten documentation. "Thank you, I guess?"

Kayla chuckled. He heard the click of the laptop closing but didn't turn back until she rose from the stool. She placed the computer on the corner of the counter and walked toward the fridge. But he couldn't help eying the laptop like it was a snake about to strike. Something about the notion of her withholding information from him rankled, though he understood the reasoning behind it.

"Who's protecting who here?" he asked gruffly.

She pulled two bottles of water from the fridge, and handed one to him without asking. "You're willing to put yourself on the line to protect me physically. Why shouldn't I do what I need to do to protect your career and therefore your ability to continue protecting me?"

He uncapped the bottle as a burst of harsh laughter erupted from him. "Wow. You are a lawyer. I think your reasoning is somewhat convoluted."

Kayla smiled at him. "Not at all. Everyone has decided I need you to guard me from big, bad Del. You can't protect me if I put your job in jeopardy."

"Withholding information can be dangerous," he insisted.

"Withholding unsubstantiated suppositions helps us refrain from muddying the waters," she countered. "For the record, I ordered enough food to keep us full for the next week if Ethan and Michelle don't do their part to put it away."

He shook his head, unwilling to step into the web of her circular reasoning, but also frustrated by her ability to deflect. "Good. They should be here soon. I was half-afraid they'd want to get carryout from the dairy bar."

"I love the Daisy Dairy Bar," Kayla retorted, clearly affronted.

"Hey, I like a burger and rings as much as the next guy, but I have to admit I'm developing a general wariness for pineapple milkshakes. Apparently, they are addictive."

"That's the word on the street, though I have to say I'm partial to—"

A fist banging on the front door drew them both up short. Kayla slid off the stool, her eyes wide with surprise. Ryan felt a flash of annoyance. He might never get to hear exactly what Kayla Powers was partial to, and damn it, he wanted to know. But the shouts coming from the front of the town house quickly squashed his irritation.

Ethan and Michelle had arrived, but rather than the warm greetings of friends coming to share an evening in, they were both shouting about for them to unlock the door before they broke it down.

Both he and Kayla started for the front of the town house, but he quickly inserted himself in front of her. "Stay in the living room," he ordered. "Let me see what's going on."

He didn't wait to see if she wanted to argue with him. There didn't seem to be time. Two armed agents were standing on the doorstep threatening to bust into the place, and he had to find out why.

"Sergeant Ryan Hastings, Arkansas State Police," he shouted back. "Identify yourselves."

The pounding ceased as abruptly as it started and there was a beat of silence before Michelle answered him. "Special Agent Michelle Fraser, FBI, and Lieutenant Ethan Scott, ASP-CID."

"Why are you pounding on the door?" Ryan demanded as he approached it, leaning down to touch the sidearm he had strapped to his ankle beneath his jeans.

"Are you both okay?" Ethan countered.

Ryan straightened halfway, gun in hand, but a quick glance through the peephole confirmed the only people standing on the threshold were indeed Ethan and Michelle. In one fluid movement, he returned his firearm to its holster and disengaged the locks as he rose again. He yanked open the door and ushered them in. The second they crossed into the foyer, he slammed the door shut and locked it. "What's going on?"

Michelle held an enormous brown paper bag with handles. It was emblazoned with the logo of a local food-delivery service and appeared to be loaded to the top with carryout containers.

"Where have you been? Did he ring the doorbell?" Ethan demanded, brandishing a piece of lined paper torn from a spiral-bound notebook. A scrap of silver duct tape with frayed edges was stuck to the top of the page.

"We've been here waiting for you," Ryan said impatiently. "And no. No one rang the bell. Why?"

"This was taped to the bag and sitting on the welcome mat," Ethan replied, waving the note in the general direction of their dinner delivery.

"Wha—"

Neatly drawn black marker letters glared back at him.

YOU TRADED LAKEFRONT PROPERTY FOR THIS?

"Holy—" Ryan blew a soft swear out on a gust of air.

"Someone knows you're here," Ethan concluded.

Ryan shot him a glare he hoped conveyed how little he appreciated statements of the obvious. "Excellent deduction, Holmes."

Michelle raised both eyebrows and stepped between the two men as if she and a bag full of fragrant food could shield Ethan from sarcasm. "Let's all take a breath," she said in a measured, but firm tone. "Someone knows where this order was being delivered. They don't necessarily know who is here."

"If it was the food-delivery driver, I want my tip back," Kayla said, stepping into the foyer.

"Did you order the food?" Ethan asked without preamble.

"What? Yeah. Why?" she asked, eyes narrowing.

Ryan swiveled to face her. "Did you use your own name or credit card?"

She shook her head as if to clear it. "No, I used the account you had me set up," she replied, her tone shaky. "The one in Frank Farmer's name."

"Frank Farmer?" Michelle repeated, her brow crinkling. "Why does that name sound familiar?"

"Kevin Costner's character in *The Bodyguard*. It was a joke," Kayla said briskly. "What's happening?"

Ryan felt the intensity of her stare down to his bones. She addressed the question to him, rather than to Ethan, who still held the note. "We don't know it was him." He met his friend's gaze and knew he was grasping at straws.

"What was who?" Kayla demanded.

Ryan snatched the note from Ethan before Kayla spotted it and could do the same. How had Powers figured it out? The only people who were fully clued in were the four of them, a couple of local deputies who had helped with checking locations and Ryan's superior.

The *how* didn't matter now. Once Kayla saw this note, she would know his brilliant master plan for keeping her safe by keeping her moving had failed. He had failed.

"There was a note attached to the food delivery," Michelle reported. She pulled the long strip of receipt stapled to the bag closer to her face to inspect it. "The restaurant receipt shows the name as Frank Farmer."

"But somehow he knows who Frank Farmer is, and where Frank Farmer has been staying," Ethan said grimly.

"He?" Kayla interjected. "He, as in Del?" she asked, turning to Ryan for confirmation. "How?"

Ryan's jaw tensed, but there was no point in trying to put her off. "I don't know how, but yes. Someone knows we've been moving from property to property, and we have to assume that person is Del Powers."

Michelle lowered the sack of food to the floor by its handles. "Before we get too far afield with this, I suggest we call for backup and another dinner."

"Another dinner?" Kayla asked, her tone bewildered.

"It's probably some fairly advanced paranoia on my part," Michelle admitted with a grimace of a smile, "but I don't think I want to eat this. If neither of you heard the delivery, or anyone else outside before we arrived, we have no way of knowing if he tampered with it."

"He must have intercepted the driver," Kayla whispered, her gaze falling to the bag.

Ethan pulled his cell from his pocket and speed-dialed a contact. "Hey, it's Scott here. I need a patrol car parked outside the address I'm sending to you. Someone has the drop on where Mrs. Powers is staying."

Ryan's gut churned as he turned over every move they'd made in his mind. Where had they slipped up? Was he the weak link? Had someone followed him back to the town house after he met with Ethan?

Ethan ended the call with a sigh. Nudging the enormous bag of food that would go uneaten. "I asked Sheriff Stenton to have the deputy he's sending over pick up pizza for himself and for us."

"Are we staying here tonight?" Kayla asked.

Again, she turned to him for confirmation and Ryan wanted to personally hunt down Del Powers and make him pay for the frightened look in her eyes.

"No sense in going anywhere else," he answered gruffly. "We'll have a deterrent outside—"

"And three armed agents inside," Michelle interjected.

"Armed?" Kayla turned to look at her friend quizzically. "You brought your gun to dinner?"

"Kayla, sweets, we're cops," Michelle said in a cajoling tone. "We don't go anywhere unprepared." She wrapped an arm around Kayla's waist and turned her back toward the kitchen.

Ryan met Ethan's gaze and gave a defiant lift of his chin even as he fought back his body's natural inclination to blush.

"We need to come up with another plan," Ethan said quietly.

As if Ryan needed to have it explained to him. He couldn't resist lashing out. "No kidding."

"I'm not criticizing," Ethan said, raising his hands in surrender. "I was trying to remind you there are four of us here, and among us we have plenty of brainpower to figure out where this went sideways."

"I've already narrowed it down," Ryan said grimly.

Ethan gave him a wan smile. "Me, too."

Somehow, his superior had to have given up enough information for Powers to track them down. How and why, Ryan didn't know. He'd have time to figure it out later. For now, he had to keep his focus on his primary.

Kayla was going to be even more resistant than she'd been at the start. He'd been able to use the scare of the shots fired at the lake to his advantage for a couple of days, but this turn of events would turn the tide against ducking and hiding. He'd learned enough about her over the course of the past week and a half to know the clock had already been ticking.

Kayla Powers was not the type to stand down for long.

Chapter Nine

Kayla allowed the conversation to swirl around her. In the hour since Michelle and Ethan's arrival, she'd found it difficult to do more than ask the most rudimentary questions.

Everyone had an opinion. They needed to move tonight. No, morning would be soon enough. Perhaps someplace out of state? Could Michelle's contacts at the FBI help find a place outside of Del Powers's comfort zone? Surely there was a safe house they could use.

Each of them had questions, but no one asked her opinion.

Where should she go? What were the odds the note had been left by someone other than Del? Was Senator Powers involved? Was all of this tied to Harold Dennis's money-laundering schemes? Was Harold behind Del's attack on Kayla? Had Harold, Del and the senator concocted an elaborate scheme to take control of the Powers fortune? Were they cold-blooded enough to kill their own family to secure their futures?

They talked over each other, voices rising with each objection and growing more strident as their speculation dove deeper. Kayla sat quietly at the town house's small dining table, while all around her the people she'd grown closest to talked about her like she was some kind of rare porcelain doll they needed to store in an airtight, unbreakable box until they deemed the world safe enough for her to emerge.

Inside she seethed.

At her friends. At Ryan. She saved a good bit of her inner vitriol for Del, of course. And in fairness, she added in Harold Dennis, Bill Powers and the world in general. Afraid to open her mouth for fear of unleashing her rage, she sat quietly and stared at a spot beyond her untouched slice of pizza.

It was impossible to eat when she was biting her tongue.

But no one seemed to notice her reticence. Or maybe they were too keyed up to tune in to her feelings. It was just as well. If she let them run their course, eventually, they would run out of steam and look to her for some sort of validation.

Then she'd tell them what she would do.

"What if we look for someplace in a more metropolitan area?" Michelle suggested. "Dallas? Tulsa? Kansas City? Someplace where it's easier to get lost in a crowd. Someplace not located directly in the Powers family's backyard."

"Someplace out of their sphere of influence," Ethan chimed in, pointing a half-eaten pizza crust at Michelle as if it helped hammer home the point.

"Cities present a whole other set of variables. If you're going to stay regional, I'd almost rather we head for Little Rock. At least I know the lay of the land there and would have plenty of backup."

"Good point," Ethan conceded, slumping back in his seat and dropping the uneaten crust onto his plate. He glanced over at Michelle. "What do you think of Little Rock?"

"Personally, or for Kayla?" she asked. But it was clear from her tone the question was rhetorical.

They fell silent for a moment. Ryan reached into the pizza box for another slice. He was about to lower the lid when he caught sight of her plate and frowned. "You're not eating."

A sneer twisted the corners of her lips, and a rush of indignation heated her blood. "I was sitting here waiting for one of y'all to tell me how to do it," she replied in a tone as cool as her blood was hot.

All conversation stopped. Michelle and Ethan turned to look at her, then down at her untouched plate. Michelle met her gaze again, her expression troubled. Kayla could almost see the other woman weighing whether she needed to be in friend mode or put on her lawyer hat.

"No one is telling you what to do," Ryan replied in what she assumed was his best hostage-negotiations tone.

"For the past thirty minutes the three of you have discussed how best to 'handle' me right in front of me," she snapped, raising her arms to be certain everyone appreciated her use of air quotes.

"We were talking about security," Ryan countered.

"My security," she replied. "The guarding of my body. My person. As if it didn't come with a functioning brain included in the package."

"Now, Kay—" Michelle began.

"No." Kayla turned her glare on her friend. "You were doing it, too. Talking about me like I'm some kind of valuable painting, or delicate statue you have to tuck away in a vault somewhere."

"We know you aren't those things," Michelle said, her manner forthright, "but the issue at hand is protecting you. Your person, as you said. Including your brain," she added with a lift of one perfectly groomed eyebrow. "No one is excluding you from the discussion."

"No one has asked for my input," Kayla pointed out.

Ethan had the good grace to look down at his own empty plate before busying himself with liberating another slice of pizza from the box.

"I believe we all assumed we were brainstorming," Ryan said gruffly.

"I'll refrain from repeating the old bit about assumptions and move on to telling you what happens next," she said, her voice taut.

There was a moment. A split second where the other three seated at the table froze for a heartbeat. The conversation resumed when Michelle cocked her head to the side and asked, "Yes? We're listening."

"I'm moving back to the house on Table Rock," she announced.

The words came out of her mouth before she'd even given the decision much thought, but she wasn't admitting as much to this crew. Not when they were stumbling over one another to voice their objections. She let them go for a minute, sitting still, but feeling surprisingly serene about her decision.

And while she was grateful for all the time and effort Ryan had put into his plan to keep them moving, it obviously wasn't the right answer. Unless she was willing to leave the area, possibly even the state, someone would likely have eyes on her. And she couldn't walk away now. Not with Ty's murder unsolved and his child growing in her belly.

No. Her heart had spoken. Or maybe it was her gut. Either way, she knew in her bones she needed to be on her own turf to see this through.

When their objections spluttered to a stop, she sat up straighter and folded her hands on the edge of the table, pushing the plate away a few centimeters. Ryan's gaze dropped to the uneaten pizza as if she'd issued an ultimatum. And maybe, in a way, she was. After all, they couldn't force her to accept their help.

"Listen, I appreciate all of…this," she said, gesturing to the town house, then catching Ryan's eye. "But it's not working.

Someone is watching us. Whether it's Del or not, I can't say, but it's safe to assume he has eyes on us one way or another."

He lifted his chin, the muscle in a corner of his jaw working as he formulated his response.

"Ryan, it's not working," she repeated, gentling her tone. "They know where we are and they know where we've been."

He broke eye contact, tucking his chin to his chest as he nudged the plate toward her again. "Doesn't mean we should make you a sitting duck," he grumbled.

"I'm willing to do whatever we need to do to make you feel better about me being there," she said, keeping her tone even, but firm. "We can upgrade the security system."

"A new system would be the bare minimum you'd have to do," he countered.

"We can make it top-of-the-line," she assured him. "You're welcome to come and stay there as well. The place is enormous."

His head jerked up. "Not a plus in this situation," he informed her. "We need less space. There's too much out there. It's uncontained."

"Exactly my point. I am also uncontainable," she declared. "I'm a human being trying to live my life. If you want to keep me under wraps, you're going to have to arrest me first."

Ryan and Ethan exchanged a glance. Both Kayla and Michelle leaned in, on high alert.

"What?" Michelle demanded.

"Nothing," Ethan replied. He took an enormous bite of his slice, no doubt to avoid having to answer their interrogation.

"It wasn't nothing," Kayla growled. "Tell me, or I'll refuse protection entirely."

"You shouldn't use your life as a bargaining chip," Ryan retorted.

"The point being, it's my life. If anyone gets to use it as a bargaining chip, it's me. What have you two been discussing? Behind my back?"

"There's been no discussion," Ethan said through stuffed cheeks.

"There was something there," Michelle insisted. "I thought we were all supposed to be on the same team here. Team Kayla alive." She sent a pointed look at Kayla herself. "Part of being a team means no pronouncements from on high. No backroom double-dealing," she said turning her gaze to the two men. "If we're going to figure this out as a team, we need to discuss options, not argue."

"Hard not to argue when three out of four of the people sitting at this table are lawyers," Ryan grumbled.

Kayla had to smile at his assessment. Turning back to Michelle, she said, "I wasn't making a pronouncement from on high," she said. "I was simply saying I wanted to go back to my own house. I don't think it's an unreasonable request given the fact we know trying to evade detection has not worked."

"Your house is too exposed," Ryan said gravely.

"Not to mention it's not actually technically your house. Senator Powers still holds interest in it, and that interest could mean Del has some rights to it, too," Ethan reminded her.

"I haven't forgotten," Kayla assured them. "I can assure you Bill Powers isn't going to risk his career by coming anywhere near me or northwest Arkansas until the stories about Tyrone's death and Harold Dennis's financial indiscretions have faded entirely," she insisted.

"I'm still wanting to know what the look meant," Michelle said, pinning Ethan with a penetrating stare. "Given the tenor of the conversation, I can't help wondering if you're playing with the notion of arresting my client."

"Arresting me?" Kayla said, snapping to attention.

"Not for real," Ethan said, holding up both hands placatingly. "But you have to admit, it wouldn't be a bad idea to let people think you've been taken into custody."

"Wouldn't be a bad idea?" Michelle growled.

"Are you kidding me with this?" Kayla demanded.

"Were you going to say anything to me about this, or were you planning on popping in and cuffing her without a shred of hard evidence?" Michelle said, glaring at Ethan.

"Is this some sort of asinine keep-her-under-wraps-at-all-costs sort of ploy?" Kayla asked Ryan as she rose from her seat.

Both men raised their hands in a gesture commonly used when a guy was about to deploy the old calm-down tactic, but neither was reckless or brave enough to actually utter those two fatal words.

"It was only an idea we tossed around," Ethan said, digging his hole a little deeper.

"Not a serious one," Ryan added quickly, shooting daggers at his friend and colleague. He almost saved himself with a single glare, but then he opened his mouth again. "But you have to admit, it would be a pretty good way of keeping you safe. Let the Powerses think we've caught the culprit…"

"They'd come crawling out of the woodwork the minute word leaked you were in custody," Ethan added.

"Then we set something up to get Del to implicate himself," Ryan said, nodding.

Ethan grimaced even as he nodded in agreement. "At least in the shooting at the lake house," he amended.

Kayla gaped at them, incredulous. "And exactly how long were you planning to keep me in custody?"

"As long as it takes," Ethan replied, his expression grim.

"Oh, you can't be serious," Michelle cried.

"I've heard some cock-a-doodle schemes, but how exactly do you think you're going to get someone to confess to a double homicide when you have a suspect in custody?" Kayla demanded. "Why wouldn't they want me to take the fall?" She threw her arms open wide. "Heck, they'd probably throw a parade for you."

"You'd be surprised how often guilty parties give themselves away once they think their getaway is assured," Ethan said soberly.

Beside her, Michelle stiffened in her seat. Kayla cocked her head, staring down at her friend and attorney in stunned disbelief. "You aren't about to buy in to this plan, are you?"

To her credit, Michelle shook her head with brain-sloshing ferocity. "No. But I do have to tell you, Ethan's right. Most people who think they've gotten away with a crime feel compelled to flaunt it in some way."

"It would be a way for you to ensure you are able to secure your late husband's legacy," Ryan said quietly.

Kayla gripped the back of her chair, shocked disbelief pulsing through her. Ignoring the thrum of her blood pounding in her ears, she stared down at the man she thought she'd come to know over the past week and a half. Her rage barely contained, she spoke through clenched teeth.

"If I'm no longer willing to move from one short-term rental to another, you can bet your badge I'm not about to give birth to Tyrone's baby in prison, Sergeant."

She bit off the last syllable and turned on her heel to stalk from the room. Unfortunately, the town house's open-concept floor plan didn't lend itself well to dramatic exits. She made it to the foot of the stairs before an explosion of voices tore through the aftermath of her pronouncement.

Ethan spoke first. "Nobody said anything about prison... Wait. She's pregnant?"

"Tyrone's baby?" Michelle asked, her tone dazed.

"What the— No way," Ethan said. "I can't even do the math."

Chairs scraped laminate flooring and Ryan let out a loud groan. "Oh, man. Kayla, wait," he called after her.

She reached the top of the stairs as Michelle barked a breathless but commanding "Hey!"

Closing her eyes, Kayla stilled, but did not turn back to face her friend.

"Are you really?" Michelle asked, her tone softening as she trotted up the steps.

Kayla could feel the other woman standing firm and unflinching at her back. "Yeah, I am."

"Are we happy about this?" Michelle whispered.

Kayla couldn't help but smile at the solidarity implied by the other woman's use of the plural pronoun. Glancing tentatively over her shoulder, she let the smile grow a fraction before she answered with an unwavering, "Yes."

Michelle gave a single decisive nod at the pronouncement. "Well, wow. Okay, then." She gave a huff of a laugh. "Okay. Well, come back downstairs. I promise not to let Ethan arrest you."

"Like you could stop me," Ethan mumbled, flashing Kayla a shamefaced smile as she reached the bottom of the staircase. "It was only a spitball."

"Yeah, well, it fell short," she retorted. Without bothering to look at Ryan, she asked, "What do we need to do to beef up security enough to make you feel comfortable with the move back to Table Rock Lake?"

"You know a good way to fence off waterfront?" he asked.

"You were okay with us being on Beaver Lake this past week," she reminded him.

Ryan quirked an eyebrow. "I was okay with it because I believed no one knew we were there. Now I know different."

"Proving that hiding from him isn't the answer," she countered.

"We've been through this," he growled.

She crossed her arms over her chest and lifted her chin. "Either you're coming with me or I'm going alone. It's up to you, Sergeant."

"You're not going alone," he barked.

"Then tell me what we need to have put in place. I'm booking rooms at a B and B I know in Eureka Springs for three nights, then I'm moving back home."

She felt a twinge at calling the lake house *home*. It wasn't the house she shared with Tyrone. The house and the parcels of land surrounding it weren't even hers to call her own. They belonged to the Powers family, and would in perpetuity, given the complex trusts put in place by Ty's father. But her child would be a Powers, and as Ty's only living offspring, they would inherit his share in the estate along with the personal wealth Ty had amassed on his own.

"I have ample resources, Ryan. Tell me what's needed, and we'll get people on it first thing in the morning."

"Unless you have enough cash to build a force field, it will be nothing more than a drop in the bucket," he countered.

Ethan and Michelle's heads swiveled like spectators at a tennis match, but they said nothing.

She pursed her lips. "Perhaps I should speak to someone at the state police about finding a more cooperative agent to work on my security detail?"

"Stop threatening me," he said, taking a step closer.

Kayla held his gaze, closing the distance between them until they stood toe-to-toe. "Stop trying to bully me."

A growl of frustration ripped from his throat, but he didn't back down. "I am not trying to bully you. I'm trying to make you face reality."

"Face reality," she repeated, blinking up at him in disbelief. "You seriously think you can give me a reality check?"

Her voice rose on the last bit. Michelle hastened to her side and exhaled, "Uh oh."

Ryan ran a hand through his thick, russet hair. "No, I didn't intend—"

But it was too late. "Face reality," she said with a sneer. "Well, maybe you're right, because it was pretty darn surreal to walk into my family room and find my husband and his son shot dead."

"Kayla—" Ryan began.

"And you know what's a real trip?" she interrupted. "Standing up against people who've intimidated me since the moment we met. But I did because my husband wanted me to be the custodian of his precious law firm."

"I know you have—" he said, but was cut off again.

"To weather the investigation, speculation and social ostracism in the days and weeks after. To have no one but Michelle by my side as I grieved as quietly and decorously as I could because heaven forbid I made a scene," she raged.

"And you did," he insisted.

"Suspicion clings like the stink on a skunk." In her agitation, the drawl she tried so hard to modulate came creeping in like kudzu. "I spent night after night alone in a hotel room drinking myself to sleep, wondering how I'd ever measure up. But you know what? It turns out I didn't have to," she said, lifting her chin in defiance. "Because there was nothing to measure up to," she continued, undeterred.

Ryan tried to interject in a soothing tone. "Kayla, we know—"

"It turns out the people I thought were so much better than

me were nothing but common criminals. Harold Dennis with
his stealing and double-dealing. Bill Powers, who only comes
around when he wants to soak people for money. And Del..."

She let loose with a harsh, self-deprecating laugh.

"Quiet, good-natured Delray Powers, who takes cheap
shots at unarmed women, and possibly murdered his own
uncle and cousin." She threw up her hands. "You're right,
Ryan, this cannot be reality. Someone had to have made all
this up because it's too bizarre to be real."

"But it is," Michelle interjected.

Kayla's head whipped around. She'd been so focused
on confronting Ryan Hastings and his plans to bulldoze
her, she'd forgotten they had an audience. She met her best
friend's eyes, then blinked. As always, the worry and compassion she saw in Michelle's steadfast gaze grounded her.

"But it is," she agreed in a whisper.

"And you've made it through all of it, all on your own,"
her friend continued. "But you aren't alone, Kayla. We're
here to help you. Let us help you."

Kayla swallowed the hot lump of emotion lodged in her
throat. "All I want is to go home."

Michelle pursed her lips as if weighing the demand, then
nodded. She turned to Ryan, her expression serious and her
tone unyielding. "As my client said, she has money at her
disposal, Sergeant Hastings. Let's spend some of it to make
the Powers family estate on Table Rock Lake as secure as
it can be."

Ryan nodded his assent and pulled out his phone. "Get
out your credit card," he grumbled as he scrolled through his
contacts. "If you're going to go bragging about your money,
then I'm going to be crowing about how much of it I spent."

Chapter Ten

Ryan kicked a rock and sent it tumbling across the leaf-strewn ground. It came to rest at the base of a spindly pine tree, and so did he. Planting his hands on his hips, he turned to survey the property from ten feet beyond the invisible perimeter protected by the new security system installed at the Powers's lake house. Truthfully, he was happy to be out of the frilly B&B.

It was too close, as far as he was concerned, but there wasn't much he could do to secure the exterior.

The interior, on the other hand...

He smirked, recalling Kayla's furrowed brow as she tried to follow the directions for accessing the smart home features. She made the technician repeat the various voice prompts three times. On the last attempt, she made the man turn on the voice-recording feature and run through each option. Then, she cross-examined the poor guy on the capabilities of each and every application.

Ryan had tossed his duffel into one of the upstairs guest rooms. It was two doors down from the primary bedroom. Far enough to give her the privacy she craved, but close. Maybe not as close as he'd like, given the massive scale of the place. But close enough.

Cutting through the woods, he circled the house, head-

ing for the lakefront. When he broke from the trees onto the
neatly maintained stretch of lawn, he made a mental note to
see if he could get hold of an aerial view of the estate. If he
was going to try to keep her safe out there, he needed a feel
for the entire property from every possible angle.

Things had been quiet since the night of their intercepted
food delivery. Too quiet.

Ryan had the uneasy feeling their every move had been
watched and noted, but for the life of him, he couldn't pick
up any trace of Del Powers in the area. Huffing from frustration more than exertion, he crossed the sloping expanse
of grass, half-wishing he had at least one more rock to kick.
He'd stepped onto the native stone pavers leading down to
the swimming dock and boat slips when his phone rang.

"Hastings," he said in a brusque, business-like bark, even
though the name on the screen informed him the caller was
Ethan.

The lieutenant must have been in a similar mood because
he didn't bother with even the most cursory greeting. "What
do you think about leaking the fact Senator Powers's son
might be a person of interest in the deaths of his uncle and
cousin?"

Ryan stopped in his tracks and let out a low whistle. "I
think you're a braver man than I am. Why not try poking the
hornet's nest before yanking it down and wearing it as a hat?"

"Can't be any worse than the heat I'm getting from the inside. I swear, the only person not calling to badger me about
this case daily is Kayla."

Both men fell silent for a moment, unspoken questions and
hypotheses as to why the victim's widow wasn't heading up
the line of people pushing the lead investigator on the case
swirling around them.

"I think she's still in shock," Ryan said at last, breaking

the tension. "I know she speaks to Michelle every day. And her therapist from Briarwood. Maybe she's getting enough information about the investigation from Michelle to keep her satisfied? Besides, I think she trusts you," he added after a thoughtful pause.

Ethan was quiet on the other end of the call. "Yeah. No. You're right. I'm grasping at straws." At last, he sighed. "I'll call if I come up with a better approach."

Ryan ended the call and made his way down to the dock. He stood with his feet spread wide, listening to the soft slap of lake water against the hulls of the boats docked in the nearby slips. He glanced over. The passenger compartment of the slick ski boat he assumed belonged to Trey Powers was covered with a canvas cover.

He thought about the girl who'd either fallen or been knocked off the boat as he stared out at the lake. The water was a near-impossible blue in the bright sunlight. A steady breeze out of the northwest sent ripples skittering across the surface. The day was warm, but the sticky humidity of summer was fading. Months had passed since Mallory Murray had gone missing, but there'd never be any resolution to the case. Not unless one of the people who'd crowded onto the back of the boat changed their story, which wasn't likely to happen. Accident or not, no one had bothered to pull poor Mallory out of the lake.

And now, the murder of the man who'd left her for dead could possibly go unsolved. He totally understood Ethan's desperation. The higher-ups were not going to be satisfied until he brought in the killer—or, at least, the person who'd paid the killer—wrapped in a bow. But trying to bait the son of a sitting senator into showing himself was probably not the best path to justice a man with career ambitions could take.

"Hey."

Kayla's voice jolted him from his thoughts. He turned to find her standing on the edge of the terrace, hand on her hips and a curious tilt to her head.

"Hey," he replied, pivoting to face her. "You shouldn't be out here like this," he admonished. Hurrying up the stone path, he tried to figure out the best angle to place his body between her and whoever might be watching them from the edge of the waterfront.

She glanced down, then back up at him with a puzzled expression. "What do you mean? I'm wearing pants, aren't I?"

He quickened his pace, fully intending to hustle her back into the safety of the house. "You're standing up there exposed for everyone to see," he half-shouted, hooking a thumb over his shoulder.

By the time he reached her, both of Kayla's eyebrows were riding high. "I hate to break this to you, but we're the only people out here. Well, other than Deputy Warren, but I doubt he can see me parked at the gate."

He huffed, ignoring the twinge of pain in his knee as he climbed the last few feet. "You know what I mean," he grumbled, catching her by the elbow and not breaking stride.

"Okay, if you're going to pull the caveman moves, I'd appreciate it if you'd either toss me over your shoulder or drag me by the hair, because my arm is sore and—"

He released her as if she was radioactive. A chiding voice in the back of his head reminded him her arm had healed, but logic didn't play into it. He wasn't there to inflict harm, he was there to protect her from it. They stood staring at one another, as stubborn and entrenched as TV news anchors in a tug-of-war of wills.

"Your arm is fine," he accused, narrowing his eyes, challenging her to say otherwise.

Kayla's chin popped up, but her mouth curved into a smile. "It is. Thanks for asking."

"Kayla," he said in a low, warning tone.

"Ryan," she countered. He gave an involuntary grunt, and her smile grew exponentially. "Come inside. I have a surprise for you, and I want to ask a favor."

She didn't wait for his response. Kayla Powers was a woman who'd grown accustomed to getting her way. As he watched her walk toward the glass doors that opened onto the terraced patio, he felt a sharp stab of recognition.

Suddenly, he was nineteen again, standing bewildered in the upstairs hallways of his mother's massive home in Little Rock. He'd skipped an afternoon class to come home for the weekend, hoping to surprise his mom and spend some time hanging out with a couple friends from high school. But rather than the warm welcome he'd been anticipating, he'd found himself listening in shocked disbelief as the woman who'd raised him on the paltry salary of a chain-hotel, front-desk clerk fired her assistant for not hanging his stepfather's dry cleaning in his closet properly.

"Ryan?" Kayla called to him, jolting him from the memory.

He met her gaze. But unlike the cool disparagement he'd seen in his mother's eyes that day, he saw only concern, warmth and maybe a hint of mischief in Kayla's. "Oh. Yeah. Right," he murmured.

Ryan tried to maintain an air of indifference as he crossed the massive patio with its built-in firepit and brick pizza oven, but his knee was aching and his pride was wounded. This woman played him too easily. She got under his skin. He needed to be on his guard—not only for her, but also with her.

"What is it?" he asked, injecting a note of perturbed impatience into the question in hopes of putting her on her heels as well.

It worked. Kayla blinked in surprise, then her forehead creased with worry. "Is your knee hurting?"

Damn if the woman wasn't the most frustrating mass of contradictions. How could someone so oblivious to her own peril be so attuned to someone else's pain? He fell back on his standard response. "A twinge. I'm fine." He nodded for her to precede him into the house. "What did you want to ask me?"

She shook her head as she crossed the threshold. "Surprise first." Turning back to face him, she said loudly, "Play Ryan's song."

A disembodied voice replied from an invisible speaker. "Playing Ryan's song."

Before he could process what was happening, Whitney Houston's voice blared from the whole-home audio system, belting out the crescendo of the song she'd resurrected for the movie *The Bodyguard.*

He shook his head in mock dismay, doing his best not to crack a smile, but it was not an easy thing to do when bombarded by professions of unending love.

She reached for the high note at the climax, and their eyes met. Seeing the devilish delight lighting Kayla's face made it impossible for him to remain stoic. Grinning back at her, he shook his head, not even attempting to speak over the soaring declarations.

Then, as if she'd tuned in to the lyrics for the first time, Kayla's eyes widened, and her cheeks colored. Ryan didn't bother trying to stifle his laughter as he watched her succumb to the mortification of possible misinterpretation.

"Stop," she shouted over the music.

But the song continued to play.

"Stop the music," she ordered again.

But Whitney sang on.

"Mute," she shouted in frustration.

The command did the trick. Silence roared through the cavernous house, and for an uncomfortable moment, Ryan almost wished she'd let the song play to its conclusion. At least then, the echoes would be filled with wistful longing rather than gut-wrenching emotion. Hoping to ease the tension, he tore his gaze from her flushed cheeks and looked up at the ceiling as if searching out the concealed speakers.

"Wow, no one has made a joke about me being Kevin Costner in at least five minutes," he said in a bored drawl.

To his relief, Kayla laughed. "You have to admit it made for a good entrance."

"Now I'll expect nothing less each time I walk through a door," he answered, making a point of meeting her gaze again. "I take it the song was my surprise. What is the favor?"

With a huff, Kayla blew a lock of blond hair from her cheek. "I want you to walk down to the mailbox with me."

"The mailbox?" he repeated, puzzled. "Do you need to have something sent?"

She shook her head, but she couldn't quite meet his eyes. "No, I want to go check the mail."

"You expecting a big check or something?" he joked, then, with a frown added, "Do people even have checks anymore?"

"Yes, they do, and no, I am not expecting one." She gestured for him to follow, then took off in front of him again.

Ryan caught up to her in two strides, but this time he didn't make a grab for her arm. "I don't get it," he said as she made a beeline down the corridor leading to the front entrance. "What's in the mail?"

"Nothing's in the mail," she countered as they reached the heavy double doors.

He watched as she disarmed the alarm with a few taps of

the keypad, then twisted the locks. She reached for the handle, and he stepped closer.

"Hey, you going to tell me what's going on here?"

Kayla pressed her lips together, and for a moment he thought she might bolt without explanation. He caught the edge of the heavy door as it started to swing into the foyer, his forearm effectively blocking her way until he was given a more satisfactory answer.

"Kayla?"

"I was checking the mailbox the day he shot me," she answered, her gazed fixed on the middle distance beyond the door.

"The day Del shot you?"

She nodded.

"What were you looking for in the mail?" he asked, hoping for some more clarity.

"Nothing," she answered with a huff of impatience. "Would you stop fixating on the mail?"

"I will if you explain to me why we need to go check the mailbox," he retorted, pushing the door closed and leaning into it, his palm flat on the polished wood, his fingers splayed wide.

Kayla tucked her chin to her chest, and for the briefest moment, he thought she might concede the fight. Then, she jerked her head up and glared at him.

"It's a thing, okay? Once I checked out of Briarwood, I started doing it daily. The walk down the drive and back was my exercise."

He tactfully refrained from mentioning the state-of-the-art home gym he'd spotted on the lower level of the house.

She exhaled dramatically and her shoulders drooped as if he was wringing the information out of her. "It was nice.

It was a nice walk down to the road. I'd check the mail, I'd walk back."

"Except it wasn't so nice the last time you did it," he concluded.

"I don't want it to be the last time," she said stubbornly. "I don't want to let him destroy those memories," she said, a wistful note creeping into her voice. She cleared her throat. "And then after… I liked who I was becoming," she admitted. "Me, on my own. Without anyone to tell me what I should do or how I should act. And without a bottle of wine as a crutch."

"I get you," he said quietly.

She tilted her head and looked up at him from the corner of her eye. "Do you?"

"Yes."

"I won't let him take it from me," she said, the steel of determination sharping her tone again. "Either you can walk with me or wait here until I get back."

"I'll walk with you," he answered without hesitation. "Let me tell Deputy Warren it's us coming down the drive. He was a little too excited about a 'stakeout' for my comfort," he said with a smirk.

"Okay. Yeah," she said with a nod. The young deputy on duty had been disconcertingly enthusiastic. "Good thinking."

He called the deputy's number as he followed her out the front door and down the steps to the brick driveway. They walked in silence until they rounded the first bend and the bricks gave way to the well-tended gravel lane lined with trees. As they walked, he maneuvered Kayla to the center of the lane, and for once she didn't fight him on it.

"This is a nice walk," he said, tipping his head back as if to admire the canopy the trees provided.

She chuckled. "You're freaking out as much as I am, but for different reasons."

He looked over at her. She appeared calm, cool and completely in control. "Are you freaking out?" he asked, genuinely astounded.

"Of course I am," she scoffed. "The last time I took this walk, I got shot."

"True." They continued in silence until a strange thought slotted into place and he let loose with a chuckle.

"What's so funny?" she asked as they navigated the next graceful curve in the drive.

"I'm freaking out because the last time you took this walk you got shot, so I guess we're both freaking out for the same reason."

Kayla gave her head a rueful shake as she paused to pick up a bright red maple leaf. Twirling the stem between her fingers, she shot him a sidelong glance. "Is this your way of saying we have a lot in common?"

"It was an observation, but yeah, I guess in this case we do." He paused for a moment to let the thought sink in. Feeling suddenly exposed, he deflected by cracking a joke. "Which is nice, considering you and Whitney have already declared your unending love for me," he added with a playful nudge of his elbow.

"I was thinking about the movie, not the song," she grumbled, ducking her head to hide her smile.

They trudged along, the soles of their shoes crunching the gravel underfoot and occasionally sending a few rocks skittering along the surface. Ryan caught a glint of sunlight reflecting through the trees and drew to an abrupt halt.

Kayla stopped on a dime. "What?"

"Reflection over there," he whispered, motioning to his left.

She squinted in the direction he'd indicated, then a moment later exhaled loudly through her mouth. "I think it's

Deputy Warren's car," she informed him. "The drive does a little switchback not far from the gate, remember?"

"Right." The moment she said it, he knew in his gut she was correct. He let the breath he'd been holding seep silently from barely parted lips. After all, someone had to play it cool out here.

Sure enough, they came around the next corner and found the young deputy lounging against the side of his vehicle. "Afternoon, sir. Ma'am," he said, touching the brim of his hat as he straightened away from the car.

"Hello, Deputy," Kayla replied, her voice warm. "Are you okay out here? I asked our caretaker to put a minifridge in the guardhouse. Did you find drinks and snacks in there?"

"Oh, yes, ma'am. Thank you, ma'am," he said, a flush coloring his barely stubbled cheeks.

Ryan refrained from rolling his eyes. "Mrs. Powers wants to check the mailbox."

The young man nodded and hurried to the control panel to open the gate. "I saw the delivery truck go by about thirty minutes ago. If there's something you're waiting on, ma'am, I can check the box for you and call up to the house," he offered.

"You are kind," Kayla said smoothly, "but no. I like the exercise."

Deputy Warren nodded, then stepped back and he and Kayla walked around the gate to the metal box set into the stone pillar.

Sure enough, the box held little more than a bundle of bulk-mail advertisements, postcard reminders and a few standard business-size envelopes. "Hey, look, I'm preapproved for a home-equity loan," she said, waving the envelopes at Ryan.

"Congratulations," he said dryly.

Kayla laughed and flashed another winning smile at the

young deputy as they passed. "You call up to the house if there's anything y'all need out here, okay?"

"Yes, ma'am. Thank you, ma'am," Deputy Warren replied eagerly.

Anxious to be away from the road, Ryan hustled her back the way they came. "You can't smile at the young ones like that," he said under his breath. "It scrambles a guy's brain."

"What?" she answered distractedly, a crease appearing between her eyebrows and her steps slowing as she gazed down at an envelope.

Ryan had taken three full steps before he realized she'd slowed to a halt. Turning back, he closed the distance between them. "What is it?"

"It's from P, P and W," she murmured, tracing a fingertip over the return address, then letting it trail down to the place where her late husband's name was printed in bold black ink. She wet her lips, then offered it up for his examination.

It was all Ryan could do to keep from snatching it from her hand. "Why would they—"

"Mailing list," she answered, cutting him off. She shuffled the envelopes until another piece of PP&W stationary appeared. She was the addressee on this piece of correspondence.

"Mrs. Ayers probably forgot to fix her list," she murmured, almost to herself.

"Fix her list?"

"Nancy Ayers keeps a database. All official firm correspondence is copied to Tyrone at both the house in Bentonville and here. Bill gets copies sent to DC and his place here. Anthony Walton is copied, too, even though, as a judge, he has removed himself from the day-to-day running of the firm."

They walked back to the house in silence, Ryan riffling the

pages of the flyers while Kayla turned the envelopes around and around in her hands. The moment they reached the front door, Kayla stopped and took a deep breath. "I'm probably being ridiculous. These are probably nothing but copies of some financial statements or something."

She tore into the envelope addressed to Tyrone and extracted a single sheet with engraved letterhead. Printed in the center of the page in standard twelve-point Courier font was a blunt message.

YOU SHOULDN'T HAVE BETRAYED THE FAMILY.

Ryan peered over her shoulder, then snatched the envelopes from her trembling hands. "In. Get inside. Now."

"It wasn't addressed to me," she said in a bewildered tone.

Ryan dropped the mail onto the foyer floor in his haste to lock the doors and rearm the alarm system. He heard the rip of heavy paper behind him, and his heart plummeted into his stomach. He turned in time to see the envelope addressed to Kayla flutter to the floor.

There must not have been much of a message for her, either, because barely a second passed before she thrust the sheet of expensive paper into his stomach, crumpling it at the edges. But rather than admonishments about loyalty, the message sent to Kayla was much more succinct. The page had only two words printed on it.

WELCOME HOME.

Chapter Eleven

They fought about the messages all day.

Of course, Ryan wanted to leave right away, but she dug in. They were playing a game with her. One with rules she wasn't privy to, but a game, nonetheless. The timing and delivery of the messages didn't make any sense. Whoever it was, intended her to receive the letter addressed to Tyrone. Neither envelope was stamped or postmarked, which meant they'd been hand-delivered after he'd been killed. And after she'd been shot.

Kayla stubbornly refused to go.

Instead, she'd instructed Michelle and Nancy Ayers to comb through the piles of mail that had accumulated from their Bentonville address to see if anything had been sent there. Sure enough, they found two identical envelopes and messages on PP&W stationary buried in the stacks of statements, information disclosures and other nonessential, but first-class, mail. Michelle handed them over to Ethan, and Kayla carefully placed the duplicates into a plastic storage bag, then escaped to her bedroom to avoid further conflict with Ryan.

They ate dinner separately, each slipping down to the kitchen when the other wasn't around.

A strange, buzzing tension filled the house. Kayla found

it disquieting. After all, this was hardly the first time they'd clashed over his plans for her protection. But even after hours of mind-numbing television and an attempt to read a book couldn't hold her attention for more than two pages, she had trouble sleeping.

She had an appointment with an obstetrician in Eureka Springs the following morning. With all that was happening, she'd had little time to concentrate on her pregnancy beyond trying to eat decently, get some exercise and try her best not to be killed.

Scheduling regular prenatal visits in Bentonville, Springdale, Rogers or even Fayetteville without anyone finding out would be next to impossible. Arkansas's northwest corridor might be busy and expanding, but since the towns along the interstate tended to bleed one into another, the region was like a stretched-out small town. Gossip spread faster than mayonnaise on a hot day. All it would take would be one whisper about Ty Powers's widow being pregnant and the speculation would fly.

The tension rode with them into Eureka Springs the next morning. Kayla had to bite the insides of her lips to keep from being the one to break it. She had to stand her ground on staying at the lake house. Her intuition told her it was the right place to be. But how was she supposed to explain the certainty of a gut feeling to a man who lived to make plans?

She assured him she'd booked in using her maiden name, something that earned her an approving nod from Ryan. The man sat still as a statue in the waiting-room chair, his eyes fixed on the toes of his boots as they waited for the nurse to call her back to be examined. She'd sipped water all the way here in preparation for the ultrasound she'd requested. She'd also hear the baby's heartbeat today. According to the books she'd read, she should already have passed some of these milestones, but nothing about this pregnancy was textbook.

She closed her eyes and said a silent prayer it would end better than it began.

So far she hadn't had morning sickness. At least, nothing too severe. There'd been a couple of times the scent of food she usually loved repelled her, and one morning when she discovered the taste of any fruit-flavored yogurt made her stomach curdle, but for the most part she'd been extremely lucky.

She hoped luck held out.

"Kayla Maitland?"

Kayla rose and murmured, "Back soon."

Ryan hummed an acknowledgment, and she gathered her purse.

She froze when the nurse spoke again. "Mr. Maitland? Would you like to come back, too?"

Kayla's cheeks burned as Ryan continued his study of his footwear, blessedly oblivious to the fact the nurse was speaking to him. "Oh, um, I don't think he…" she stammered, casting an apologetic glance at Ryan as he tuned in and his head popped up.

"What?"

"Would you like to come back as well?" She glanced down at the chart in her hand, then back up at them. "This is going to be an action-packed visit," she added with a cheerful smile.

"You, uh, you don't—" Kayla began again, but the words fell away when she realized Ryan was rising to his feet.

"Yeah, um, sorry. I was zoning out," he said, flashing a winning smile at the other woman. Glancing down at her, he let the smile stretch until the dimple in his cheek appeared. "Where you go, I go, right?"

Ears aflame and face so hot she was sure it would melt off like something out of a sci-fi movie, Kayla fell into step behind the chattering nurse. Before she knew it, the two of them were in an exam room painted a soft pastel green, and the nurse was asking her to strip down.

Kayla glanced around the minute the door clicked shut behind them, but saw no curtain or privacy screen to hide behind. Picking up the neatly folded gown at the foot of the exam table, she turned to Ryan and asked, "What do you think you're doing?"

"It's better this way. If anyone ever figures out you were here, they will assume I'm with you for a reason," he told her. "If someone you know finds out you're pregnant, you can let them think the baby isn't Ty's. It might be safer for both of you."

She couldn't argue the logic, but the subterfuge annoyed her enough to get her hackles up. "You realize I'm about to get naked and have a gynecological exam right in front of you, don't you?"

She had the pleasure of watching him redden from the collar of his shirt to his hairline. "I did not, no," he admitted gruffly. "I was thinking about…" He trailed off, gesturing to the window and the world beyond it.

"Right," she said grimly. With a huff, she shook out the fabric of the gown. "Well, turn around. And no peeking."

She kept her eyes glued to his back as she hurriedly stripped off the soft cotton dress she was wearing and slipped her arms into the gown, bra and panties still in place. Then, feeling adequately covered, she wriggled her way out of her underwear, and placed it all in a bundled wad on the counter beside the small sink.

Holding the front of the gown closed, she shook out the plain white modesty sheet and hopped onto the end of the exam table. She made certain she was covered from head to toe before she lied back with a huff. "Okay. You can stop staring at the wall."

To his credit, he kept his expression carefully blank. "Sorry, I didn't think this part through."

She nodded, clutching the sheet over her chest. "Yeah. Uh, stay up by my head," she instructed. "Or better yet, take a seat." She jerked her chin toward the chair wedged into the corner of the room. "They're usually good about keeping things covered as they go."

Ryan dropped heavily into the chair. "Sorry. I—"

"I get it," she assured him. "Don't worry, this doesn't automatically sign you up to be my Lamaze partner."

But though she'd hoped to lighten the mood with the joke, the realization she would be going through this pregnancy and marking all her baby's milestones alone blanketed her with a heavy melancholy. She blinked back the threat of tears, then swallowed hard as she stared at the mosaic of pastel painted ceiling tiles above her. Maybe Michelle would be her birth partner? Or maybe she'd ask her mom? Either way, this should be the one and only time Ryan Hastings would be asked to go above and beyond his call of duty.

A sharp knock on the door served more as a warning than a request. Before she could respond, a petite, dark-haired whirlwind blew in.

"How are we doing today?" she asked, beaming first at Kayla, then scanning the room until she spotted Ryan. "I'm Dr. Vargas," she said, offering Kayla a hand to shake. "I understand you're new to the area?"

Kayla nodded, then launched into the cover story she'd been concocting since the day she made the appointment. "Yes. With the stress of moving I didn't know I was pregnant." She gave a self-conscious grimace. "I had a little accident a couple weeks ago, and they treated me in the ER. I realized I was late and asked for a test."

Dr. Vargas nodded then made a note on her chart. "It looks like they ran a test at the hospital?"

"Yes, ma'am," Kayla replied "With getting settled and all, this was the first time I could get in."

Dr. Vargas gave her leg a reassuring squeeze as she moved to the foot of the table. "I understand. Sometimes life sweeps in and carries us away, doesn't it?" She patted the end of the table and tugged the modesty sheet down a few inches. "I need you to scoot down a bit."

Dr. Vargas set the chart aside and carefully raised the stirrups on the exam table. "Quite a surprise for you too, huh, Dad?" she said to Ryan as she set about getting things arranged to her liking.

To his credit, Ryan didn't hesitate long before answering. "Yeah, you could say so."

"Well, you're here now." She grinned at Kayla again. "You're young and your vitals all appear to be good," the doctor said, dividing her attention between the two of them. "Nothing in the family history other than what you noted on the intake paperwork?"

Kayla shook her head. "No. I'm healthy as a horse."

"Good to hear." The doctor rolled the stool closer to the edge of table then helped Kayla position her heels in the stirrups. "A quick peek under the hood to make sure everything looks okay, then you're getting a twofer. We're going to hook you up to a couple machines—you'll get to hear the baby's heartbeat today and we'll do your first ultrasound." She beamed at Kayla over the tented edge of the sheet. "Most moms have to spread these trips out."

Kayla laughed. "I guess it pays to be oblivious."

"Sometimes it does," the doctor agreed.

She was true to her word and the examination was quick. As she stripped off her sterile gloves, she assured them everything looked good and seemed to be on track. She discussed possible dates of conception with Kayla and then confirmed what the doctor in the ER doctor had guessed about her progress.

"I'd say you're about at the halfway mark, so you could be holding your new little sweetheart right around Valentine's Day."

"Valentine's Day?" Ryan croaked, breaking his silence. "In February?"

"That's when it usually falls," Dr. Vargas said cheerfully. "Better plan on buying twice as many roses, Dad."

"I'm already nineteen or twenty weeks along?" Kayla confirmed, doing the calculations in her head.

"Yep." Dr. Vargas gave her a reassuring smile. "You're one of the lucky ones. You skipped all the pukey stuff at the start. Hopefully, you'll sail right through the rest." She made a note on her chart. "We'll set you up for regular visits every four weeks for now. We'll get down to every week once we're in the home stretch."

"Okay," Kayla responded with a nod. "Thank you."

"No need to thank me. I have the easy job," the doctor replied. "In the meantime, relax, sleep, eat well, get some exercise. Keep things as low-stress as you possibly can, and you'll barely need me at all until the big day."

"Low stress," Kayla said with a laugh.

"I know," Dr. Vargas, said with a winsome smile. "We can always dream, right?"

"Right."

"Okay. Our technician, Stacy, will be in shortly. She'll get you hooked up and we'll take baby's first pictures," she said as she slid her pen into the pocket of her white coat. "Any questions for me?"

Kayla shook her head. "No. I think I'm good."

Dr. Vargas looked over at Ryan. "Dad? You good, too?"

"Good." His voice cracked on the single word, and he cleared his throat. "All good. Thank you."

They were quiet on the ride back to the lake house. Kayla didn't want to talk. She didn't want the radio. She didn't want to hear anything but the technician's confirmation over and over again.

It looks like you're having a boy.

She held her breath as the gate at the foot of the drive swung inward. Deputy Warren had been replaced by an equally fresh-faced recruit named Bennett this morning. She and Ryan waved simultaneously as they passed, but neither broke the silence. Gravel crunched under the tires as they wound up the drive. It transitioned to the rumble of bricks as they approached the house. Unwittingly, she scanned the front of the house for any sign of intrusion as the SUV crept past the main entrance, then around the side to the garage.

Sunshine bounced off the glasslike surface of the lake. Kayla stared out the passenger window, making no move to open the door even after Ryan killed the engine.

When Ryan spoke, his voice was as rough as the gravel they'd driven over. "Congratulations, Kayla. I'm happy for you."

"Thank you," she responded, unable to tear her gaze from the water. "A boy," she whispered, saying the words aloud for the first time since repeating them back to Stacy for confirmation. She glanced over at Ryan, feeling awkward and exposed in a way she hadn't felt when she was lying on the exam table. "Sorry. Still processing."

"It's a lot."

"Yeah. It is," she said, not bothering to mask the emotion thickening her voice.

She'd cried the entire time they printed out the remarkably clear ultrasound screenshots. Apparently, tears were not an unusual reaction because Stacy hadn't been fazed by them in the least. What she hadn't expected was to look up and find Ryan standing beside the table, his gaze locked on the monitors.

"Would you like to go for a walk?" he asked, nodding to the lakefront. "Some fresh air might do you good."

She laughed at his suggestion. "Aren't you the guy who's always trying to make me stay inside?"

"One-time offer," he said, all stern solemnity.

She smiled at him, blinking back tears she couldn't explain. "I'll take it."

Ryan was out of the car and at the passenger door before she could gather herself. Walking companionably side by side, they skirted the side of the house and cut across the patio. Kayla dropped her purse on one of the chairs, but carried the small clutch of ultrasound printouts with her as they started down the path to the dock. She knew eventually, she'd tack one to a fridge with a magnet and walk past it without ever seeing it again, but for today, she wanted to look her fill.

Ryan shoved his hands into his pockets as they walked out to the end of the swim dock. She didn't miss the way he scanned the shoreline at regular intervals, but she couldn't worry about that now. Now, all she wanted to do was drink in big, greedy gulps of crisp, clear air and hug her baby's first pictures to her chest.

A boy. She was having a boy.

"Will you name him Tyrone?" Ryan asked, giving voice to the question she hadn't allowed herself to ponder.

"I don't know," she answered honestly. "I've thought about

it, and I probably should." She turned to him, her nose wrinkling, and confessed, "But I don't want to, though. Is that bad?"

He shrugged. "I can't blame you. It hasn't been the luckiest name to pin on a kid."

She huffed a laugh. "Nope. And you can bet Delray is out of the question," she added.

Ryan looked over at her, his face a mask of seriousness. "He'll thank you one day."

This time, she laughed out loud. "No doubt." She turned, gesturing for him to follow her. "Did you know Ty's dad named his boat the *Stingray*?" she asked.

Behind her, Ryan snorted. "No." She led him back up to the shore, then pointed to a beautifully restored and maintained sailboat, its glossy wooden hull glinting in the sunlight. "There she is. It's a giant pain to take out, but Ty liked to run it around every once in a while. Boat nerds flock to any dock where she's moored."

"No doubt. It looks to be a beautiful boat." He followed her as she made her way along the shore to the boathouse. "I assume the red one is Trey's. I saw photos in the files."

Kayla nodded. "I would have thought it would be impounded, but no doubt Ty made some calls," she said, her tone dry and tinged with disapproval.

"I'm assuming the crime lab got all they could from it," he answered diplomatically.

"Ty was nearly apoplectic," she said softly. "There was no way they were keeping anything that belonged to his precious Trey." The moment the words were out of her mouth, she regretted them. "Sorry. That was inappropriate. Ty was a good father. Maybe a little blind to his son's faults, but I think most parents are."

"Probably," Ryan agreed easily.

Unspoken questions hung in the air between them as they approached the boat slips. Kayla was about to tell him to spit them out so they could get it all over with once and for all, but then she noticed something amiss.

The door to the boathouse, where they stored life jackets, fishing and other water sport accessories, was wide open. One side of the thick hasp had been pried from the bolts securing it to the cedar-shake siding. The other clung to the door, its padlock rendered useless.

"Someone broke into the boathouse," she said, throwing her arm out instinctively to block Ryan's progress.

He grasped her arm, but rather than pushing past her to investigate, he swung her around and hustled up the sloping lawn to the terraced patio. Before she knew it, they were safe inside the house, and Ryan had his phone in hand.

"Reset the alarm. I'm calling the sheriff. Someone must have come around by boat."

Kayla picked up the remote for the smart system and spoke a few commands into the receiver. A second later, the computer-generated assistant assured her the system was fully armed.

Barely a minute passed before they heard the squeak of brakes out front. Ryan took off for the foyer and she followed hot on his heels. Deputy Bennett pulled up in front of the house and Ryan swore softly under his breath. "Go wait in Ty's office," he ordered as he disarmed the alarm. "Remember to lock yourself in."

Kayla watched as he headed out to speak to the young deputy, clearly displeased he'd left his post. When Ryan mapped out the additions he wanted made for the sake of security he had insisted she had a safe room. As one of the few rooms with no exterior access, Ty's office made sense. Still, she had no intention of locking herself in there every time Sergeant Bossy issued an order.

She waited in the foyer, watching Ryan speak to the younger officer through the paned sidelights. She could see the reluctance in the deputy's movements as he climbed back into his cruiser, but Ryan had clearly issued an order for him to return to his post at the gate. She backed up a few steps as Ryan came back inside.

The moment the door closed behind him she ordered the alarm to reactivate.

"You're supposed to be in Ty's office," he reminded her sternly.

"I could see you from where I was standing."

"Which means anyone who was out there could see you, too," he argued. He ran a hand over his face, then shook off his frustration. "If you won't do it for yourself, Kayla, you could at least do it for the baby," he said, gesturing to the pictures she clutched in her hand.

"I don't need you to tell me what I should do for my baby. I'll go in the office and stretch out on the couch, but I won't be locked down."

"We had an agreement—" he began.

"I agreed you could turn the office into a safe room. I never agreed to lock myself in it," she countered.

"Lawyers," he growled.

"Know-it-all cops who don't know a darn thing," she stormed.

"Then tell me, Kayla. Tell me what I don't know so I can do my job better," he challenged.

She sighed, all the fight going out of her. She was tired of butting heads with Ryan. He was right. He was only trying to do his job. She inhaled deeply, then blew out a breath.

"Okay, fine." She looked him straight in the eye. "Before

the sheriff gets here and you make a big deal out of this being Del, I need to tell you people break into the boathouse all the time," she said calmly.

"What?"

"I admit, it freaked me out a little, given the situation, but it's not uncommon. We're in an isolated area. People around here know the place is unoccupied most of the time. We've had boating gear, fishing tackle and all sorts of skis, tubes and boards stolen out of this boathouse."

"How often?"

"Probably a half-dozen times since Ty and I got married, so multiply out over however many years," she said with a wave of her hand.

She lifted her chin a notch. "Now I'm going to go lie down for a bit to keep things low-stress, as per doctor's orders. I trust you can handle things with the sheriff now that you know."

Chapter Twelve

Kayla was right, and it didn't make him happy. According to the Carroll County sheriff's deputies who responded to the call, vandalism and theft from lakeside storage buildings was a common occurrence. But knowing was no comfort.

The storeroom hadn't simply been ransacked by a thief looking for the good stuff. It looked like a tornado had ripped through it. Boating gear and sporting equipment had been tossed around with the kind of random ferocity meant to create mayhem and not to procure merchandise.

After the deputies finished taking their notes and photos, they assured him they would confer with the Powers family's caretaker to determine if anything of value had been taken. After waving them off in the driveway, he placed a call to the sheriff himself, who repeated much of the same information his deputies had imparted. After receiving his assurances of continued vigilance and support, Ryan hung up with an exhausted sigh.

He trudged back into the house and reset the alarm via the keypad rather than the voice commands he could never remember, then made his way to what was Tyrone Powers's home office. There, he found Kayla cozied up on the leather sofa under a chunky knit throw reading a book.

"You get all your reports filed?" she asked without looking up.

"Yeah." He rubbed the back of his neck, wondering where to begin with her. Being in the exam room with her that morning brought her pregnancy into focus. When he'd heard the *whoosh-whoosh-whoosh* of the baby's heartbeat, the reality of it hit him. Kayla's baby wasn't some vague complication they'd need to work around. This was happening. She was pregnant. He'd had visual confirmation of the small human growing inside her.

Should he ask how she was feeling? Would she want to talk about it? Until she'd mentioned the appointment, she'd barely mentioned the topic, so he wasn't sure if it was fair game or not.

"How are...? Are you...?" he began and stopped.

What he'd witnessed that morning was an intimate moment he'd inserted himself into without her prior consent. It was painfully clear to him they needed to talk about the boundaries of their working relationship, but he didn't have the foggiest idea how to approach the conversation.

He chickened out and settled on something else. "What are you reading?"

She held up the book so he could see it. "A classic—*What to Expect When You're Expecting*," she said with a wan smile.

He nodded, then lowered his hand from his neck and pointed to one of the chairs situated in front of the desk. "May I?"

"Sure." Kayla shifted to sit up straighter, marked her page, then placed the book on the low table in front of the sofa.

He turned the chair to face her, then dropped into it. Only then did he notice she'd marked her place in the book with the sonogram photos. Seeing them gave him the launchpad he needed for his apology.

"Listen, I'm sorry about this morning. I wasn't thinking about anything beyond sticking close to you. I had no business barging my way in there, and—"

Kayla held up a hand to stop him. "No. It's okay. Actually, other than the whole awkward gown-and-sheet conundrum, I was glad to have someone there. Have you there," she amended, meeting his eyes. "I do appreciate what you're trying to do for me, Ryan. And maybe this morning's doctor's visit was the eye-opener we both needed." She drew a shaky breath. "It made it so much more real, didn't it?"

Ryan nodded. "Yeah. Scary real," he added with a smile.

She tipped her head to the side. "I keep circling back to the name thing," she told him. He must have frowned because she waved a hand dismissively. "Oh, I know I have months to go, but it's in my head." She gave a short, self-effacing laugh. "Maybe because I feel so much of my life is out of my control. Since Ty isn't around, what to name this baby is the one thing on which I get the absolute last word."

"Makes sense."

"What do you think of Tyler?"

"I think it only matters what you think," he countered.

She grinned. "Excellent evasive maneuver."

He inclined his head in acknowledgment. "Thank you."

"I could call him Ty, like his dad, but he wouldn't be the next Tyrone Delray Powers. He's going to be born into a lot of stuff. The last thing I want is to add the weight of a name, you know? I don't want him to grow up feeling like he has to be a lawyer, or a senator, or even take over the family firm."

She covered her stomach with her hand, and for the first time, Ryan noticed the slight curve beneath the thin cotton fabric. Good manners told him he should look away, that he had no business ogling a pregnant woman, much less one who was also someone he was supposed to be protecting. But what he witnessed this morning had crossed so many lines, he didn't know how he'd ever back up enough to regain any level of detachment.

Uncertain what his role was supposed to be in this conversation, he simply nodded and said, "It sounds like you have been giving it a lot of thought."

"I have. It's all I've thought about since I found out. How do I protect all this for him? Can I keep his birthright intact, but not thrust a whole passel of expectations on him? How do I help him understand the privilege he'll be born into is a blessing and a responsibility, but not a predetermined path?"

Curious, he asked, "Did your husband feel like he didn't have any choice in becoming a lawyer?"

Kayla laughed. "Oh. He didn't. His father made sure both Ty and Bill knew they had to toe the line. Tied things up in trusts. I'm told his will had so many codicils and contingencies it took them days to parse it out." She shook her head. "Another reason why Tyrone wanted to rewrite his will. Apparently, the old one was only slightly less convoluted than his father's, mainly because the trusts and such had already been worked out. Tyrone wanted something simpler. Cleaner. One allowing for more…options."

"Wasn't Trey supposed to take over the firm?"

She nodded. "Yes, but Tyrone didn't stipulate anything beyond immediate succession. If Trey were alive, he could have dissolved the partnership."

"And now you can," he concluded.

"I can, but I won't." She gave him a wan smile. "I talk a good game about not wanting to put too much on him, but it is his legacy." She dipped her chin to her chest, then plucked at one of the thick strands of yarn. "Once this madness is all over, I'll do my best to hold it all together in case he wants it."

"I have no doubt you'll do more than hold it together," he assured her.

"Anyway," she said, swinging her legs down, and turning to face him. "What did the people from the sheriff's department say?"

He gave her a lopsided smile. "They said it happens all the time."

She nodded. "I called Mr. Johnson. He takes care of the grounds for us. He said he'd come by later today to sort through the mess and see if anything significant is missing." She paused, then shot him a sly smile. "He probably won't come to the house, so if you see a man who's about seventy and has six hairs on top of his head poking around out there, don't shoot, okay?"

"I'll do my best to refrain," he assured her.

That night, Ryan was lying stretched out on the bed in the guest room, remote pointed at the large wall-mounted television. It was late, and the programming available was unsatisfactory. Kayla had gone off to the main suite of rooms hours earlier, but he couldn't settle. He was too keyed up from the day's activities to relax.

Giving up, he pushed the power button and the screen went black. Swinging his legs over the side of the bed, he sat for a moment debating whether he should go down to the kitchen for a snack or try to find something boring to read. His gaze landed on his abandoned sneakers. Glancing down at his gym shorts and T-shirt, Ryan thought about the home gym on the lower level and was forced to admit to himself he'd let his physical therapy slide over the last few weeks.

Blowing out a resigned breath, he picked up his sneakers and padded down the hall to the staircase. A single lamp in the foyer cast a gentle glow over the shadowed furniture in the open living area. Swiping his thumb across the screen on his phone, he turned on the flashlight and headed down the dark corridor beyond Tyrone Powers's home office.

He flipped the switch inside the door of the workout room and let out a low whistle as he took a good look at the assortment of high-tech equipment inside. In addition to a treadmill and elliptical trainer, there was one of those virtual reality bicycles. The far wall was covered in floor-to-ceiling mirrors. Opposite the wall of mirrors sat a large universal weight system complete with bench and leg presses.

Pulling up his favorite workout playlist, he started the music and adjusted the volume to where it was loud enough to hear, but not enough to carry through the house. He began his workout with an easy five-minute walk on the treadmill to get his blood moving and muscles loose.

Then, to get his heart rate elevated, he allowed himself to take a spin on the fancy bike. The program he had selected was called easy mountain trail, but five minutes into the ride, his shirt clung to his back. Moving to the weights, he stripped off his shirt and used it to mop his face.

He was reaching for the shoulder extension bar when he glanced to the right and saw they even had a station complete with water cooler, towels and what he assumed to be a bottle of disinfectant spray to wipe down the machines.

He thought about the gym in Little Rock where he paid ten dollars per month as a membership fee and chuckled. It was nice to avoid doing his sweating and straining, moaning and groaning in a public forum. He worked his way through his arm routine, then allowed himself a trip to the water cooler before putting in the dreaded reps on his legs. He'd crushed the little paper cone in his hand and dropped it into the wastebasket below the cooler when the entire house lit up like a Roman candle.

Three ear-splitting beeps ripped through the silence, then

the voice of the virtual assistant built into the security system boomed from the speakers concealed throughout the house.

"Perimeter alert. Security breach. Sector four. Coordinates one-twenty-eight by ninety-eight."

The next set of beeps had him pressing one hand to an ear and patting his hip in search of his weapon.

"Perimeter alert. Security breach. Sector four. Coordinates one-twenty-eight by ninety-eight."

His gun was upstairs.

"Kayla," he shouted as the alert cycled through to the piercing beeps again. Cursing under his breath, he took off at a run through the brightly lit house. "Kayla!" he shouted as he took the stairs two at a time.

He'd nearly reached the top when she burst from her room with a gleaming golf club cocked like a baseball bat. Ryan drew up short at the sight of her. She had on a set of pajama bottoms printed with coffee cups and a tank top. Her feet were bare, and her hair was mussed from her pillow. He met her gaze and found her eyes wild.

Holding up both hands, he assured her, "It's me."

"You set off the alarm?" she asked in a rush.

He shook his head then grabbed her hand and pulled her with him to his room.

"No, I was in the gym."

In his room, he released his hold on her and crossed to the dresser, where he grabbed his sidearm from the pile of detritus he'd off-loaded earlier in the evening. On his way back through the door, he took her by the hand again. The heavy head of the golf club thumped down the stairs, but she didn't relinquish her hold on her weapon.

"Where are we going?" she asked breathlessly.

"We need to get you to Ty's office. It's the safe room, and we can monitor the cameras from his computer, remember?"

The system-generated voice kept blaring out its alert, and the tension inside him rose with each repetition. When they reached the office, the door was locked.

"It worked," Kayla said in an almost reverent hush. "Fingerprint. Do the fingerprint thing."

Ryan nodded. They'd had biometric technology installed on the door locks to this particular room. When the house went into lockdown, the locks could only be opened by Kayla or him using a fingerprint.

He pressed his index finger to the small glass pane, and the locks disengaged. He ushered Kayla into the room, then closed the door behind him, using a similar screen to reset the locks.

"If you ever have to come in here without me, you have to remember to lock the door behind you," he instructed.

"I will."

"It's not perfect, but at least no one else can lock you in. Always run to this room," he shouted, wincing as the alarm screeched again. "If someone follows you in and tries to trap you here, they can twist those knobs all they want, but the door won't lock unless you use your fingerprint."

"I remember."

"We should have practiced," he muttered as he hurried over to the desk and wiggled the mouse to awaken the massive monitor. "We're going to practice," he vowed under his breath.

With two clicks of the mouse, he had the complete video surveillance displayed. Clicking through the multipaned display for close-ups, he checked every interior room before moving on to view the exterior cameras.

"It looks like we're clear in here. I don't see any movement in the house."

"Good."

"I'm not seeing much outside, either. Look at the key, will you?" he instructed, nodding to the map the security consultant had left out on the desk. "Where is sector A?"

Kayla scanned the sketch of the property. "South side. The woods beyond the garage." She pressed her hands to her ears like a child. "Can I turn it off now?"

"I need the coordinates," he reminded her.

The system cycled through its warning again and this time the disembodied voice and Kayla spoke in unison. "Sector four, coordinates one-twenty-eight by ninety-eight."

"System mute," Ryan commanded before the technology could take up its litany again.

"System muted," the virtual assistant said, but the alarm continued to emit its staccato beeps periodically.

Ryan scanned all the screens but the only movement he saw was the deputy's patrol car skidding to a stop in front of the house. "I'll go meet the deputy," he said, straightening to his full height and snatching his gun from the desktop. "Locking you in. Don't go anywhere until I give you all-clear." He stopped at the door to scan his print, turning to pin her with an I-mean-business glare. "I mean it, Kayla. I need you to stay put while we clear everything. Promise me."

She must have been more shaken than she wanted to let on because she didn't even attempt to argue. "I promise."

The app on his phone lit up with a full-screen image of a Carroll County sheriff's deputy in a rumpled uniform. This one was considerably older than the fresh recruits who'd pulled guard duty on previous shifts.

Lifting the phone to his mouth he said, "Sergeant Ryan Hastings, Arkansas State Police. I am armed."

"Deputy Mickey Sallings," the man replied. "My sidearm is holstered, sir. I have backup on standby."

Ryan confirmed the man was unarmed, then keyed in the

code to cut off the alarm. The front door locks disengaged, and he swung the heavy wooden door inward, peering out at the uniformed officer. He had his gun pointed down and away, but his grip was sure and his paranoia running high. If anything went sideways, he could get at least one shot off before the deputy could draw.

"Did you see anything?" he asked without preamble.

The deputy gave a short nod. "Yes, sir. A big, beautiful buck ran into the woods yonder," he said, indicating the area on the south side of the garage. "I'd say between ten and twelve points on those antlers." He pulled a face. "Made me wish I had my rifle."

Ryan could only assume it was the general vicinity of sector four. "The only things we're hunting tonight, Deputy Sallings, are intruders."

"I believe he was big enough to set things off, but I'll cruise around back and check the dock. With this place lit up like Las Vegas, I'm betting anyone looking to cause trouble took off as fast as the buck."

"I'll check the garage and inform Mrs. Powers. Let me know if you find anything on the exterior. If not, let the backup know they can stand down."

The officer's gaze slipped down to Ryan's chest and a smirk twisted his lips. "Will do, sir," the older man said, turning away with a salute.

Ryan frowned at the lumbering figure of the deputy as he headed back to his cruiser, then glanced down at the gun in his hand, wondering what the guy found so amusing about being met at the door with a SIG Sauer.

Then he remembered he was shirtless.

Groaning, he closed the door firmly, then reset the alarm via the master panel in the foyer. He was making his way down the hall to the back of the house, planning to go through the breezeway and into the three-car garage before returning to Kayla. He made it to the garage door before he heard a soft hiss and crackle.

"Did he see anyone out there?" Kayla asked, her voice carrying high and clear through the speakers.

He stopped and looked up, even though he knew he wouldn't find the concealed speaker. Setting his jaw, he wished he'd been paying closer attention while Kayla had been interrogating the security specialist. This system had more bells and whistles than any he'd dealt with before. Between the cameras, the speakers and the omnipotent virtual assistant, he was getting a creeping sensation along his nape. Freezing in his steps, he tried to recall exactly what rooms interior cameras covered.

For all he knew, she was sitting there watching him creep through her house like a prowler. A half-naked prowler, he amended, feeling instantly self-conscious. Looking up at the ceiling with a stern glare he half-hoped she could see, he said, "He thinks a deer may have tripped the perimeter alarm. Saw a large buck running into the woods on the other side of the garage."

"Oh." She exhaled loudly, then gave a little laugh. *"Of course. A deer. A buck, no less. Surprised the deputy didn't try to bag himself a trophy."*

"Believe me, he's wishing he was in a deer stand and not a cruiser."

"Where are you?" she asked, her voice husky with exhaustion.

His shoulders slumped with relief when he realized she couldn't see him after all. "I'm about to check the garage. Check the interior cameras again, and if everything looks clear, head on back to bed. I'll shut everything down."

"I'm not seeing anything on any of the monitors," she reported as he unlocked the door to the garage.

"Okay. I think we're good," he murmured as he peered into the cavernous space.

Tyrone Powers hadn't kept any of the usual junk in his garage. Tools and paint cans were for mere mortals, not the kind of people who had their concrete floors coated with shiny swirls of epoxy, and sleek canister lighting designed to showcase even sleeker vehicles. The sight of her sparkling white luxury SUV parked beside his dusty, state-issued domestic model drew him up short. Even the classic Range Rover that Powers kept on the estate looked better suited to the space.

"Okay. Well, I guess I'll take my nine iron and head back to bed," Kayla said, interrupting his thoughts.

"Driver," he corrected without thought.

"What?"

He shook his head then turned to head back into the house to start taking everything down a few threat levels. "Your club. You grabbed a driver. A nice one, too." He shook his head as he recalled the glint of gold he'd seen on the bulbous head of the club. "You were about to tee off on someone with a custom driver. Looked like a Honma, but I'm no pro."

"Could have been a club sandwich for all I know," she replied. *"Ty always kept this set in his closet."*

He chuckled. "I'm glad you had something close at hand. Tomorrow, we'll talk more about security procedures, but for now, try to get some rest."

"Okay." The sound of a massive yawn swooshed through the speakers and she gave a helpless laugh. *"Sorry."*

"No worries," he said as he headed back into the kitchen area. Glancing out at the spotlit terrace, he spotted Deputy Sallings trudging up the path from the lakefront. "Try to get some sleep. I'll make sure everything is good down here."

"I have no doubt," she answered. *"Good night, Ryan, over and out."*

"Good night, Kayla," he replied. Then, lifting the remote control she'd left on the kitchen counter, he spoke directly into it. "Intercom off. Reset lighting. Set system to standby armed."

The lights dimmed and Ryan flipped the switch on the terrace lighting to signal the deputy to stand down. Blowing out a breath, he looked down at the gun gripped in his right hand. His phone weighed down the left side of his gym shorts. His knee throbbed; a reminder he wasn't quite up to full-on sprints up and down sets of stairs. The sweat from his workout and residual adrenaline cooled on his skin, making him shiver, but he dismissed the notion of heading back to the gym to retrieve his shirt.

It would be there in the morning, he decided as he made his way to the staircase, his feet heavy as blocks of cement. Suddenly, he was so tired he wasn't sure he'd make it upstairs to his room before he collapsed in a heap.

Chapter Thirteen

Despite the late night, Kayla awoke before the sun rose. Pulling a robe she rarely used from the back of her closet, she slid it on over her pajamas and padded from the room. She wasn't going to get any more sleep, no matter how badly she wanted it.

Though she knew there was no sense in worrying about things she'd done prior to discovering she was pregnant, Kayla couldn't help but fret about the copious amounts of coffee and wine she consumed in those early weeks. As if she could undo the damage done, she began guzzling water like she could detoxify in preparation for the new arrival. She knew it didn't make sense, but logic had hightailed it out of her life months ago.

She held tight to the rail on her way down the stairs, and let loose a monstrous yawn as she shuffled into the kitchen. Humming tunelessly, she pulled a pitcher of filtered water from the fridge and carried it over to the island.

Water sloshed over the side of the glass when she first took aim, but soon it was filled to the brim. After setting down the pitcher as if it was a hand weight, she lifted the glass to her lips and began the day's hydration staring out into the predawn haze that hung low over the lake.

The first rosy hints of the coming dawn reminded her of

the inspirational poster she'd had in her first apartment after college. It was an ode to ambition and determination, complete with a pithy one-liner she'd thought doubled as a mantra back in the day. After grinding her way through law school, she'd practically wallpapered her fridge door with sayings about living each moment of her life without remorse.

Now, her fridge was a spotless expanse of expensive stainless steel, her life was more exhausting than exhilarating and she toted around a full set of baggage stuffed with regrets. Some big, most small, but every one of them painful in its own way.

She cringed to think of all the times she'd gone to bed in a snit because one of Ty's friends or her old colleagues made a sly remark at her expense. Taking off the day after her fight with Trey at the gala to lick her wounds and drown her sorrows in wine. The short, terse texts were meant to make him feel guilty, but so rarely worked. Refusing to return her husband's one call that fateful Saturday evening. Hoping he wouldn't be home so they wouldn't have to repeat the argument about the way Trey had treated her. Not somehow sensing the man she loved had been killed long before she'd deigned to come home.

The last one stung the most.

Contrary to popular opinion, she had loved Ty. She'd loved him so much that not fitting into his world had nearly destroyed her. And now, because he'd changed his will to reflect her place in his life, someone had killed him.

Del.

Del had killed Ty.

Or maybe he'd hired someone to do it.

For weeks the possibility cycled through her head. No matter what she'd seen, or thought she'd seen when she'd been winged at the mailbox, it was still hard for Kayla to accept

Del Powers had been the one to kill Ty and Trey. It was one thing to shoot at someone who bore no relation to you and threatened your livelihood from a distance. Killing the uncle who'd always doted on you and a cousin you'd grown up with at close range...walking into a man's home and shooting him and his son before they even had time to react...

No, those things were something entirely different.

The coroner's report came back indicating no signs of defensive wounds. The scene showed no real sign of struggle. It had to have been a professional hit.

The Del she knew would not be capable of committing a crime so coldhearted.

The mists shifted, casting shifting shadows across the smooth surface of the lake. A tiny ripple cut through the flawless surface like a concealed zipper. It was the barely perceptible wake of a small boat. A canoe? A kayak? A flat-boat with a trawling motor? Her eyebrows drew together as she stepped closer to the window, her gaze mapping the trajectory of the track.

Was someone out there? A fisherman? Was it Del?

The wake was subtle. If the morning hadn't been so still, the water so mirrorlike, she might never have noticed it. About a quarter mile south of the house, the shoreline protruded into the lake. One of dozens of fingerlike spits of land divided the underpopulated end of the lake into the coves and inlets fishermen adored.

She blinked to clear her vision. No, she hadn't been seeing things. Tiny waves were absorbed by the relentlessly placid lake, but there was a disturbance taking place somewhere.

As if on cue, a large bird swooped from a low tree limb, nearly skimming the surface of the water as it made its way from one side to the other. She lowered the glass and forced herself to take a few calming breaths, all too aware her heart rate had spiked.

"An owl looking for breakfast," she murmured to herself, curling her hand in until the cool glass pressed against her throat.

She forced herself to stand there, unflinching. She and Ryan had been as jumpy as toddlers hyped up on sugar these past few days. The scare last night had pushed them both to peak paranoia. It was high time one or both of them got a grip.

Lifting the glass to her lips with a trembling hand, she forced herself to gulp the contents. Staring sightlessly out at the lake, she drank until she drained the glass dry, then topped it up again. She was halfway through guzzling glass number two when a gravelly male voice nearly made her jump out of her skin.

"You're up early."

She spun around and set down the glass so hard she was surprised it hadn't shattered on the granite countertop. Her heart in her throat, she glanced back at the lake, but all hints of the ripple had disappeared.

Drawing a calming breath, she pressed her hand to her hammering heart and focused on the intruder she could see clear as day. "I cannot believe you'd sneak up on me after a night like last night," she accused.

Ryan winced and a flush of red crept up his neck. "Sorry. I thought you might have heard me coming."

She glanced pointedly at his bare feet, then noted with some relief he was wearing a shirt with his plaid pajama bottoms. "I guess you're pretty light on your feet."

He chuckled, then made his way to the single-cup coffee maker. "One thing I've never been accused of being."

"I like to be first," she said, adding a playful little sniff as she lifted her glass of water in a silent toast. "Good morning."

"Morning."

He placed a mug under the spigot and lowered the boom on the coffee pod. In one fluid move, he rolled to his right and stood facing her, his hips propped on the edge of the counter. He crossed his arms over his chest, and she did her best not to fixate on the way the bulge of his biceps pulled the cotton sleeves tight.

She put the glass to her lips and drank as if she needed to put out some internal fire.

Ryan's state of undress the previous night had been beside the point in the moment. As a matter of fact, it hadn't even registered he was shirtless until she was watching him leave Ty's office dressed in gym shorts, sneakers and carrying a sleek black gun. It had taken hours of tossing and turning to put the image out of her mind.

First, there was the fact her personal-protection officer was ripped. Equipped with the rippling muscles she thought only underwear models sported. Then, there was the fact she had not only noticed how built the man was, but the ensuing tsunami of guilt had also engulfed her the moment she'd allowed herself to dwell too hard on it. And finally, the righteous indignation flew in on the heels of guilt. After all, she was a single female swimming in a whole sea of pregnancy-induced hormones. She would have had to have been dead not to notice him.

It wasn't until he tipped his head to the side inquiringly that she realized she'd drank all her water and stood holding an empty glass to her lips as she soaked in the sight of him.

"You doin' okay?" he asked.

She lowered the glass and grabbed the pitcher again. Slopping the rest of the water into the glass, she nodded a shade too vigorously. "Yeah. Fine." She hesitated, then gave in with a wan smile. "Well, obviously not fine. I didn't get much sleep."

"Yeah, me, either." He pushed away from the counter and reached for the now-empty pitcher. "Here, I'll get a refill while my coffee brews."

Her first impulse was to argue, but she relented and allowed him to remove the pitcher from her hand. The busier they were, the better. She didn't need him in her direct line of sight, given her poor impulse control. Her gaze fixed on the water beyond the windows and she stifled a yawn.

"What time was Michelle heading out here?" Ryan asked, his voice still husky.

"I'm pretty sure it'll be sometime this afternoon," Kayla said. "I'm curious to see what it is she'll think she'll find in Tyrone's office. We've gone through most of the files in there, and all of the paperwork in both his home and office safes."

"Did she say which case she was focusing on?"

Kayla shook her head. "No, but I get the feeling it has something to do with Harold Dennis. She said she'd been working with some of the forensic accountants on her team and wanted to dig a little deeper."

Ryan gave a noncommittal hum as he pulled the steaming mug of coffee from beneath the spigot. She watched as he inhaled deeply, his eyelids lowering to half-mast in appreciation before he blew across the surface of the coffee and chanced a quick sip. His wince told her he hadn't been patient enough.

"What's on your agenda for the day?" he asked, setting aside the mug to let it cool.

"Nothing much," she said with a shrug. "I thought I'd get dressed and maybe we could take a walk around. I'm feeling cooped up."

He nodded his bottom lip for a moment then dipped his

head assent. "Yeah, I think it might be good for both of us to have some fresh air. Clear the cobwebs."

She offered him a half-smile. "We can go looking for deer tracks."

"Oh, boy," he said, deadpan, and reclaimed the mug. "Let's give it a little time, though," he suggested. "I have a feeling I'm going to be waking up pretty slow this morning."

Kayla smiled. "I was thinking maybe I'd head back to bed for a couple hours."

He nodded. "Not a bad idea. What do you say we meet back here at about ten?"

Kayla tipped up her glass and drained the last of her water. "Sounds great," she said as she placed the glass in the top rack of the dishwasher. "See you in a little while."

True to their word, they met back in the kitchen, but well before ten o'clock. She'd managed to doze for a couple of hours and felt far more refreshed than she had earlier. Still, the restless night tugged at her energy levels.

The sun was high and bright in the sky when they stepped onto the patio. Ryan carried the voice-activated remote control for the alarm system, clutching it tight in his hand like a talisman.

"Good thing I'm not into jogging," she said dryly. Lifting her arms over her head, she allowed herself a long luxurious stretch. "If you made me go through those security protocols one more time, I might have taken off at a dead run to get away."

"You'd probably succeed. I think my days besting people in foot races are over."

She glanced down at his leg. He'd never tried to hide his limp, but it was clear Ryan didn't particularly want to talk about it. The one time she had asked, he'd simply said it was a severely torn meniscus and left it at that. No further explanation as to the how or what happened.

Feeling emboldened by the previous night's activities, and considerably more friendly toward him than she had been in the beginning, Kayla worked up the nerve to ask him again. "Did you tear up your knee diving in front of a bullet?"

The question startled a laugh from him. "I wish." He gave his head a rueful shake then gestured to the lake. "By land or by sea?"

She consciously didn't mention anything about the small waves she'd seen on the surface of the misty water morning. The last thing she needed was for Ryan to go into full lockdown mode because she was bleary-eyed and letting her imagination get the better of her.

"Let's walk along the shore to the woods then come back around to the garage and the driveway. We'll look to see if the buck left any tracks behind."

"Who knew you'd be so into the wildlife scene?" he teased.

"I'm an Arkansan. This won't be the first time I've gone tromping around behind a deer." As they walked down to the dock, she cast a sidelong glance at him from under her lashes. "I'm not so easily distracted, you know."

He sighed heavily. "You don't know how badly I'd like to tell you I was injured while doing something epic," he said, his tone bone-dry.

"Ooh, the story gets more intriguing. It wasn't heroic?"

"Not in the least." An expectant silence between them. "I got pushed around by a bunch of eighteen-year-olds who were super-stoked about heading to the Big Dance."

She glanced over at him quizzically, trying to sort out what kind of school dance could possibly require the presence of state-police officers. "A dance? Like homecoming? Prom?"

He let out a scornful laugh. "No," he said, wagging his

head hard. "The. Big. Dance. The NCAA basketball tournament." Her blank expression must have given her away because he continued. "I was providing security for the university's head basketball coach. A win would give them a spot in the tournament for the first time in years," he explained patiently.

Recognition dawned. "Oh! Big Dance," she said, nodding sagely. "I'm with you now."

"Yeah, so nothing as dramatic as throwing myself in front of an assassin's bullet."

"I'd like to see the person brave enough to take a shot at the first coach to lead our team through its first winning season in years. I'm betting the crowd would have taken them down in two to three seconds flat."

"It took some frat boy about three to take me down," he said wryly. "I had a prime seat on the floor. If you check the footage you can see me clutching my leg as I watched my primary protectee get carried away by a throng of freshman who probably haven't figured out how to work the laundry machines in the dorms yet."

"Yet they took you out," she said dramatically. "I'm starting to get worried." She leaned in to bump her shoulder against his, letting him know she was pulling his injured leg.

"You probably should."

"I'm only kidding. And I am sorry."

He accepted her sympathies with grace, inclining his head, then motioning to the lawn leading to the large garage built out of the same native stone as the house and its extensive terraces. "There are the tracks," he said, pointing to dark impressions in the neatly maintained lawn.

Kayla followed the direction indicated by this index finger, then gave her head a slow shake. "Ty would have been so excited," she said softly. She drew to a halt and looked up at the sky, blinking back the heat of unexpected tears. She could feel a flush prickling her skin, but she was beyond worrying about embarrassing herself with Ryan Hastings. They had been living in close quarters for weeks now. He'd seen her at her best and her worst, and everything in between.

"Was he a hunter?" he asked quietly.

Kayla smiled a little as she tried to determine the correct answer to his question. "He went to deer camp every year, but I think it was more for the socializing than anything else. He liked to be out in the woods, tracking, waiting, watching. He wasn't big on trophy hunting, though."

Ryan nodded. "I pretty much feel the same way. It's nice to get out. Peaceful to sit in the woods and listen to the sounds all around, but I couldn't care less if I ever took a shot or not. But I admit I am a fan of a well-cooked venison steak."

They followed the tracks from where the deer had entered the perimeter not far from the lakefront. It was clear to see the spot where the animal found itself caught up short by the clamor and clangor of the high-tech security system. Recalling the cacophony of noise from the night before, Kayla couldn't blame the poor, frightened creature for turning tail and running for the safety of the woods.

Glancing over at the house, she gestured to the driveway. "Let's walk down to the bottom of the drive again."

"You expecting more mail?" he asked, instantly wary.

She shook her head. "No, but I don't want to be afraid to walk on my own property."

"Deputy Warren was on duty, but he got called out to check an accident. Maybe we should stick close to the house."

"We won't open the gate," she promised. "We'll walk down and back. I need the exercise."

He acquiesced without another word of protest, tactfully failing to mention the well-equipped home gym he'd obviously been using the night before. She didn't ask if he was carrying his gun. She'd once watched her best friend pull a gleaming gun out of a holster she wore beneath a pair of exquisitely tailored suit pants. The quilted vest he'd shrugged on before going out didn't fool her. Ryan Hastings was armed to the teeth.

They continued in companionable silence until the brick pavers gave way to the gravel. "How come they never paved the whole drive?" he asked, their footfalls crunching on the rocks.

She shrugged. "Ty said something about wanting the driveway to be as inconspicuous from the road as possible. But given how ostentatious the house is..." Ryan chuckled as she let the thought trail off. "I can't tell you. I will say from everything I heard from Ty and Bill over the years, Tyrone Senior was a fairly mercurial man. He had a reason for doing things the way he did them, and he didn't appreciate being questioned about his motives."

"The architecture is a bit...eccentric for the area."

"A nice way of putting it," she said with a laugh. They rounded the last bend and the paved road beyond the gate came into view. "It's strange to admit, but as over-the-top as the house is, I feel more at home here than anyplace I've lived since I left my parents' house."

"Maybe because deep down you're over-the-top?" he said, a teasing note in his tone.

"Oh, def—" Before she could get the words out, the stench of rotting fish hit her right in the face.

And the gut.

"Oh!" She covered her mouth with her hand, but it was too late. Stumbling to her left, she hurried to the spot beyond where the deputies had been parking while on duty and tossed her breakfast.

"Stay here," Ryan ordered.

As if she could take off running while she was bent over retching. He came back a minute later, the toes of his shoes wet with dew from their trek across the lawn and now coated with dust from the gravel. She glanced up to find him pulling his shirt up over his mouth and nose, but there was no quelling the rebellion in her abdomen.

"Fish," Ryan confirmed. "Someone probably tossed what was left of their catch out of a car."

She wiped the back of her hand across her mouth but didn't dare lower it as she inhaled through her mouth. The last thing she wanted to do was trigger another round of retching. "Happens all the…" The words died on her tongue as she raised her head and spotted a shadowy figure melting into the shadows of the woods on the far side of the drive.

Her mouth was dry.

Eyes wide, she could only stare at the spot where the man had stood a moment before.

He was gone, of course.

Gone, but not forgotten.

When her wits returned, all she could do was extend a pointed finger at the spot near the base of a spindly pine as she whispered, "Del."

Chapter Fourteen

He didn't think, he reacted.

But he should have thought. He should have thought of her safety. He should have made certain she was locked down and there was no way Del Powers could get to her. But he didn't do any of those things.

"Go! Get in the gate house," he instructed, propelling her in the direction of the stone outbuilding.

He didn't look back to see if she followed his instructions. He was too busy responding.

Ryan took off after the shadowy figure like a rookie. He ran headlong into the woods, forgetting his mission. Completely disregarding years of training. Like a greenhorn, he plowed into the underbrush, his weapon drawn and Del Powers's name bellowing from his lungs.

He knew better. But he couldn't stop charging forward.

Branches tore at his arms and underbrush tangled around the legs of his jeans. Scanning the area, he caught sight of a shadow ahead and to his left, heading away from the house. He ran another fifty feet deeper into the woods before his toe caught a tree root.

He went down on his knees. Hard.

The impact sent a jolt of pain radiating through his body. He lost his grip on his gun. The thick mat of pine needles and fallen leaves swallowed the weapon like quicksand. A sick dread twisted his stomach. The fall did something to his already injured knee. Something he knew in his gut was bad. Career-changing bad.

The realization brought him back to his senses.

Scraping around on the ground in search of his weapon, he muttered under his breath, "This is it. You're done. And you should be done. You should be canned for—" He allowed the self-recrimination to trail off as he fingers closed around the stock of his weapon.

A guttural growl ripped from deep inside him as he pushed to his feet.

His knee was toast.

But he couldn't think about the pain now. He had to focus on heading back to the gatehouse.

He'd left his primary unprotected.

A mistake he'd never made before, and one he'd never have the opportunity to make again. Which would be a good thing. Because if he was enough of a fool to go tearing off into the woods chasing shadows while the person he was protecting cowered in an unsecured outbuilding, he deserved to be handed a radar gun and busted down to patrol.

Limping, he made his way back to her, making deals with whatever higher power that might be listening the entire way.

If something happened to Kayla or her baby, he'd never forgive himself.

He checked over his shoulder every few steps. At the edge of the trees, he paused to catch his breath and check the area. He cursed himself for acting like a wounded wildebeest trying to make his way from the watering hole back to safety without a lion spotting him.

From this vantage point, he could see the stringer of gutted fish tied to the wrought-iron gate. Someone had left them a calling card.

And he'd left Kayla alone.

"Kayla," he grunted as he pushed away from the tree trunk and hobbled his way across the gravel drive toward the gatehouse.

The woman in question came out of the woods from the opposite direction. "Here. Sorry." She waved her hand in front of her face. She stopped in her tracks and frowned as she watched him approach. "You're hurt. Did Del—"

"I fell," he admitted through gritted teeth. "No one to blame but myself."

She hurried to his side, slipping up under his arm as if she could support him. Ryan appreciated the thought, but at the moment his pride was throbbing about as insistently as his knee, and he was angry at the world.

"I told you to stay in the gatehouse," he snarled.

She scowled at him when he shook off her attempt to drape his arm over her shoulders. "I had to get upwind. Let me help you."

"If I try to lean on you, I'm more likely to topple us both over," he groaned. "Don't worry about me. We have to get to the house."

"Did you see him?" she asked, sounding breathless as she kept pace with his determined clip.

"I saw something. Not sure if it was him, or our friend the buck," he admitted. "Are you sure you saw Powers?"

She paused long enough for him to glance over at her. At last, she shook her head. "I'm not sure of anything these days. For all I know, it wasn't even Del who shot me. I don't know."

Her insecurity proved to be as difficult for him to handle as his own. "Don't. Don't start doubting yourself now. If your gut says you saw him, you need to trust your intuition."

Sage advice from a man whose own instincts had him chasing off into the woods rather than doing his duty by her.

"Do you think you reinjured your knee?" she asked quietly.

The driveway sloped downhill toward the waterfront, which made controlling his momentum breathtakingly painful. The trek back to the house seemed ten times as long as the walk to the gate. He was winded, sweating and, much to his consternation, leaning heavily on Kayla by the time they reached the house. He managed to pull the security-system remote from his pocket and disarmed the alarm.

"Who should I call about your leg?" she asked as she deposited him on the large sectional sofa in the open-plan living area.

"Set the alarm," he instructed from between clenched teeth.

Without much finesse, he tossed the system remote in her direction. It clattered to the floor at Kayla's feet. Not bothering to ask permission, he swung both legs onto the sofa with a harrumph of agony, then fell back against the cushions, flinging an arm over his eyes.

He was too wiped out to even pretend he could tough it out.

Dimly, he registered the computer-assisted confirmation that the system was armed. Kayla sat on the edge of the large, square coffee table right in front of him. He could feel her stare but couldn't bring himself to meet it.

"Ryan? What can I do to help?" she asked gently. "Do we need to go to the emergency room?"

He shook his head as he lowered his arm, but kept his eyes screwed shut against the double whammy of pain and humiliation. "No. No need."

There would certainly be another surgery in his future. Months on crutches. Endless sessions of physical therapy. But for now, the best anyone could prescribe for him would be rest, ice and painkillers. He asked for the most palatable of those three.

"Do you have an ice pack?"

She bobbed her head. "Ty's back would go out on him every once in a while. I think there's one in the freezer."

Without being asked, she grabbed a throw pillow from one of the oversized armchairs. "Lift," she commanded. He did as he was told, biting the inside of his lips as she placed the pillow under his leg. "Do you have anything you can take?"

He thought of the bottle of pills in the bottom of his shaving kit but shook his head. He was not willing to take a narcotic while he was responsible for her safety and well-being. Plus, she'd recently completed a stint in rehab. Though he was pretty sure that pills were not a problem for her, he didn't want to be the one to tempt her. Particularly after his hubris had left her vulnerable.

"I can take a couple over-the-counter anti-inflammatory tablets, if you have some handy."

"We do," she said with a brisk nod. "Be right back."

He wanted to let her go without asking for anything more, but to do so would only protect his ego.

"And Kayla?" he called before she could get away entirely.

"Yeah?"

"Better call Ethan. Tell him you're going to need someone else up here with you," he said gruffly.

"Someone else?"

He allowed his eyes to drift shut even as he heard her coming close again.

"What do you mean get someone else?" she demanded. "Are you quitting?"

He grimaced, then opened his eyes to find her glowering down at him, her hands on her hips.

"No, I'm not quitting," he replied, letting his disgust at the notion seep into the words. "But I'm not any good to you like this." He waved a hand at his knee, where the pain throbbed in time with his pulse.

"You're quitting," she concluded.

"It's not about me or my commitment to the job. I'm getting you someone who can literally chase down the bad guy, Kayla."

"I'll get a German shepherd," she said as if a dog was the obvious answer to all her problems.

"Kayla—"

"Ryan," she countered.

He sighed, then leveled his best cop stare on her. The woman didn't flinch. "You need someone who isn't banged up."

"You're my protection agent," she announced. "Bring in anyone else you think might be helpful, but you're stuck with me."

"You didn't even want protection," he argued.

"I've gotten used to you," she replied without missing a beat.

"You fight every plan I try to put in place."

"I'm a lawyer. We're trained to argue."

"I'm a liability to you now," he pointed out.

"You are one of the handful of people I trust most in this world," she said plainly.

He sighed and closed his eyes. "Fine. Tell Michelle to bring Ethan with her. If I'm sticking around, we need to talk out next steps, and you are going to have to agree to go along with the plan." He pointed at her, his expression stern. "You got me? No arguments, no pushback."

She hesitated only a moment before nodding. While she went to hunt down the ice and analgesics, he almost convinced himself the hesitation was a good thing. If she'd agreed too readily, he would have been suspicious. Then again, the fact she'd agreed at all made his scalp prickle. If the sensation hadn't felt so darn good in contrast to the pain pulsating in his leg, he might have stopped to question her too-easy acquiescence.

HE WAS STILL on the sofa with his leg propped up when Michelle and Ethan arrived. They came bearing another freezable ice pack, along with a box of small single-use packs he could employ between more serious rounds of chilling.

Ryan knew he must have looked as wretched as he felt when Ethan failed to greet him with the expected razzing an agent was usually subjected to following an on-the-job mishap.

"Hey, man," Ethan said as he took a seat in the chair adjacent to the sofa. "How bad do you think it is?" he asked in a low voice as Michelle followed Kayla into the kitchen to see to the ice-pack rotation. "Game-ending? Season?"

The guys they came up through the ranks with often referred to the stages of career denouement using sports analogies. When he wasn't the one who was laid up, shifting the dialogue from medical jargon to athletics seemed to make conversations easier. Now he realized the lightheartedness of those conversations had been entirely one-sided.

Meeting Ethan's gaze, he said, "Career-ending."

"Nah," Ethan said with a dismissive shake of his head. "I mean, I know it's bad, but another few months of desk duty and you'll be on your feet again."

"Maybe," Ryan said, but his tone was dubious. "But even if I am, I can't do the kind of work I have been doing."

"You can always switch lanes," Ethan interjected.

But Ryan was already shaking his head. "The only place for me to go is behind a desk, and the thought of being glued to an office chair for the rest of my days…" He let the thought trail off and gave a visible shudder. "Nope. Not for me. I could do it for a while when I thought I'd be back at it again, but to be sent from the dugout to the front office is too depressing to even think about."

"There are other options," Ethan argued.

"Not ones I would want," Ryan said, shooting his friend a pointed glance. "Listen, I know you don't mind spending your days kicking over rocks to see if anything slithers out, but I like to be in the thick of things, you know?"

"You like to run with the big dogs," Ethan teased.

"I'd like to be able to run at all," Ryan said morosely. "But, yeah. I like what I do, and there's no way for me to keep doing it with a bum knee."

"Maybe, maybe not," Ethan said, glancing up as Michelle and Kayla reappeared with one of the instant packs. "You don't have to decide anything today."

"Decide anything about what?" Kayla asked.

"About where to go next," he said, meeting her stare directly.

"Go? I'm not going anywhere," Kayla insisted.

Before he could open his mouth to retort, Michelle jumped into the fray.

"Before we get into all that, I need to tell you what we've discovered in the case against Harold Dennis."

Ryan and Kayla glowered at one another for a moment longer. But Ryan couldn't miss the look of puzzled annoyance on Kayla's face as her natural curiosity got the better of her.

He was glad for the reprieve. He needed more time to build his case in his head.

"What about Harold Dennis?" he asked, hoping whatever tale Michelle had to spin would be a lengthy one.

Michelle took a seat on the arm of the chair where Ethan

had settled himself then waited until Kayla set in the chair opposite before beginning her story.

"Okay, so you know we suspect Harold Dennis was funneling money through his client, DevCo. The company itself is nothing more than a shell corporation he was using to launder money for a real-estate-investment scheme among other streams of income." She paused long enough to give each of them a chance to nod or murmur affirmations they were all up to speed.

"You know the tricky thing with laundering cases is they're often shell corporations within shell corporations within shell corporations… It's basically the three-card monte game played out in legal paperwork."

"Sometimes it can be nearly impossible to find where it all started," Ethan agreed with a nod.

"Yes, it can. Anyway, we've had some of our best IT people wading back through the lineup of entities, trying to find the origin story. Since no one's talking, it's up to us to sort through the data we've acquired and make sense of it."

Ryan snorted. "Which means you're basically wading through data up to your armpits," he interjected.

Michelle gave him a rueful smile. "Feels like it."

"Did you catch a break?" Kayla asked, cutting to the chase.

Michelle shot her an exasperated look. She seemed miffed by the notion of anyone wanting to cut out the elaborate buildup of months and months of painstaking research and investigation. Ryan couldn't blame her. Then again, Kayla was a lawyer, not a cop. She didn't appreciate the unraveling of the story the way the rest of them did. She only wanted to know the facts so the attorney in her could poke holes in them.

"We believe the development firm at the start of this whole thing was called DelCo, rather than DevCo," Michelle answered, a small smug smile tipping the corners of her mouth upward.

"DelCo?" Kayla repeated.

Michelle smile grew even more smug as it stretched. "Interesting, isn't it?"

Kayla hummed noncommittally. "I don't suppose he was kind enough to list himself as the principal when he filed articles of incorporation."

Michelle shook her head, but her Mona Lisa smile stretched into a grin a mile wide. "Well, no. Not his name," she answered, her tone coy.

"Oh, my God." Kayla threw her hands up in exasperation. "Fine, yes, you've done a wonderful job digging this all out. You're amazing. Mindblowing. Now tell me whose name was on the paperwork and what you think this all means," she demanded.

To her credit, Michelle refused to let Kayla's impatience rain on her parade.

"DelCo was a small real-estate holding consisting of three area mobile-home parks. They were purchased as an investment holding by William Powers, on the occasion of his eldest son, Delray's, eighteenth birthday."

"Good enough for me," Ryan announced.

Turning his gaze directly on Kayla, he said, "These people are all tied up in each other, and you are the one standing in their way. You are the one throwing the wrench into them getting what they want. They are not going to be satisfied until you are—" he paused "—neutralized."

A startled laugh burst from her. "Neutralized," she repeated, holding his gaze. Then, she rolled her eyes and turned her attention back to Michelle. "You're telling us you can pretty much tie the three of them up tightly on the financial malfeasance," she concluded.

"Given the activities they ran through DevCo's accounts, I can say with a strong degree of certainty each of the parties were aware the money moving through the company, and by proxy, through the firm. From what we can trace, a good portion of it went into Harold Dennis's personal accounts, as well as accounts owned by William and Del Powers. A significant amount found its way into Senator Powers's Powers for the People campaign coffers as well."

"If they know you know all this, why keep stonewalling?" Kayla asked. "Why not cooperate in exchange for leniency?"

"Because they've gone too far," Ethan responded, his tone grave.

"From what we can tell, they did their best to keep this client's transactions off Tyrone's radar. But, of course, someone got greedy," Michelle said, making a helpless gesture to the inevitability.

"Someone? Singular?" Kayla persisted.

Michelle shook her head. "It appears all three of them were using DevCo for their own purposes, but I don't know at this point if any of them were aware of how deep the others might be playing."

"You think they were all dipping into the money?" she asked.

But, in an instant, Ryan realized they weren't asking the right question. It popped into his head like a flashing neon sign. And the answer might be the key to unlocking this mystery and so many more.

"Where was the money coming from?" he asked gruffly.

"Various sources," Michelle replied. "One of the more lucrative was some sort of time-share investment scam." She made a face of utter distaste. "From what we can tell it was marketed primarily to retirees moving down from up north."

"Snowbirds," Kayla murmured.

Ryan nodded. Arkansas saw more than its share of seniors looking to escape harsh northern winters while still enjoying a full four-season cycle.

"Exactly," Michelle said. "They stayed low-rent as far as income properties. Mobile homes, small apartment complexes, a few single-family dwellings in neighborhoods. Coincidentally—or not—most of the properties are in areas that have become eligible for public-housing vouchers since Senator Powers took office."

"You're telling me they were triple-dipping senior citizens, people who are economically disadvantaged, and the federal government?" Kayla asked.

The two women locked gazes and Michelle issued a clarification. "Federal and state governments."

"Those are some pretty high stakes," Ryan observed. He fixed his attention on Kayla, watching her absorb the information.

Michelle said softly, "You said your husband was suspicious of the company as a client, and of Harold's handling of the account."

"Yes. He saw there was a higher than customary rate of investment exchange, and startlingly high billable hours being spent on a client that until a few years ago had been reasonably insignificant to the bottom line at P, P and W."

"Do you think he suspected his brother's involvement?" Ethan asked.

Ryan watched Kayla closely as she turned over the possibility in her mind. In the end, she sighed and shook her head. "No. I don't think he believed Bill was involved in anything suspicious."

"Do you think he might have suspected Del?" Michelle persisted.

Again, Kayla shook her head. "He only said something

to me about Harold. Not surprising. Bill and Del are family, and while Hal may have been something like family, there was no actual blood connection."

She sighed heavily, and Ryan saw her slip a protective hand over her abdomen.

"Family was the unbreakable bond to Tyrone. It blinded him to their faults in many ways. Particularly with Trey. All he wanted was for the family to get along and for everyone to be happy."

"Do you believe your husband may have resented the extra financial support he gave to his brother?" he queried.

She shook her head. "No. He was proud of Bill. He would have done anything for him."

"I presume as a member of the family, Del was more than adequately compensated," Ethan mused.

Kayla gave a sharp laugh. "Oh, yeah. Next to Tyrone and Bill, Trey and Del had interests in the firm exponentially larger than the most senior associates. Even Harold. Of course, they couched Bill's income as profit sharing, like they do for Judge Walton."

"It makes sense, considering Trey and Del were actively working at the firm," Michelle conceded.

Kayla shook her head. "I'm willing to believe they were stealing pensioners' Social Security checks, and defrauding Uncle Sam, but I can't see any of them taking it so far as to have Ty and Trey murdered."

"Maybe you're suffering the same sort of blindness your husband exhibited," Ryan suggested quietly.

She turned to look at him, but rather than anger, he saw hurt and betrayal in her bright blue gaze. "What do you mean?"

"You can't see any of them purposely wanting to harm Tyrone and Trey because they were your family, too. Because, like Ty, you believe the possibility of them inflicting harm on Ty and Trey to be unfathomable."

"You're saying you think Del pulled the trigger," she concluded, her voice breaking.

Ryan inclined his head slightly. "The only thing wealthy people like more than money is more money," he said quietly. "And the only thing they fear more than anything in the world is somebody taking their money away from them. Didn't you tell me Ty was laser-focused on maintaining the family's wealth?"

"I can't imagine—"

Ryan cut her off by raising one hand. "I know you can't. It should be unthinkable for you. For any person with a conscience. But would it be for them?"

"You think he did it," she said softly.

"We have to assume he did, Kayla." He held her gaze, ignoring the searing pain in his leg as he sat up straighter on the sofa, planting his good foot on the floor for leverage. "And we have to assume they will stop at nothing to clean up any loose ends."

"Loose ends like me," she repeated, her expression disconcertingly placid.

"Yes."

"I can't hide from them forever," she argued.

He shook his head at her stubbornness. "As far as I'm concerned, you can't risk them catching up to you. Remember, you said you'd do things my way. You promised you wouldn't fight me on this."

"But—"

"No buts. You agreed you wouldn't push back. I'm holding you to your promise now. We're leaving here, Kayla. Tonight." Turning to Michelle, he asked, "Were you able to set something up?"

She nodded once, then met Kayla's gaze with a wince. "I'm sorry, but I agree with Ryan on this one. You have to go. I've arranged for you to stay in an FBI safe house a few hours from here. I can't say where, but Ryan will get you there. We have to know you're safe so we can focus all our energies on flushing Powers out of the underbrush."

Ryan studied Kayla's profile, but she'd remained disconcertingly stoic throughout Michelle's recitation. Every muscle in his body tensed as she rose gracefully from her chair. If he was going to have to go toe-to-toe with her, he wished he could actually do it on two feet.

"Kayla, it is for the best," Ethan interjected.

But Kayla remained true to her word. She didn't argue. She didn't push back. Instead, she turned to Michelle and asked, "How long should I pack for?"

Which left him feeling even more agitated than any argument she might have mustered.

Chapter Fifteen

True to her word, she didn't argue, or push back in any way. She sat quietly while Ryan, Ethan and Michelle mapped out next steps, seething inside as she toyed with the remote connected to the smart-home system.

All around her, plans swirled. They'd leave after nightfall. It was smarter to use the old Range Rover stored in the garage in case they needed to go off road. Del Powers knew their vehicles, so there's no way they could take her luxury car or Ryan's state-issued SUV, but hopefully he'd forgotten about the ancient four-wheel drive stored in the garage.

She had no clue what their destination would be. The only thing she knew for certain was they would drive north, over the border into Missouri. Michelle had arranged for them to stay a night at an FBI safe house, but they would have to move on the following morning. When her friend apologized to Kayla for the inevitable rounds of movement, both Ryan and Ethan insisted it was the best plan for the immediate future.

She couldn't go anywhere Del Powers would expect her to turn up. She couldn't risk being seen in any of the places where she might be recognized. Heaven only knew how many snitches Del and his father had stashed around the northwest corridor.

Like the good soldier she was, she'd gone upstairs and

packed a weekender bag of casual, comfortable clothes and only the barest necessities in terms of cosmetics and toiletries. For the first time since she'd left law school, Kayla Powers was planning to travel with only two pairs of shoes—the trainers she wore, and a pair of hiking boots.

Exhausted by the thought of living out of a bag for the foreseeable future, she dropped heavily onto the edge of the bed. Pulling her phone from her pocket, she saw she had a missed call from an unknown number. Normally, she wouldn't have paid it any mind, but she saw the icon for a voice mail was lit. Curious, she pressed Play.

"It doesn't have to be like this."

Her heart thudded to a stop when she recognized Del Powers's voice. Sitting up straighter, she darted a glance at the open door before pressing the phone to her ear hard. Her instincts told her this call from Del might be the key to her freedom.

"We always worked well together, Kayla. You can't hide forever," he said, his tone disconcertingly calm. "We need to meet. You and me. No cops. We need to sort this out once and for all."

The call ended, but his final words sent a chill racing down her spine.

Once and for all.

Did he expect her to hand over everything Ty had entrusted to her and walk away? Or maybe he didn't expect her to walk away at all.

Either way, Del's calm demeanor was what scared her most. How did he expect this to play out? There was no way this could end well. Would it ever end?

After dropping her phone, she propped her elbows on her knees and dipped her head into her hands.

"Are you all set? We need to get moving."

Ryan's question should have startled her, but she was beyond being scared at this point. She'd heard his heavy footfalls and uneven gait coming down the hall. Ryan was treating his injury as if it didn't matter. But it did. If Del did get to her, Ryan would throw himself between her and danger, and she wasn't sure she could stand it if he was hurt any worse than he already was.

"Almost." Leaving the zip half-open, she headed into her bathroom, needing one more minute to think without the weight of Ryan's watchful gaze on her.

She drew three deep breaths to steel herself, then grabbed a handful of hair bands and a tube of facial cleanser she didn't need. Given the promises she'd made, stealing moments to sort her thoughts was the only acceptable means of rebellion available to her.

She could claim she was being coerced.

An argument could be made he'd put her in an untenable position, coaxing a promise from her under duress, but it would do no good.

Catching sight of his face as she reemerged from the bathroom, Kayla registered the stubborn resignation hardening his jaw. Sergeant Hastings had dug in, and unless she was willing to engage in endless hours of tug-of-war, she needed to cooperate.

Or give the appearance of cooperating.

She tossed the random items she'd grabbed into her bag and zipped it shut. Looping the strap over her shoulder, she let it fall against her hip as she walked away from the big comfortable bed.

Kayla had no idea what sort of arrangements to expect at an FBI safe house, but she was certain 2000-thread-count sheets wouldn't be one of the amenities.

She drew to a halt in front of him, lifting a single eyebrow in challenge, but he didn't step aside to allow her to leave.

"How about you? Do you need help packing?"

Ryan snorted. "My bag is in the car."

"Ah, you came to hurry me along."

"You being cooperative makes me nervous," he admitted bluntly.

She tipped up her chin and met his gaze. "Me being cooperative feels unnatural," she said with an edge to her voice. "But a promise is a promise. I am not arguing, and I'm not pushing back."

Ryan tilted his head. "Thank you."

"You're welcome. Shall we?" She waved her hand to indicate he was standing in her way. But he didn't move.

"Thank you," he repeated. "I'm not trying to make you unhappy. I only want you to be safe."

Instinctively, she covered her stomach with her hand and drew a steadying breath. "I appreciate your efforts."

They stood staring at one another for the space of a few thrumming heartbeats, then Ryan seemed to snap out of a trance. "Okay," he said a shade too briskly. "Here—" he reached out to lift the strap from her shoulder "—let me take your bag."

Kayla swiveled so the bag swung out of his grasp. "I can carry it. You need to hang on to the banister as we go down the steps. If you topple, I can't catch you."

No sooner were the words out of her mouth, Kayla regretted them. She didn't want to infer his injury made him incapable of doing whatever he needed to do to protect her. She had all the faith in the world in his dedication to her safety. The only issue was, she was not on board for the plan to cut and run that the rest of them had concocted.

"I'm not going to fall down the stairs," he said mulishly.

She gave a sympathetic chuckle. "Don't take this as an indictment of my faith in you, but I'm sure you won't mind if I walk behind you. I don't want to risk being crushed in the avalanche."

"Ha. Ha," Ryan said dryly over his shoulder as he made his way to the staircase.

Stiffness in each of his steps made her wince. As they painstakingly made their way down the steps, she couldn't help replaying the scene at the gatehouse in her head.

The stomach-roiling stench.

His hand warm on the center of her back.

The shadowy movement in the trees.

Del.

Now she had absolutely no doubt whatsoever she had seen somebody in a small boat that morning. If given a stack of bibles to swear on, she would affirm to the entire world she had spotted Delray Powers watching her from the woods as she heaved up her guts.

As they rounded the landing and started down the final flight of steps, she kept her gaze squarely centered on Ryan's broad shoulders. She'd watched him run toward danger, willingly placing himself between her and whatever lurked in the woods surrounding the house.

He hadn't hesitated. He hadn't locked up. He'd taken off in pursuit of the person he believed to be a threat to her and her unborn child.

As long as she lived, she would never forget the sight of Ryan running headlong into the trees. She'd never get over those endless minutes she'd waited, panting for breath, doing her best to escape the stench of Del's unsubtle message, but staying within range of the spot where Ryan had disappeared.

When she'd finally found a precious pocket of fresh air around the curve in the driveway, her worries had shifted from battling back another round of dry heaves to the notion she may have seen Ryan for the last time. She'd stood frozen, her hands braced on her knees and her eyes fixed on the tree line, listening for gunshots or calls for help.

She'd heard none of the above.

But when Ryan emerged from the trees, she could see right away something was wrong. He must have literally been running on adrenaline because his limp had not been as pronounced as it was now. Whatever happened in the woods, it had done some serious damage.

"Stop watching me like I'm about to tumble over," he grumbled without looking back at her.

"What makes you think I'm looking at you at all? Sheesh, the ego on some people," she teased.

"Your eyes are like laser beams. I can feel the heat," he growled. He drew up at the foot of the stairs, his hand clutching the newel post as he waited for her to join him on the main level. "Stop worrying about me," he ordered.

"Stop telling me what to do," she retorted.

"I'm afraid I'm going to be doing a lot of telling you what to do for the foreseeable future, so you might as well get used to it," he said, quirking an eyebrow. "No arguing. No pushback."

"Have I argued? Have I pushed?" she asked, being sure to keep her tone maddeningly patient and calm.

"No, and your cooperation is making me nervous."

"So you keep telling me." She gave him a sweet smile. "I like keeping you on your toes."

"I feel like a ballerina." He nodded in the direction of the garage. "Michelle is sending us a GPS pin in about thirty minutes. She asked you to text her once we're in Missouri."

Kayla rolled her eyes. "I can't help wondering if Del is getting a charge out of being treated like such a big threat."

He leveled a gaze on her. "He is a big threat. And the sooner you let go of your old notions of who Del Powers is or was, the safer and better off we'll all be."

Kayla raised both hands in surrender. "Okay, fine, you're right." She closed her fingers then flicked them open again as if chasing the notion away. "Del Powers is a stone-cold killer, and he's out to get me."

She'd intended the words as a joke. A little bit of dark humor to offset the seriousness of the scene, but the moment she'd spoken the words, she realized they rang true. At least on some level.

Drawing a deep breath, she squared her shoulders and gestured for Ryan to lead the way to the garage.

He picked up the security-system remote and issued instructions.

"Arm alarm system in five minutes," he ordered.

"Alarm system will be armed in five minutes," the computer-generated voice confirmed.

"Begin random security lighting sequence at twenty-two hundred hours," he instructed.

"Random security lighting sequence will commence at twenty-two hundred hours," the voice replied.

Satisfied, Ryan placed the remote on the edge of the kitchen counter and led the way into the breezeway to the detached garage.

The hatch on the Range Rover was open, awaiting her luggage. Kayla tossed her bag in beside his duffel and shut the rear door.

She made her way to the right side of the vehicle. It wasn't until Ryan had flung himself bodily into the front left seat that he realized she'd tricked him.

The vehicle was an import, and the steering wheel was on the right.

"What the—"

She cut off his protest by holding out her hand for the keys. "Ty had this shipped over years ago," she said, wiggling her fingers in a gimme motion. "Before they even started selling them here in the States."

"I can drive," he countered.

"I know you can," she said with the patience of a kindergarten teacher, "but it's a manual transmission. You won't be able to handle the clutch for long."

Kayla wasn't above enjoying the look of horror on his face as he took in the vehicle's stick shift and lack of modern communication devices. "I'm guessing there's no Bluetooth," he said as he slid into the passenger seat.

"Nope." She cranked the engine, pressed the button to raise the garage door, then put the car in Reverse, slinging an arm over the back of his seat. She craned her neck to look out the rear window. "No time to fuss about it now, though. We can't get trapped in here by our own security system," she reminded him.

Ryan grunted when she hit bumps in the rutted gravel drive at a speed slightly faster than she would normally undertake. The sensor on the gate picked up their approach, and the rusted iron swung inward. The second she could clear it, Kayla floored the accelerator and turned onto the secondary road, tires spinning on the loose rocks at the shoulder of the road.

Ryan glanced over at her as she ran the Rover through its gears, a wry smile tucked into the corner of his mouth. "Feel better?"

Kayla glanced up at the rearview mirror in time to see the gate swing shut. "Marginally."

Taking her foot off the gas, she allowed the car to shift

down to a more reasonable speed. Once she heard the clunk of the gate latching, she took off toward the highway.

They rode in silence. Shifting smoothly through the progression of gears, she allowed her thoughts to swirl until they coalesced.

She turned onto the highway and pointed the SUV north, toward the state line.

"We're going to have to get some gas," she announced, checking the gauges. "We don't use this car often, so we have a little less than a quarter of a tank."

"What kind of mileage does it get?" he asked gruffly.

She shrugged. "Heck if I know." She glanced over at him and offered a small conciliatory smile. "I'm sure we've got enough to get to the next gas station. There's always one just inside over the state line. Most of these counties were dry up until a few years ago."

He nodded. "Selling beer, cigarettes and lottery tickets to Arkansans desperate for vice has always been a big moneymaker for the state of Missouri."

Sure enough, less than a quarter mile beyond the state line they were greeted by a brightly lit gas station advertising specials on 30-packs of beer and crowing about their low, low cigarette prices.

She pulled in at the pump, then chuckled at herself as she realized the tank was on the opposite side of the car. "Oops. Hang on a second."

When she had the vehicle properly aligned, she killed the engine and reached into her purse to extract her wallet. But when she pulled out a card, he waved it away.

"No cards. We can't risk being monitored. Need to use cash to pay for things as much as we can. Fake names and dummy accounts haven't worked for us so far," he said grimly.

Kayla clasped her wallet for a moment, debating. She'd

extracted a wad of cash from the safe in Tyrone's office, she didn't volunteer to pay for the gas. She could see her chance to put her plan into action shimmering like a mirage in the distance.

Luckily, Ryan was already rolling out of the car. "You stay in the car. I'll pay, then we can pump,"

"Okay." She watched as he made slow, steady progress across the deserted apron and disappeared into the store.

The moment he was out of sight, a large pickup truck jacked up on mud tires and loaded with roof-mounted lights pulled in at the pump on the other side of the island. Two young men jumped down from the elevated cab. Knowing she'd never have a better opportunity, Kayla cranked the engine and pulled away from the pump.

Hooking a left onto the highway, she headed back in the direction from which they'd come. She prayed she had enough gas in the tank to carry out the plan she'd hatched while Ryan, Ethan and Michelle had discussed what to do with her.

When he emerged from the gas station mere minutes later, Ryan Hastings swore under his breath. He hustled back to the pump, but he wasn't imagining things. Kayla was gone.

She'd left him stranded.

And judging by the taillights glowing in the distance, she was heading back to Arkansas. He swore again, this time louder.

"Oh, dude," a young man in sagging jeans and a stretched-out Cardinals T-shirt crooned. "Was that your ride?"

"What?" He shook his head to clear it then turned to look at two twentysomethings staring at him with their mouths agape.

"Did your girlfriend take off and leave you here?" one asked.

"She's not my girlfriend," he said, latching on to one irrefutable fact.

"Well, not anymore, I'd say," he said with a laugh.

"Was it your car or hers? Cool how it's got the steering wheel on the wrong side and all," the second guy chimed in.

"Did you guys get in a fight or something?" the first guy asked, glancing over to where Kayla's taillights were disappearing over a rise in the road.

"Must have been one heck of a fight," the other said with a sympathetic grimace.

"No fight," Ryan replied numbly. "No pushback," he added, almost as an afterthought. He hadn't been wrong. Kayla's capitulation had come far too easily. "Damn," he said under his breath.

"You're better off, man. I mean, she was hot and all, but leaving a guy high and dry out here," the shorter guy said. "Totally cold."

"Do you live far? Do you need a lift somewhere?" the first guy asked, removing the pump handle from his gas tank.

"What?" Ryan asked. Then he shook his head hard. "No. I mean, yes," he said, unable to get his thoughts and words in the right order. Coming to his senses, he fumbled for his wallet and flipped out his badge and ID. "Arkansas State Police, Sergeant Ryan Hastings. I need your vehicle."

The taller guy edged closer to the driver-side door. Ryan could literally pick him up and physically set the scrawny kid aside if he had to, but he was looking for their cooperation.

The kid reached for the door handle and hauled himself up into the cab of the truck again. "Dude, I understand you're having lady trouble, but I'm not giving you my truck."

"I'm not asking," Ryan said more forcefully, stepping into the open doorway and blocking the kid's ability to shut him out. "This is official business. I need to borrow your vehicle."

"Don't give it to him, Danny," his friend exhorted, scuttling back to the passenger side. "He's Arkansas State Police—this is Missouri, he doesn't have jurisdiction here," his buddy said as he hoisted himself into the vehicle.

"Please," Ryan said in a clipped tone. "I'm asking for your assistance. The woman you saw is being stalked. I need to go after her. She's about to put herself in grave danger."

"Grave danger," the kid named Danny repeated in a tone half awed and half terrified. "How do you mean?"

"There's somebody after her," Ryan explained in a rush. He placed a foot on the running board and grabbed the handle inside the open door.

"How do we know you're not the stalker?"

"The woman you saw is being harassed by a guy who's already killed two people. I've been tasked with protecting her," he said looking the driver directly in the eyes. "I'm asking for your help."

Danny eyed him skeptically for a moment, but then his curiosity won out. "Okay, man, you can get in, but I'm driving."

"I can't lead you into what might possibly be an ambush," Ryan insisted.

"Our way or the highway, Mr. Arkansas State Policeman," his friend said in a singsong voice.

"This isn't a joyride. I'm serious about the danger," Ryan insisted, holding eye contact with Danny and ignoring his annoying buddy.

Without breaking the stare, Danny leaned forward and pulled the lever to move his seat forward. "Then you'd better climb in. She's getting a good head start on you."

Ryan gulped down the urge to shout at this stubborn guy. Despite the pain in his leg, and the fury roiling in his gut, he launched himself into the truck's sad excuse for a rear bench seat. "Head south as fast as you can. I'll tell you where to turn off."

Danny revved the engine and powered up the array of

after-market lighting. With a whoop and a holler from the guy riding shotgun, they took off after Kayla with a squeal of oversized tires.

Chapter Sixteen

She was five miles into Arkansas before he called the first time.

"What the hell do you think you're doing," Ryan demanded.

Kayla chose to believe he was shouting to be heard over the roar of a barely muffled engine, and not yelling at her. "I'm heading back."

"I figured," he said in a disgruntled shout. "The question is why? You said you'd go along with the plan."

"I said I wouldn't fight you. I said I wouldn't give you any pushback." He muttered something unflattering about lawyers, and she could swear she caught the rumble of masculine laughter.

"You're failing to make your case, counselor," he said in an ominous tone.

"Where are you? Who are you with?" she asked when she heard another man say something she couldn't quite make out.

"This is your idea of not fighting me?"

Kayla bit her lower lip. She heard the hurt and worry he tried to cover up with grumbles and complaints. "I didn't fight you. I simply came up with an alternate plan," she said, her tone patronizing in its patience.

"You cannot go back to the lake house, Kayla," he said sternly.

"I am going back. What's more, I'm inviting Del over for a visit—"

"How? He hasn't been big on returning phone calls and texts lately."

"No one is calling the right number," she informed him.

Her assertion seemed to knock him off balance. For a moment, all she could hear was the rumble of an engine running at full throttle.

"He's been in contact with you," he concluded, not bothering to mask the disgust and betrayal in his tone.

"I had a voice mail today," she informed him. "It *was* Del we saw in the woods. He must be using a burner phone because the call came from an unknown number."

"Forward it to me," he ordered.

Kayla pulled the phone away from her ear as she glanced nervously at the winding mountain road ahead of her. "I can't right now. I'm driving."

"Kayla," he growled in a warning tone.

"I don't have hands free," she reminded him.

"Use the voice command," he insisted.

"I will, but first, I need you to call in the cavalry. I'm going to lure him to the house, but I need people ready to spring the trap."

"Kayla, you are not—"

"I'm the only one he'll come for, Ryan," she interrupted. "I'm the one who is in his way."

"You can't...the baby," he responded, but his words were broken into pieces.

She was entering one of the deep valleys where cell reception grew choppy. Knowing she needed to get her call in to Del as she came over the next rise, she spoke over his objections.

"I have to go now. Call Ethan, Michelle, whoever you want, but tell them to wait until I give the signal. I don't mind being bait, but I refuse to be chum," she warned him.

"Kayla, wait—"

"Ryan, believe me when I tell you I know I have a lot to live for, but I want to be able to live. Really live. You must trust me."

She paused, hoping he'd give her his blessing, if only grudgingly, before she ended the call, but he said nothing.

"I'll send you the contact information. Goodbye, Ryan. And thank you," she added, almost as an afterthought. "I do appreciate what you tried to do for me."

She dropped the phone into her lap, her fingertip hovering over the icon that would end the call. She didn't want their connection to end, but if she wanted a shot at being able to crawl out from under the specter of Del Powers, she needed to draw him out of the shadows.

"Kayla, I—"

Whatever Ryan was about to say was lost when she hit a bump in the road and her finger grazed the touch-sensitive screen, ending the call.

The drone of worn tires on ancient asphalt hummed loud in her ears. She wet her lips as she glanced down at the now-darkened screen. "Yeah. I know. Me, too," she whispered into the darkness around her.

She drove the rest of the way back to the house as fast as she dared on the dark country roads. The moment she turned off the highway, onto the private road leading to the lake house, she rolled her shoulders back and gripped the steering wheel with both hands. Calling out to her phone's virtual assistant, she issued a command. "Replay last message in my voice-mail box on speaker."

The moment Del's voice pierced the safety of her vehicle, she cut it off by ordering the assistant to return the call to the stored phone number.

Del did not answer. She didn't expect him to. Instead, she continued to play the game, offering herself up as the mouse to his cat.

"It's me. I've ditched Sergeant Hastings, and I'm back at the house on the lake. This is your one and only chance, Del-ray," she said, drawling his full name as she waited for the gate to creak open. "You think I took what's rightfully yours? Well, come and get me. If you have the guts."

Then she shot up the driveway, leaving the gate wide open.

She parked the Range Rover in its usual spot, strode through the breezeway and entered the house the same way they'd left it. Grabbing the security remote, she ordered, "Disarm system. Standby mode."

"System disarmed," came the reply.

Her mind reeling with all there was to do, she made a mental list.

Light. She needed to light every corner of the house up. She wanted no dark corners where Del could slip into the shadows.

"Lights on, all rooms."

Every bulb in the house sprang to life. *"Lights on,"* the virtual assistant confirmed.

Moving through the kitchen, Kayla made her way over to the glass sliders. The patio, dock and boathouse were flood-lit. Catching her bottom lip between her teeth, she manually flipped the switches to shut off the exterior lights.

Satisfied, she hurried down the hall to Ty's office. There, she locked herself in and moved to the safe. She removed the gun her husband kept there. Her father was a hunter, so respect for firearms had been drilled into her from an early age. Ty had taken her with him to the shooting range a few times, insisting it was important she knew how to load and use the handguns he kept in both houses.

Kayla opened the safe and withdrew the gun and the clip of bullets. She wasn't particularly fond of the notion of carrying a loaded weapon around, but she wasn't about to face down Del Powers unarmed.

If her plan worked, she wouldn't actually have to face him at all.

With the gun loaded, but the safety on, she reached into the safe one more time, this time withdrawing a key attached to a neon yellow foam floater. The boat key hadn't been removed from the safe since the state police had released Trey's precious ski boat. It was the only time she'd ever known her husband to take something away from his spoiled heir.

The key dangled by a beaded chain as she lifted the security remote and pressed the button. "Intercom on," she ordered as she headed for the sliding doors.

"Communications system activated."

To test it, she lifted the remote again and said, "Can you hear me now?"

The echo of her own voice bounced back at her from the depths of the cavernous house.

"Record all video and audio," she ordered.

"Recording in progress," the system confirmed.

A grim smile curved her lips. She moved to Tyrone's computer and woke the system. The oversized monitor displayed a grid of all camera angles. One by one, she cycled through them, inspecting each frame for anything out of the ordinary. Only those arrayed along the back of the house were dark and grainy, but the ambient lighting from the house lit them enough for her to make out shapes and movement.

Everything was quiet. For the moment.

She held her phone poised, ready to call Ryan the moment she spotted any sign of Del's truck. But no one came.

Or so she thought.

It seemed like hours had passed before the front door opened and closed, but it was likely only minutes.

"Kayla?" Del Powers called up to the cathedral ceiling of the entry.

Panicking, she dialed Ryan's number. This wasn't what she planned. She thought she'd see him come up the drive and slip out the back. Now she was stuck. Ryan answered on the first ring.

"What the hell are you doing?" he snapped. "Answer my calls."

"Shh." She turned down the volume on her phone as low as it would go. "Del is in the house."

Ryan let loose with an expletive, and whoever was with him immediately asked what was wrong.

She moved over to the office door and pressed her thumb to the biometric pad that would engage the locks. "I'm in the safe room. I'm armed. I have a plan, but I need you to calm down and listen."

"Oh, dude, you're in deep now," one of the guys in the background said on a guffaw.

"Shut it, Jimmy," another man snapped. "I think this is serious stuff, man."

"Who are you with?" she asked. But before she could answer, Del called out for her again. "Never mind. Mute your phone. I'm going to leave the call open. You have backup coming?"

"Yes," Ryan replied tightly. "Kayla—"

"Mute it. I can't have you giving me away."

Almost immediately, all the noise on the other end went silent.

She eyeballed the video capture of her late husband's nephew. His hair was longer and messier than she'd ever seen. He wore tree-patterned hunting camouflage from head to toe and sturdy boots. This version of Del Powers looked nothing like the tax attorney she'd known for years. This Del Powers had tried to shoot her, stalked her and wanted to take everything Tyrone had treasured from her. Maybe even her baby.

She lifted the smart remote with a trembling hand. "I'm upstairs," she said over the intercom. "I, uh, I spilled some wine, so I needed to change clothes."

On camera, she saw Del sneer as he turned his face toward the staircase. "I guess the trip to rehab didn't take, huh?"

His sarcastic tone set her teeth on edge, but she did her best to keep a rein on her temper. "Hard to focus on staying healthy when someone is trying to kill you." Drawing a shaky breath, she continued. "We always got along, Del. I don't get it. What did I ever do to you?"

He gave a short bark of laughter, then strode to the steps. "You married into the wrong family."

Kayla held her breath as she watched him slowly creep up the first few stairs. "Come on," she whispered under her breath encouragingly. "Come and get me."

Del climbed another two steps. "It was supposed to be you, you know," he said with such equanimity her blood ran cold.

Glancing down at her phone, she saw the call to Ryan was still in progress, but she didn't dare try to take on multiple conversations. Not when she was watching a man who wanted to kill her creep up her stairs.

She tapped out a quick text. You getting all this?

His reply came in an instant. 10-4

Focusing on the footage of Del, she lifted the remote. "Supposed to be me what?" she asked, dreading the answer she was fairly sure she already knew.

"You cuddled up on the couch with good old Uncle Ty," he said, his voice growing louder with remembered anger. "I don't know why I thought that hillbilly Harley Jenkins could do the job right."

"Harley Jenkins? What job?" she asked, needing more information.

"You and Uncle Ty."

Kayla stared at the monitor incredulously. Had he shrugged and told her he planned to execute her? Genuinely bewildered, she spoke into the remote. "You hired Harley Jenkins to kill Tyrone and me?"

Del snorted, then started taking the stairs two at a time. "He took my money, but said he couldn't go through with it. You know what they say about wanting a job done right."

The moment she saw him reach the upper gallery, she moved away from the computer and to the door. "You did kill them."

"If it's any consolation, it was quick," he said in a mocking tone. "They never saw me as any threat."

Needing to draw him out, she asked the burning question. "Why? How could you?"

"Why? Why should you have everything I had coming to me?" he demanded, his voice rising again.

"What do you mean? You didn't know Ty changed his will."

"Oh, but I did. My jerk of a cousin made sure I knew."

"Trey knew? How?"

"He found a copy of the will in Daddy's office. You thought you were so smart, having someone else draw it up, but you underestimated how much of a mama's boy old

Trey was. He didn't like you taking his mommy's spot on the gravy train."

Shaking her head, she spoke into the microphone. "I didn't—"

Above her, she heard a door slam against a wall. "Where the hell are you?" he shouted.

Knowing she had to get out while he was occupied, she pressed her thumb to the scanner. It was risky to leave the safe room, but if Del realized there was no way he could get to her, he would flee the scene. She would lose her chance to be free of him.

But nothing happened.

She juggled her phone, the key chain and the remote, shifting them all into her left hand. Squaring up in front of the scanner, she pressed her right thumb to the screen again, whispering a prayer under her breath.

Her shoulders sagged as the locks disengaged.

"Kayla!"

She knew she had to come up with something quick. "Oh, I'm in the blue suite," she said, trying to control her breathing. "Couldn't stay in the master after…" She let the thought trail off as she made her way down the hall, her sights set on the back of the house.

His heavy footsteps seemed to echo through the house. "Why not? It's all yours now," he replied.

Inside the service door of the kitchen, she stopped to taunt him one last time in hopes of getting a full confession. She lifted the remote again. "It wouldn't have been, though. If you killed Ty and me, you'd still have to deal with Trey."

"Turns out, he was easier to deal with than you," he growled. "Stop wasting my time."

"You know you aren't going to get away with this. You know the police are looking for you."

"They can look all they want. I can make it so they never find me."

She opened the door but drew up short at his answer. "Then, why? You know it will never be yours now. Why go through all this?"

"Because it should have been," he growled between gritted teeth. "It should have been mine all along. My father should have made sure everything came to me, but as usual, Daddy was too busy being a big shot. Well, he won't be for long, will he?"

Kayla's eyes widened as she realized Del had planned to take them all down one by one. She wanted a moment to process it all, but she didn't dare hang around one second longer. Time was not on her side. There would be no reasoning with him. Del had nothing left to lose.

With the house lit up brighter than an octogenarian's birthday cake, she moved away from the windows as quickly as possible. Heading alongside the darkened patio, she hurried toward the boathouse. Once she felt the darkness close in around her, she shoved the security remote into her pocket and raised the phone to her ear.

"How far are you?" she asked, breathless.

"Close to the drive. County guys are behind us. Ethan and Michelle twenty minutes out."

"Were you able to hear—"

"I heard it all," he assured her. "Get out of the house."

"I'm out. I'm recording, and I can talk to him, but I won't be able to hear him anymore."

"Get as far away from him as you can. It's dark, so head for the woods."

Kayla shook her head and headed for the dock. "I have a better idea. Listen, something tells me he'll keep talking, but we both know whatever we get may not be admissible in court. Del will know it, too," she informed him, her sneakers slapping against the aluminum planking of the boat dock.

"Where are you?"

"Getting out of here," she panted as she reached for the strap attached to the canvas cover of Trey's flashy red ski boat and yanked it free with one hand. The boat was in its slip, covered tight as a drum and untouched by anyone in the Powers family since the night Mallory Murray had gone overboard.

Moving frantically, she unlatched two straps along the side, then realized she couldn't peel back enough of the cover to get to the driver's seat. "Hang on," she huffed into the phone, then shoved it into the front of her shirt so she could use both hands. Moving to the other side, she quickly released three straps, yanked the cover back far enough to open the cockpit and stepped over the gunnel into one of the pristine white seats.

Taking her spot behind the wheel, she closed her eyes and prayed the engine would turn over.

Kayla winced when the powerful boat roared to life, but she couldn't worry about the noise now—she had seconds to get this boat free of its slip and out of range of whatever weaponry Del may have brought. She let the engine idle at a purr as she unwrapped ropes from the cleats and gave as powerful a shove as she could. The boat drifted back, the bumpers tied to each side knocking against the aluminum dock. She didn't have the time or inclination to worry about being careful.

Easing the throttle up, she reversed until she was well clear of the other boats. Then and only then, did she allow herself to glance at the house. Flashes of blue lights streaked the trees. The police were arriving.

Del's tall, lumbering figure appeared at the sliding doors

to the patio. She cranked the wheel and brought the nimble boat around as a shout of frustrated rage echoed across the still waters of the inlet.

She didn't turn on the running lights. She knew the sound of the engine was a giveaway, but in the darkness it would be difficult for him to pinpoint her exact location once she got far enough from the shore. Something skipped and plunked into the water to her left, but it was too dark and she was too panicked to see what it was. A fish? A bullet?

Pointing the nose of the boat toward the widest part of the lake, she pushed the throttle forward and prayed she could make it past the spit of land that marked the entrance to the cove. Once she was beyond the curve, she could risk a light. Hopefully, once she was around the corner, maybe the police would have Del in custody.

This time, she heard the crack of a rifle being fired, but she had no idea where the bullet went. As long as it wasn't into her or this boat, she didn't care. Let him keep firing at her. Keeping his focus locked on her would allow Ryan and his backup to get the drop on him.

Hair whipping around her face, she sped into the darkness, and shouted into the wind, "You can't take my life. I won't let you."

Then, as she cut the wheel to arc wide left to follow the jagged shoreline, she pulled back on the throttle and glanced back at the house before it disappeared from view. Blinking in disbelief, she gave her head a shake.

"What the—"

She could have sworn she'd seen a jacked-up pickup complete with a half-dozen rooftop lights parked on the lake-house patio.

She steered the boat closer and spotted Special Agent Ryan Hastings kneeling beside a person stretched facedown on the ground, his head turned toward the water. Cranking the wheel, she pushed forward on the throttle. A plume of water rooster-tailed behind the boat as she came around.

She fumbled for her phone, the remote for the security system tumbling out of her pocket as she yanked it free. "Are you there?" she panted into the phone.

But Ryan didn't respond. She watched as two officers rushed over to take the person she assumed was Del into custody. She tossed the phone onto the seat as Ryan pushed to his feet. She kept her gaze locked on him as he stumbled.

Was he hurt?

She sped up. As she approached, she spotted his gun dangling at his side as he raised his free hand as if to shield his eyes. She saw him scanning the water beyond the glow of the light spilling from the house.

He was looking for her.

Her hammering heart slowed to a steady *thud-thud-thud*. She flipped on the boat's running lights and gave a short blast of the horn.

A flood of calm washed through her the moment he spotted her. She killed the engine, allowing momentum to carry her toward the shore.

"Are you okay?" she shouted. But he clearly couldn't hear her. Remembering the remote, she scooped it from the deck of the boat and pressed the button. "Are you okay?"

Ryan glanced back at the house, then turned back to the water. She could see the smirk twisting his lips. He shouted something back, but though the sound carried, the words were too garbled for her to hear.

She shook her head. Then, she saw the deputies behind him helping a handcuffed man to his feet.

Del.

They had Del. It was done.

"We got him," she whispered to herself.

She saw Ryan reaching for his back pocket as two gangly guys in T-shirts and baggy jeans started down the dock, gesticulating to the action on the patio. When he raised his phone to his ear, she grabbed hers again.

"Are you okay?" she said breathlessly.

"I'm fine," he answered gruffly. "You?"

"I'm…" She paused, breathless. "We got him."

"We got him," he confirmed.

In no hurry to be lectured on her scheme, she continued to let the boat drifted closer to the dock rather than piloting it to its slip.

"Dude, that was so cool," one of the guys approaching him crowed.

"You totally took that guy down," the other chimed in.

"Ryan?" She couldn't contain the smile spreading across her face as she recognized the tricked-out pickup from the gas station. "Did you make some new friends?"

Chapter Seventeen

Ryan didn't answer her impertinent question.

She tried to hide her smile when he made an impatient gesture for her to bring the boat in, but she could see the relief written all over his face. She'd scared him almost as much as she'd scared herself. But she did what she had to do to stop this madness, and no matter how fiercely Ryan Hastings scowled, she would do it again.

Del had confessed to killing Tyrone and Trey.

He was in custody.

She was free.

Letting the boat drift, she lifted her gaze to the pseudo castle the first Tyrone Delray Powers had built as a testament to his wealth and power. The place where she'd fallen in love with his son. The house that became her refuge when she was miserable, and eventually, the key to her freedom.

A gentle wave of sadness washed through her as she realized she could never live there.

The happy memories she had there, the solace she'd once found within its walls, would forever be tainted now. Shadows of Trey's negligence, the emptiness left behind by Ty's murder and this terrifying night would lurk in every corner. But she would retain control of the firm. Or what was left of it, if the fallout from multiple scandals didn't bring the place down entirely.

Her thoughts were interrupted by Ryan shouting her name.

She glanced up to find him standing firm at the end of the dock, his hands cupped around his mouth. Giving her head a shake, she raised a hand in acknowledgment, then pointed to the boathouse and slips, her eyebrows raised in question.

He shook his head and pointed an emphatic finger at the swim dock where he was standing. His visible relief had transformed into a thunderous expression. Behind him, the two young men she assumed belonged with the pickup truck jostled and crowed about the scene around them.

Biting her bottom lip to keep from smiling, she gave the boat enough juice for her to turn the starboard side perpendicular to the end of the dock. Cutting the engine, she allowed the wake to carry the craft closer as she yanked back more of the half-loosened cover to look for a line she could toss to him.

The bumpers she never bothered to pull into the boat nudged the dock. She heard a groan of pain and looked up to see Ryan struggling to lower himself enough to grab one of the bumpers and haul the boat closer.

"Don't! Your knee," she cried, finally coming up with one of the nylon ropes used to tow inflatable tubes. She loosened one end, then tossed the gathered line to Ryan. "Hold on to this."

He straightened, not bothering to mask the twist of pain that contorted his handsome face. "Get up here."

"I'm trying," she said as she secured her end. Then, diving under the canvas, she extracted another rope and went about unfurling it. "This would have been easier at the boathouse," she grumbled, scooting around to find a spot to attach the second rope.

"Hey, we can help," one of Ryan's companions said, boots clomping as he hurried to help Ryan's side. "That was awesome."

"It wasn't awesome, Danny," Ryan growled, shoving the rope at the taller guy. "It was foolish. Reckless. Deadly."

Kayla smirked as she nodded to the shorter of the two, who stood poised to catch her rope. "He's right. Don't try this at home."

With the boat tethered to the end of the dock, Kayla climbed onto the seat, then stepped onto the side of the boat, holding her arms out to maintain her balance.

"Give me your hands," Ryan ordered.

"No," she said briskly. She waved at the man he'd called Danny. "You help me. He's hurt."

Danny and his companion hurried to the edge to do her bidding, but not without cracks about how the old man should step aside, in addition to offers to fetch Ryan a walker. The second her feet hit the dock, she thanked them politely for their help, then turned to face the music.

Ryan stared at her, his expression cycling from fury to relief, from admiration to agony. She was certain there were a half-dozen others to come, but the pain etched into the brackets around his mouth tugged on something elemental inside her.

She wanted to kiss him and make it all better.

Grasping his beautiful face in both hands, she stepped into him, her thumbs smoothing the lines of pain. She searched his eyes for signs of resistance as she stretched up to meet him. She saw none, so she gave in to instinct and pressed her mouth to his.

Ryan's arms closed around her, clasping her to him tightly. A tremor ran through them both. She shifted her hands into his thick, soft hair and held him there, angling her head in an invitation to deepen the kiss.

Behind them, the guys who'd helped Ryan whooped and hollered. Kayla found she couldn't stop smiling when he shifted to take the kiss deeper. Ryan's lips curved against hers in response, and he pulled back and pressed his forehead to hers.

"Well, this is an interesting turn of events," said a familiar voice.

Kayla was too drawn into Ryan's intense gaze for her brain to process it. He was panting softly. Each puff of breath whispered across her damp lips made her ache to pull him back into the kiss.

"Ethan, don't," Michelle said in a harsh whisper. "Leave them alone."

"I've wanted to kiss you since the day I met you," he said, ignoring the commentary.

"Liar," she whispered in a shaking voice. "You thought I was a pain in the backside."

"Still wanted to kiss you."

"When you two get a minute," Ethan called to them.

"Hush," Michelle snapped.

Kayla drew a deep breath, resigning herself to the interruption. Looking deep into Ryan's eyes, she said, "We need to talk."

"Understatement," Ryan replied.

"But first we need to fill in Ethan on Del, then we need to get someone to look at your knee."

His hands came to rest on her waist, his thumbs grazing the curve of her belly. He maintained eye contact as he pulled up to his full height. "You should be checked out, too."

A sudden rush of doubt swamped her. She was pregnant.

What was she thinking? No man was going to want to get involved with a woman who was carrying another man's baby.

Her thoughts must have shown on her face, because Ryan swooped in and pecked another gentle kiss to her lips. "We'll talk."

"Okay."

"I'm not done with you," he said, holding her tight and gazing deeply into her eyes. "Things will be complicated and confusing, and a giant mess, but I won't be your Frank Farmer."

"Huh?" She reared back, searching his eyes for some clue as to what he meant.

"I'm not going to let you kiss me then take off on your private jet. You get me?" he asked, bending to pin her with a penetrating stare.

"I don't have a private jet."

"Good." He nodded briskly, then glanced over his shoulder at the small crowd gathering at the end of the dock. "As long as we can keep our feet on the ground, I think we'll figure everything else out."

* * * * *

UNDER COLTON'S WATCH

ADDISON FOX

For the wonderful city of New York. You captured my teenage heart all those years ago and it's my great privilege and pleasure to call you home.

Chapter One

A woman became surprisingly productive, Ciara Kelly thought, when she was supposed to be dead.

Murdered, to be more precise.

She shuddered at the thought and laid a protective hand over her belly. For the past few weeks—ever since she'd nearly been run over by a killer who had a damned fine shot at an insanity plea—Ciara hadn't been able to slow down. To settle.

She couldn't erase the endlessly racing thoughts that kept her up to all hours of the night and drifting off in nightmarish daydreams during the day.

She'd already carried so much fear and worry for Humphrey since her husband's disappearance at the start of the year. Four and a half months of hell as she'd waited for news. Or a call. Or any clue, no matter how meager, that her husband was okay.

Only to have it all finish with Humphrey's murder at the hands of a seductive older woman the police had dubbed a black widow killer. Maeve O'Leary had eluded the cops and what felt like four different federal agencies, based on the endless reams of questions Ciara had faced since Humphrey's disappearance.

It was a case the cops believed had wrapped up with Humphrey's death—until Maeve had turned her sights to Ciara.

It seemed implausible anyone would want to harm her, but the memories of an oncoming sedan, bearing down on her with increasing speed, had left an indelible impression.

She was sure Maeve had found out about the child Ciara was carrying—now nearly five months along—and that was what had put her squarely in the crosshairs. Especially since it had become evident that Humphrey was caught up in some sort of emotional spell Maeve had wrapped around him. There was no way he hadn't revealed his wife's pregnancy—or rather, her attempts at getting pregnant prior to his disappearance, since he hadn't known she was successful—during the months under Maeve's influence.

It seemed unthinkable, yet no matter how much she wanted to deny Humphrey's descent into Maeve's clutches, the truth was clear. The woman wanted her—and, by extension, her unborn child—dead.

It didn't matter that Ciara had done everything she could to keep her pregnancy a secret; Humphrey's disappearance had been major news in New York. And his anxious and worried wife was prime fodder for the news outlets—those that dealt in respectable reporting as well as the ones who managed far less savory pursuits in their attempts to broadcast "news."

Especially when that news concerned his considerably younger widow.

Her pregnancy had been whispered speculation, but since nearly all her clothing now no longer fit, Ciara had finally needed to acknowledge there was no hiding her growing baby bump.

A fact she'd have to reveal to her "roommate" as well.

Frowning at that thought, even as she was well aware there was nothing to be done for it, she refocused on the syllabus she was in the process of refining for her summer school students. Students who'd gamely agreed to gain her wisdom through remote learning, all while they spent their days out on a boat in the waters surrounding New York City and northern New Jersey with Ciara's best teaching assistant.

She hadn't wanted to step back. She lived for being out on the water, but with her husband's death, her pregnancy and the increasing reality that the black widow who'd murdered her husband now wanted to finish off Ciara, she'd needed the reprieve. And her long-standing record of being a good, hardworking professor, and a popular one, in Rutgers University's Department of Marine and Coastal Sciences had ensured her department head had been willing to work with her.

And boy, had she needed the break this year.

Between Humphrey's disappearance in January and the ensuing stress of wondering what, exactly, had happened to her husband, Ciara had been torn between burying herself in work and having days where she could hardly concentrate. And then there was her pregnancy, carefully planned yet not at all what the average person would expect of her. She'd been fortunate to avoid morning sickness in most of the early days.

It was all the days that had come since—navigating the ups and downs all by herself—that had been the real challenge.

Humphrey had indulged her in this area, and while they'd had an understanding on how she'd become pregnant, she had expected to share some of the experience with him. Even if it was only as two dear friends who shared a home.

What did you expect, marrying a man who had secrets?

She'd asked herself that question over and over for the past six months, and she knew it was an honest assessment—as well as a daily reality—of her late husband's life. His responsibilities as one of New York's most respected psychiatrists meant he was in demand from a lot of high-profile individuals. People who had reason to keep secrets of their own, even if they did share them in the confines of a doctor's office.

Secrets, Ciara reflected, had become an increasing reality of her life. One she couldn't escape, no matter how deeply she buried herself in work. Especially since she'd landed herself a roommate and what felt like an endless stay in a safe house.

A roommate with secrets of his own, she already suspected. US marshal Aidan Colton had far too many shadows behind the compelling brown eyes that were so dark they were nearly black—she knew he was keeping his own counsel. A state she could appreciate when she did it herself, but that was rather frustrating when she was on the opposite end of the same treatment.

The subtle knock on the front door—tapped in the exact code they'd practiced—was an odd reinforcement to her thoughts of said roommate and, in a matter of moments, the tower of locks on the door frame all flipped, one by one.

But it was the chiseled face peeking through the door, immediately followed by one strong forearm holding three reusable bags of supplies, that caught her attention from where she sat at the dining room table, tapping at her computer.

She refused to smile at him, her small, personal brand of mutiny the only thing she could control in this entire situation.

Despite her lacking welcome, he seemed unfazed, as usual. In fact, she could have sworn his smile grew broader as he kicked the apartment door closed with one foot.

"Honey! I'm home!"

TWELVE DAYS, AIDAN COLTON thought with an inward sigh as he kicked the weathered apartment door closed. Twelve days of that cold, withering reception despite all his best efforts to get past Ciara Francis Kelly's defenses.

Humor hadn't worked.

Cajoling honesty hadn't done much, either.

He'd even tried his own personal brand of law-enforcement-official-with-a-bad-attitude, which she'd roundly ignored.

The woman was impervious.

It should have been a relief. They weren't stuck in this safe house to become bosom buddies or even friends. He had a job, and he was doing it.

Every damn day.

Twelve of them and counting.

So why was he so irritated at her seeming inability to respond to him, no matter what tack he took?

There wasn't anything in the US marshal rule book that said a safe house guest needed to bond with you. In fact, he'd had buddies through the years who'd made that mistake and had nearly lost assets because of it.

He had a job to do, nothing more.

Which made the fact that he couldn't stop thinking about the woman—and his complete inability to get any sort of reaction out of her—a frustration in its own right.

He'd studied her before taking on this job. His family was involved in the Humphrey Kelly case up to their eyeballs, his cousins all close to the late psychiatrist while growing up. Now, in their various roles in New York law enforcement, each had been a part of this case from the start. And even if there hadn't been a family connection, Aidan would have needed to purposely put his head in the sand to miss such high-profile news.

It was Aidan's involvement, along with his sister's, that had ended up being the real surprise, he had to admit. Pulled in by his cousin Sean to help with the federal aspects that fell outside local NYPD jurisdiction.

His sister, Deirdre, with her FBI background, had been tapped first when the reality of Humphrey's situation became increasingly clear. Wealthy, well-respected doctors didn't simply go missing from the federal courthouse. Yet that was exactly what had happened back in January, and Sean, a NYPD detective known for cracking cases in record time, hadn't been able to get anywhere with Humphrey's case.

Nor did those same doctors disappear without leaving a trace. The boon for law enforcement that was modern technology made escaping the prying eyes of a video camera a challenging feat, especially in a dense setting like New York City.

And when that video camera was inside a federal facility? Well, disappearing was for all intents and purposes, impossible.

Yet Humphrey had vanished all the same, walking into a supply closet at the federal courthouse and seeming to disappear from there.

Of course, common sense had dictated that no matter how badly the technology had failed them, Humphrey Kelly hadn't just vanished from the courthouse. And several months of detective work by his Colton cousins had unearthed the truth.

Humphrey had been brainwashed by Maeve O'Leary. She'd gotten him out of the courthouse in a heavy disguise and had proceeded to keep him a willing captive for months. It had only been Maeve's attempt on Sean's life—the reality break Humphrey obviously needed after a lifetime of watching out for Kieran Colton's children—that had Humphrey jumping in front of a bullet Maeve had meant for Sean.

And now here he was, Aidan thought with no small measure of disgust, babysitting Humphrey's young widow and putting up with her seemingly endless supply of attitude.

"I picked up groceries. I thought I might cook something tonight. I'm getting sick of takeout."

"Okay." She shrugged but never looked up from her computer.

"You up for pasta primavera or sweet and sour chicken?"

"Whatever you prefer."

Still, that gaze never left her laptop screen.

"Maybe I'll go with option three. Liver and onions."

It was a dumb joke, meant only to get her to raise her eyes from that damn screen, but it had an odd effect on her. The eyes he knew were an enigmatic green widened before her face went ghostly pale. She slammed a hand over her mouth at the same time she leaped out of her chair and ran from the room.

The shift was so swift and immediate, it was all Aidan could do to stare after her before his own training kicked in.

What the hell had happened to her?

He followed the same path she'd taken, racing down the hall toward the bedroom and en suite bathroom she was using. Although he'd been very careful to give her space, only entering the bedroom to do the initial sweep for bugs, repeating the exercise only two other times after they'd left the apartment, he ignored any sense of propriety as he heard retching from the bathroom.

Following the sound, he found her huddled over the toilet bowl, a miserable look on a face that had gone even paler than when she'd run from the dining room.

And in that moment he knew exactly what secret Ciara Kelly had been hiding.

As she turned her head toward the bowl, in obvious distress as her stomach revolted once more, Aidan moved forward to hold her shoulders. He laid a soothing hand over her back and rubbed in large circles as she lost whatever meager contents were left in her stomach.

There'd be time enough for answers.

For now, he simply helped her through the worst of the sickness. And when she finally sat back, he gathered her into his lap and held her close as she shivered in his arms.

CIARA WASN'T SURE what was worse.

Being sick in Aidan Colton's arms.

Or huddling in those big, strong arms like a quivering baby bird fallen who'd fallen from its nest.

Even in the depths of her mortification and the still-roiling nausea in her stomach, she had to admit those arms felt nice.

Soothing.

They had an unexpected strength she hadn't realized just how much she'd missed.

Her own relationship with her mother had been bad, growing horribly worse instead of closer as her mother had suffered through her life-ending cancer diagnosis the year before. But Ciara had borne up under the pressure, caring for her mom through the very worst.

And Humphrey had been an emotional source of strength, but, if she were honest, he'd been a means to an end as well. She loved him, albeit platonically, but he hadn't been a physical source of strength. He'd provided financial security and a deep, abiding friendship she missed terribly.

But well-built, strength-filled arms that wrapped around her and held her through one of her worst moments?

No, that had been absent in her life.

"You doing okay?" Aidan's deep voice rumbled against the side of her head, his lips pressed against her temple.

"Getting there."

"Do you think you can stand? If so, I'll leave you to it and meet you in the living room with a cold ginger ale."

"That sounds nice."

Suddenly recognizing she'd nestled deeper into his arms instead of pulling away, she scrambled to sit up, even as Aidan tightened his hold.

"Easy. I'll help you up."

He was never inappropriate, but his big hands settled at her waist as he lifted her to her feet. He did it easily, his palms settling against her increasing stomach.

If he noticed—and she had no doubt he did—he said nothing, instead getting to his feet beside her. "I'll get that soda for you."

Ciara stared at his retreating back in the mirror before shifting to assess her appearance, the hair she'd pulled up haphazardly to work on her syllabus now falling in strands around her face. She made quick work of redoing her topknot and then reached for her toothbrush, determined to remove the lingering memories of tossing her meager lunch.

She hadn't thrown up much since her first trimester—and even then she'd been lucky the morning sickness hadn't been too bad—but she was triggered by certain things. The smell from a piece of raw chicken the month before had done her in for the rest of the day, and a nasty whiff of garbage one morning walking back to her apartment had done the same.

Who knew the mere mention of liver could signal the same response?

Unwilling to dwell on it now that her stomach was settling, she brushed her teeth, dried her mouth and hands, and took a deep breath.

The time had come to tell Aidan the truth. She'd known her days were numbered—her pregnancy was growing impossible to hide—and she'd have to talk to him at some point during this safe house stay.

It looked like the time had come.

She padded back down the hallway and back into the living room. As promised, there was a large glass of ginger ale on the coffee table, its golden hue still bubbling with its recent pour from the can.

And sitting opposite was Aidan.

"How are you feeling?"

She took a sip, strangely comforted by the crisp coolness. "Better. Thank you."

"You want to tell me what's going on?"

"You can't tell?"

"I'd rather hear it from you."

Although his dark eyes brooked no argument, she didn't sense any hostility in his voice, either. Recognizing that the more information he had, the better armed he was to do his job, Ciara considered how to address her pregnancy.

Because addressing that piece led to a bigger reveal about her marriage, the personal reasons she and Humphrey had even married in the first place, and what all of it meant for her life moving forward.

In the end, Ciara realized as she took another sip of soda, it was easier to start at the beginning. She'd done the same with Sean Colton and he hadn't judged her. Granted, Sean had been focused on solving Humphrey's murder, but she had to hope that his lack of judgment was a good sign.

With the increasing knowledge that Aidan Colton would respond however he chose, she dived in. "I don't expect you to understand what I'm about to tell you."

Again, those features remained impassive, even as she got the distinct sense Aidan was interested in what she had to say. "Why don't you try me?"

"I got pregnant in January."

"Did Humphrey know?" When she didn't answer immediately, he added, "Before he disappeared at the courthouse?"

"He knew about the trying to get pregnant. But no, he never officially heard the news from me. I suspect, though, that Maeve found out the details."

"Why do you think she knows?" The question beneath his question—why Maeve O'Leary might know when the US Marshals didn't—was beside the point.

"Let me start from the beginning." When he only nodded, Ciara continued. "Humphrey and I had a marriage of convenience. One of deep care and affection, though, as he's an old family friend and he's always watched out for me. When my mother got sick with cancer, I had to spend all my savings on her treatments."

"I'm sorry for that."

"It was worth it."

"I'm not suggesting otherwise, but I'm sorry you lost her."

Ciara was, too, but for a whole different set of reasons she wasn't comfortable going into. Her relationship with her mother was...complicated, and the odd mixture of anger, guilt and relief still warred in her heart whenever she thought of her mother's last months.

Yet Humphrey had understood all of that, somehow. He'd understood and done something so deeply kind and supportive for her.

"As a stipulation of my grandmother's will, I needed to be married to inherit her fortune. And the ruin of my finances from my mother's treatments being what they were, Humphrey kindly offered to play the part."

"That's some friendship."

"Humphrey was some man. A good man. I know he had his secrets and these past five months have called everything about him into question, but I tell you, Aidan, he's a good person. Was a good person."

Hadn't Humphrey proved that in the end? Taking that bullet meant for Sean Colton and ultimately losing his life?

"And the baby?"

"I've wanted a child for so long. I thought I'd find someone to share my life with and make a family, but time kept passing and I never found a relationship that lasted into the serious phase. Or to a point where I could see making a marriage and a life. And then my mother got sick and that area of my life was put on hold.

"I didn't want to wait any longer."

How could she? She was thirty-five, and the increasing reality was that if she hadn't acted, she knew she might miss her chance. So she'd forged ahead, with Humphrey's support every step of the way.

Save one.

"So in a matter of a few months you got married, got pregnant and lost your husband."

She considered Aidan's observation, thinking back to the whirlwind that had been the back half of last year and the start of this one. Her wedding to Humphrey. Her visit to the sperm bank in January. And the horrifying reality only a few days later that her husband was missing.

Vanished, really.

"So why do you think Maeve O'Leary knows? Especially if Humphrey didn't know you were actually pregnant."

Ciara wanted to believe that she'd kept her own counsel, never letting on to anyone that she was pregnant, but Maeve's attempt on her life had suggested otherwise. Perhaps under her influence Humphrey confessed Ciara had been trying to get pregnant?

Or maybe Maeve was just jealous.

Either way, the woman was tying off loose ends, and Humphrey's widow—his pregnant widow—certainly fit that bill.

"Based on your cousins' investigative work, she's not just a black widow, but she'd somehow managed to brainwash Humphrey. Although he was a wonderful man, he was a strong one, too. Determined. And someone who most definitely knew his own mind. If she'd broken through those defenses, then I have to assume he shared my plans."

"But now that Humphrey's gone, how does it benefit Maeve to kill you and the baby? The law enforcement community is on to her and she's on the run."

"I stood in the way of her getting what she wanted. A child only reinforced that."

"And you think she'd want to eradicate Humphrey's child out of spite?" Aidan shook his head, the first chink in his cool facade coming through in his deep frown and the small line that furrowed between his eyes. "I'm sorry. That's cruel of me to speak of your and Humphrey's child that way."

"If only if it were that easy."

"I'd hardly call her reaction easy."

"No, but if she knew the truth it might put her even further over the edge. One more point of evidence that even while she thought she was manipulating Humphrey, the situation was already beyond her control."

"The truth of what?"

"My baby. It isn't Humphrey's."

Chapter Two

Aidan had seen a lot in his near decade with the marshals. Little surprised him any longer, and he'd learned early—even before he'd begun his professional life—to trust very little of what other people said or presented to the world at large.

But what was this?

And who the hell was this woman?

She got married for money and then pregnant by someone else all in a matter of weeks?

He knew he needed to check himself, but something in her story stuck a hard landing in his gut. Humphrey Kelly might have led a large, extravagant lifestyle way out of Aidan's reach, but everything he'd learned about the man suggested he was a decent human being. He'd been there for Aidan's Colton cousins after their father died. He'd clearly been willing to help Ciara out when she was in a tough financial spot.

Why would she cheat on him?

On some level it wasn't any of his business. Her personal sexual choices had zero bearing on his responsibilities to watch out for her and protect her in the safe house.

Yet even as he knew that truth, something in her casual affirmation that the baby wasn't Humphrey's bothered him.

Because it flew in the face of what he thought he knew

about her? Or something else? Something even sharper at the idea that she was an adulteress?

Words fell from his lips before he could pull them back.

"Sure. Because every newlywed goes out and cheats on their husband."

"It's not—" Ciara's eyes widened and her mouth opened before she snapped it shut so hard he heard her teeth click. "Sure, Marshal Colton. You go ahead and marinate in that all that lovely, self-righteous attitude."

She stood, even as a shot of remorse was already threading through his system at his misplaced anger.

Why did he even care about her personal choices?

Those choices weren't any of his business, nor did they have anything to do with him. And as soon as they got Maeve O'Leary off the streets and into custody, Ciara Kelly wouldn't be his problem any longer, either.

"Ciara." He managed to snag her hand as she passed him through the narrow passage between the couch and a chair angled toward the couch for conversation.

"What?"

"I'm sorry. That was out of line."

Something flickered in her hostile gaze, but the firm line of her mouth didn't so much as quiver. Quickly retrenching, he added, "You caught me by surprise, is all. I didn't know your, um, situation with Humphrey, so I've assumed you were in love with him. That you were a couple in love."

Her lips were still set, but her gaze did soften a bit at the reference to her late husband. "Humphrey and I might not have been in love with each other, but we did care for each other. Deeply."

She seemed to consider her words before taking a seat again. "He supported me during a time when I didn't have anyone, and I will always be grateful. It's also why I wouldn't have done anything to hurt him."

"And the baby?"

That hard set of her jaw finally relaxed. Although she didn't owe him an explanation, it was a surprise to realize that she was going to give him one all the same.

"Humphrey and I had an agreement. He knew I wanted a baby, and he was determined that he never wanted to father a child. A fact we discussed before we got married. So he was willing to give my baby his name, but he asked that I go through a sperm donor to get pregnant."

Whatever Aidan anticipated, this was more news he hadn't braced for, yet alone even considered. Humphrey Kelly didn't want to father children, even when presented with an opportunity where he could do it with little attachment.

Why?

Aidan had his own personal reasons for avoiding marriage and fatherhood, so he was hardly in a position to judge another man. And yet...

What's really bugging you, Colton?

The world around him while he was growing up had offered little care or comfort or emotional support, so he'd learned to live without all of it. It was in that very learning that he'd come to accept he had no place raising children of his own. He'd been raised by terrible examples and refused to continue the cycle.

But would it be so bad with a woman like Ciara? One who obviously had her own goals and ambitions and still fought to make her dreams of having a child come true?

As he turned that over in his mind, Aidan had to admit there was another ramification, unspoken yet underlying her words. He wouldn't approach it after his already-careless comments, but it hung in that unspoken space all the same.

She and Humphrey weren't intimate.

And once again, he'd entered that strangely personal realm that was none of his business.

Aidan was good at his job specifically because he didn't get involved with his assignments. Yet something about Ciara had been different from the start. His determination to break through her underlying aloofness. His frustration that nothing seemed to work. Even the weird need he had to see her smile.

That wasn't him.

He steered clear of intimacy—in his professional life and his personal life—a keen lesson sharpened repeatedly throughout his life at the knees of his parents. Even if his sister, Deirdre, had managed to escape their childhood example with her new and unexpected tumble into love with Maeve O'Leary's estranged stepson, Micah Perry.

He and Deirdre had never been close, their parents' mostly cold relationship resulting in him and his half sister being raised in separate homes. But with both of them being pulled into Humphrey Kelly's case, her through her role in the FBI and him in the US Marshals, they'd spent more time together, forging new sibling bonds in the process. He'd been happily surprised to realize that he appreciated the opportunity to get to know his sister better.

Aidan considered the various facets of the information Ciara shared, turning each piece over in his mind. If Maeve knew about Ciara's pregnancy—and knew that the baby wasn't Humphrey's—would she be as determined to see her revenge on the young widow?

His gaze drifted over Ciara again. She was slight, very slim and willowy, even as that delicacy was easy to dismiss because of an inner strength that seemed to light her up. It was only now that he was really looking that he admitted he could see the outline of her pregnancy. That, along with the sense memory of his palms resting against her stomach when he helped her up in the bathroom, filled his mind. Willing the sensation away, he ran his hands over his thighs.

And focused on her stomach.

Had Maeve seen the same?

"Okay. So let's operate on the theory Maeve knows you're pregnant but doesn't know Humphrey isn't the baby's father. It plays more clearly into the revenge theory we've been operating under."

"She's not exactly proven herself to be a stable personality. Does it even matter?"

"It might not have when this all started, but that stability has no doubt suffered as the months have passed. It's likely she's become completely unbalanced since her plans have been so thoroughly thwarted."

Ciara nodded at that, seeming to consider his points. It was the first time she'd actually engaged in a conversation with him since they'd started living together in the safe house twelve days ago, and Aidan was oddly heartened by her involvement in the discussion.

Especially since he'd fumbled so badly over her pregnancy and what it suggested about her marriage vows.

Once again, Aidan thought about the strange intimacy of their living situation. He'd come into this ready to do his job and had quickly become focused on getting some sort of response or reaction out of her. Now that he had, he also had to accept that he was living with her and her unborn child.

A wholly unexpected shot of protectiveness filled him at that new reality.

Even as Aidan had no idea what to do about it.

CIARA WASN'T SURE what had changed, only that something had. One moment she was fighting off the hard offense of

Aidan's insults over her marriage and her seeming lack of fidelity. But after she'd corrected him, she'd then sensed a deep layer of protectiveness wash over him.

To be fair, she'd felt that already, but it had hovered in the safe house apartment almost like an invisible blanket, wrapping around her.

But now?

Now she felt it, in his gaze, in his attitude and even in the tone beneath his words.

He was an impressive man. Formidable. She'd seen that from the start. Although she didn't know many men in law enforcement jobs, she knew enough that it wasn't a casual decision, nor was it easy, to get into the US Marshals program. It took dedication, irrefutable skill and a larger-than-life quality to hold the job.

This might have been her original perception when she'd been told she would receive safe house protection from the marshals, but her additional internet searches had helped round out that perspective.

Meeting Aidan Colton had only reinforced it all—and more.

He was striking and deeply attractive, which she'd done her level best to ignore. She was a pregnant, widowed woman, for heaven's sake. It did no good to think about someone off-limits, even if there was an odd sort of safety in the fantasy.

But no.

She'd noticed how attractive he was from their first meeting, but she'd diligently tamped down on any lingering flutters beneath her skin or that sly, not-so-subtle warming in the belly.

Refocusing herself on the grim direction of their conversation, she considered what she did know.

And what she didn't.

"Has anyone figured out how Maeve set her sights on Humphrey in the first place?"

"Humphrey wasn't the first wealthy man she'd focused on. It's a pattern."

"The black widow pattern." A shiver struck the length of Ciara's spine, down to her butt and right back up to her shoulders in a rolling shudder. "I'd always assumed that was the purview of thriller novels someone read on the beach or a Sunday afternoon woman-in-jeopardy movie on cable."

"Sadly, it's real. Uncommon, but real all the same."

"But why Humphrey? Of all the people a manipulator could go after, it doesn't make sense she'd choose a psychiatrist."

"It's an interesting point. But it could be the seeming unconquerability of a personality like Humphrey's that proved challenging to her."

As ideas went it was as good as any, even as it still felt elusive. But hadn't all of Maeve O'Leary's actions felt that way? Baby or not, Humphrey was gone. Sticking around to try and kill his widow instead of just finding a way to escape New York didn't suggest a lot of rationale or reasoned thinking.

Despite Maeve's depravity—and Ciara's gratitude for the protection—it seemed like an incredible amount of effort was going into keeping her safe. With a sudden realization, Ciara took a hard look at Aidan.

"This case has to be taking up a considerable amount of time for you. Staying here. Watching out for me. Why's all this effort going into capturing this one woman?"

"It is a lot of effort. A worthy one, too. Especially since her crimes have been committed over decades and across various state lines. But to your bigger question, I do have other work."

"Isn't it suffering because of me?"

He grinned, the smile broad with a lot of teeth. She should

have read it as cocky, but for some reason all Ciara could do was smile back. "I'm a pretty good multitasker."

"Maybe so, but I have to imagine a job like this one is tedious."

His eyes narrowed at that, oddly inscrutable even as his smile dimmed. "My job has various facets. Protecting innocent people in danger is nothing I take lightly. Add on their innocent unborn babies, and that goes double."

Although she'd avoided any outward signs of the life growing inside her, Ciara did lay a protective hand over her stomach at his words. Her baby bump was still small, but it was there all the same. She'd already felt the telltale flutters of her child's movement, and her thickening waist had begun to take on a more rounded shape over the past few weeks.

"I know this is the safest place for me." She glanced down at her stomach, the truth even more clear. "Us. But I can't stay here forever. I've already put so much of my life on hold these past months as we've tried to understand what happened to Humphrey. Now I'm teaching my summer school classes remotely to avoid being out in the open."

"You're where you need to be, Ciara. I know it's frustrating, but there's work, constant work, going on to catch Maeve O'Leary. You have to know this is the best place for you."

"I know that. Truly, I do. It's just—"

Goodness, didn't she sound so selfish? Aidan was here to protect her. To watch over her. And all she could do about it was complain?

But when would life go back to normal? First there was that last year with her mother. Time she wouldn't trade, but her hours had been made up of worry, endless doctor's appointments and all those arguments and bitter words.

Words she'd have to live with for the rest of her life.

She'd endured them because she knew her mother had no

control over her pain or her disappointment with how her life had turned out, but oh, how many days had they simply lost to anger and sadness?

That had been her real catalyst for getting pregnant. Ciara had seen that bitter emptiness and had vowed not to live life that way.

No regrets.

No living halfway.

"I know you're a professor. I'd like to hear more about that."

Aidan's question pulled her from the dismal thoughts—ones that she simply had to find a way to live with—and focused on his kind efforts to make conversation.

"If we're being specific about it, I'm a marine biologist who also teaches. My first love is the sea, but I found it was a lot easier to tie my research to educational funding."

"Do you like teaching?"

Ciara grinned at his question and figured that same slightly cocky light that had come into Aidan's eyes earlier had likely hit her own. "I might have gotten into it for the research funding, but I quickly found that I'm pretty good at it. Add on that the marine community is a deeply passionate lot, and I found that through teaching I got to share my own knowledge with like-minded individuals."

"Which only amps up the fun factor of it all."

"Yes!" She was surprised to realize how closely he'd hit the mark. "It is fun. And there's so much value in learning about the creatures that share the planet with us. Do you know that the whales have come back to this area, living in pods in the Atlantic waters off the coast of New York and New Jersey?"

"I thought that was a social media hoax. Whales in the Hudson."

She'd seen those images, too, the large whale tail rising

up out of the Hudson River, set against the backdrop of the western side of the Manhattan skyline. That particular photo might have suspicious roots in social media doctoring, but the whales were back. "They spend more of their time physically in the Atlantic Ocean, but yes, it's real. Oh, and speaking of the Hudson, there are the oysters! New beds growing and thriving every day.

"Sorry." Ciara broke off, suddenly self-conscious. "I'm getting carried away."

"Consider me hooked." He wiggled his eyebrows at the dopey pun. Ciara laughed in spite of herself, even as he pressed her on. "But please. Tell me about the oysters."

"Are you sure?"

"Wow me."

She wasn't sure her story had much wow factor to many people besides her, her students and a few of the city's more adventurous chefs, but she pressed on. "New York Harbor used to house over a billion oysters in the beds on the harbor floor."

Aidan looked confused at such a large a number. "When? Like in the '60s and '70s?"

"Sadly, no, they didn't make it nearly that long. Overfishing began in the colonial period and the pollution that followed during the industrial revolution pretty much decimated the oyster population around the city. One of my passion projects is working with a STEM program in the city's high schools that revolves around restoring the oysters."

"That's amazing."

Ciara sighed, realizing she had gone on too long. "I'm sorry. I really do get carried away."

Aidan only smiled back. "What's the saying? Do something you love and you'll never really work?"

"Something like that. Although…" She broke off as memories of how she used to eat oysters during her college years, especially the summer she did work in the Chesapeake Bay, suddenly had her stomach growling.

"Although what?"

"I have to admit I do miss eating them." She rubbed her midsection. "Oh, how I miss oysters."

Aidan's eyebrows narrowed. "You didn't seem particularly pleased with my dinner joke earlier, yet the thought of eating raw oysters makes you sigh with longing?"

Ciara laughed at that, settling her hand lightly against her belly. "I guess the baby wants what it wants."

Aidan shook his head, even as a small smile danced in his eyes. "And what drives his or her interest?"

"You know," Ciara suddenly realized, "I have absolutely no idea."

"Does that mean baby might be up for that pasta primavera I mentioned earlier?"

Ciara nodded, oddly pleased they'd found their way toward more level ground. "I think that works."

As HE STOOD at the counter peeling a garlic clove, Aidan knew they'd turned a corner. A particular surprise, since getting to that outcome had involved his making Ciara sick first, followed by insulting her character.

Yet here they were.

The kitchen had a lot of room for a city safe house, and they both fit comfortably at the counter. It was tight—it was still a New York City apartment, after all—but they were able to keep a respectful distance as they stood side by side preparing dinner. Aidan knew it had taken a lot for her to come around, and he was anxious to keep the peace and ensure she continued talking instead of reverting to the cold-shoulder treatment.

A situation that seemed increasingly unlikely since she'd started in on chopping vegetables while he put the water for pasta on to boil and had started a light béchamel sauce, their conversation flowing easily.

"I know I've been a bit aloof since we came here," Ciara started in as she sliced long, precise straws of zucchini. "But I wonder if you'd be willing to answer a few questions."

Although her admission went a long way toward echoing what he'd already thought, he was oddly touched she'd hit it on the head instead of simply avoiding the reality of her silence up to now.

"You did just lose your husband."

"That's kind of you," she said, eyeing him sideways as she cut and chopped. "But that doesn't change the fact I haven't made the best roommate."

"Water. Bridge. I'm good."

Oddly, Aidan realized as he stirred the béchamel, he spoke the truth. She didn't owe him any explanations, and he really didn't need one. They weren't talking before, now they were.

Time to move forward.

"What's your question?"

"Sean's done a great job of keeping me informed, but why are there so many law enforcement officials taking such an interest in Humphrey's case?"

Aidan hadn't expected the astute question. He was wrong to keep underestimating her. Ciara was bright and sharp, and her lack of conversation up to now hadn't been because she didn't have questions. Rather, she'd simply sought some distance, and that aloofness, as she'd described it, wasn't because she wasn't interested in what was happening around her.

"Initially it was a mix of things, I think. Humphrey's high-profile standing in the city and the fact that he was kidnapped out of a federal courthouse were the primary reasons. I also wouldn't discount his relationship to the Coltons. Sean, Cormac, Liam and Eva have a lot of weight in the NYPD—Sean in particular. He kept attention on the case and doggedly pressed for answers."

"Humphrey always spoke so highly of Sean. Of his siblings, too. Humphrey really watched out for all of them when their father died."

Aidan didn't fully know the details, his relationship with his cousins not close until recently, but he did know Humphrey Kelly had been an outsize influence in their lives.

The man's disappearance—and some of what they'd discovered after he disappeared—had raised questions. There were areas of Humphrey's life that were darker than they'd ever considered. Ciara's late husband had been an important man, but his client list had been more varied and more dangerous than Sean had initially understood.

It left questions.

Including ones directed at the years-younger wife. Sean had ultimately worked past his concerns about Ciara, but it had taken time, even as the gaps in Humphrey's past grew murkier.

It was that murkiness, Aidan knew, that still lingered and kept the law enforcement community's interest high. But how did he say all that to the man's widow? Worse, did he risk ruining whatever image and memories she had left of her husband?

"I want to answer you as best as I can, but I have to admit to a bit of selfishness."

Ciara looked up from one of her zucchini strips, a slight frown edging her lips. "About what?"

"We're having a nice conversation and I don't want to upset that."

"Because you know something about Humphrey?"

"Enough to know that your husband has left suspicion in the wake of his disappearance and his death."

"In what way?"

"How he lived his life. Who his associates were. How he came under Maeve O'Leary's influence. People thought he was above reproach, and it's been jarring to learn otherwise."

Ciara had set down the knife she was using on the zucchini and backed away from the counter. Color rode high on her cheeks, and he could see the telltale throb of her pulse at her throat.

And in the face of that rising anger, he braced himself for an onslaught of emotion.

So the sudden welling of tears was a surprise.

"I'm sorry." She waved a hand as the other reached for a hand towel on the counter. Pressing the towel to her eyes, she let out a harsh breath before heavy sobs filled the kitchen.

It had been instinctive earlier, when she was sick, to pull her into his arms. Did he dare do the same again?

Did he dare leave her alone?

Her anguish was real, palpable. And as he reached for her, pulling her against his chest, Aidan knew he'd made the right decision.

The water bubbled on the stove, ready for the long fettuccini noodles, but Aidan simply reached over and flipped off the gas burner. They could deal with dinner later. For now, Ciara had five months of fear, worry and, with his new knowledge of her pregnancy, a hell of a lot of hormones driving her reaction.

So he'd let her cry it out.

And see her through to the other side.

Chapter Three

Hot, wet tears spilled from her eyes and Ciara fought her weird, immediate reaction to Aidan's description of Humphrey's client base.

Hadn't she worried about that, too?

While she knew her husband and had obviously trusted him with the next several years of her life, that trust had come with an internal willingness to wear blinders, too.

What did that say about her?

Had she been so desperate to get the spoils of her grandmother's will in order to move on with her life that she'd inadvertently tied herself to a man with secrets darker than she'd ever believed possible?

"You doing okay?"

The gentle rumble of Aidan's voice against the side of her head had Ciara swiping at her eyes as she stepped out of his embrace.

"I'm fine. I'll be fine."

"You will be. That doesn't mean you need to beat yourself up because you aren't right now."

It was one of the kindest things anyone had ever said to her, and as she stood there, staring up into his deep brown eyes, Ciara had to admit to herself that whatever she had expected from Aidan Colton, it wasn't this deep well of understanding.

No matter how hard she looked for it, she didn't get any sense of judgment or censure from him at her situation since their initial misunderstanding over her pregnancy.

Instead, he seemed genuinely willing to acknowledge that her circumstances weren't ideal or normal.

Or safe.

"It's just that—" She broke off. She and Aidan had shared a few kind moments, but she didn't know him. Did she dare voice her fears about her husband?

Did it matter any longer?

She'd long ago stopped caring about the court of public opinion. She'd grown up with wealthy grandparents and had seen how the public's attitudes toward her family had shaped her grandmother's behavior. Hadn't that been the root cause behind that stupid clause in Betty Francis's will?

Ciara had never worried overmuch about the family money. If her grandmother had wanted to spend every last dime on herself, it was hers and she'd have been entitled to do it. Instead, in cahoots with her lawyer, Ciara's grandmother had created this elaborate inheritance clause that harkened back to something from the nineteenth century. In order to inherit any of it, Ciara had to marry. Her father had left and eventually died before he could inherit anything, so the family finances had shifted to her. Even her mother's sickness and the endless bills couldn't be accounted for out of the Francis family trust.

"It's just what?" Aidan gently probed.

"It's just that I've known Humphrey for most of my life. He's a good man. I know he is. And it eats me up inside that since this whole Maeve O'Leary thing and his disappearance, I've begun to doubt that."

"He was a powerful man who counseled powerful people. That's bound to generate some secrets."

"Yes, but some of those people were quite shady. I had no idea, and I'm not sure if that makes me naive or stupid."

"I don't think you're either."

"I'm one or the other, and neither scenario makes me feel any better."

"Well, how about if I give you a third, then?"

Aidan moved back to the stove, flipping the water back on to boil. She glanced at him, trying to be unobtrusive but failing miserably as she caught sight of the flexing muscles in his forearms as he began chopping garlic for the pasta.

Were forearms sexy?

Since Aidan Colton's flexing muscles were kindling something dangerous beneath her skin, Ciara had to admit the answer to that question was a resounding yes.

Focus, Ciara, focus.

"A third what?"

"A different scenario you maybe haven't considered yet."

She stilled her knife over the red pepper she'd just begun to slice, shifting to give Aidan her full attention. "What's that?"

"People have different facets of their life. Humphrey was a well-respected psychiatrist, and he built his practice and his reputation in tandem. With that sort of success, you attract the powerful and those who wish to be."

"But why would he take on the sort of people that he did? Your cousin Sean told me in the course of the investigation he learned that Humphrey treated Wall Street sharks and even a few murderers."

"Your husband was a doctor, Ciara. He had to respect patient confidentiality."

"Yes, but—"

"And because of that there were things he couldn't tell you." Aidan seemed to debate something before he continued. "And things he shouldn't tell you. People are entitled to their private matters in the confines of a doctor's office."

It was more than fair and in a small way did make her feel better. She'd been so focused on the things she'd discovered about her husband that she hadn't given much thought to the other side of things. Humphrey's practice wasn't some sort of public town square; those who received his services were entitled to their privacy.

"That's true."

"It doesn't change the fact that it's hard to hear difficult things about people we know and respect and thought of differently."

"You sound like you speak from experience."

She wasn't sure why she asked the question, but it was impossible to miss the way Aidan's dark eyes shuttered and his shoulders stiffened.

"I just recognized a long time ago that everyone keeps pieces of themselves private."

His answer belied nothing—not even that obvious discomfort—but his focus did move determinedly toward getting the pasta into the boiling water.

Ciara left him to it, turning back to finish her pepper, even as his words played over and over in her mind.

Everyone keeps pieces of themselves private.

It was a true statement—and she'd be a hypocrite if she didn't acknowledge she had secrets of her own—but it still couldn't diminish her curiosity.

What secrets did Aidan Colton keep private?

And, maybe more, who'd kept secrets from him that had put such deep-seated knowledge in his dark gaze?

IT WAS RIDICULOUS to stiffen up like a man facing a firing squad, so Aidan worked on relaxing his stance. Worked on getting them back to the easier conversation of a few minutes ago.

Yet even he couldn't deny the strange sensation that Ciara had gotten too close.

Which was especially ridiculous considering that until about an hour ago, the woman hadn't said more than a hundred words to him in the entire twelve days they'd spent together.

Why had he even mentioned people and their secrets?

I just recognized a long time ago that everyone keeps pieces of themselves private.

Or, more to the point, why had he phrased it in just that way? As if he had personal knowledge.

Because you do, his conscience taunted him, reminding him of all the things that had shaped him into the man he was today.

He was proud of that man. More, he was proud of what the child had overcome to become that man.

But he didn't talk about what had shaped him.

Ever.

Yet an hour of actually talking to Ciara and he was opening up and intimating things even his extended family of Colton cousins didn't know.

"You ready to hand over those vegetables? I'll get them in the béchamel."

"Sure." She picked up the cutting board and carried it over to the stovetop, gently dropping all the various vegetables into the sauce.

He caught the light scent of her over the lingering smell of the heating garlic. He'd noted it earlier in the bathroom and again as she'd cried against his chest. A subtle scent that made him think of summer nights at the beach, threaded with a freshness that came into the air after a heavy rainstorm.

It was likely his mind playing tricks on him, a sort of mental blending of knowing what she did for a living along with the late-spring air blowing in through the open windows of the apartment.

Yet it spoke to him.

Tugged at him.

And made it abundantly clear that Ciara Kelly had gotten under his skin.

After dropping the veggies into the sauce, she backed away quickly, seemingly as aware as he of the tension that had filled the kitchen. But it was the shy words that followed that confirmed his suspicions.

"I need to finish up a few things for my summer school class and email them out. I'll be back in a few minutes and I'll set the table."

"No need. I can do that while you're taking care of your work and meet you back at the table when dinner's ready."

"Okay." She smiled softly before ducking her head and heading out of the kitchen.

He watched her go, helpless to turn away. She was small, petite in her frame, with that long hair that he knew spilled down her back in a dark wave twisted up in a thick mass on top of her head. It set off the slim column of her neck to perfection and made him itch to take the pins out of her hair. To tangle his fingers in that mass and see if it was as soft and as tempting as it looked.

There was something enticing about her, a siren calling to him even as he knew he needed to turn away.

Even as he knew she wasn't for him.

Since he'd now considered the scent of the ocean, the waves of her hair and mentally likened her to a siren, Aidan figured he needed to turn his damn brain off.

He hadn't made it up before when she'd asked—he was

working a few cases in addition to the Kelly case—so he'd sink himself into a few emails and try to forget about his ridiculous leanings that had turned fanciful.

Opening the encrypted email files on his phone with his thumbprint, he was surprised to see an email from the informant he'd been chasing for a few weeks now.

And nearly dropped the wooden spoon he'd used to stir the béchamel as he read Guy Sands's latest message. The message was brief and his encrypted program had already confirmed Sands had sent it through a secure connection the marshals had given him. All he needed to do was sign in from any public computer, like at a library, and the encryption would keep him off anyone's radar.

The message was brief and had Aidan cursing as he took in the single line of text.

I can't do it.

"Can't or won't?" Aidan muttered, exiting the program and shoving the phone into his back pocket. "Damn it to hell."

He'd been working with Guy Sands for months. The man was a key witness in one of the US Marshals' biggest cases in the Southern District of New York. Guy was the proverbial scapegoat for an organized crime front, their unwitting and unknowing accountant, managing what he'd believed were legitimate books.

The man was a key witness and a treasure trove of information.

And he'd gone rabbit just when his testimony was needed the most.

Aidan considered their conversations to date. He'd clearly laid out the details for protection in a safe house, how they'd manage the man's security and how they'd ensure he had a life after this was all over. Sands had seen a lot of thrillers and wasn't convinced Aidan and the other professionals in his office could keep him safe, but it wasn't true.

They were good at what they did, and Sands had a leg up, more than most. He was a single guy with minimal attachments. He had no children of his own, and he'd lost both parents in his early twenties. It was a shame, and Aidan didn't want to minimize the man's loss, but that lack of connection also ensured he was a fantastic candidate for witness protection.

They'd get him a new identity and a new life, and the minimal link to an old life meant he could literally start over.

Aidan had presented that all to Sands, convinced he'd gotten the man on his side. So the message wasn't just a surprise, but it felt like a failing, too.

Even if Aidan could still remember that light veil of skepticism in the man's eyes as Aidan had detailed how WIT-SEC worked.

And even if Aidan himself had carried the strange sense of staring into a mirror at he talked to Guy. Though his parents were still alive, they spent as little time with each other as possible. He hadn't even had a real relationship with his sister until the past few weeks, when they'd made some inroads on their sibling bond.

Was he all that different from Guy Sands?

Could he point to that many personal connections in his own life?

On that jarring and surprisingly dismal thought, Aidan reopened the encrypted program and composed a reply. And hoped like hell he could get the man to understand a new life was the only real shot he had at a future.

MAEVE O'LEARY FLIPPED through the lockbox of aliases she maintained and considered each piece of forged identity. Each persona staring back at her from the identification photos had been carefully crafted to present a different style. A different memory to each person she encountered. She never repeated herself, well aware giving anyone a connection between those personas would be the key to her downfall.

It had been an incredible plan, one she'd managed easily due to her bland yet easily transformed looks.

A smart woman knows how to play up her assets, her mother had always said. Maeve had taken that advice to heart.

She'd used the long-haired, dark wig when she'd run cons in Rome, modeling her wardrobe on a blend of Sophia Loren and Anna Magnani. When seeking one of her husbands in Germany, she'd had a blond bob and deeply sculpted eyebrows over liquid blue contacts to transform her eyes into a cool, shuttered temptress. And when she'd worked Amsterdam, she'd transformed yet again, to a long-haired redhead with deep brown eyes who kept up a casual athleticism as she biked all over the city.

That had been fun, she remembered with a wistful fondness. Amsterdam had been early in her career, before she'd fully settled into her calling. Before she'd found the real rhythm of the con.

All she'd intended was to seduce the head of a competing business in order to secure inside information for her own boss. He'd promised her a significant cut of the revenues if she helped him win the contract, and Maeve had embraced the job with gusto.

And had realized she was far better at seducing men by becoming the embodiment of their deepest fantasies than she'd ever be at being a dutiful yet devious secretary.

So she had evolved, like a butterfly coming out of its chrysalis, and had built her life's work.

Men were so easy, after all.

So simple.

It was a matter of tapping in to the urges they didn't even understand they had to drive their behavior.

She'd been successful up to now. Or mostly successful, if she didn't include that damn sap Len Perry. It had been early days, less than a decade after Amsterdam, and she'd learned from the experience. She'd gotten better because of it.

But that time still chafed in her memory.

She'd worked hard to lure her second husband in and set the proper trap, but Len hadn't ever fully given in to her entreaties. She still believed she'd have gotten his full loyalties if he didn't have that brat of a kid, Micah, that he was so damned devoted to.

She'd done her level best to turn father against son, using the boy's surly teenage attitude as her lure, but Len had held on.

Had defended his son.

And in the end, she'd had no choice but to get rid of her "beloved husband" and run. She'd held on until Micah turned eighteen, ensuring the kid lost any rights he'd have had as an orphaned child. And then she'd acted. The untraceable poison had done its work on Len, all while she mapped out the precise moment she'd clear the bank accounts.

And then she'd poofed.

It wasn't hard. After all, Ariel Porter Perry didn't really exist. And with Len dead, she'd simply faded away, enjoying the spoils for a few months as she lay low and considered her next target.

Yes, seducing and entrapping men was her craft, and she was damn good at it.

Yet here she was, once again, churning through the actions of a man who hadn't quite fallen under her spell. With Len she'd known she never fully had him convinced, but Humphrey hadn't been the same way. She'd roped him in by making herself a tempting package who fawned over his power and played up all he'd built for himself. More, she played up all he deserved.

For all he knew about New York City's wealthy and powerful, he deserved more of that for himself, didn't he? She'd all but purred the enticement, pleased when he'd begun to repeat her words.

When he acknowledged that she was right and he did deserve access to the highest echelons of power and privilege in the city.

He could have had it, too. For a time. After she'd taken over his home and the wealth he'd spent a lifetime accumulating. After, of course, she'd gotten rid of his little wife.

Ciara Francis. Now Ciara Francis Kelly. That had been a sticking point. All her work to brainwash Humphrey to her cause had nearly fallen apart when he'd magnanimously stepped in to help his old friend.

Maeve had nearly come apart then—until she'd gotten Humphrey babbling again. Rushing to explain why he'd married the little bitch in the first place.

Ciara needed money.

And as she allowed Humphrey's words to penetrate her own personal fury that he'd married, Maeve had suddenly realized the pot was a hell of a lot bigger when you added the Francis family money to Humphrey's. So she'd waited. Plotted. And decided to use the simpering young wife, so fearful her husband was dead, to her advantage.

It had been the perfect plan.

Lure Humphrey.

Keep him hidden, all while bolstering his ego and using his talents for other cons.

Kill Ciara, ensuring the wife's money rolled up neatly with Humphrey's.

And then marry Humphrey herself.

It was the perfect plan.

Until Humphrey had suddenly come to his senses and taken a bullet meant for Sean Colton.

All Maeve's plans had come crashing down with that lone act of heroism. One she'd never planned on or even considered Humphrey had in him.

Her work. Her plans. Her future.

All of it was gone.

The one truly responsible couldn't pay any longer, but someone could. Someone would.

Maeve had already done the mental exercise of putting a bounty on the little wife's head.

There was no reason to change her plans now.

Chapter Four

Aidan had deliberately avoided checking his messages for a response from Guy Sands all through dinner, but now that he and Ciara had settled in for the evening, their meal long since enjoyed, he was back to checking his email every ten minutes.

Even he was sick of himself.

Which was why it shouldn't have come as a surprise when Ciara glanced over from the other side of the living room. "Watched pots, Aidan."

"Hmm?"

"You keep checking that thing with a level of attention that borders on obsession. Who is she? Are you waiting for her to text you back?"

He was so focused on the response from an informant that it hadn't crossed Aidan's mind his constant phone checking would be seen as something related to dating. "Who is who?"

"The woman who must be on the other side of that text message."

"There's no woman. I'm waiting to hear back from a scared informant."

It struck him as an interesting shift that in the past few hours they'd gone from tense roommates to a couple of people who could easily tease each other.

And if her casual questions about his chasing after another woman also suggested she had no jealousy at the idea?

Well…that was good, right?

Very good, his instincts screamed, especially since this was a job. His job. One he had to do with his full attention, his focus on her safety unwavering.

Even if it felt sort of bad that she didn't seem to mind the idea of his dating someone.

"What are they suddenly scared about? I'd think someone would work through the risks before taking on the job of an informant. Before even exposing themselves to law enforcement as a potential source of help."

He studied her face, the clear lack of concern there. It was funny, he had to admit, but she'd proven herself to be an eminently practical person as they'd worked through a variety of topics.

From her reasons for marrying Humphrey to the whys of taking on her teaching work to her desire to get pregnant. She was a woman who knew her mind and didn't make apologies for it or prevaricate about her motives.

It was oddly refreshing and made him realize just how rare it was to meet a person who simply took responsibility for their choices.

As someone who'd been raised by parents who had given in to an attraction for each other that had not only put his father's high-powered political career at risk but had also destroyed his father's first marriage, personal responsibility wasn't in evidence in his upbringing. For his entire life, Aidan had watched how those decisions—a result of taking exactly what they wanted—had led to any number of demands for their loved ones' tacit approval of their choices.

Aidan had never quite known what to do with that, and he'd checked out of the mess of relationships because of it.

But getting to know Ciara a bit better, he had to admit there was another side. One that gave a lot of credence to making choices and then living with them.

"You're right on the informant front. Whether Guy likes it or not, he's on my radar now. I can't force his help, but I can keep an eye on him."

"Well, what's going on? Can I help at all? Even if it's just to be a sounding board."

"I'm trying to find out more, but he won't respond to my encrypted email."

"Ah." She smiled. "That's the obsessive phone checking. Not a hot date after all."

"I wouldn't do that—" He broke off, not sure why he had the immediate need to defend himself to her on the personal front. Yet even as he questioned it, his mouth kept running. "I'm here to keep you safe, Ciara. I'm not dating or trying to date anyone right now. You're my priority."

"Thank you." She reached for the mug of herbal tea she'd fixed before they'd settled in the living room. "Truly, thank you. For taking my care so seriously, obviously at the expense of your personal life. And especially because I haven't been the easiest person to room with."

"Your life is in upheaval and completely out of your control. I'm here to help you while everyone works to put Maeve O'Leary away."

She stared down into her mug before seeming to come to some conclusion. Squaring her shoulders, she sat up straighter in the overstuffed chair that currently enveloped her. "I do thank you. Which is also why I want to help with this informant of yours. Why don't you walk me through it and I can try to give you a few ideas? I am, after all, currently hiding away from the bad guys, too. Maybe I can help you come up with a few arguments so that he'll participate."

As ideas went, it was a good one. He was so close to this case that it was entirely possible he'd lost a bit of perspective, if not full-out objectivity.

And if it also gave him a chance to talk to her a bit more, well, side benefit.

"His name's Guy Sands. He's the star witness in an upcoming trial, and I'm responsible for escorting him to court each day."

"Because he needs protection?"

"Yes. He's a whistle-blower who discovered extremely corrupt practices in a major construction outfit here in Manhattan. His testimony can swing the balance of about twenty billion dollars in real estate deals."

"Wow." She pursed her lips for a moment, her expressions a pleasant change from the automaton-like responses he'd gotten for the past twelve days. "I stand corrected from before. I get why he's scared and why this would be hard, even if he felt he was doing the right thing with his initial whistle-blowing call."

"I know it's hard," Aidan said. And he did. A case of this magnitude didn't come along every day, and with the consequences tied to such large amounts of business, there were a hell of a lot of interested parties who'd be happy if this case was tossed out altogether.

Aidan did understand the risk to Guy's life. People killed for far less than payouts in the billions, and his testimony would destroy a lot of unsavory practices, along with the unsavory individuals who practiced them.

But the key witness vanishing—the one the prosecution's case hinged on—was a serious problem.

Even as Aidan did recognize Guy's very real concern that he wasn't going to come out the other side alive.

"Where has he been up to now?"

"We've had him in a safe house, but based on my last call, he was getting increasingly nervous staying there. And then with the message I got earlier saying he can't go through with this, I'm concerned he's going to take off."

"Where do you think he'd go?"

"No idea. He lives a fairly solitary life, which has made him a great candidate for our protection. He doesn't need to worry that he's got a family at risk."

"But he's still scared." She traced a fingertip over the cloth of the chair arm. "It goes through your mind, over and over. How you can get your old life back."

As Aidan listened to her, he realized that he had someone sitting right here who understood, in every way, what Guy was going through.

"And?"

"Along with it all is this terrible realization that not only aren't you getting your old life back, but it's so far gone that it doesn't exist any longer. It's a tough road, Aidan." She looked up from that steady tracing. "And it's a hard day when you wake up and admit to yourself that all you knew is gone."

Not only hard, he acknowledged, but an aspect of his career he'd never considered. He'd always remained so focused on the good they were doing—protecting people, ensuring they stayed safe and alive—that he'd given little thought to the fact that part of living a life was having control over it.

Witness protection offered a solution to staying alive, but it didn't do a heck of a lot when it came to the quality of that life. And it certainly couldn't restore what the person had to leave behind.

"I can see how that would be an incredibly difficult thing to accept," Aidan finally offered.

"So if I had to guess, he's going back to the places that are familiar to him, even with the risks involved. At least until he gets to the place where his heart can catch up to the realities his mind already knows."

CIARA HAD TO admit that after spending nearly two weeks of petulant, frustrated time mentally processing the fact that her old life was gone, it felt good to focus on something else.

A new challenge that didn't involve her, yet where she could offer some real, tangible help and perspective.

Talking about this man Aidan was also responsible for protecting—although his situation was quite different from hers—made sense to her in so many ways. She understood what he was going through. The challenges of having your life tossed upside down through no fault of your own.

Even his whistle-blowing call likely felt inevitable, because he was already in a situation that was out of his control.

Hadn't that been her decision to marry Humphrey? She'd be grateful for the rest of her life to her friend for taking on a marriage of convenience to help her get back on her feet, but the problems had started long before that. They began with her mother's cancer diagnosis and the expenses that came with that and her grandmother's staunch and, frankly ridiculous, notions about when and how a woman could inherit money.

Although Humphrey had never said a word about it, Ciara did believe part of why he'd offered to help her was that he understood how misguided and ridiculous her grandmother's notions were.

Notions that, in the end, only added to the overarching problems Ciara faced.

"You look like you've gone to a few of those familiar places."

Aidan's insightful words pulled her from her own memories. "Maybe. I'm not a person used to dwelling on the past, so it's been a bit of a surprise these past few weeks to realize how easy it is to sink down into that place."

"Are you doing okay with things? You did lose your husband after spending four months not knowing what happened to him."

Ciara stared at him across the small expanse that separated her chair from the couch where he sat and, for the first moment in all of this, felt a kernel of understanding from another person.

"Thank you for that."

"For what?"

"For recognizing that even if we didn't have a traditional marriage, Humphrey was my husband. He's a person I loved and cared for very much. And it's been terrible not knowing what happened to him. Wondering why he'd been targeted and where he was."

"I am sorry for what I said earlier. It was unprofessional and out of line."

She considered those moments of misunderstanding, over her pregnancy and the underlying realities of her marriage that both she and Humphrey kept confidential between them.

"It's funny, really. Before entering into my marriage, I'd have likely had the same reaction."

That acknowledgment seemed to catch him off guard, and Ciara continued. "I came from family money, but I've never spent all that much time thinking about it or worrying about it. As far as I was concerned, that money belonged to my grandmother. Someday it would go to my parents. If there ended up being any for me, I'd worry about it then."

"Not everyone can say that. Most people are counting, to the penny, what's supposed to come to them."

"Then I pity them. Our loved ones aren't checkbooks."

Yet even with her convictions, she knew her insouciance

about money was one of the contributing factors to her inability to fall in love and settle down. The men who ran in her rarefied New York society circles weren't interesting to her, and the men who *were* interesting thought she was more debutante than any sort of real woman to consider making a life with.

"Anyway, I was focused on marrying for love. That I'd do the work that makes me happy and somewhere along the way I'd meet the right person."

"But that never happened?" he asked softly.

"No, it didn't." She let out a quiet sigh, no more able to change the past fifteen years than she could her current situation. "And my disregard for money caught up with me when my mother got sick. Cancer is a nasty taskmaster, and she needed a lot of treatments. I never understood why my grandmother, who sat on that pile of money, refused to give it to her daughter-in-law. Refused to use it to help her get well.

"It's why, when Humphrey offered to marry me to get my inheritance, I didn't feel bad. That money should have been for my mother all along, and by marrying Humphrey it went to pay off the debt of her medical bills."

She shrugged. "I don't expect anyone to understand it, but I'm not ashamed of my choices. Of my decision."

It was only when she glanced across that small space between them that Ciara realized how good it felt to see encouragement and understanding in Aidan Colton's eyes.

Because while she didn't regret her choices, she had begun to feel some shame in the presence of the Colton family.

Sean Colton and his siblings had done some amazing police work trying to find Humphrey these past months, but she'd not been able to shake the fact that they'd carried judgment on her life, too.

"You shouldn't be ashamed. In any way. Your life is yours

to live as you choose. You and Humphrey entered into a marriage between two consenting adults that you both obviously wanted to be in. I'm sorry it ended so soon."

"If you look at only the time we were a married couple under the same roof, it was only a few months. It's hard to believe how such a short time could have such a monumental impact on my life."

"You can lay that squarely at the feet of Maeve O'Leary. The woman's diabolical."

"What I can't understand is how she managed to get Humphrey under her spell. He's a smart man, Aidan. Well educated. And he spent his life as a psychiatrist. He knows the mind and he understands, at a foundational level, what it means when a mind is manipulated."

Hadn't that been the most difficult part to understand in all this? Their age difference had always put him more firmly in the seasoned grown-up category, but they'd developed a genuine relationship since she'd been an adult. Monthly dinners to catch each other up on their lives and a real friendship between them. And through it all, he'd always spoken like a highly competent professional who understood human nature and the workings of the mind.

Most people hadn't ever understood it. Her friends teased her about her "sugar daddy," and she knew she and Humphrey got looks whenever they walked into a restaurant. But through it all, he was just her friend.

She *knew* him. And she knew him to be an infallible judge of character.

So how did he ever get wrapped up with Maeve O'Leary?

"She's a powerful con artist. My sister, Deirdre, saw that firsthand last month. She went to Wyoming to try and get a few leads from Maeve's stepson, Micah."

Although Ciara had gotten the broad basics on the events

that had led up to Humphrey's shooting upstate, at Aidan's description she realized she was still woefully ignorant of what had led to that moment.

"Your sister was there when Humphrey was shot?"

"Maeve was aiming for my cousin Sean, but Humphrey dived in front of the bullet. For as brainwashed as he had been, clearly there was a part of his mind Maeve couldn't touch. A place that still knew who he was and who he'd cared about in his life."

A shiver ran down her spine as she imagined Humphrey's last moments. And with it came a deep pride that the man she knew had done what was right in the end. "Is that why Maeve is after me? Because I represent all she can no longer have?"

"It's a working theory, but I wish we knew more. We rounded out much more of our understanding of her after Deirdre went to Wyoming and got to know Micah. But even the profilers are struggling to get a full representation of her. Is all this behavior tied to some sort of internal madness that she keeps in control? Or is it the persona she's adopted to kill with impunity?"

"The black widow killer."

"A fanciful idea, to be sure. And while I'm not suggesting it's the wrong one, there's a lot wrapped up in there."

"Like what?"

"Where does she go in between husbands? There's recent proof she had a husband several decades ago that resulted in a son. And we know about her time with Micah's father about twenty years ago."

Another one of those shivers skittered down her spine at the underlying implication of Maeve's deadly choices. "She's been at this for decades?"

"So it seems."

"Where has she been since Micah's father?"

"We don't know, and we can't account for her time."

Whatever Ciara had imagined about the woman who'd taken her husband's life, nothing came close to this reality. It sounded like something out of a fantastical news story or a crime thriller.

There were actually people in the world who killed so callously? And more, Ciara acknowledged, so *manipulatively.*

Humphrey hadn't just been kidnapped out of the federal courthouse downtown. He had been lured away, brainwashed and kept in a sort of semikidnapped state, stuck in a real-life game of moves on a chess board.

And now not only was she at risk, but her child was, too.

She'd resented being put into this safe house, her life turned upside down and out of her control. Just like Aidan's informant.

Only now?

Now that she better understood what they were up against, Ciara had to admit that she hadn't simply lost her old life, those remembered days vanishing like smoke.

Her new life was in jeopardy, too.

Her child's future was in danger, and the only thing that stood between them and a madwoman was a determined US marshal and Ciara's continued prayers the cops could outrun a killer.

She'd spent the past few weeks struggling with all she'd lost. The unfairness and the nonsensical aspects of it all. Was there really a woman running around New York plotting to kill her?

Since the answer to that question was a resounding yes, Ciara needed to focus on her future, too.

And do everything possible to help outrun a madwoman.

AIDAN SENSED HE and Ciara had turned a very large corner. He'd felt it building ever since he'd walked in with the groceries, and, as each hour passed, they'd grown more and more like partners in this whole situation and less like adversaries.

But now, as he considered all they'd discussed, he realized something else.

There was nothing he wouldn't do to protect this woman and her unborn child.

As always, because it was his job.

But now?

Now, something had changed. And in a short amount of time, she'd come to matter.

She'd excused herself a short while ago to get ready for bed, and he'd used the time alone to catch up on emails as well as update his daily reports. It was quiet, easy work at the end of the day, and he'd always used it to both settle his mind and document details while they were still fresh.

But as he typed out the detail report on Guy, Ciara's comments kept drifting through his mind. Was it possible Guy had rabbited to his home? The small apartment in Morningside Heights wasn't a palace, but Aidan had made a home visit there, and it was clean and full of the personal things the man cared about.

Had he simply disappeared there for a few days to regroup and think?

Or were they at risk of losing him altogether?

He considered the various angles and, after wrapping up his reports, he tried one more encrypted email to Guy. Aidan acknowledged how hard this was and how the US Marshals would protect him. That Guy's decision to come forward mattered and his ultimate testimony was important. And as Aidan closed the email, he reminded the man of why he was doing this in the first place.

As he hit Send, he hoped he'd gotten through.

He'd just closed the lid on his laptop when Ciara padded back into the living room. Her face was scrubbed free of makeup, and her hair was gathered on top of her head.

For the briefest moment, Aidan was speechless.

The intimacy of spending time in a safe house with a witness always had its ups and downs, but he'd never had an issue keeping his emotional distance.

This was a job, nothing more.

But there was something about the woman…

Something that felt a lot like attraction. Even knowing she was nearly five months pregnant hadn't managed to diminish his interest. Not that a child was a problem, but a child that was someone else's was a quick way to cool a man's ardor.

And yet…

This child wasn't another man's in the sense of a relationship.

For reasons he didn't want to examine too closely, Aidan had to admit that reality did make a difference.

Chapter Five

Ciara read through her syllabus with fresh eyes. She had already tweaked a few of the assignments for the midpoint of the class, realizing the students' skills by then would be up to some slightly more challenging tasks. But as she re-reviewed the last two assignments, she also acknowledged those were a perfect fit for the end of the program. They would come far throughout the summer, expanding their skills and preparing themselves for the graduate work that would come in the new school year.

"'The improvement of New York Harbor for the benefit of bivalve populations,'" Aidan read over her shoulder. "That sounds like some serious reading."

Ciara pushed back in her seat, surprised to realize an hour had passed already and she'd barely touched the herbal tea she'd fixed with her toast for breakfast. "It is. And since I bored you yesterday with the majesty that is the mighty oyster, I won't do it again. But I will say they are a significant area of study for my students."

"I enjoyed it."

She picked up her small notebook and swatted him on the shoulder. "Liar."

"I enjoy any topic when the speaker shares it with such passion."

She stilled, the appreciation in his gaze as he stared down at her filling her with something determinedly soft and receptive.

The last things she needed to be.

She was glad she and Aidan had moved past the cold détente they'd lived with from the start of her stay in the safe house, but she didn't need her flights of fancy to get away from her, either.

But goodness, he was an attractive man.

She'd noticed *that* from the first.

Broad shoulders and an incredibly fit frame. He had a job that required a certain physicality, but the hard lines of his body suggested a man who kept up with his strength training beyond a basic ability to do his work. He was attractive in a classically handsome way, and Ciara recognized her immunity to him was waning.

Quickly.

She knew what people thought of her and Humphrey, and she'd never minded it. She understood and accepted the truth of their relationship, and it didn't really matter what others speculated about her marriage. She cared for him and that was all that really mattered.

She'd also made the decision, when she accepted their marriage of convenience, that she wouldn't seek a relationship outside her marriage for its duration. Humphrey was an attractively robust man in his midfifties, and she'd accepted he would likely seek discreet relationships on his own, but she was willing to remain true to her vows.

Only now…

To spend time with a man closer to her own age?

Well, she'd become a bit more aware of those stirrings of attraction and desire.

And she'd become *very* aware of what she'd willingly decided she could give up for the next five years of her life.

None of which was practical at this moment in time.

Aidan Colton had a sworn duty to protect her. In return, she needed to keep her little fantasies to herself and focus on all that lay in front of them: a madwoman with a vendetta who wanted Ciara and her unborn child dead.

His gaze had lingered after the passion comment, and he seemed to catch himself, because he headed into the kitchen and reached for the fridge door. He came back with two waters and took a seat beside where she'd set up her workstation. "I have a potential outing for today. If you're up for it."

"Up for it?" A level of excitement she'd never have expected came spilling out, and she slammed down the lid on her laptop. "Tell me more."

"I've been thinking about what you told me last night. The idea that Guy might have gone to ground back at home. It made me realize that you must miss your home as well. I could take you there if you wanted to get anything or just spend a few hours. Sean also called, and he wants to do a family meeting tonight to provide some updates on the case. We can go there after you get your things."

"I love it. And I'm in."

She was already mentally racing through the list of items she'd pick up, especially since some of the clothes she'd brought with her were already getting a bit too tight with her expanding belly. She'd purchased maternity clothes, most of which were sitting in her closet, and the idea of finally getting to wear them was an exciting thought. Especially since she'd never expected to spend two weeks in the safe house when she was rushed out of her own home.

It was only the other part of Aidan's explanation that stilled her mental packing list. "You want me to come to your family meeting?"

"I do. Humphrey was incredibly close to Sean and his siblings, but he was your husband. You're a part of this, and you deserve to hear how the case is progressing."

"Thank you." She reached out and laid a hand on Aidan's forearm. "Really, thank you. It means a lot that you want to include me. That you trust my involvement in what's going on. Up to now, I didn't get the sense your family felt the same."

Aidan took a moment, obviously weighing his words, before he took a seat that cornered hers at the dining room table.

"Although Sean, Liam, Cormac and Eva have been a bit proprietary about Humphrey, I think they've come around to the idea there's a bigger game afoot. The new focus on Maeve O'Leary and her background as a black widow killer has shifted the entire case."

Ciara couldn't quite stop the twitching of her lips. "'Proprietary' is what we're calling it now?"

"Calling what now?"

"Suspicion and assumption of guilt before innocence?"

It stung—or it had stung at the time—but she had to admit some of that initial pain had faded over the past few months. While she was dealing with all the questions that surrounded her husband's disappearance, Sean and his siblings were handling Humphrey's abrupt vanishing as a criminal matter. They wouldn't have been doing their jobs if they hadn't looked at things through a critical lens. And spouses always got an extra-close look when a person disappeared.

But it had still really bothered her to be the recipient of that watchful and suspicious eye.

"Sean Colton's a good man, and I know he was doing his job." Aidan stilled, clearly choosing his words. "If I'm being honest, I care for my cousins in that broad, semivague *family* sort of way." He put a distinct emphasis on *family*. "But we don't really know each other that well, either."

"Did you know each other growing up?"

"Distantly. A few Colton family gatherings as kids that bonded us in the moment but nothing all that lasting until now."

"Are you sure you want me entering into that? I may not be under suspicion any longer, but I'm not convinced my presence is going to calm anyone's nerves."

"You'll calm my nerves." Aidan smiled, the grin bordering on sheepish. "And I'd love to have someone I know and trust in my corner."

Trust?

They'd come a lot farther since yesterday than she'd realized. Yet as she tried that thought on for comfort, she had to admit that she trusted him, too.

They were allies and partners in whatever was going on, and she couldn't deny she was happy about that fact.

"You're not close with your cousins. What about your sister?"

Whatever she expected, the clear remorse and sadness that carved grooves in Aidan's face wasn't it. "We weren't close growing up. It's taken us a long time, but I think we're finally getting there."

"I'm sorry. I guess I assumed—" She paused, thinking about it from someone else's perspective. "I'm an only child, so I often romanticize the idea of siblings."

"Our parents are more the reason Deirdre and I didn't have a close relationship. We have different mothers, and while my father gave me his name, my mother spent a long time frustrated he didn't give her the same with marriage."

"That must have been hard."

"It was, but it also made me realize I didn't want that in my life."

His conviction was obvious, and there was something

about all of it that made her inexplicably sad. She didn't know him well and she had no business trampling over sensitive emotions, but there was also a big part of her that wanted to argue.

Wanted to tell him that when you found the *right* relationship, it was all worth it.

She'd always believed that. But if she were honest, over the past few years, since her mother got sick and Ciara saw her own hopes for finding a life partner slipping away, she had to wonder.

And acknowledge perhaps she wasn't one to give him advice or question his feelings.

For all her care for Humphrey and their deep friendship, none of it changed the fact she'd accepted a sham marriage as a means to an end. She wasn't exactly the poster child for healthy, long-lasting relationships.

Suddenly sad with the direction of her thoughts, Ciara shifted to focus on Aidan. "Well, I'm glad you and your sister are finding your way to a strong relationship. One the two of you can create and craft all on your own."

"I am, too." Aidan took a sip of his water. "I think for a long time she labored under the impression that my dad favored me in some way. Whether it was because I was a son or because I'd done something noble like going into the law enforcement community. I've always gotten the sense that was one of the things that drove her into the FBI, despite the fact that she's incredibly gifted at the work."

"Do you think she was right? That your father favored you?"

"I think my father has a degree of pride in both of us that is still never quite as bold or as big as his love for himself. So trying to decipher what will or won't make him happy is useless, because neither of his children have that ability."

She'd experienced similar challenges with her mother. While she'd never regret the time they spent together through her mother's cancer battle, she'd hardly call them close.

It was a difficult place to come to as an adult when you made the decision to accept what that person could give and stop taking the rest of it all on you. But she had. And she'd vowed that she'd build a different relationship with her own child.

One based on mutual love and respect and affection and less on unrealistic expectations or a desire to see her child become some image of herself instead of exactly what he or she really would be—wholly themselves.

"I'm glad you're finding a way to have a relationship that's free of that."

Aidan smiled at that. "I think we're finally both starting to understand that as adults. We can thank Humphrey for some of that realization as well."

"Oh?"

"This case has brought Deirdre and me much closer. Sean pulled us both in, her for her FBI work and me with the marshals. Because of it, we've found some way back to a relationship, too. I'm grateful for that."

She'd give anything to have Humphrey back. To have this horrible nightmare over. But in Aidan's words, Ciara also found some measure of hope.

If something good could come out of Humphrey's tragic death—something good and lasting—then there were happy things to be found.

In a situation that had very little positive, that was something to be grateful for.

And as she looked at Aidan Colton, she realized something else.

She was grateful for him. For his protection and his care, yes.

But she was grateful for *him*, too. For the man she was getting to know, day by day.

One more thing to thank Humphrey for?

As Ciara let that idea sink in, she had to admit that it fit. And for the first time since her husband disappeared, she realized that there might be some good to come out of the bad. It was a thought more comforting than she ever could have imagined.

AIDAN KNEW THINGS were changing. He'd felt it since Sean had pulled him into this case, and that feeling had only grown steadily since he'd taken on the duties of watching out for Ciara.

And yet...he couldn't help but feel he was changing, too.

His relationship with his sister was better than it had ever been. Their strained relationship growing up—being raised separately by a different parent—had continued into adulthood, so it had been incredibly rewarding to see them both able to change their perspectives.

Even with that personal growth, there was more to what he was feeling, and he knew himself well enough to acknowledge it.

He was attracted to Ciara. His need to protect was as strong as ever, but now entwined with it was the distinct interest and attraction that came with desire.

They were feelings that had no place in this case, yet he'd only be lying to himself if he denied them.

But what to do?

He could no sooner change how he felt than stop the earth from turning. Besides, she was an amazing woman. Even the conversation about his family had shown how fundamentally kind and caring she was. All while also demonstrating her ability to see beyond a personal slight.

Although Sean and his siblings would never behave in a way that was out-and-out terrible, Aidan also didn't doubt they'd made their suspicions of Ciara very clear. In the early days of Humphrey's disappearance, his young wife had been a suspect, and they would have treated her that way.

Even if everyone had moved on, their focus now rightly on Maeve O'Leary, he knew that would be a harder transition for Ciara.

Yet she was willing to come with him. To take an active part in the case and help them talk through all they knew to understand the bigger picture of what was going on.

And to stop the mad mastermind behind Humphrey's kidnapping and killing.

"I want to thank you for telling me about your sister."

"Oh?" He glanced up at Ciara.

"What you said, about something good coming out of Humphrey's case. That means a lot. I know—" She broke off, and he was surprised to see tears shimmering in those enigmatic green eyes.

"Ciara?"

"I am fine." She waved a hand before offering up a rueful smile as she pointed toward her belly. "The hormones get me now and again. But even without them, it means a lot. That I can point to something good coming out of Humphrey's kidnapping and death."

She could blame hormones all she wanted, but as they'd spoken of their lives over the past twenty-four hours, Aidan had come to accept that Ciara wasn't at all what he'd assumed.

What anyone had assumed.

She had cared for her husband. To assume because their marriage hadn't been a traditional one somehow that meant there wasn't grief at the man's death was a fool's errand.

And simply wrong.

"You don't need to try and take that in all at once, Ciara. A lot has happened. Your life has been upended, and someone you care about was taken from you. Pregnancy hormones or not, you're entitled to your grief, too."

"I know, but it does help to ease some of the shock and the pain of it all. To know about those positive outcomes. He was a good man, and there were a lot of months there where I doubted it. It plays with your mind, forcing you to wonder if you were ever right in the first place."

"I didn't know Humphrey personally, only through the stories Sean, Liam, Cormac and Eva have shared. But he made an impact on people, and he clearly saw himself as having a duty to the generation after his. He did that with his support of you and your life, and he did the same for my cousins after their father died. It takes a good man to do those things. To see where he can provide help and care like that."

Her gaze was still watery, but he saw a smile through the tears. "That's such a testament to him and his life's legacy."

"Then that's what you need to hold on to, Ciara. On the days when it's hard to remember the good times, those memories are what's real. Not these last few months of his life that were the direct outcome of a twisted and devious mind."

She reached out and laid a hand over his. "Thank you."

Without thinking of the implications, Aidan turned his hand over so their palms met, the touch more intimate.

More profound.

Just...*more*.

And recognized that whatever he'd expected this case to be, it had become so much *more*, too.

CIARA'S HAND STILL tingled from where it had lain against Aidan's across the table at the safe house. Hours had passed, ones where she'd showered and finished up her last few details for work and then been driven up to her Upper West Side apartment in a government-issued SUV.

Now here she was, pulling various items from her closet and still experiencing those sense memories of how it felt to touch Aidan.

She had no business feeling this way. It was the steady refrain she kept practicing over and over in her mind, yet she couldn't say the message had sunk in yet.

Of course she'd noticed he was an attractive man, but there were lots of attractive men in New York. It didn't mean she went around touching them or fantasizing about them or feeling anything beyond the basic visceral sense of appreciation for what they looked like.

But with Aidan, she was in real trouble.

Because the attractive package was just the wrapping. What was truly compelling—and entirely too captivating— was the man beneath that wrapper. Tough, strong, caring. Even his reticence over relationships because of his parents' poor model was compelling.

And she needed to get a grip.

A thought punctuated by the maternity clothing she was currently pulling off hangers and folding into a small travel bag.

She was pregnant and recently widowed.

Was she actually allowing herself to have runaway fantasies about a US marshal?

Sure, on some level she got it. Those damned hormones she'd complained about earlier were raging through her system in full force, a frustrating and unsatisfied by-product of this child she wanted so much.

As if to reinforce her ridiculous behavior, the baby kicked in her stomach. The sensation had grown stronger and stronger over the past few weeks, and what had initially felt like flutters was now firmer and more determined, as if to say, "I'm here!"

She laid a hand over the area where she felt movement, the sheer wonder of it all filling her.

This was what she'd wanted. What she'd always wanted. How was it possible she could be this happy and anticipating the future when her present was so upside down?

A knock from the farther direction of her room filtered back to the walk-in closet. "Come in!"

In a matter of moments, Aidan filled the doorway of her closet. "You getting what you need?"

"I am."

"I was thinking about picking up some lunch. Do you have any favorites around here?"

Immediately a sharp longing for the pot stickers at her favorite Chinese restaurant filled her. "Wok Palace is around the corner. Want to walk over there?"

"I was thinking I could go pick something up. This way you can stay safe, here. We've got security downstairs, too, posing as your doorman."

Their trip uptown had gone smoothly, so Ciara couldn't fully reconcile the external danger with the seeming normality of her surroundings.

"Couldn't we walk over? I hardly think anyone's waiting to attack me in the middle of lunch hour."

"I'd like to do a sweep first."

It still struck her as strange that the concept of a "sweep" was even necessary, but she knew it for truth. *And* she recognized the compromise he was offering.

"It's two blocks away. Why don't you go check it out and I'll wrap up what I'm doing in here? I've only been woolgathering anyway, sort of standing here marinating in my surroundings."

His smile was warm. "This is your home, and you've been

away from it for a while. Marinate all you like. I'll do the check and come right back."

"Sounds like a plan."

He stood there for an extra moment, his gaze roaming around the closet before coming to land back on her. "You have a beautiful home."

"It was Humphrey's and I just—" She shook off the words. This was her home. It had been before her husband's death, but it fully was now, as he'd generously left it to her in his will. "Thank you. I do love this place. The vaulted ceilings and vast rooms and being in walking distance of the park."

She did love this apartment. Aside from the fact that Manhattan real estate was an experience all by itself and this was a standout of a home in a well-regarded building, the apartment was more to her.

So much more.

She'd come here for visits since she was young. The apartment had always been a welcoming space, and Humphrey had encouraged her to make it her own once they'd married. She'd made a few light decorating choices but hadn't wanted to change the elegant character she'd always associated with the place until they'd grown a bit more comfortable in their marriage.

What would have been decisions they'd made together had felt crass and grabby to do after he'd gone missing. So other than the decorating she'd done in her bedroom, she hadn't changed much else.

"It was his home far longer than it's been mine. It's hard to think about living here permanently after—" She took a hard breath. "If this is ever all over."

"It will be, Ciara. I can promise you that."

She wanted to believe him. The conviction in his voice alone was something to hold on to. And still…

"I am trying to stay focused on that. On the future that's coming." The baby gave another one of those hard flutters again, one more punctuation of the life she envisioned for them both.

Even as her present had crumbled around everything she thought she knew.

Her husband.

This home.

Even her own sense of personal safety.

All of it had vanished along with Humphrey that January day at the courthouse.

Chapter Six

Aidan did the quick two-block walk to Wok Palace and had to admit Ciara had a point. The crowded Upper West Side streets around her apartment were full of people out and about, rushing to lunch or to various errands.

It was hardly a den of danger, he thought as the bright if somewhat distracted faces passed him by in a rush.

And still, he couldn't shake that need to protect. Nor could he shake the persistent feeling that even if Maeve O'Leary had seemingly gone to ground, it was only to regroup, lick her wounds and plan her next attack.

And that didn't sit well with him at all.

The woman had set her sights on Ciara, and a few days of inactivity didn't mean she'd forgotten her quarry. Or whatever vendetta was brewing in her unstable mind.

Although he wasn't close to his cousins, Aidan had to admit getting together to go over all they knew and all they'd discovered these past months since Humphrey's disappearance would help. He and his sister had been brought in on the case several months in, and while he'd familiarized himself with the files, it would be helpful to get his cousins' perspectives.

What they'd seen and uncovered throughout the investigation. What theories they were investigating. And, maybe most important of all, what Maeve's intentions were.

Sean had been working the O'Leary angle since they'd discovered her involvement and connection in another case, and, based on Aidan's last conversation to set up the family meeting, it sounded like the woman now had Sean's full focus. They'd all been shocked to discover the linkage between Humphrey Kelly's case and Wes Westmore's. The slick hedge fund manager was awaiting trial for the murder of his girlfriend, Lana Brinkley, and the story had gotten prime coverage in the New York news.

Despite the preparation for the trial having gone on for months, a declaration had shown up in the file a few months later...from Humphrey. The esteemed psychiatrist had declared that Wes was incapable of murdering anyone. While not a slam dunk in and of itself, the fact that the cops had struggled to find evidence that unequivocally tied Wes to the murder had made the declaration more powerful than it might have been.

But it had also tied two seemingly unrelated cases quite firmly together. Why would a man—known to have disappeared a few months prior—suddenly have an endorsement in Westmore's files?

Had that been Maeve's sole purpose in kidnapping Humphrey Kelly?

It was a theory that had grown deep roots as the investigation progressed. But it was the review of DNA from Humphrey's kidnapping that had indicated a woman was involved. The connection of that DNA ultimately led Sean and his team to Maeve, which had further uncovered the fact that the black widow was Wes's mother.

Coincidences never sat well with Aidan—in life and especially not in cop work—and the connection had shifted the focus that much more onto Maeve and Wes Westmore.

And his senses were all clamoring that Humphrey's testimony, suddenly showing up in Maeve's son's case file, was a very large flag.

He further used that highly unlikely coincidence as the linchpin in his push to take Ciara into the marshals' custody.

With one last glance up and down the sidewalk in front of Wok Palace, Aidan turned to head back to Ciara's apartment. He'd escort her over here and they'd take a small table in the back of the restaurant. It was a quick in and out, but he could understand her desire for something that felt normal and ordinary in the midst of spending days that were anything but.

The hard tap on his shoulder caught him off guard, and he turned, surprised to find Guy standing beside him.

"Don't look at me, Colton."

"You'd rather it looked like I was talking to myself?" Aidan kept any hint of humor from his voice, but he couldn't deny Guy's introduction, like something out of a bad TV cop drama, was nearly laughable. Add on he'd been so wrapped up in his own thoughts that he'd missed the man's arrival, and it only spiked his irritation.

At Guy.

At the situation.

Most of all, at himself.

Just because Guy Sands had made his professional life an endless frustration didn't mean he could get soft on the job or let his guard down.

"Don't draw attention."

"Then get talking, Sands. You've ignored my emails and my promises of protection." Aidan heard that frustration coming through loud and clear in his own voice, and he opted to use it. He didn't like scaring his witnesses, but Sands needed to understand what he faced. And what real danger he was in. "Now you want me to play cops and robbers on a busy sidewalk?"

"I'm not a bad guy," Guy practically whined. "I'm in over my head."

"Yeah, you are. That's why I'm assigned to help you. To see that you can do the right thing and get out of this alive. So you can move on with your life."

"What life? You think those goons from that construction empire are going to let me walk after testifying? I'll be lucky if I can get out of the courthouse."

Although Aidan didn't want to encourage the man's flights of paranoia, he wasn't entirely wrong. One of the most delicate parts of his job was the transportation of witnesses. But just as the bad guys had advanced their skills, the federal government wasn't too shabby, either. Between disguises, an ability to jam various frequencies and a careful, focused plan to move a witness to safety, they were damned good at their work.

Hadn't he been trying to convince Guy of that from the start?

And hadn't he also been the one walking a busy New York street woolgathering about Ciara?

Aidan shook off the self-recrimination. He was keeping her safe and his mind *was* on the case. Just because it was also focused on her and the time they spent together didn't mean he'd lost his focus.

He'd make sure he didn't.

"We need to discuss the trial and moving you to a new safe house location."

"What's wrong with the one I've been in?"

"The one you walked out of, blithely unaware of who could be watching or who has watched you these past few days?"

Again, Aidan pushed as much harsh truth as he could into his words. "We need to scrap where you were and move you."

"I didn't realize. I didn't know. I—"

Aidan got the distinct sense Guy was going to run, and he clamped a hand on the man's forearm to hold him in place.

"Let me help you. It's my job."

"I don't know. I just don't know. I need to think." He shook Aidan's hold off. "I'll email you back once I've decided."

Before Aidan could try once more to convince the man, Guy slipped away through the crowd. For all of five seconds, Aidan considered going after him before reconsidering.

It's a tough road, Aidan. And it's a hard day when you wake up and admit to yourself that all you knew is gone.

His conversation with Ciara the day before had haunted him ever since.

He'd never intended to treat his charges with a cavalier attitude or lack of understanding about what they were dealing with. But he knew his job. And he knew that part of what was required of him also mandated he keep his distance.

He'd managed it with Guy Sands. If he were honest with himself, he'd done a damn fine job of it with all his charges throughout the past decade of his career.

Until now.

Ciara had made him lose his objectivity.

As he walked into the lobby of her apartment building, his gaze reflexively scanning one end of the space to the other, he acknowledged the truth.

He hadn't just lost his objectivity.

He'd begun to suspect he was in serious danger of losing his heart.

CIARA LEFT A small bag packed near the front door and had busied herself with cleaning out the fridge. She'd intended to get herself a fresh glass of water through the small, filtered tap inside the appliance and had instead caught a whiff of decaying food that would have had her losing the contents of her stomach only a few short weeks ago.

"At least we've got better control over smells," she abstractly remarked to her belly as she dragged a container of takeout off a shelf and dropped it straight into the garbage bag.

It was a pleasant surprise, especially considering her reaction to Aidan's joking dinner suggestion the day before. Deciding not to think about it and just be grateful her stomach remained still and holding, not a whiff of nausea in sight, Ciara continued her ruthless purge of the fridge.

One of her beloved avocados followed the takeout. She then pulled out a half-eaten bag of grapes that looked about to resurrect itself for the zombie apocalypse and ruthlessly tossed it. And as her final act, she pitched a loaf of bread that would likely be vying with the grapes if she dared open its wrapping.

Satisfied she'd removed all offenders, especially since the only things remaining were housed in glass jars, Ciara closed the fridge and fit one of the garbage bag's drawstrings over a kitchen drawer handle. She'd make one final turn around the apartment before she and Aidan left, collecting any last things that needed tossing, satisfied that even if she couldn't live here, she'd left her home in as good a condition as possible until she could come back.

And as that thought hit her, she took a seat at the kitchen table.

What if she never came back here?

She'd worked so hard to remain positive and believe that she'd get her life back, but as item followed item into her garbage bag, she had to admit that the idea of returning to her old life felt like more of a distant possibility by the day.

Maeve O'Leary was still out there. No matter how long she waited to strike, Ciara knew that she would. The woman had proven her determination and focus—and she'd already tried once.

And even if they did catch the woman, it still didn't solve what came next. Ciara's sole focus was her child, but even she wasn't naive enough to think that her future was going to be easy.

Or that she had anything worked out.

Even her home felt foreign to her. Like she was a visitor who'd overstayed her welcome.

The apartment had felt so empty without Humphrey, and after being away for two weeks, it was hard to say she'd missed it. This place where she'd laid her head all those months when he was missing.

All those months struggling to figure out where she belonged.

When she'd believed her husband was coming back, she had been able to convince herself that things would work out. That they'd find their way back to the tentative equilibrium they'd crafted in those first few weeks of their marriage.

But now?

For as hard as those endless months had been, worrying over Humphrey, she was saddened to realize having the answers hadn't made her situation any better.

Yes, she now knew what had happened to her husband.

But the danger to herself and her child was shockingly real as a result of it all.

Was this some sort of punishment? A divine sort of retribution for using the clauses in her grandmother's will to her own benefit instead of as Betty Francis had intended?

She'd made this choice, Ciara admitted to herself. No matter how misguided she'd believed an old woman's intentions, in the end, it had been Ciara's own decision to circumvent her grandmother's will that had gotten her into this situation.

"Ciara?"

She glanced up and felt the hot wash of tears spill down her cheeks as Aidan moved into the kitchen, dropping to a knee in front of her.

"Are you okay?"

"Fine, I'm fine. It's just—"

A hard sob escaped her, the result of all those pent-up feelings that had somehow been let loose by cleaning the fridge.

"It's just what?"

She let out a hard exhale, willing the sobs back. "It's just hard. To know that Humphrey will never come back here. To know I don't really belong in this apartment. And to know that I've created this mess all on my own."

For all Aidan's stoic willingness to do his job, she didn't miss the gentleness that settled in his deep brown eyes or the tender way he pulled her from the chair and led her to the softer, more comfortable furniture of the living room.

"Let me get you some water and you can tell me about this. About how some soulless woman who has set her sights on you is somehow your fault."

Ciara heard the skepticism in his tone at the idea she had any role in what was happening. Moreover, she heard the innate care and concern that threaded right along with his disbelief that she held any fault for her current circumstances.

How could she make him understand?

He pressed a cool glass of water into her hand, and she took a long, fortifying sip. Funny how it was her intention to get some water that had started her whole fridge purge and all these emotions she couldn't seem to keep shoved down.

She'd done fine for so long, so why now?

Why did everything suddenly feel so present?

And so very, very real?

"Are you ready to tell me what's upset you?"

Ciara took another small sip before setting the glass on a nearby end table. As dispassionately as she could, she walked him through the endless impressions that had assaulted her since they'd entered the apartment.

The sense that this was Humphrey's place and she was just living here.

The regret that her choices over her grandmother's will had pushed so much of this into motion.

Even the sense that she'd never get out of this situation came tumbling out in her rush to explain herself.

Aidan nodded, his gaze solemn. "Why don't we take this point by point, then."

"There are no points, Aidan. I did these things. I'm in this." She flung a hand out to encompass the living room, still decorated in the style Humphrey had chosen decades ago when he'd moved in. "I'm living in Humphrey Kelly's home like a freeloader."

"You are Humphrey Kelly's widow. You were his partner in life, a choice he made freely. If you're no longer comfortable here, that's fine, but don't assume that's because of your marriage."

For someone who'd carried a clear judgment about her relationship with her husband when she'd first told him, it was a bit startling to realize what a 180 Aidan had made on the subject.

"You're defending my actions?"

"I'm saying you and Humphrey made a mutual choice. Something you both wanted. What has happened since is deeply unfortunate, but it's not a result of your marriage."

"But none of this would be happening if it weren't for my marriage."

"I'll grant you that Maeve's interest has turned to you as a result of your being Humphrey's wife. But her sights were clearly set on Humphrey already, regardless of the status of his personal life. You were only married a short time when he disappeared. The type of crime she's committed? Kidnapping a grown, free-thinking man? That took some planning."

"But why?"

"I think it all hinges on her trying to protect her son."

Whatever Ciara was expecting, the news that the woman trying to kill her had some sort of maternal streak was a surprise.

"What does Humphrey possibly have to do with it?"

"Maeve's son, Wes Westmore, is awaiting trial right now. I think Maeve set her sights on Humphrey to add weight to some fabricated evidence that Wes wasn't capable of the crime."

"That's what all this is about? My husband was killed over some made-up evidence?"

"That's the working theory. Or at least where this all started. It's what we'll discuss with my cousins later as well, but it is the information Sean's been operating against."

"Sean mentioned Westmore when he spoke to me after Maeve's attempt to run me down. I don't know if I was in shock or just not putting the pieces together, but I had no idea that detail was so significant."

"Not only is it significant, but the entire case Sean is building hinges on that connection. Maeve needed Humphrey's spotless reputation as a psychiatrist to add weight to a fabricated doctor's note that said Wes wasn't a killer."

"And Humphrey did it? He wrote the note?"

Aidan's grave expression told her all she needed to know.

"He did. Humphrey's written endorsement of Wes mysteriously showed up in his case file about six weeks ago."

"What do you mean, mysteriously?"

"My cousin Eva has been working the Westmore case for months. She knew everything in that file, and Humphrey's sworn statement wasn't in there."

"Was it possible she overlooked it?"

"I asked the same, but even I know that's a long shot. My cousin is very detail oriented. She's still a rookie, and she's very determined to prove herself beyond her Colton pedigree. *And* Humphrey was a good family friend. It would have somehow escaped her notice that someone she knows and cares for provided sworn, affidavited testimony?" Aidan shook his head. "No way."

"I see your point."

"Add on, while they don't have the evidence they need, reports are pretty straightforward on Westmore. The guy's bad news."

"Which only adds reinforcement to the theory that Humphrey was kidnapped and brainwashed to provide the sworn testimony?"

"Exactly."

"Layers on top of layers." Ciara tried to process it all, realizing just how tangled the web really was. "How did Humphrey even get on Maeve's radar?"

"He's got a stellar reputation here in New York. Since Maeve's got a suspected pattern of seducing men, she'd likely have believed he was still single when she started planning this whole thing."

"It also adds to the weight that I need to be eliminated because I got in her way."

"Sadly, yes."

Although his agreement shook her, cold fingers weaving

up and down her spine, she also appreciated Aidan's honesty. She couldn't fight a faceless threat if she didn't know what she was up against.

Or why.

But Aidan had shot straight with her from the beginning. He wasn't keeping her in the dark, and she appreciated it. Knowledge was power. And understanding what you were up against went a long way toward preparing yourself for when those threats inevitably became real.

LAY THE TRAP.

Set the trap.

Close the trap.

It was a tried-and-true formula she'd spent her entire adult life using to maximum effect.

So why had everything gone sideways on the Humphrey Kelly job?

Maeve had asked herself that over and over these past few weeks. Things had started off so well, but just as her plans really began falling into place, that trap closing neatly around Humphrey Kelly and all he held dear, the bastard went and ruined it all.

His one last hurrah of good will and a seeming desire to save his soul.

Ever since that last act, when he'd put himself in the direct line of a bullet meant for Sean Colton, Maeve's plans had gone to seed.

Although she was always in the market for her next husband, she'd originally set her sights on Humphrey Kelly as a means to an end. An easy mark who could help her free Wes from prison.

She loved her son, but he'd always been impetuous. One

more check mark in the evidence column that men simply could not keep cool heads.

Especially when they were thinking with parts south.

And this time his impulses had gotten the best of him. Lana Brinkley was one of his endless parade of beauties. Nothing about her had indicated Wes would go so far as to commit a crime of passion, but there were some things a mother and son didn't discuss.

All she did know was her idiot son had killed the woman, leaving dear old Mom to clean up the mess.

And damn it, she'd had it well in hand. Humphrey had come to heel and taken on all her hypnotic suggestions as she'd brainwashed him. It had been close at first—she'd needed to slip him a few drugs to make him more suggestible—but once she'd gotten him under her spell, he'd come along quickly enough.

But then, piece by piece, it all began to unravel.

Humphrey's heroic actions to save Sean.

His brainless young bimbo of a wife who'd scrambled out of the way of Maeve's oncoming SUV at the last minute.

Even Wes's case wasn't progressing quickly enough, the "recommendation" from Humphrey planted in his file not doing nearly enough to set her son free.

It was infuriating.

Those damn, meddling Coltons. She knew of their reputation, of course. A woman didn't spend a lifetime evading law enforcement without knowing whom to diligently avoid.

But this time, simple avoidance hadn't been enough.

She'd cut and run if she could. No, she didn't want to leave Wes behind, but if this were just about him, she'd bail out and leave him to his own defenses. She'd taught him well, and those were *his* damned impulses, after all. A few years in jail wouldn't hurt him.

They might even get him to work on that lack of control.

But it was Humphrey's wife who left the real problem. The young widow was a loose end, and Maeve hated those. She'd spent a lifetime escaping detection and the close eye of the law specifically because she knew how to tie up loose ends.

The one dangling thread she'd left alone—Micah Perry—had sure as hell come back to roost. He was the whole reason she and Humphrey had fled the city, ultimately drawing the cops out to follow them.

Lesson learned.

No matter how urgent the need to flee, snip every single loose thread clean off.

It was the only way to stay ahead of the cops.

To stay ahead of her past.

Which meant, Maeve thought as she pulled up a map on her computer of the Upper West Side of New York and began cross-referencing it with obstetricians in the area, that she'd keep to her original plans.

Even if it meant staying in the city a few extra days.

Because much as she'd love to leave, there was one loose end that needed very careful tying.

Ciara Kelly had to go.

Chapter Seven

Ciara took a bite of her egg roll before setting it down to focus on wrestling open her boxed portion of sweet and sour chicken. The food—which after her crying jag Aidan had suggested they order in instead of going back out into the neighborhood—had arrived quickly, and she'd tried to focus on the delicious smells and forget the lingering idea that a madwoman was plotting her demise.

"I'm not sure that color is actually found in nature." Aidan pointed at the sauce-smothered chicken she was even now pouring over the bed of rice she'd spread onto her plate.

Although she had questioned the color a time or two herself, she wasn't going to think too hard on what could be in one of her favorite treats. "That's the most delicious sweet and sour sauce on the entire island of Manhattan."

"It's a crime against food." Aidan leaned forward, studying the plate closely. "Is that neon pink?"

She laughed in spite of the tense day and handed over her carton, still half-full of the chicken. "Try it, oh doubtful one. One bite and you'll be hooked."

He did as she asked and she didn't miss the quick flutter of his eyes as he got that first real taste. After chewing and swallowing the first piece, he reached for the carton. "Okay, you win. I'm definitely having some of that. You can have my steamed chicken and broccoli."

"Spare me," she said with a smile.

Although she'd worked hard to eat well with her pregnancy—a habit she'd always followed, really—there were a few treats she enjoyed and refused to feel guilty about.

Wok Palace was one of them.

Chocolate sandwich cookies were the other.

"You doing okay?" Aidan's question was casual, but Ciara recognized his interest went far deeper.

"I am. A meal helps, no doubt. I love being pregnant, but I have to be better about my eating schedule and remember that I am eating for two."

"Is it strange?"

"Is what strange? Being pregnant?"

"Yes, but more the idea you're going to be responsible for a human being. For their whole life."

It touched her, Ciara realized, that gentle question.

"I suppose. At times it is a little overwhelming, especially lately as I have *felt* more pregnant. In those early days, when it was just morning sickness, it was hard to imagine the reality of it all." She laid a hand over her stomach. "But now that the baby is growing? He or she feels so much more real to me."

"It's never something I was interested in, personally. Being a father." Aidan appeared to weigh his words, and Ciara found herself, surprisingly, holding her breath at what he might say.

"I didn't have the most orthodox upbringing. And my parents aren't exactly role models for strong, healthy relationships or positive parenting."

"Did they hurt you?"

A hard laugh escaped his lips. "If you mean intentionally, I feel quite confident in saying no. But did they hurt me? Deirdre, too? Yes."

Although her relationship with her mother had always been strange, she had understood from a very early age that it was not her fault. Her father had left the picture when she could barely remember him, abandoning the two of them, and her mother had never really gotten over it. Ciara wasn't sure what it said about her, that she was able to move on far more easily from that abandonment than her mother did, but she had.

From a very young age, she had understood that someone's inability to care for her was on them, not on her.

Perhaps that was why she had been so determined to get pregnant on her own.

She knew she wanted this child, in every way. She knew her own personal commitment to being a parent and how deeply loved her child already was.

"I think that is one of the things we forget. About people."

"What's that?" Aidan asked.

"That some people, for one reason or another, aren't prepared to handle life. Whether because they're too self-involved, or too selfish, or simply unable to face the world around them." She stopped, trying to find the exact right words. "It sounds judgmental, but I mean it far more practically."

She could see her words captured his attention, especially when he pressed her. "You don't sound judgmental. But I am curious what you mean."

"It's like Maeve. And from what you said, maybe her adult son, too. Everyone grows up. They become spouses. Parents. Co-workers. And sometimes they're not very good people."

Ciara considered his earlier question. "You asked me if it's strange being pregnant. Yes, of course it's a little strange, the changes my body's going through and knowing that there's a baby growing inside me. But it's those other things. That's the scary part about becoming a parent. Knowing that you're not just responsible for raising someone, but also hoping you can help them become a good person."

"It's an awesome responsibility."

"It is," she said. "But it's also one I'm ready for."

Whether it was her increasing ability to read him based on the close quarters they'd lived in for the past two weeks or just her growing awareness of him, Ciara wasn't sure. But as they sat there enjoying their lunch, she saw the transformation come over Aidan.

How his thoughtful questions morphed into additional observations. And how those further observations then expanded to their situation.

"Maeve is a mother."

Although *monster* felt like the more appropriate moniker, Ciara nodded. "She is."

"Is it possible every bit of this is about what she's doing to protect her son?"

Ciara weighed that, considering, before coming to her conclusion. "I'm not sure I'm the best one to answer, since she did try to run me over and I've got nothing to do with her son."

"Maybe it's that lack of involvement that makes you exactly the right person."

"Although…" At Aidan's encouraging look, Ciara continued, "Maybe it's a bit of both. She's opportunistic, we know that."

"Right."

"What if this all started as a way to help her son and then became something more?"

"Something more *what*, though? Kidnapping Humphrey and smuggling him out of the courthouse took a lot of planning. But it appears it was designed around the purpose of brainwashing him to get the testimony for Wes."

"Maybe it was only after she had Humphrey that she realized a bigger game. A bigger payoff."

Aidan clearly followed her, his interest sharp as they batted the subject of Maeve back and forth. "Of what?"

"She had the next victim in her black widow trap."

CIARA SHOOK HER head across the table, a slight blush suffusing her cheeks. "You do realize that sounds like something out of a nighttime soap opera."

"It doesn't mean it's wrong."

"I know, but really? Are we truly talking about a woman who has made her life out of seducing wealthy husbands and killing them?" A small sigh whispered from her lips. "I know we are, but there are moments when it's just too unbelievable to wrap my mind around."

Although he agreed, he had to admit that there was a surprising thread of truth here. His sister, Deirdre, had experienced it firsthand when she went to find Micah at his ranch.

"Deirdre had similar questions when she went to Wyoming to interview Micah Perry. His hale and hearty father died mysteriously as soon as Micah turned eighteen. And the man's wife was Maeve, under an assumed name."

Ciara laid down her fork and held up a hand. "Hear me out for a minute."

"Okay."

"I realize I don't do this for a living, so my theories may be off, but here's what I don't get."

When he laid down his own fork, his attention fully on her, she continued. "Maeve makes her life seducing wealthy men and then killing them. In a world where technology wasn't so prevalent, I get it. When she started this all, maybe. When her son was young and perhaps she was just trying to find a way to survive. But now? How would a person actually do that?"

"There are people who find a way."

"Yes, but if you want to land a wealthy husband, you need to be in a large city or a well-established place. No offense to the boondocks, but it's pretty hard to create a wealthy, high-powered life without any modern trappings around."

He had to admit, her point made a ton of sense. How would someone actually stay off the grid? Really and truly off, especially if they were engaged in a life that required being in places with street cameras and cell phones and the general sort of surveillance that made up modern life.

When Maeve seduced a man nearly two decades ago, it might have made sense.

But now?

"She did have to jump through an awful lot of technological hoops to smuggle Humphrey out of the courthouse," Aidan acknowledged.

"Exactly. And we also know she's in New York because she tried to hurt me just a few weeks ago. If she's here because she's helping her son, she's not going to leave until she gets what she wants."

"What are you suggesting?"

"You have the same tools she does. Better ones, really. Why don't we use that in reverse?"

We?

A subtle tension tightened his shoulders at Ciara's words.

When had this become a *we* sort of situation? She was under the care and protection of the US Marshals and, by extension, the city of New York. There was no *we* here.

No contribution that she needed to make other than to sit tight and let the cops work the unfolding case.

"Sean's team is scouring the city's cameras and whatever information they have on her. They haven't been sitting on their hands on this."

"I know my early experiences with Sean weren't ideal, but I don't doubt he's an excellent cop. What I mean is, why not lure Maeve into her own game? Move things along, as it were."

The law enforcement professional in him loved where she was going. Her ideas were thoughtful. Precise. Determined.

They were traits he prized and ones he knew as absolutely necessary for success in law enforcement.

But the alarm bells that had begun ringing at her use of *we* now went nuclear at the clear excitement building in her gaze.

"What are you proposing, Ciara?"

"If she's so determined to come after me, let's use that. Let's lure her out."

"No way." Aidan shot out of his seat, nearly toppling the chair as he pushed back. "Are you hearing yourself? You're five months pregnant and you want to act as bait for a madwoman?"

It shocked him, really, as he stepped away from the table, how much the mere idea of it all upset him.

And how it had his heart racing at the clear risks she casually proposed over her neon-pink lunch.

"I'm highly protected bait that is under the watchful eye of the US Marshals."

How could she sit there and remain so calm about this? So casual, really?

It only notched his ire higher.

"It's ridiculous and rash. And much too risky."

"It's the only way."

"Hell no, it isn't." Aidan strode back to the table, coming around to her side. Planting a hand on the back of her chair and the other on the table, he leaned down, their gazes clashing as his face came within inches of hers. "Hear me well, Ciara. Not only is it a piss-poor idea, it's a bad one in the extreme. This woman has snuck out of range of law enforcement for decades. She's smart and crafty and has a hell of a lot riding on being successful at this game. She's also proven herself damn near soulless in the process."

He took a harsh breath, willing her to understand.

"Do you actually think she'd blink or have a moment of hesitation at hurting you? At hurting the baby?"

His words hung there, and Aidan was startled to realize how hard his pulse was racing. How the thought of Maeve hurting Ciara and the baby had him upset.

Nearly out of his mind, really, at the idea they could be in danger.

But it was the gentle hand she laid against his cheek that was nearly his undoing. "I'm not talking about taking risks, Aidan. I'm talking about a very specific, focused op where I'm under full protection. All eyes and backup and attention on me so that she can be captured."

He still didn't like it—didn't even like her thinking about such an approach—but he did have to admit she was thinking less rashly than he was at the moment.

Aidan raised his hand and laid it over hers where it still rested against his cheek. "I still don't like it."

"Then I'll keep working on you." A small smile hovered over her lips. "I'm nothing if not persistent."

Since that's what he was afraid of, Aidan was about to offer additional admonishments as to why this was a bad idea when she shifted gears straight into another one.

And lifted her lips to his.

CIARA KNEW THE phrase *pressing her luck*. She'd done it throughout her life, pushing to get into a highly competitive marine biology program in college. Pushing to get the best care for her mother, despite the odds of survival. And pushing forward with her personal plans for a baby.

She'd never been particularly good at taking no for an answer, and, when faced with an obstacle, her natural inclination was to simply press through.

But kissing Aidan Colton?

Well, that was something entirely different.

Gloriously, life-affirmingly different.

He resisted the kiss for the briefest of moments before leaning in from his standing position, taking full advantage of their meeting of mouths. His tongue swept past her lips, and she opened for him, glorying in that carnal meeting. His kiss was all she expected and yet so much more. The banked heat she always sensed in him suddenly spilled forth in a glorious rush.

Had she ever been kissed like this?

A sort of gentle ruthlessness that was thorough and yet promised so much more.

It was that promise that ultimately had her pulling back.

Yes, she'd initiated this, but in the whip-quick sparks of attraction flaring between them she recognized she played a far more dangerous game than she ever could have imagined.

What had felt like basic attraction—something to flirt with and possibly give her fantasies free rein—was so much more.

And she risked so much if she allowed this to continue.

She was a pregnant widow under the intense focus of a killer. There was no time to lose her own focus or allow dreamy fantasies to cloud her thinking.

That reality was what had her pulling back, dropping her hand from where it rested against his cheek. "I'm sorry. That was forward of me."

He stood to his full height, those dark eyes shuttering all emotion. "I'm the one who should apologize. You're under my protection, and you didn't deserve that sort of behavior from me."

"Aidan—" She broke off at the steady peal of his phone, a sharp interruption in the ocean of quiet that had suddenly descended between them.

And she knew there was nothing more to say when his gaze turned dark as he read the number. Answering, he snapped out, "Colton."

Although she wasn't able to get a clear sense of the situation on the other side, Aidan's references to "Guy," "Yes, I understand" and "Stay right there," gave her a pretty sizable clue.

"I need to go," Aidan said as he disconnected the call.

"Guy Sands called?"

"Yes. He's in the park, and he's been rethinking his behavior and his choices."

"Then I'll come with you."

"You need to stay here."

"I'd rather be with you. And we can come back here after and get my things before we go see your cousins."

He looked about to argue, so she pressed whatever slight advantage she might still have over his lingering guilt for the kiss.

Push forward, Ciara Francis Kelly, she admonished herself. *Press that luck like you always do.*

"You said yourself I have an understanding of what he's going through. I can help you and maybe give him a bit of comfort in the process." When Aidan looked about to acquiesce, she added, "He's scared, Aidan. Give him that much credit—that he's frightened and he's still trying to do the right thing."

As she pressed her point, Ciara recognized the truth of her own life.

She was scared, too. Yet she kept pushing forward. Kept trying to keep her head above water and her emotions in check so that she could get her life back. So that she could see that a woman who'd terrorized so many in addition to Ciara herself was put away forever.

That mattered.

It had to.

Otherwise, what was any of this for? What good was it to try to live a life and work toward your own dreams and your own happiness if you let the chance at it go without a fight?

RIVERSIDE PARK WAS a long, rambling strip of public space that ran along the west side of Manhattan. Living at the southern tip of the island, Aidan hadn't spent much time there, but he was able to get his bearings quickly. Ciara had spent time in that park since she was young, and she was able to quickly navigate them to where Guy said he was waiting, near an entrance not far from Columbia University.

They'd driven up from Ciara's apartment, and he'd been lucky to find a spot not far from a street entrance near Grant's Tomb.

"I love this monument," Ciara said as she got out of the car, waiting as he'd asked until Aidan had come around to open the door for her.

"I don't know I've ever been up here," he said, looking toward the stately monument that commanded real presence at the edge of the park, buildings and traffic zooming by on its eastern flank.

"The Upper West Side is pretty vast and it makes for a great focal point when taking a weekend walk. I did this jaunt up here one Saturday after I moved in with Humphrey, before I got pregnant. Before—" She broke off, the word hanging there. "Just before everything changed."

He reached for her hand, helping her cross from the street toward the entrance into the park. But he held on, even as he felt her fingers slacken in his, as they began down a small sloping walkway.

He wanted to keep her safe, yes. And he wanted to give comfort. But neither of those reasons, if he were being honest with himself, was why he held on. Their kiss might not have been the best idea, but as the taste of her had lingered on his lips ever since, he couldn't quite argue with its power.

Or his conflicted desire to kiss her again.

Even if his hasty apology afterward likely put another kiss out of the question anyway.

"It's just down here." Ciara pointed toward a walking path that cut through the center of the park, and, in the distance, Aidan saw Guy standing along a jutted-out overlook near the Hudson River.

Aidan was still cursing himself for giving in and allowing her to come, but he also couldn't deny that he felt better having her in his sights. That strange push-pull he couldn't quite manage, of keeping her safe and keeping her with him. The two should be interchangeable, but as he looked at the vast park that spread out around him, Aidan began to wonder.

And then he reminded himself that they were in broad daylight, there were people everywhere and the odds that Maeve O'Leary would be expecting Ciara to show up in Riverside Park on a random afternoon were fairly slim.

And still, he kept her hand tightly wrapped in his.

Because the park was a long, narrow strip running along the Hudson River, it didn't take them long to cross to where Guy stood, his gaze on the water.

Aidan approached, positioning himself so that Ciara was flush along the wall overlooking the river and his body was between her and anyone potentially in the park. He didn't miss her slightly askance eye roll, but she remained quietly at his side.

"Who's this?"

Guy's tough attitude would have gone over a lot better if there wasn't a quaver beneath his words, but Aidan ignored it. Before he could answer, Ciara had a hand out, extended to the other man. "I'm Ciara Kelly. I'm under Aidan's protection."

"So he brought you out here in the open?"

Her smile remained bright, but her voice was pure steel. "You mean he's keeping me close to him even though we're in a public place with people all over? Yes, that's right."

Her correction knocked a bit of wind out of Guy's sails, and his puffed-up chest noticeably deflated. "I guess I get it."

Ciara glanced down to where their hands were linked. "I really can't see any reason not to give you two a chance to talk."

"Ciara—"

She shook her head, cutting him off as she pointed to the park around them. "Really, Aidan, what's going to happen? It's a quiet afternoon, and I'll keep my guard up. I promise."

He recognized her point. And while her protection was his responsibility, just like Guy, she wasn't his prisoner. She had the right to some space and to come and go as she pleased.

And whether he liked it or not, he had a job to do. One that involved another witness who hadn't been nearly as co-operative.

"You promise not to go far?"

"Take the time you need. I'll just be enjoying the pretty day."

The blue sky overhead and the vivid sunlight glinting off the Hudson seemed to punctuate her point, and Aidan finally nodded. "Okay."

He watched Ciara wander a bit, her steps careful as she

navigated the mix of paved pathway and grassy areas running alongside.

"You've got it bad, dude."

Aidan glanced back sharply at Guy. "What do you want, Sands? An hour ago you wanted nothing to do with me."

"Yeah, well, I've been thinking about what you said. That it's your job to help me."

"That's what I've been trying to tell you from the first."

"And I do want to do the right thing." The man scrubbed a hand through his hair, his initial jitters morphing into a sort of resigned weariness.

Oddly, it made him think of Ciara's discussion about luring out Maeve. And that underlying sense he'd taken away that she wanted to move things along as quickly as possible to just get past it all.

To get back to normal, whatever that was.

He tended to look at a case through the lens of law enforcement. To find clues and work cases and ultimately wrap them up and move on to the next. Wasn't that what he'd always done?

Moved on.

He'd done it both because the case was over and because it was his job to face the next problem. To tackle the next challenge.

But for the individuals involved, was there ever a chance to truly move on? That idea Ciara had spoken of—that your old life didn't exist any longer—continued to haunt him.

But it had also given him an idea.

"Look, Guy. I can't promise this will be easy. But we're committed to your protection. And more than that, we're committed to helping you set up your new life after the trial is all over."

"You keep saying that, and I know you mean it."

"Then let's get your new location set up and you can start getting prepped for the trial."

"And then you go right there." Guy let out a hard sigh. "It's not that easy, man. I need to know I'm not gonna end up dead the moment I set foot in the courthouse."

"It's my job to make sure you get to that courthouse to testify and then get out. I take that job very seriously."

"It's not like weird crap doesn't go down in that place. That guy. The famous shrink guy. He went in and no one knew how he got out for months." Guy's eyes widened as a slew of pieces obviously slid into place for him. "Her. Ciara. She's that dude's wife."

"She's under my care."

"Because her husband was kidnapped and then killed. Jeez, if you're focused on her, how much are you going to be worried about me?"

"Haven't I been doing my job?" Aidan glanced toward the sky, willing some sort of answer into his mind that might make Guy understand.

It was only as his glance descended back to earth that he realized he no longer had Ciara in his sights.

With a raw panic settling deep into his gut, he turned away from Guy, his sole focus on the area surrounding them. Scanning the area in quadrants, he looked for Ciara left, center, then right, keeping the broad expanse of the Hudson at his back.

Where was she?

And what the hell had happened?

On a hard scream of her name, he took off at a run.

Chapter Eight

Ciara laughed at the sight before her, delighted by the small herd of goats as they worked their way up a high-sloped stretch of ground.

She'd read about the Riverside Park goats for a few years now but had never seen them in action. And quite beyond herself, she was charmed by the handlers who'd introduced her and the rest of the small crowd that had assembled to watch the voracious eaters as they worked their way through their lunch.

Although she was aware the city was full of far more wildlife than a person would expect in such a densely populated environment—both onshore and off—it was still something else to see the farm animals. They'd been brought to the park to do the important work of clearing out the weedy plants that took stubborn root in places difficult for humans to reach, especially on the steeply sloping land that made up this edge of the island.

There was a young mother beside her crouched down with her little girl, who was pointing and screaming with happiness each time one of the goats lifted its head, those pointy ears twitching in the light breeze.

It made Ciara think of her own child and how much she looked forward to having those same moments. To see the sheer delight in her own child's face as they learned about the world around them.

With that image warming her, she suddenly realized that she'd wandered a bit farther away from Aidan than she'd intended. With one last look at the small herd, she turned back, only to come face-to-face with a hard-breathing Aidan.

"Ciara!" He pulled her close, his grip firm as he shielded her with his body. "Are you okay?"

"Aidan, I'm fine. I'm—"

"Didn't you hear me? I've been calling for you."

She realized the people nearby had begun to stare, and she kept her smile broad, even as her grip tightened on one of his forearms. "I'm fine, Aidan. Can we please quiet down?"

He looked about to argue when she lowered her voice on a soft hiss. "You're making a scene when these people are just trying to enjoy the park."

That seemed to do the trick, and he quieted, his grip loosening as he carefully helped her over the slightly uneven ground. It was only when they were out of earshot of the crowd, back on the well-worn footpath in the center of the park, that she turned on him. "What is wrong with you?"

"Me? I've been calling your name for five minutes. What happened to 'I'll stay close'?"

"I was a hundred yards away from you. If you hadn't panicked, you'd likely have realized that, instead of tearing off like a wild boar through the park."

"I didn't tear off."

"Yes, you did. And while I appreciate the concern, I did exactly as I promised. I remained close. You're the one who panicked."

She wanted to be angry about it all, but the sheer, stark terror she'd witnessed on Aidan's face had gone a long way toward assuaging her feelings. On some level, she was even touched by his concern.

But it didn't mean she'd sit back and allow him to put her in her place.

It was only when she saw that same look flash over his features a second time that Ciara realized something else had happened. "What is it?"

Aidan didn't immediately respond as his gaze roamed over the park. It was only when he turned back to her that she saw his remorse. "Guy. He's in the wind. Again." He shook his head, his words bitter. "Damn it, I was close. I could feel it."

"Aidan, I'm sorry." She reached forward to lay a hand on his forearm, but he pulled it back, turning to scan the area around them once again.

She deserved that. She knew she did.

But as she watched the protector turn into the cop, she also recognized that she needed to back down.

And accept that no matter how intense the moments they'd shared up to now had been, his time with her was about one thing and one thing only.

Doing his job.

AIDAN HAD SENSED a change in Ciara and knew he was responsible for it, but he wasn't sure how to address it. He stood by his actions. It was his job to protect her, and he wasn't going to back down on that or second-guess himself. But she'd also been okay. *He* was the one who'd panicked.

So here they were.

He'd asked her a few times if she was okay, and while he'd been a grown man long enough to know a woman using the word *fine* wasn't necessarily a sign she actually was, he'd also been unable to detect any real upset in her.

In fact, he'd sensed the opposite on some level. She was

serene as they'd walked back to the car and then drove to her apartment. She'd quickly finished pulling together her small overnight bag of things while he'd taken what was left of their lunch out to the common area trash collection. And she'd even suggested he take the time to try to reach Guy once more before they headed over to see his Colton cousins.

From all angles, she really did seem fine.

So why did he sense that they'd returned to those distant days where they'd started, albeit with a bit more direct conversation between them?

"I'll bring the car around to the front of the building and you can come down once I call you."

"We've been through this, Aidan. I'll sit here in the apartment with the door locked until I get your call. As soon as you do, I'll lock up, take the elevator down and walk out the front of the building."

"Why does it feel like you're humoring me?"

"Maybe because I am. And because I know how to follow directions."

"I never said—"

Her green gaze glittered, whatever she'd banked since their drive back to her apartment suddenly sparking to life. "I hear you. I'm listening to you. And I'm trading off any sense of independence because you're convinced danger is lurking around every corner. Okay?"

He nodded, recognizing yet again that she was putting up with far more than any human should.

And, to be fair, he had gotten a bit heavy-handed with his instructions.

To her credit, she hadn't wandered that far in the park; he'd simply been convinced she had been kidnapped instead of calmly seeking her in the crowd. A tactical error he wouldn't make again.

Especially since he'd not only tested her patience and possibly hurt her feelings in the process, but he'd also lost whatever tentative bridge he'd built with Guy.

Shaking it off, Aidan focused on the rest of the day. He'd already called ahead, and Sean had said that Carmine DiRico, Eva's fiancé and a well-respected NYPD detective in his own right, would be waiting in the lobby of Sean's apartment building to escort Ciara up while Aidan parked the car. All the details were in place.

So why couldn't he shake the notion that Maeve was lurking, just waiting to strike?

And why did that very fear seem to have gone nuclear since Ciara mentioned acting as a lure to draw the woman out?

Was that the real problem?

He was so convinced she'd push forward with her ridiculous plan that he wasn't willing to trust the evidence in front of him. Because despite suggesting such an outrageous approach, Ciara had done nothing to put herself in danger. Even the visit with the goats had been in the midst of a group of people—Aidan had even seen a few NYPD officers at the far edges of the crowd keeping watch.

She'd never been in danger.

He did recognize the risks of swinging too far in the opposite direction. It was his job to keep her safe, and if that carried a solid layer of paranoia and suspicion about the world around them, then so be it. But he also couldn't alienate her or cry wolf so many times she let her guard down.

"I'll get the car and come around." He picked up the bag she'd left near the front door, turning to face her. "I just want to keep you safe, Ciara."

"I know." That glittering fire receded, banked once more behind a serene visage. "When I get over my snappish frustration, I do understand that. It's just a lot. Can you appreciate that?"

Once again, that thought flitted through his mind that she wasn't a prisoner. Far from it. Yet the more time he spent with her, the more precious she became.

He couldn't risk anything happening to her.

Yet that was the very reason he couldn't alienate her and upset her to the point that she did something rash in frustration or anger.

"I can, Ciara. I can appreciate it a whole damn lot."

"Okay." She gestured toward the door. "Go get the car, and I'll be waiting right here until you call."

Their plan went as intended, and in under ten minutes, he'd retrieved the car, pulled around to the front of Ciara's building and jumped out to escort her into the passenger seat once he saw her waiting in the lobby through the front door.

"Then we're off." Ciara pulled her seat belt around her, and Aidan didn't miss the baby bump that was visible as she fitted the lap portion of the belt low under her stomach.

It was moments like that—when he could visualize the child inside her—that nearly stopped his heart. Because it made this whole job so much *more*.

He took every person under his care seriously, but something had been building in him as he and Ciara had grown closer. It had happened so fast, and as such a natural outgrowth of their finally breaking the ice between them.

But it was his feelings about the child she carried that had truly surprised him.

He recognized attraction, and, on some level, he'd felt it for his pretty charge from the very first. Appropriate or not, he was able to admit his attraction to himself, if for no other reason so he could keep it under proper control.

It was his continued thoughts for the unborn baby she

carried that had struck him with a depth of feelings he was wholly unprepared for.

"Aidan, are you okay?"

Her question pulled him from his suddenly heavy thoughts, and Aidan busied himself with his own seat belt. "Good. You ready to go? I already spoke with Carmine, and he's waiting to greet us in front of Sean's building."

"Let's go, then."

They'd come to a sort of emotional truce there in her foyer, but he hadn't quite shaken the feeling he needed to make an apology for the park.

"Those were cute goats. Before."

"I've read about them and seen a few news stories, but I hadn't actually seen them in person."

"You looked like you were enjoying yourself until I showed up. I'm sorry for that."

Ciara did sigh this time, but it was tempered with the gentle hand she reached out and settled on his shoulder. "I'm sorry for my outburst before. I know you're doing your job. Really, I do. And I'm grateful for it."

"While I appreciate it, this is completely on me."

"We can argue about that later. I was actually thinking about something while waiting for you."

Effortlessly, she shifted the conversation, and whatever reticence he'd heard earlier had vanished. It was odd, Aidan realized, to feel the tension in his shoulders ease at the idea they might be moving back to common ground.

"What was that?"

"So I realize I didn't put much stock in the idea Maeve would magically know I'm in the park at precisely that moment, but how is she getting around? Minus a scrying mirror and flying minions?"

Although they ran the risk of letting their guards down if

they thought of Maeve O'Leary in such charactered ways, Ciara's description was still funny. "Does she have a pointy hat, too?"

"Hmm, let me consult my mental image." She hesitated for effect before adding, "Yep."

"Why are you worried about how she's getting around?"

"Because I'm curious. And I keep going over and over that part in my mind, trying to figure out the *how*. How she's moving from place to place. Does she have an apartment? A hidey-hole? A place outside the city where she plots and plans? And what about other people? Are there others in her life? And her son. He's in prison, but she must be contacting him some way."

"Are we back to the idea of putting you out as bait?"

"Not exactly."

He'd just slowed for a stoplight, so the pause gave Aidan a chance to face Ciara. "Not exactly or not at all?"

"A hard no, then. But I am struggling to figure out the woman's methods. She had to plot her kidnapping of Humphrey. And while he certainly wasn't free to roam around out of her clutches, the coroner's review of his body didn't indicate he'd been deprived over the months leading up to his death, either. He might have been a prisoner, but Maeve cared for him in some way."

It was an interesting line to tug, and, once again, Aidan was impressed with her logical assessment of the situation. It wasn't something he'd considered up to now, but perhaps they'd underestimated the value of Humphrey's widow to the investigation. Her genuine care and affection for Humphrey gave her the desire to help solve things, but the fact the couple hadn't been in love also gave her a bit of space to look at it all objectively.

It felt callous on some level, Aidan recognized, yet her

ability to focus on the situation *was* different. It gave her the capacity to ask all those astute questions, yet also indicated a perspective that rose above the exhausting, all-consuming upset that grief asked of a person.

She was a real asset to this investigation.

"As we discussed before, Sean and his team at the NYPD are scouring street cameras and any public cameras they can use to get a handle on where she might be. Facial recognition technology keeps improving every year, and the NYPD's got some pretty great resources."

"And it's still not working out all that well. What information have they gotten since Humphrey's death?"

He wanted to argue, but it was difficult to dispute the truth. "I can't speak for his team, but since he hasn't flagged anything, you may be right."

"So what if she is in the city but moving around another way? The investigation said she somehow manipulated Humphrey into a disguise to get him out of the courthouse. A good one, since it took so long to understand what happened."

He did smile at that. "I'm not sure I'd put it that way to Sean."

"Put it what way?"

Genuine surprise filled her gaze before Aidan looked away to drive through the intersection.

"That he and his team were stumped for quite a while on how Humphrey vanished from the courthouse. It's the same sort of slight that says all their fancy technology can't find one lone woman on the loose around the city."

Ciara let out a hard laugh at his assessment. "I'm not subtle on the best of days. I'll work on holding some of that back tonight."

"You don't have to hold back anything. But I do see it

from the other side. It's hard being a protector and admitting when you're wrong."

"That would be difficult. Deeply disappointing, too."

He felt her gaze on him and once again was struck by her ability to quickly pivot from one idea to the next. Eve more, that she wasn't so set in her ways she couldn't accept an alternative opinion, either.

It was a special skill. And it was one more aspect of Ciara Francis Kelly that was unique.

And very, very special.

"The stakes are high when you have a career in law enforcement. Minimizing failure is essential."

MINIMIZING FAILURE.

The words tumbled around in her mind, over and over, and Ciara had to admit it gave her a perspective she hadn't had up to now.

Sean Colton had initially been heavy-handed with her when Humphrey first disappeared. He'd softened over the months, increasingly proving to her that he was her champion. She'd done her best to give him the benefit of the doubt, based on both his own love for Humphrey and the weight of his job, even if she hadn't appreciated that early tension.

But Aidan's earnest efforts to do his job—in his words *and* in his actions—gave her a new understanding of Sean's behavior as the case evolved.

It was enough that she vowed she'd find a way to say something to Sean privately tonight.

And it was also enough to have her revisiting her and Aidan's earlier visit to the park.

"I have to admit, I keep forgetting that aspect."

Aidan didn't say anything as he navigated them past a taxi waiting for a fare to pay out, but she pressed on.

"I keep seeing this through my own well-being, but in the process I keep shortchanging you and everyone else working the case." She took a deep breath. "And each time I think that you don't understand or you're being overbearing, I'm forgetting the great toll this is taking on you, too."

"You don't owe me an apology, Ciara."

"No, I think I do. You're in this, just like me. The stakes might be different, but that doesn't mean they don't exist for you. The same is true for your sister and your cousins."

"Thank you."

He navigated the last few blocks to Sean's apartment building and, just as promised, there was a man waiting out front whom Aidan pointed to as they pulled to a stop. "That's Detective Carmine DiRico. He's going to take you up to Sean's apartment while I park."

Ciara's gaze found the attractive detective. His smile was broad and, she quickly recognized, his eyes had a devilish twinkle that was incredibly compelling.

"I'm sure I'll be in good hands."

"He and my cousin Eva were the ones to crack open the connection between Maeve and Wes Westmore. He's an excellent cop."

Ciara heard something beneath the words. "He works with your cousin?"

"Even better, the grizzled detective and my rookie cousin are a good match. Both on and off their NYPD schedules."

"They're together?"

"A happy outcome of the case."

Once more, it was a reminder that another good thing had come out of all this sadness surrounding Humphrey's kidnapping and death, and Ciara couldn't help but take heart from that.

Carmine opened her door, extending his hand to help her out. "Hi, Ciara."

"Carmine."

Although that twinkle remained, there was no mistaking the laser focus of a cop beneath the easygoing demeanor. He had her protected with his body and through the front door of Sean's apartment building with minimal fuss…or exposure.

"That was impressive."

He kept an arm around her, managing to be protective yet not at all proprietary as they crossed to the elevator bank. "What can I say? This is a full-service family meeting."

She laughed at that and allowed him to help her into the elevator before moving to the back of the space. He followed her in, his large frame still blocking the entrance until the doors closed fully.

"Are we the first ones here?"

"You're actually almost the last ones to arrive, but you're not late. Sean mentioned setting up here at his place earlier, and we've trickled over all afternoon. Cormac and Emily got here about an hour ago and Eva and I came over as soon as our shifts ended. Liam and Ellie had a commitment so will try to stop by later."

The elevator doors opened, and Carmine swept through, his attention on the hallway before he nodded, gesturing her to exit.

It was only as he turned back and caught sight of her that a soft, compassionate smile creased his very attractive face once more. "It's a lot, I know."

"That's one way to put it."

"Let me give you another, then." That gentle protectiveness was in evidence once more as he escorted her down the short hallway. "We're one hundred percent committed to your safety and to putting an end to this nightmare. I say that as a sworn officer of the NYPD as well as an honorary Colton."

She could only nod around the heavy tightening in her throat.

"We're going to catch her, Ciara." He pulled a key from his pocket and quickly unlocked the door to Sean's apartment.

"I know you believe that."

Carmine closed the door behind them, dropping the dead bolt before turning to face her. "It's a promise. And DiRicos are very big on promises. So's the rest of the force, as a matter of fact."

Ciara heard the heavy din of voices but gave herself the extra minute to stand there with Carmine. "You're new to this crew. Will you be honest with me?"

"They'll be honest, too, but ask away."

"I know the Coltons have questioned my loyalty. My marriage and my involvement in Humphrey's life. Even my personal secrets throughout this." She laid a protective hand over her stomach, and it was enough to have Carmine's deep brown eyes going wide, recognition dawning instantly at the secret she'd been hiding. "But know I can make promises, too. I will help all of you in any way I can. I want this monster stopped.

"I want the woman who killed my husband to pay for it with the rest of her life in a cage."

Chapter Nine

True to his word, Sean Colton seemingly had moved past his earlier suspicions of her. It was all Ciara could think as he routinely addressed her throughout the family gathering and discussion of the ongoing case, not just with respect, but with a genuineness that was at the core of all the reasons Humphrey had always spoken so well of the man.

Sean Colton is a damn fine cop, but he's also a damn fine man.

Humphrey's words rolled over and over in her mind, her late husband's love for Kieran Colton's children something he carried plainly on his heart.

It was one of Humphrey's finest points and something she'd felt, too, in his care and protection for her. Her late husband had never wanted to be a father himself, but he took his role as elder statesman to the young people in his life seriously.

One more thing that made it so hard to believe he was gone.

"Hey there." Eva Colton took a seat beside Ciara on the couch after stepping away from the huddle of people all theorizing and shouting around a police case board that had been set up in the center of the living room.

"Hi." Ciara made room for the pretty redhead, even as Eva

waved her to stay still. "You're keeping up quite well with them for a rookie. If this is how good you are in your first year, the city of New York had better look out as you continue solving cases."

A light blush suffused Eva's cheeks, but her green eyes glittered with triumph. "I take that as the highest compliment."

The younger woman glanced around the room, her three brothers in heated discussion with Aidan and Carmine as they pointed and tapped on the board or at various files clasped in gesturing hands. Although Ciara didn't miss Eva's eager attention to the work, the tension of having Maeve go so long without capture was clearly taking its toll.

"The longer this goes on, the harder it gets. We'd expected an open and shut case, and this has been anything but."

"From all Aidan's told me, as well as my own experiences with her, Maeve is a formidable opponent. One who's been getting away with her crimes for a long time."

"I keep telling myself that, but it doesn't make it any easier. She's also vulnerable, in a place where she's licking her wounds. It makes her extra dangerous—but desperate, too, and it frustrates the hell out of me that we haven't been able to capitalize on that."

Ciara understood the frustration—wasn't she living it?—but she also knew a fresh set of eyes could help shift things. "Aidan mentioned earlier you and Carmine helped figure out she was involved at all."

"We went undercover. Played a couple having issues so that we could get close with two marriage counselors."

"The Westmores?"

"Yep." Eva pointed toward the open file on the coffee table in front of them, Wes Westmore's photo on top. "Wes's father and Orrin Westmore were brothers. Orrin and his wife,

Kitty, always believed his brother was murdered but never could prove it."

Ciara considered that. The four months she'd gone not knowing where Humphrey was or what had happened to him had been some of the worst of her life. How much worse would it be to live with a certainty you could never actually get real evidence or closure for your family?

"That must be an awful burden to carry. Never knowing what happened to someone you love."

At the word *love*, Eva's gaze drifted to Carmine. Even in the midst of his active discussion with the other Coltons assembled around the case board, his eyes locked with hers, heat arcing so quickly across the room Ciara was surprised she didn't have singe marks on her own clothes.

What must that be like?

It was a wholly misplaced thought, her current situation not exactly the right time to be thinking about steamy attraction and falling in love. So it was interesting and more than a little frustrating to realize how often her thoughts had drifted in that direction over the past few weeks.

She'd believed herself happy. She was living a life that fit her, with a job she loved and a settled personal life that would give her the child she wanted so desperately. And yet…

Sitting here, in the presence of real, genuine connection, Ciara couldn't help but feel she'd sold herself short.

That somewhere in all those plans and the determined march forward toward the life she wanted, she'd willingly put romance on the back burner.

Not like there'd been a long line of men she'd somehow brushed aside, a small voice whispered. Sure, she'd dated before her mother got sick and she'd shifted into caregiver mode, but there'd been no one who'd looked at her the way Carmine looked at Eva.

No one who looked at her like Aidan did, a small voice whispered from somewhere in the vicinity of her heart.

And wasn't that the real rub?

She'd finally gotten her life to the place she'd planned and worked for, and now, Ciara realized, other than the baby, she no longer wanted any of it.

AIDAN GLANCED AROUND the crowded table at the assembled crew of Coltons and their significant others and had to admit he was far more comfortable than he'd expected to be. He hadn't misled Ciara earlier—he was quickly warming to his family but prior to the Kelly case he'd had a distant-at-best relationship with them.

So it had been startling to realize that the evening had felt far more like a real family than he could ever remember before.

Most of his cousins were at Sean's, all focused on solving the various twists and turns of the case. His sister had returned to Wyoming and she continued to support the investigation from a distance, but it was time for her and Micah and his little boy, Derek, to settle into their new life. Aidan even looked forward to visiting them once he wrapped up everything here in New York.

At the anticipated visit out West, an image popped into his mind, unbidden, of taking Ciara with him.

What?

The thought was so clear—from getting on a plane together in New York to stepping off in Wyoming, the wide-open West welcoming them—that Aidan nearly bobbled the glass in his hand.

Setting it down and trying to keep his movements as natural as possible, he reached for one of the serving plates Orla, Sean's fiancée, had set out on the table earlier. It was only when Ciara tapped him on the arm, her voice low, that he realized what he'd done.

"You must really like mac and cheese."

He glanced down to see a surprisingly large heap of cheesy noodles on his plate and quickly put the platter back to the center of the table.

Conversation continued to fly back and forth across the table, and while he figured others had noticed—a table full of cops missed little—it was Ciara who continued to speak in low tones.

"Thank you for bringing me. I can see how hard everyone's working, and I'd like to help."

"I think your questions about how Maeve is getting around are good ones and worth bringing up for this crew to think over."

"You don't think I'll insult anyone?"

"Not in the least. If you add on how many dead ends we're all facing right now, even after two hours with that case board, I think everyone will relish trying out a few new theories."

He reached for her hand, giving it a soft squeeze. "No one's going to be upset."

"Okay, then."

"I sense some deep thinking down there." Sean's voice was hearty as it boomed out over the table, reminding Aidan of the few times he'd been with his Uncle Kieran. It was fascinating to see how smoothly Sean had shifted into the role of patriarch. Even more interesting to see it was a transition that sat well on the man's shoulders.

Aidan glanced at her, offering a small nod of encouragement before turning back to Sean. "Ciara's had some really good insights as we've been discussing the case."

"Please, let's hear them."

Aidan had kept close watch over Ciara since they'd arrived, conscious that while his family wouldn't intentionally be unkind, their brusque determination to solve the case might still leave her feeling vulnerable.

It had been a pleasant realization to find the exact opposite. Most especially when it came to Sean.

Whatever tension might have existed between his cousin and Ciara over the past few months had fully vanished. The man had been welcoming to her from the very first moment she entered his home, and he'd continued to create a warm atmosphere and sense of camaraderie throughout dinner.

It was also the obvious encouragement Ciara needed to speak her mind.

"I just wonder how she's getting around. She had to plot and plan Humphrey's kidnapping and then all the time after when she was holding him as her prisoner. That whole time, they were in New York."

Aidan saw the head nods around the table and the sharp expressions that had settled on each face.

"Go on, Ciara," Cormac encouraged.

"So she was here in the city, but we all know she's been working on so much more. Whatever's happening with her son. The attempt on me. The situation that led to Humphrey's death." Her voice hitched slightly at that last example, but Ciara pressed on. "You're using some of the best facial recognition technology available anywhere, but it's like the woman's a ghost. She's evaded it all."

Sean had nodded throughout Ciara's comments, but it was Carmine who spoke first.

"When Eva and I were undercover looking into the Westmores, we discussed her past quite a bit. When we finally broke through and got them to talk to us, they were afraid of her and what she was capable of."

"Genuinely afraid." Eva nodded. "Which adds even more weight to your points, Ciara. Maeve has a lot of tools in her bag of tricks, and she's been using them for a very long time."

"She's gotten away with a hell of a lot, too," Cormac piped up. As a private investigator who was on near-constant speed dial with the NYPD, he'd spent a lot of time looking into the woman's background. "But where she seems to excel is in disguises. We've been digging into that angle, but maybe we have to dig harder. Costume and professional makeup stores, for example." Cormac pulled out his phone and tapped a few notes. "I'll start pulling together a list tonight."

"That's good work, Ciara," Sean said before adding, "I'm grateful for your help."

"As someone who has made my career studying marine life, I'm not much of a detective, but I want to find this woman. She's a menace in every way."

"Our very own version of a shark," Aidan murmured.

"More like a tuna." Ciara made the joke before something changed, a new idea transforming her face with excitement.

"She's a big fish," Carmine joked, but Aidan could already see the wheels turning in Ciara's mind.

"A tuna. That's it. Or it might be it." Ciara shook her head. "Or it *is* it."

Aidan laid a hand over hers. "Tell us what you're thinking."

"Tuna actually move through the waters fairly safely. Their silver skin gives them an edge and makes it harder for predators to detect them. But they don't change what they are. They just blend in. What if—"

She broke off, but it was Orla who quickly swooped in to finish the thought. "What if she's just blending in? Between her clothes and makeup and some subtle tweaks to her chin and nose, she could go undetected for quite a while. Especially if she added a hat and large sunglasses. Even changing up earrings and jewelry might be enough to keep the recognition programs guessing."

"The facial recognition software is a bit more sophisticated than that," Sean argued.

But Eva was already pushing forward, waving at her brother. "Yes, but we're talking just enough to trip it up. If she kept making subtle tweaks and changes to that look so that there wasn't a continuous pattern detected."

Sean looked intrigued with the idea, but his forehead remained creased in confusion. "But we're tracking people around the courthouse as well as throughout the city's network of cameras. She can't change that fast."

"Don't think she doesn't know that," Carmine added. "She damn well knows it and could make those changes easily. The earrings, sunglasses and hats would be easy enough to change out so that she's not captured and recaptured looking the same in any given outing."

"And her reputation with disguises would make it easy enough to tweak facial features and wigs," Eva finished off before turning to give Carmine a big, smacking kiss on the lips. "We've got something new to dig into."

"Look for big bags," Cormac added. "She's got to carry it all with her if she's going to make these switches."

Aidan watched the ideas bat back and forth across the table, the genuine excitement between everyone palpable.

"This is good, Ciara. Really good."

She beamed beside him, her smile wide. "It's good to feel useful."

He leaned toward her and pressed a quick kiss to her forehead. Even as the impulse was unexpected, Aidan acted before he could check himself.

Nor did he really want to, he realized, as their gazes locked.

"It's even better to be right."

"THAT WAS GOOD work earlier."

Ciara turned from where she stood at the kitchen counter to find Sean standing in the doorway. She'd busied herself with helping Orla clear plates while the team moved back into the living room to add theories and ideas to the case board and was nearly done placing the last few forks in the dishwasher.

"Nor do you have to do this. I can handle it later."

"I'm here and I can easily help." She shrugged. "It's a few plates."

For all her talk earlier of wanting to build a bridge with Sean Colton, now that she had the chance, Ciara had to admit she felt strangely shy. It was still a bit unnerving to think that he'd seen her as a suspect in Humphrey's disappearance, even if those doubts were short-lived.

"I also owe you an apology. For all that's come before. For not respecting your privacy." He glanced down to her stomach. "My sister would swat me if she were standing right here, but how far along are you?"

She smiled at Sean's reticence to deliberately ask about her pregnancy, but also knew she no longer had anything to hide from the Colton family. "Five months."

"That was your big secret?"

"Yeah, it was."

"It's happy news. But—" He broke off, realization dawning. "It's dangerous news, too. Especially with Maeve on the loose."

"Even more if you consider the reasons for my marriage. If she set her sights on Humphrey's money, my involvement and a child she'd assume is Humphrey's would only complicate things."

"What do you mean, assume?"

"We don't know what Humphrey told her while under her

influence. He could have made her think the child was his or he could have told her about our arrangement and the fact that the baby was conceived through a sperm bank. There's no way of knowing."

"He wouldn't have done it willingly."

"No, but he may not have had a choice."

"He wanted the best for the next generation," Sean said. "He wanted to see all of us not just succeed, but thrive."

"I know. Which is why I also know he'd never willingly have told her unless he wasn't being brainwashed."

And it was with that knowledge that Ciara felt the full weight of grief wash over her. The tears burst forth in a rush—goodness, were the waterworks her only emotion anymore?—and it was Sean who pulled her close to his chest, allowing her to get it out.

The stress.

The tension.

The heartbreak.

"It's okay, Ciara. We're all here, and we will take care of you. We're in this to the very end, and we're all bearing the same weight of grief."

"He cared for you and your siblings so much."

"Just as he cared for you." Sean reached out and snagged a napkin off the counter, handing it to her so she could dry her eyes. "That care and affection he had for you was real. Even at my worst moments, trying to work the various angles of his disappearance, I knew that."

His focus was intense as he stared down at her. "I hope you can at least take a bit of comfort from that."

"You wanted to do right by him with your investigation." She wiped away tears with the napkin. "Take heart that you did that, Sean, every step of the way."

"No," he said, his gaze going hazy. "It was Humphrey

who did right by me. Even at his lowest, when that woman had him brainwashed and acting against his own thoughts, he still protected me. Still jumped in front of that bullet meant for me."

Ciara saw the light sheen in Sean's eyes and fully accepted that she wasn't the only one grieving here. Humphrey had given up his life for Sean's safety and, while it was a gift beyond measure, it was a weight the man would carry for the rest of his life.

One more facet of how special Humphrey was. One more reminder that even though he'd been a difficult man to know fully, since he kept his thoughts so close to the vest, he was also a man of deep care and affection.

That last hard wave of grief receded as Sean spoke, his voice steady. "Liam and I were talking about something the other day. He and Humphrey had the most strained relationship, but they found their way forward over the last few years. And he was the one who suggested we hold a memorial service for him. Just us, as a private celebration of his life and what he meant to us all."

"I like that." She nodded, the idea taking root quickly. "And I think it's fitting. He was a deeply private man, and I don't think he'd want a big show. But to know how much we all cared for him? I think that would be something he'd have loved."

"It's decided, then. That's what we'll do." He hesitated before seeming to come to some decision. "So what's going on with you and my cousin?"

"Nothing. I mean, I... Nothing."

"You sure about that?"

"He's keeping me safe, Sean. It's a job, and he's focused on my well-being and keeping me out of Maeve's clutches."

"If you say so."

"I know so." The baby moved, and she laid a hand against her stomach. It was the perfect reminder that she needed to keep her head firmly in the here and now.

And her heart even more firmly locked down.

AIDAN HAD WATCHED Sean quietly slip out of the living room and head into the kitchen, where Ciara was helping out with the after-dinner cleanup. He'd briefly considered following but knew that whatever had gone down between Ciara and Sean in the past required them to have a conversation in order to move forward.

Sean had made great progress in his attitude toward Ciara, but it couldn't change all that had happened in the course of this investigation. And Aidan had noticed a distinct change in his cousin since Humphrey had taken Maeve's bullet.

That shot had been meant for Sean, and no matter how much support and care and love he received from those around him, that act would take time to process. Aidan was glad his cousin had found Orla in all the mess of the case and was sure the bodyguard would use her own personal strength and no-nonsense attitude to keep them on solid ground, but that didn't mean it would be easy.

So maybe it was for the best that Sean and Ciara worked through all that had come before.

Knowing *why* Sean had been suspicious of her motives didn't change Ciara's rightful upset that he'd eyed her in the first place.

The two of them walked back in from the kitchen, and Ciara crossed toward him while Sean sought out Orla. He and his fiancée spoke in low tones, their connection unmistakable. It was a bond Sean needed. A match he likely hadn't even realized he'd been looking for, yet now that Orla was in his life, it was obvious how much they needed one another.

Maybe not a lone wolf after all, a small voice tickled in the back of his mind. *Just like you?*

"Thank you for inviting me here tonight. It's good to be here, and it's even better to know how hard everyone is working to find justice for Humphrey."

Ciara laid a hand against his arm as they stood there, a part of what was going on, yet somehow separate, too. His role in the marshals ensured that he was part of the case, yet he had no formal jurisdiction over the work.

His focus and his job were Ciara.

But as the evidence piled up and their time stretched out, day after day, Aidan recognized, she'd become so much more.

If he wasn't careful, she might become everything.

Chapter Ten

The drive back to the safe house was quiet, and Ciara let the vivid street life wash over her as she stared out the window. People gathered in groups on corners and spilled out of various bars, enjoying the summer sidewalk seating. Pretty women in sky-high heels tottered in groups over the concrete while handsome young men on the prowl looked to gain their affections.

Had she ever been that young?

Empirically, she knew she had, but looking back, it was getting harder and harder to conjure up how it had all *felt*.

Had she simply been going through the motions? Or was it all a prelude to what she was really searching for?

Her life to begin.

"Do you remember those days?" Ciara asked the question, half musing to herself even as she was genuinely curious to Aidan's answer. "Or maybe you still have those days."

Aidan carefully navigated through an intersection, several of those tottering women ignoring the Don't Walk sign. "The going-out days? I still go out from time to time, but that's never really been my scene. I've been somewhat grateful to grow out of it, if I'm honest. You?"

She felt his gaze on her, and she shook her head. "I enjoyed going out for a few drinks with colleagues after work or meeting up with friends on occasion, but the whole get-dressed-up-and-go-to-the-bar, week in and week out, was never really what I enjoyed socially, either.

"No disrespect to those who did," she added, well aware there was nothing wrong with the rite of passage. "It just never felt as fun as I wanted it to be, you know?"

"That's a great description, actually. It was never as much fun as I expected. My mother always called me an old soul." His hard bark of laughter belied something far deeper. "I know she never meant it as a compliment."

Once more, that sense of his strained and difficult childhood came through, and Ciara was reminded that not all hurts were physical.

"She enjoyed the nightclub experience?"

"I expect so, since it landed her straight into my father's orbit."

She'd pieced a lot of Aidan's background together but recognized the darkened car and his need to focus on driving might give the additional emotional security he needed to share.

"Which is a polite way of saying she and my father had an affair and I was the result. I refer to Deirdre as my sister and I think of her that way, but she's actually my half sister. We both have the same father."

"I see."

"It's a strange way to grow up. As the dirty secret."

"Aidan, I'm sure you're not—"

"No, Ciara. *I'm* sure. My father accepted me and gave me his name, but my mother and I were baggage, plain and simple. Public baggage, since he's in politics. Illegitimate children, with a famous last name or not, are always dirty in politics."

Although her own childhood was hardly free of land

mines, especially with her father's disappearing act, she'd never been made to feel like she was an embarrassment. Aidan's clear feeling that he was one notched a hole in her heart. One that drew her to him, even closer than she already was.

She willed back her emotions, because she wanted to remain a safe space for him to talk about his situation. Adding in her own confusing feelings wasn't the best way to do that.

"Do they still speak? Your parents?"

"They go through cycles." He made the one-way turn that would lead to the apartment building with their safe house. "There's an odd drama to their relationship that keeps them coming back for more. But if you mean do they have an active romantic relationship, then no."

He pulled into the parking garage at the end of the block, and she sensed his internal battle with getting her back to the safe house. "I'm going to leave the car here and walk you to the apartment, if that's okay?"

"It's fine, Aidan. We've been okay today, and it's only half a block. I promise to stay close."

It was late, and there'd been no sign of Maeve for days. Add on that she was exhausted from the very full day of activities and all Ciara wanted was to get inside and get ready for bed.

Aidan took the ticket from the valet and requested she stay in her seat until he had her bag out of the trunk and could come around to get her. Although there were still aspects of the safety routine that chafed, the cop talk all evening had gone a long way toward putting her antennae back up. Maeve was a threat, and just because she'd been quiet didn't mean she'd forgotten them or whatever she'd been planning before Humphrey's death.

If the vast amounts of detail filling the case board in Sean's living room was any indication, Maeve had quite a few tricks still up her sleeve.

So she'd wait, Ciara thought. And she'd allow Aidan to take care of her however he needed to in order to feel that he was doing his job.

The June day had gotten hot, showing summer's promise, but the evening had cooled things off, nature's reminder that it was still, for a few more days, at least, spring. As she and Aidan walked toward the safe house apartment building, the cool night air surrounded them. He'd positioned her on the inside of the sidewalk, his body and the additional layer of her bag on his shoulder a measure of protection from the street.

And still, she felt the energy emanating off him in sharp waves.

"Half a block to go," she reassured him as she kept up a steady pace beside him. She'd begun to feel her pregnancy, but the additional weight was still manageable and the physicality of her work ensured she was in pretty good shape overall.

She used that now, moving at a swift clip beside him.

Which made the sudden screech of tires and change in the air that much more ominous.

They were prepared.

They were walking in a way that should have protected them.

But clearly Maeve had planned this go-round a bit better.

Aidan shouted, his arms wrapping around her as he half dragged, half carried her toward the safe house.

But it was the distinct ring of gunshots that had him suddenly taking her down to the ground.

AIDAN FELT THE solid form beneath his body, and since she was still moving, he took that as the best sign she was untouched by bullets.

"Aidan. Aidan! Are you all right?"

"I'm fine."

"Let me up."

"Stay low."

The squeal of tires shortly after the shots had gone off left him fairly confident that Maeve had taken off, but he wasn't going to leave them there on the sidewalk like sitting ducks in the event the woman decided to take her shot at round two.

People were already coming out onto the street, and he shouted to the doorman in the building next to theirs to call 9-1-1.

But it was Ciara who held his focus.

"We need to get inside."

"Is she still out there?" Ciara's eyes were wide but her voice was steady.

"Not that I can tell, but we can't sit here to wait and find out."

Using his body as a shield, he wrapped himself around her as they shuffled sideways toward the front of the building. He got her inside the lobby and took his first easy breath, but Aidan knew there was so much more to be done.

They'd been compromised.

Safe house details were a closely guarded secret, not even widely available across the marshals. There was too much risk to a successful protection detail if all employees of the organization had access.

Besides, easy access made for easy marks. Even the most well-intentioned individuals could fall on hard times and take a payoff for passing a small bit of information.

Which made this breach even more concerning.

The elevator doors swished open, and Aidan gestured Ciara in before following her, immediately turning to scan the lobby before the doors closed once more.

"How did she find us?"

"You can bet I'm going to find out."

"Someone told her."

"Or she hacked into our systems. Neither is an answer we want."

The doors swooshed back open on their floor, and Aidan did a full sweep before gesturing her out. He moved them down the hallway at a steady clip before quickly unlocking the door.

"I'm going to call for backup. Please pack whatever you need, because we're getting out of here."

Her eyes were wide, her dark pupils blown in those green depths, the trauma of the past few minutes finally sinking in. "Who are you going to call?"

"A colleague. We need to get you moved out of here."

"You can't call anyone. What if it's someone in your organization who gave away the safe house? What if that's why this happened? You can't call. Then they'll find us somewhere else."

She'd already lain a protective hand over her stomach as she paced back and forth in front of the table.

Had they sat there only that morning?

"Ciara, it's fine. I just need to—" He broke off as she snatched his phone clean out of his hands.

"Listen to me. Someone in your organization let her know. Or she's hacked into your organization and can find out whatever she wants. I'm not going anywhere with you until you give me your word that you're not telling anyone."

"Ciara, come on. These are my colleagues. I trust them."

"I don't. And I'm not risking my child's life on someone you can't be completely sure of."

"But we need to get you moved."

"Oh, I'm moving, all right. But I'll move on my own if

I have to. I'm not your prisoner, and you're not calling the shots when it comes to the life of my child."

For all the fire in her response, there was a layer of calm there, too.

One that increasingly sank in as he stared at her.

"You don't want the marshals' help?"

"I want your help. That's all."

He considered her edict and realized there wasn't going to be any reasoning with her.

Even as he recognized the truth of her worry. If someone specific was involved, she wasn't safe. If it was a technology breach, she wasn't safe.

Until they knew what they were dealing with and how Maeve got her information, they did need to steer clear of help from his colleagues.

"Get your stuff. We'll go to my place."

AN HOUR LATER Aidan opened the door to his FiDi apartment and flipped the switch in the long foyer entrance. True to his word, he'd not contacted anyone at the US Marshals, but he did text Sean on the way over to update the man on what had happened, with the promise to call once they were settled at Aidan's place.

He'd avoided going back for his vehicle, calling a local car service instead. They'd managed to arrive at his place without further incident, even if Ciara's complete quiet had gone from concerning to unnerving by the end of the ride over.

"Can I get you anything?"

She shook her head, her gaze roaming around his sparsely furnished space as he flipped on more lights.

"I'm sorry it's a bit musty. I haven't been here for a few weeks. I even called off my cleaning service this week."

"It's fine." She waved a hand. "I'm fine."

"I can show you to your room. You can get settled a bit."

A hard, bitter laugh escaped her. "Settled? Will I ever feel that again?"

"You will, Ciara. I promise you will."

She whirled on him then, that silence nowhere in evidence. "You promise? Really? You promise you can end this? That you can keep me safe? That you work for a damn organization that can keep me and my child from dying at the hands of a madwoman? Because from where I'm standing, your office failed."

What she didn't say, but which he heard loud and clear, was what came after.

You failed.

He'd lived in his own head for his entire life, so he was more than capable of recognizing what was unspoken. But more than that, he couldn't blame her.

"I'll show you to your room."

He'd had his place for nearly five years now, and it was only as he walked another person through the living room and on down the long hallway to the second bedroom that Aidan took it all in through her eyes.

His place was large by New York standards, and he'd bought into the building as soon as the contractor had broken ground in the Financial District. As an early buyer, he'd had first pick of places, and since he hated moving, he'd selected a place he'd want to live in for the long haul.

The fact that he had two bedrooms as a single person was nearly unheard-of. But his father had money, and whatever minimal affection Eoin Colton might have felt for his son, he'd always ensured Aidan had been provided for.

The lack of decoration was on him, though. The beige walls, functional decor and minimal personal touches made up his home, and now that he looked at it all, he wondered what he'd actually been doing with his time.

Working.

That's what he'd been doing. That's all he'd been doing.

And he'd still managed to let Maeve get much too close to Ciara.

She disappeared into the spare bedroom he'd directed her to, and Aidan headed back to the living room to call Sean with an update.

"Colton."

"We're back at my place," Aidan started right in. "Did you get anything on Maeve?"

"Nothing. I've had officers combing the area around the safe house on foot and more cars canvassing to see if they can find her. Street cams indicate she was in a black SUV, but we lost it the moment she hit the Holland Tunnel."

"She went to Jersey?"

"Seems like. Only problem is there's coverage of a black SUV going in on the Manhattan side and nothing coming out on the Jersey City side."

"What the ever-loving hell?"

"I know, damn it." Aidan heard the frustration in his cousin's voice along with a string of curses that matched the ones that had been running through his own head on a loop.

"Wait—" Aidan paused, the situation with the safe house coming into full focus. "Wait a damn minute."

"You got something?"

"Just now. The safe house being compromised. I still need to investigate that it's not someone inside the marshals, but what are the odds she hacked the safe house database *and* the city cameras with the tunnel?"

"No way. These are nuclear-grade protected environments."

"She's getting in somehow. Because whatever else we know, a human can't just disappear."

They argued it back and forth a bit more, but the more he chewed on it, the more the hacking angle made sense. Either due to her own skills or, more likely, an expert hacker she could pay off. His vision of a woman who'd lured and killed wealthy men for decades didn't jive with someone who also had superior dark-web skills, but he'd learned long ago never to assume in this job.

They had so little to go on, but since it was *something*, he was going to run with it.

"Don't forget Eva's at the courthouse tomorrow to watch the start of the Wes Westmore case. Emily's the prosecuting ADA on the case."

They discussed a regroup the next day to cover any new news on Maeve as well as the events of day one of Wes's trial before hanging up.

Which left Aidan to stare at his four beige walls, wondering what the hell he was going to do about keeping Ciara and her unborn child safe.

CIARA HAD SHOWERED and washed her hair and lathered shea butter into her skin and an hour later still felt dirty. Soiled by the ground and all the reasons Aidan had needed to push her onto it.

She felt dirty…and sad.

Because the man had done nothing but protect her, and she'd treated him like the enemy.

She knew Maeve O'Leary was out there. It hadn't simply been the running theme of the past few weeks of her life, but she'd spent all evening in Sean's home discussing strategies for catching the woman.

So why was it such a surprise Maeve had taken a shot at her?

Because it's been easier to pretend she's a figment of your imagination instead of very real and very dangerous.

Which, if Ciara was honest, was something of a cop-out, too.

She knew the woman was out there. It was the only reason she'd subjected herself to the marshals' protection. She'd entered custody knowing the risks to her life and further recognized that no matter how well equipped or outfitted, no law enforcement agency was infallible.

Wasn't that why Aidan's other witness kept running?

She'd had plenty of empathy for Guy and precious little for the man protecting her.

The man who'd thrown his body over hers, clearly prepared to take a bullet for her and her baby.

That was the real reason she felt dirty.

The real reason she couldn't wash off the events of the night.

Maeve might be a madwoman, but Ciara had been given nothing but support and care to ensure that threat remained at bay. And instead of being grateful, she'd tossed it all in the face of the one person who would literally have died to keep her safe.

Wrapping her robe tight around her, she tossed the small bottle of shea butter she'd worried in her hands while pacing the room and headed off to find Aidan.

She'd apologize, she vowed as she left the bedroom.

She'd make it right, she swore to herself as she walked down the hallway.

She'd—

Whatever she imagined she'd do had nothing on the wave of pain that washed over her at the sight of the lone, solitary figure that stared out into the darkened night. His broad shoulders were framed by the ambient glow drifting up to his high floor from the streetlights below, and in the distance she could see various lights dotting the land she knew to be part of the New Jersey shoreline.

He'd turned off all but a small table lamp in the corner of the room, and it allowed her to see that opposite shore clearly as she crossed the room toward him.

"Aidan?"

He didn't turn around. He didn't even move, really. But she sensed a leashed energy in him as she stared at that still figure.

"Aidan, please talk to me."

"It's late, Ciara. I'm sure you're exhausted. Go to bed. We can talk in the morning."

"We need to talk now."

"I think we talked enough. I've spoken to Sean, and only Sean. Otherwise I've respected your wishes to keep the marshals out of things."

"Aidan, please." She took a breath. "Please look at me. I need to talk to you. I need to apologize."

He finally turned, and the bleak look that covered his face hit her clear down to her toes. "Apologize for what? For speaking the truth? For recognizing that I utterly failed at my job?"

"You didn't fail."

"You were shot at ten feet from the very place you should have been safe. My organization failed you. *I* failed you!"

That last part tore from his chest in a hard rush, proof that her words hadn't just cut, but they'd absolutely shredded him.

He hadn't failed.

Far from it.

If it weren't for Aidan, she'd be dead right now. Whatever he believed, *failure* wasn't what had happened this evening.

Not at all.

She was alive. They both were. And suddenly, that felt more important than anything else.

Crossing the span of the living room, she moved right into him, wrapping her arms around his waist. Reiterating her point, she pushed every bit of her unwavering conviction into her words. "You didn't fail."

His arms remained at his sides, but she felt his heartbeat thundering against her cheek.

So she said it again, only this time she pressed her lips to the hard set of his jaw.

And when he still didn't move, she said it once more, pressing her lips to his chest, feeling the heat of his body through his T-shirt.

"You didn't fail."

It was that last whisper, nearly a benediction, that finally had him moving. His arms came around her and he held her tight against his chest, his lips pressed against her forehead.

"All I could think was she had you. That she'd hurt you and the baby and there was nothing I could do about it."

Once again, that reality of what it meant to watch out for someone else struck her as she stood there, safe in his arms.

"I'm fine, Aidan. The baby and I are fine."

Ciara raised her head, pressing her lips to his. He hesitated before leaning into her, his mouth moving over hers in the sweetest surrender.

She kept fighting this.

Kept pushing him away the moment things got difficult.

Yet it was at those moments she needed him the most.

As the kiss spun out, a magical cocoon wrapping around them, keeping them safe and secure in each other, Ciara gave in to the moment.

Gave in to Aidan.

And—*finally*—gave in to every single one of her feelings she'd mentally dubbed misplaced or mistaken.

She wanted him.

Hadn't tonight proven life was fragile?

More than that, hadn't tonight proven that life was meant to be lived?

Chapter Eleven

He needed to stop kissing her.

That thought kept running through his mind, along with all the other internal admonishments Aidan lived with on a daily basis.

He'd learned a long time ago to not just live with those frustrations but to channel them, working harder and longer than anyone else to make up for them.

His questionable parentage.

His father's determination to make him a Colton, even if it was in name only.

His up-until-recently limited relationship with his sister, Deirdre.

He kept the world at arm's length and was comfortable with that.

More, he was set and *comfortable* in that way of living.

But this?

Kissing Ciara even though he knew he needed to step back?

This was need and desire and a sort of magical madness that gripped him in a near fever.

He needed to let her go and walk away. She was his job, and he couldn't afford to lose focus. Hadn't this evening proven that?

Those were the questions that warred with the sheer ecstasy of holding her in his arms and kissing her.

And then he felt the most miraculous thing against his stomach.

The distinct movements of the baby.

"Is that—" He broke off, awe, wonder and a wild sense of joy settling over him.

"It's the baby. He or she's started to get more active this time of day." She glanced down at her small baby bump. "I didn't realize it was that noticeable. I'm sure—"

She fumbled a bit and stepped back, nearly stepping into the small end table beside the couch. He caught her before she tumbled over it, holding her steady.

"Hang on, Ciara."

She stilled, but her blush only deepened. "I'm sorry. Look, I can go. Like you said, we can talk in the morning."

Confusion warred with the distinct sense something had upset her. If he'd been too forward, he'd own that, but she'd initiated the kiss.

And they'd both been enjoying it.

"Hold on. Really, what's going on?"

"It's just that you were right and it has been a long day and I need to go."

"I'm sorry I was forward. Kissing you like that."

"You weren't! I mean, it's me. Really, it's me. And I'm excited about the baby and all, but I can see where being kicked in the stomach would be a bit of a buzzkill. So, um, I'm just going to—"

She broke off once more, and he could only imagine it was at the sheer surprise in his face.

"You think the baby is a reason to stop kissing?"

"Well, yeah. Um, I mean. Well."

He couldn't help but smile at her awkward fumbling. The

woman who'd been the physical personification of calm, cool and collected was ruffled.

Delightfully so.

"Why would the baby be a reason to stop kissing?"

"Well, come on, Aidan, it's just that…well… I'm *pregnant*. And I don't even know the father, but not because I slept with a stranger. Which I could have done and I would still love my child. Of course I would. But…" She waved a hand. "I mean, people usually get pregnant through sex, but I got it in a very clinical way, in a doctor's office so, I mean, um, well, it's just not a whole super-sexy, let's-make-out sort of vibe."

If he wasn't so amused, Aidan figured he'd likely have lost a small part of his brain trying to keep up with her rambling, so he finally just leaned in and pressed his lips to hers.

Maybe if they kissed some more she'd realize that she was supremely sexy and highly desirable.

Thoughts he most assuredly didn't need to have for a protectee, but it seemed as if that was increasingly something he needed to work through. Especially when the woman in his arms had come to him, open and welcoming of something more between them.

"Ciara?" he asked as he raised his head.

"What?"

"I think you're very sexy. And there's nothing about your pregnancy that makes you unsexy. And I don't care how you got pregnant, nor do I care that the baby decided to announce him or herself with a small kick."

She looked about to say more rambling somethings, so he leaned in and gave her another hard kiss.

"The only reason I stopped kissing you was because that kick was awesome. And it made me feel sheer wonder that there is a life growing inside you. So please don't be embarrassed about that."

"I'm not embarrassed about being pregnant." Her words were quiet. "But I thought maybe *you* would be embarrassed to be kissing me because I'm pregnant."

"You thought wrong."

"But I—"

He silenced her once more with his lips, taking her hands in his as he did.

"I mean it. I'm. In. Awe. Of you. Of the child inside you. Of the bravery it takes to welcome new life into the world." He shook his head, lifting her hands to hold them close against his chest. "Please don't be bashful or embarrassed or shy about any of it. It's life, and it's amazing."

"It is rather amazing, isn't it?"

That same fierceness she'd exhibited earlier was still there but channeled into something softer. Something still as determined but now lined with a layer of ease he hadn't seen in her before.

"Thank you, Aidan. For everything. For who you are. For taking care of us." She glanced down at her stomach as she said *us* before raising her gaze back up to his. "For caring so much about what you do. It's a gift. Please don't let a determined madwoman make you forget that."

He wasn't quite ready to let himself off the hook, but her gentle belief meant a lot.

Hell, Aidan mused, it meant the world.

CIARA SETTLED INTO the bed in Aidan's spare room, convinced she'd be asleep in a matter of moments. So it was something of a surprise when she found herself staring at the bedside clock an hour later, still wide-awake.

And still thinking of that kiss.

Of the kissing.

Of *all* the kissing.

She could still taste him on her tongue. Could feel the firm press of his lips against hers.

When was the last time she'd been kissed? Really, truly kissed, as if she were precious and fragile and strong and perfect all at the same time?

Oh, maybe never, her conscience came winging back.

She'd dated before. She'd had relationships before. If you'd asked her before meeting Aidan Colton if those relationships had been satisfying, she'd have unequivocally said yes.

But the past few weeks with him had made her rethink every one of those assumptions.

She'd fought it at first, unwilling to get too comfortable or accepting of her situation, no matter how strong and handsome and decent the man guarding her seemed. The cold-roommate act had given her a protective shell to avoid any level of attachment, no matter how desperately she'd wanted to believe the man could keep her safe.

But these past few days?

All that goodness and strength and decency she'd sensed and observed from the very first moment with him had been proven, over and over.

She might have accepted her father's abandonment far better than her mother had, but that act had set in motion a view of the world and a way of living that she'd adopted, without even fully recognizing it.

She made do on her own.

She took care of herself and made her own way.

And if she needed help, she knew how to keep it transactional. Cordial, yes, but transactional all the same.

Hadn't her marriage proven that?

Hadn't her clinical approach to pregnancy been another example?

It had been Aidan's arrival in her life that had made her

begin to rethink all of it. To realize that there were people in the world who put others first. Who saw their duty to the world through the lens of service.

It was humbling.

And it reinforced what needed to change in her own attitude.

Up to now she'd gone along with what he'd asked to stay safe, but she hadn't fully worked *with* him. She'd pressed her own agenda when it suited her or kept pushing for the way she wanted things to go.

But it was time she actively supported him, focused on addressing the threat together. Allowing him to lead.

He'd earned that right the moment he shielded her body, cradling her gently down to the ground and taking on the risk fully onto himself.

On that thought, she slipped from bed and crossed over to get her laptop. After the kissing—the amazing kissing she could still feel to the depths of her toes—Aidan had caught her up on the captured images on the street cameras and Maeve's seeming disappearance into the Holland Tunnel.

Humans didn't just disappear, which they all well knew, but the woman's ability to disguise herself was obviously her special skill.

What if Maeve had found a way to do the same with the car? All she'd need was a basic ability to cloak the vehicle to pass by or trick the cameras and get away.

The reflective scales on a tuna kept going through Ciara's mind as she turned on a bedside lamp before climbing back into bed. What if Maeve had modified some sort of lighting system on her car? Add on a small computer program that could be installed to mask the license plate, and she'd create enough diversion on a traffic cam to get away clean.

It seemed silly.

Fanciful.

And yet obvious, somehow.

Because if a traffic camera caught her going into one of the two tunnels that crossed under the Hudson River, the only answer to not seeing her come out the other side was some sort of disguise. Or the hacking capabilities Sean was already checking into.

The bigger question, Ciara wondered as she opened her laptop and quickly pulled up a search tab, was what had happened when the woman came back into the city. For all its uniqueness, one of the most defining characteristics of Manhattan was that it was an island. Which meant there were limited ways on and off. Since Maeve had made New York her home base, she had to find some way to come back home after her antics.

Because of teaching at Rutgers, Ciara knew the routes in and out on the New Jersey side of the city well. In addition to the Holland Tunnel and its sister, the Lincoln Tunnel, Maeve could use the George Washington Bridge, or she could really go out of her way and take the Goethals Bridge to the Staten Island Ferry. Those were pretty much her only options if she wanted to maintain access to a vehicle.

Without a car, her options expanded, including the train, bus service or the ferry system that ran between New Jersey and New York.

But she'd keep her own transportation, wouldn't she?

The light knock pulled Ciara out of her reverie, and she called out a "come in."

"I saw the light under your door. Everything okay?"

"Yeah, I'm fine. I couldn't sleep, so I decided to play around with an idea a bit."

"Oh?"

"The whole Maeve-disappearing-from-the-tunnel thing.

There are several aspects that bugged me, and I wanted to do a few searches."

She saw clear interest stamp itself across Aidan's face. "What are you thinking?"

"She found a way to sneak out of the city, whether via some sort of disguise she masterminded on the car or a computer hack. Neither of which would be easy, but really, I see no other option."

"You have a point there. Walk me through the rest of what you're thinking."

"First, you've been inside those tunnels. It's not like you can find a parking spot along the wall and wait a while. You get in and you move forward until you come out the other side." As an afterthought, she added, "And if she did try to slow down, all she'd do is end up backing up traffic, which didn't happen."

"Likely true, but I'll double-check that second part with Sean. All he said was she went in the tunnel and didn't come out the other side, based on the traffic cams."

"Nor did she have a toll in that direction. If she did, Sean's team could track her that way, too, but you only pay on the New Jersey side."

Aidan smiled at that. "A fact that seems to punish New Jersey."

"Not if you consider that the toll's really just doubled, and since it's an island you have leave eventually."

It was a small point but a valuable one. In order to keep traffic moving, the Port Authority had gone to tolling only on one side years ago. "Which brings me to my bigger idea. She had to come back."

"Through the tunnel?"

"Tunnel, bridge, ferry." She pointed toward her laptop. "I wanted to do a quick search to see if the other ferries ran car service, but it's just the Staten Island Ferry. So those would be her options if she wanted to keep a vehicle. Two tunnels, two bridges and a ferry."

"She could drive the really long way around and come in through the east side. Or down from upstate via the West Side Highway."

"She could. But she would still have limited ways in. All of which have traffic cams and tolls. So either she's changing out her cars outside the city or she's got ways to disguise the cars she has. Some sort of paint or covering and a way to swap license plates. But she'd still have to swap the toll tag, too."

"None of that's impossible."

"No, but it does take an incredible amount of planning. She has to know once she uses one of the disguises and emits an electronic signal with the toll, she'll trigger an alert the moment she tries to reenter the city."

"Are you sure you're a professor and not a detective?"

She flashed him a grin. "I play one on TV."

"This is good, Ciara. Really good. Sean's team is trained to look at every one of these angles, but the rush to find her is urgent. No idea is a bad idea, and if someone's already looking into it, then that only proves it was a good thought and something that needed to be run down in the first place."

"I want to help. Look. Before—" She blew out a hard breath. "I was terribly out of line before. You're doing an amazing job, and I know you and a lot of other people behind the scenes are working to keep me safe. I appreciate it, Aidan. More than I can say."

He remained at the door, and while she wanted to gesture him in, there was something oddly sweet about the way he stood in the doorway, leaning on the jamb with his hands in his pockets.

Since she could still feel the imprint of his lips on hers—and was seriously contemplating doing far more with the man than a kiss—that small bit of physical distance was likely wise.

"I told you, there's nothing to apologize for."

"I think there is. I realized something tonight. Something that I thought I knew but now understand in a foundationally different way."

"Ciara, you don't—"

"Please, Aidan. Hear me out."

When he only stood there, stoic but quiet, she continued. "I know you're assigned to protect me. Obviously my life has looked considerably different these past few weeks since moving into the safe house. But it wasn't until tonight that I fully understood what your job entails. What it means."

She took a deep breath, desperately hoping she could convey all she felt—all the gratitude and awe and a sort of fathomless appreciation—for what he'd done for her.

"You covered me and protected me, at risk to your own life, tonight. That's more than a job. That's a calling, Aidan, and it takes an incredibly special person to make that choice."

"It is my job and I do it willingly."

"I understand that now. I want you to understand that I'm going to do everything in my power to help you and support you and be part of the solution here."

He pushed off the doorjamb and crossed to her, bending down and pressing his lips to her forehead. "That means more than I can ever say."

She watched him turn to go, pulling the door closed gently behind himself as he exited, and stared at that closed door for a long time, considering all that lay on the other side.

She cared for Aidan. It had been quick and definitely born out of the intensity of what she was experiencing, but that wasn't the only reason for her attraction. On some level, it was actually an easy cop-out to think these feelings were steeped in dangerous circumstances and hero worship.

But Ciara knew better.

Aidan Colton was a special man. And her feelings for him that continued to build and grow weren't based on danger or circumstances or even the elevated hormones from her pregnancy filling her bloodstream.

She cared for him and increasingly she knew he cared in return.

The real challenge was getting through this so they could see their way to building something lasting on the other side.

Something true.

Something that didn't have a layer of cold, calculating madness draped over top.

MAEVE PARKED IN the small second garage off the side of the house and cut the engine, hitting the button for the door the moment the SUV was turned off.

Damn woman.

Humphrey's freaking widow was certainly a challenge she hadn't anticipated.

She'd planned the race out of the city if she needed it, but damn it, she'd needed it. And that left one more disguise she couldn't use any longer. Her skill was both standing out and blending in—she'd made a life out of the ability to do both effectively—but she'd never had a con that had run so long before.

She found a mark, got her money and got out.

Humphrey had been a problem from the start. First all those meddling Coltons, big brother Sean at the top of the list. And then the grieving trollop of a widow.

If Wes wasn't in so much trouble, she might have considered leaving town and skipping the widow for now. Loose ends could always be tied up later, after the dust settled and a person had stopped looking over their shoulder. But Wes's *situation* had left her no choice but to stick close.

And if she had to stick close to help her idiot son beat a murder rap, she sure as hell was going to wrap up all her loose ends.

Much as she adored New York, it was increasingly looking like she wasn't coming back. A sadness, to be sure, but necessary.

There was always Paris. Or Tokyo, London, Singapore. All were places where she could reset and build anew. Everything was in motion for Wes to get off on the murder charge, so it was just a matter of seeing that through, killing the widow and leaving.

After this, her son could fend for himself.

Birds had to leave the nest sooner or later, after all.

She made sure the garage was locked up tight, then headed for the small bungalow she'd owned for years. Truth be told, she hated New Jersey. It wasn't New York—of course, what was?—but the small, two-bedroom house was also the reminder that for years she struggled and scraped to get by.

Her city life and her luxury apartment and her closet full of furs was the life she was meant to have. Her miserable, humble beginnings were the embarrassing personal history she'd always hated.

None of it meant she wasn't eminently practical, and when she'd had a chance to buy this place in cash and put it in a late husband's name, she'd jumped at it. Everyone needed a hidey-hole, after all.

This was hers.

The small house ten miles outside New York that might

as well have been a million miles away for all the difference from her pied-à-terre in Manhattan.

"Means to an end," she muttered to herself as she slipped into the house, locking it up tightly behind her and then activating the perimeter cameras and security system.

It paid to keep an eye on who came to the house. She'd eluded the cops so far, but she wasn't taking any chances.

Heading straight for the second bedroom she used as her staging area, she dragged off the wig she'd settled on during the drive through the tunnel. Draping it over a mannequin head, she drifted around the room, discarding various aspects of her costume. Large earrings followed by the oversize scarf she'd used to cover her neck and décolletage.

Satisfied all her items were in order, she headed into her own bedroom and straight for the shower. With the failed attempt on Ciara Kelly, she'd decided to spend the night here, aware the cops would be on extra-high alert, no matter her disguise.

So she'd regroup.

She'd get a good night's sleep.

And first thing tomorrow morning she'd be hacking medical records.

Because the night might not have been all she'd hoped, but she did get one bit of confirmation she'd been curious about for a few weeks now.

After all, a woman who has had a child recognized the look in another.

When she'd gone after Ciara a few weeks ago, she'd had the distinct sense the woman was pregnant, but she hadn't gotten close enough to confirm. And then Humphrey went and got himself killed before she could ask him.

But tonight?

Oh, it was obvious tonight.

Humphrey's young widow was most certainly pregnant.

Which would make killing her and exacting her revenge that much sweeter.

Chapter Twelve

Ciara recognized she and Sean had come to something of a new understanding the day before. She was glad of it, especially knowing how much Kieran Colton's children meant to Humphrey.

But when he showed up at Aidan's apartment bright and early with a box of pastries that looked like something out of a photo shoot for a food show, she thought she might have fallen in love with him just a little bit.

"Neon-pink sweet and sour yesterday. Croissant doughnuts today," Ciara muttered as she grabbed a wickedly delightful glazed concoction out of the box. "Mother of the year for sure."

"What's that?" Aidan asked as he came back into the living room with a small stack of plates and napkins.

Sean had headed out of the room to take a call, so it was just the two of them for the moment.

"I'm questioning my nutritional choices."

"Would you like something else? I can make you some oatmeal or get you a yogurt from the fridge."

Ciara stared up from the glistening glaze on her doughnut. "It's very possible I would carve out your spleen with a butter knife if you attempted to take this away from me.

One hundred percent possible if you attempt to give me oatmeal in its place."

Aidan put his hands up in the air. "I guess we'll take 'helpful pregnancy coach' out of my job description."

"See that you do."

The light banter was fun and went a long way toward calming her nerves. She had woken up with the vague vestiges of a nightmare swirling in the back of her mind and hadn't fully regained her equilibrium, even after a shower and a cup of decaf tea.

"I couldn't help but overhear and have to say that's an impressively bloodthirsty threat," Sean said as he came back into the room. "But for the record, I'd likely do the same if I was offered oatmeal in place of one of those beauties."

Sean winked at her as he tucked his phone back into his pocket before selecting his own doughnut out of the box. He took a huge bite before reaching for a napkin on the coffee table, ignoring the plates completely.

"She's eating for two."

"She still has taste buds, cuz." Sean's defense was much appreciated and notched a few more approval points in the plus column for the man.

Aidan didn't look convinced, but he dropped the subject in favor of the matter at hand. "Did you find anything on the cameras yet?"

"The electronics team went through the films again. SUV goes in, doesn't come out. They bumped it against all the other cars coming in and out at the same time, and while they can find all the others, she basically vanished."

"No way." Aidan shook his head. "It's not possible."

"The electronics team are looking at the film for tampering, and they think they see a glitch. A damn good one, too," Sean said, "since it's practically seamless."

"She's got to be making changes to the car, too," Ciara couldn't help but argue. "Light modifications but enough to avoid detection."

"We're looking into that, too," Sean affirmed before reaching for another doughnut.

"Where the hell is she going?" Aidan reached for a doughnut of his own. "Even if it's just a place where she can further change out her ride?"

"She's got to have a place. It could be just someplace she hides, but my money's on a home of some sort." Sean shrugged. "Hell, it could even be a storage unit—we can't rule anything out yet. But she had a plan and she had a place to go. She's too methodical to do anything else."

"It's all part of the disguise, Aidan." Ciara considered it but the more she rolled it around, the more it fit. "She's not just a master of fitting in and blending and becoming whoever she needs to be—it's who she is."

Sean's already-alert gaze sharpened. "That's an interesting take. That the disguise isn't just a means to an end but it's a part of her."

"How else would she be successful at her work all these years?"

Although it pained Ciara to use a word like *work*, the truth was that it fit.

Maeve's life's work had been as a black widow. She'd had several husbands they'd already been able to account for, as well as a child who carried a different name. He didn't overtly acknowledge her as his mother, nor did she apparently acknowledge him in return, yet there was a bond there.

"Do you think Wes is going to get off on his charges?" Ciara asked, shifting gears a bit. "In talking with Emily yesterday, she seemed concerned that the case was going to go quickly and not in the DA's office's favor."

"That's the working expectation. Emily's been on this trial from the start, and while they have the boyfriend angle on the murder, they don't have DNA. Humphrey's *recommendation*—" Sean stressed the word "—puts a lot of pluses in the innocent column."

"Even with how publicly Humphrey died?"

"The evidence is still there. Emily and her team have worked on trying to cast doubt on it, but that note still carries a lot of weight because of his stellar reputation."

Ciara considered it and recognized it was yet one more facet of Maeve's wicked web.

"So that's the reason she initially targeted Humphrey. Or, maybe a better way to put it, how she initially found him."

"You have an idea?" Sean asked.

"It just seems to me that Maeve has put a lot of time and effort into someone simply to get her son off on a murder charge. A son that she doesn't publicly acknowledge."

"You think Humphrey became more to her?" Aidan said as he set his plate back on the coffee table, his gaze thoughtful. "That she initially targeted him for a way to bolster her son's file with a strong recommendation, and then realized somewhere along the way that he could be her next rich target?"

"It's an idea."

It was an idea. One that still had a lot of sketchy areas, but also one that finally felt like it fit.

"I realize her plans have all been upended, but presumably she doesn't target married men. It would be considerably more complicated than going after a single man she could manipulate and get into her good graces. But if Humphrey had been on her radar, and then suddenly he ended up married to me, quite unexpectedly, it would stand to reason why she sees me as a problem."

"You got in her way."

Aidan's words chilled her, but for the first time, Ciara felt she might have some answers.

Hadn't that been one of the worst things about this whole situation?

Not fully understanding why she had been targeted. Or why a stranger would put such intense, malicious focus on her.

Sean's phone pinged with an incoming text, immediately followed by Aidan's. Both men glanced toward their devices, even as another set of pings erupted in rapid succession.

"It's Liam."

Ciara watched as both men stared at their phones, but it was Sean's surprised curse that caught her attention.

"I'll be damned. Wes Westmore just confessed to killing his girlfriend."

AIDAN WAS STILL trying to process the details an hour later as several more Coltons descended on his home. In a near repeat of yesterday's gathering, they'd decided to regroup as a team. The attempt on Ciara's life the night before had put everyone in a mind to come to them, and all agreed to manage their arrivals discreetly in the event anyone was keeping tabs on the family.

But by lunch he had a house full of everyone except Emily, who'd stayed at work to manage the aftermath of the Westmore confession.

Aidan's sister, Deirdre, was projected up on his TV, where he'd patched her into their conversation via web conference.

"It's all over my FBI emails," Deirdre affirmed shortly after he brought her up to speed.

"Notifications came in to the marshals, too. And Sean said the NYPD is feeling all kinds of happy that the idiot made a full, unprompted confession."

"Why did he do that?" Deirdre's eyes narrowed.

"Arrogance? Stupidity? Both? Take your pick."

"They all make sense, but for my money I take arrogance. That's been his biggest Achilles' heel from the beginning. The way he comes off suggests he thinks he's smarter than everybody else. A trait he gets from his mother," Deirdre added dryly.

"That's an interesting point, and it says a lot more about her psyche than maybe we're considering. Maeve went after Ciara again last night."

At Deirdre's obvious shock, Aidan quickly brought his sister up to speed. The short walk from the parking garage to the safe house. Maeve's obvious approach by lying in wait for them. And then her apparent disappearance from the video cameras in the tunnel out of the city.

"Bureau's going to be all over that one."

"I get the sense from Sean the NYPD isn't sitting on its hands, either. Skills like that are serious problem."

"They're a problem everywhere, but a breach in the security systems in a city like New York is mind-bending."

"Without question."

Deirdre's eyebrows drew together again before her gaze drifted to the left somewhere off camera, a smile breaking over her face.

He could only assume his sister's soon-to-be stepson, Derek, had walked into the room. The two-year-old had captivated Deirdre immediately, and she was looking forward to not only becoming his mother by marriage but also adopting him as soon as she and Micah could get the paperwork arranged.

"Say hello to the little guy for me."

Her smile only got wider. "I'd tell you to say hi yourself,

but he ducked off in our newest game of hide-and-seek. He'll
be back."

Deirdre shifted seamlessly from FBI agent to mother and
back to agent again. "Aidan, when did Maeve attack? Last
night, you say? And she discovered the safe house?"

"Yeah. I'm still trying to dig around and find the leak inside the marshals, so I've kept it quiet this morning. Because
if there was a leak, I've got a problem. But if it's a data breach
of the same sort that's glitching cameras in the tunnels, we've
got a serious electronics problem instead. I pulled in our best
e-team member this morning to dig around."

"But it all happened before Wes's confession?"

"Well, yeah. Emily said Wes ran his big mouth this morning just before court started."

Based on how late he and Ciara were attacked, and Wes's
blurted confession this morning, he was hard-pressed to believe it was anything other than bad luck for both mother
and son.

"Why do you ask?"

"If Ciara is already a target because she's Humphrey's
widow, and Maeve somehow sees her as a blocker, this is only
going to make her more unstable. The initial kidnapping of
Humphrey was *for* her son. Even if she changed gears and
decided Humphrey would be a great black widow target, he
was initially her mark to get Wes out of his murder charges."

Damn it, why hadn't he seen this? Why hadn't any of them
seen this? They were good at their jobs, yet they'd somehow
continued to underestimate the threat.

"Ciara was poking around those same edges this morning. Trying to understand the timing of Maeve's interest in
Humphrey."

"We know she's unstable. Hell, Micah has lived with that

truth for years, instinctively knowing his father was murdered but never being fully able to prove it. But something like this? Such a complete ruination of her plans? That could take unstable and ratchet it up to a complete and absolute break with reality."

Deirdre leaned in, her expression as serious as Aidan had ever seen it.

"I've observed it over and over on cases. Our profilers understand those nuances and the deeds of a depraved human mind when pushed, and I can guarantee you they'll come up with it here. You're not just dealing with a black widow or an angry mother in mama bear mode. You're dealing with an individual who has completely separated from reality. Be careful, Aidan. Be very careful."

"That's the reality of what we're dealing with?" Ciara moved into the living room, her attention focused on the screen.

He hadn't realized she was standing there, but based on her expression he could only assume she'd heard the most dark and ominous parts of the conversation. Wanting to give comfort, Aidan reached for her hand, pulling her down next to him on the couch. He didn't miss the subtle widening of his sister's eyes, but otherwise Deirdre kept her professional smile firmly in place.

"I'd like you to meet someone very important to me. Ciara Kelly, this is my sister, Deirdre."

The two women exchanged hellos just as a mischievous Derek ran back into the room and immediately climbed onto Deirdre's lap.

Despite the seriousness of their discussion and the tension he still felt in her as she sat beside him, Ciara shifted quickly to focus on the little boy.

"And who is this?"

In the spirit of toddlers the world over, Derek was both delighted by the attention and suddenly shy as Ciara waved at him. He turned into Deirdre's chest, burying his head before turning slightly to eye the computer once more.

That little give was Ciara's cue to keep pressing her attentions, and in a matter of moments she had the little boy giggling with a game of hide-your-face peekaboo through the video call.

The game continued for a few minutes, everyone giggling and pleased to take a breather through the tension that had only increased all morning.

Hell, Aidan thought, by the day.

There'd been very little laughter in Ciara's life since the day Humphrey Kelly walked into the federal courthouse and didn't walk back out.

Or didn't walk back out as his recognizable self.

Ever since the day her husband, confidant and protector had been brainwashed by Maeve, she'd been in a constant state of panicked pressure.

First as a presumed person of interest in her much older husband's disappearance. Then as a purported victim of Maeve.

Ciara had been holding up admirably well, but it gave Aidan relief to see that she could still find her smile and her laughter.

That she could still take moments of joy.

Although he lasted longer than Aidan expected, Derek's interest eventually waned, and Micah's voice could be heard off camera enticing the boy to go out and visit their stables. Micah briefly popped on-screen, saying a quick hello and introducing himself to Ciara before pressing a kiss on Deirdre and then carrying his laughing toddler out of the room.

It was only once they were clearly gone that Deirdre turned her attention on Ciara. "Thank you for your indulgence. He's very quickly become my whole world. They both have."

"Thank you for sharing those precious moments. I've missed focusing on something that isn't related to kidnapping and mad criminals and my dead husband."

"We will find her, Ciara. I have no doubt in my mind."

"I appreciate that. Truly, I do. And I believe in your devotion and Aidan's and your whole family's to solving this. What I can't wrap my head around is that she's so elusive. And so damned practiced at this. She could literally be anywhere, and her use of disguise and frankly, her determined madness, give her an edge."

Since Ciara's fears only matched the clinical knowledge Deirdre had already shared, Aidan recognized he wasn't in a position to correct her.

Because she was right.

Which meant they had to be more focused.

More vigilant.

And more determined to keep Ciara alive than Maeve was to see her dead.

"TELL ME WHY we're doing this again?" Sean's attitude was good-natured, but his no-nonsense approach to police work still came through loud and clear.

"I want to drive the same path Maeve did. There's got to be something we're missing. Something we can look at differently."

Since the entire Colton clan was at his apartment, Aidan had finally felt safe leaving Ciara for a while. But he needed to see the crime scene again.

Needed to see the exact place where Maeve came after them.

Because maybe if he did, this shocking, roiling anger might subside a bit and leave him the room to breathe.

"You doing okay, man?" Sean eyed him as they came up from the subway exit a few blocks from the safe house apartment.

"Not really."

"We're going to find Maeve and put her away."

Aidan whirled on his cousin, his anger desperately needing somewhere handy to land. "You sure about that? Really sure? Because I don't see her behind bars, Sean."

"You think I'm just paying you lip service?"

"I think you think you have this under control, but every time we turn around, there's another facet that proves nothing is in the NYPD's control and we're no closer to finding the witch than you were nearly a month ago when she killed Humphrey."

"She's after the woman you love. I get it. And I get how freaking impossible it is to see straight when you're quaking in fear up to your eyeballs."

"I'm not—"

Love?

What?

Aidan stopped stock-still in the middle of the crosswalk, and it was Sean who grabbed his elbow and dragged him the rest of the way before the light turned.

"You are, Aidan. And I get it. I get how it messes with your focus. How it gets in your mind, not just the case but the woman wrapped up in the case."

"I'm not in love with Ciara."

"Suit yourself. But I was there just a few months ago. Fighting my feelings for Orla even though I was a goner the moment I met her."

"I'm not in love. She's under my protection. I don't—" He shook his head. "I'm not in love with Ciara."

Sean gave him a side eye but said nothing as they walked up to the parking garage that still housed Aidan's car. In a matter of minutes they were on their way, navigating the streets of lower Manhattan.

He was not in love. He'd vowed long ago that he had too much respect for women to subject them to his fouled-up emotional senses. He hadn't been raised by parents who loved each other. Instead, he'd seen all the ways two people who were attracted to each other could manipulate one another, putting their child in the middle.

Not exactly the proper basis for growing up to have his own healthy adult relationships.

Which was fine. It always had been before now, and it would continue to be fine.

More than fine.

He had his work, and from time to time he met a woman he wanted to spend a few nights with, and he'd always found a way to make it work. It might be a bit of a lonely way to live, but it was far better than the guilt he'd live with if he ended up subjecting a woman to a life of emotional warfare and, heaven forbid, they introduced kids into that, too.

So, no, he wasn't in love with Ciara. Nor was he in love with the idea of raising the child she was carrying, watching him or her grow up.

Which brought him right back to work.

That's what required his attention and his focus. It was the only way to keep Ciara and her child safe so they could go on to find someone who wanted that married life he was so deeply against.

Work was the answer.

So get to it, Colton.

With a renewed focus on the drive through lower Manhattan, Aidan stared at the sharp turn he'd navigate once the light turned green. "You know? This means something."

Because he lived down in the Financial District, Aidan was used to the somewhat random pattern of streets in the lower end of the city. Manhattan only became a grid—with the east-to-west streets and north-to-south avenues it was famous for—above Fourth Street. But these streets—the ones that were settled in the city in the seventeenth and eighteenth centuries—were a warren of small turns, named streets and old buildings.

"What does?"

Sean had been quiet ever since he dropped his bomb about love, and, if Aidan wasn't mistaken, the man's face wore a rather smug smile.

So he ignored it, since the ass had seemed impervious to his earlier attempts to pick a fight.

"This. Here." He pointed out the front window as he turned onto Canal Street. "Navigating these streets takes some knowledge and understanding of where you are. You can't just wing it and know you're starting at Thirty-Third and Fifth and ending up at Seventy-Second and Broadway."

"You think she lives down here?"

"Either lives or at least has spent a lot of time in lower Manhattan. You have to know this part of town. There's no other way to navigate it quite so fast."

"That's good. I'm going to tell Eva to narrow the run on property searches to lower Manhattan first. She's been coming up with dead ends, but she's likely started in ritzier neighborhoods."

"She could even have a home down here. A stand-alone row home, maybe."

"Yep, that's good, too." Sean tapped into his phone as

Aidan kept driving toward the Holland Tunnel, the two of them batting around ideas and working theories.

He pictured the traffic last night, recognizing it had been a lot lighter than now, with midday gridlock keeping them moving at a snail's pace toward the tunnel entrance.

"She's built a lot of security for herself. That's what this is." Aidan ran with the thought, giving it shape and form. "The husbands. The money. The disguises. It's all a form of security."

"A woman navigating her way in the big bad world. She's found a way to make it work for her, no matter who gets hurt. In fact, I'd say she's adapted. It might have started out as a way to protect herself. She had a young child and needed some sense of security. Some sense that they'd be all right. And then it changed. Morphed, really, when she realized that she liked the game. It morphed again when she realized she liked the killing."

As he listened to Sean describe the scenario, Aidan couldn't help but think of his own mother. Kara Dean had made her way in the world as well as a single mother. Her background had been a bit different, her modeling career as a young woman setting her up with more financial security than Maeve likely had in the early days when she'd first had Wes, but beyond that, was the scenario all that different?

Even as he thought it, he had his answer, and it was a resounding yes, damn it.

Yes, it was different.

His mother, for all her foibles and questionable relationship with his father, hadn't become a maniacal killer because his father didn't want to marry her. Nor did she have a broken mind, brought on by her maternal responsibilities.

"That simplistic definition sort of lets her off easy, you know."

"Maybe yes, maybe no." Sean shrugged. "But it's got a

certain sort of symmetry to it. If Wes wasn't important to her, why would she stick around for him? She could have cut him loose a long time ago. Hell, he's a grown man. More than old enough to know better, yet his own psychotic tendencies have shown themselves."

"You think the mother's traits are in the son?"

"Whether by birth or by circumstance, I think he's learned at the knee of a master. I think he sees her skills differently, though. For him, his mother's methods are a means to an end. A way to get him out of jail time or a savior who can get him out of trouble whenever he does bad."

"That's why he blurted out the confession this morning. He doesn't think he's going to jail."

"Probably never has. He's believed all along Mommy will take care of it."

Although his time with the marshals had always been more about protecting witnesses than it had been about profiling criminals, he'd gotten enough exposure to it through the years to understand the methodology behind the study of psychotic behaviors. From narcissism to sociopathic behaviors to full-on psychopathy, there were those who spent their professional lives studying all of it.

He'd learned a long time ago the key to understanding it was not to assume those individuals' ability to view the world around them was like anyone else's. Attempting to put yourself inside that person's head would inevitably fail, because the ability to rationalize the world around them was unique to the condition.

Which reinforced Sean's theories.

Maeve likely saw her choices as both self-sacrificing and self-supporting.

Parents and children.

Traits.

Learned behaviors.

He cycled through all of it in his mind and recognized that there was yet another woman in his life who was also preparing to be a single mother.

She didn't have Maeve's psychopathy or his mother's selfish tendencies.

But she was preparing to raise a child alone.

And for the first time, he gave in and truly acknowledged how he felt about that.

The more time he spent with Ciara, the more he'd come to care for her. Both for her and for the unborn child she was carrying.

And as he made the last turn into the tunnel, determined to track the path of a killer, Aidan acknowledged the truth.

His entire life had done a 180 in a matter of weeks. Because what might have begun as an observation from his cousin had shined a light on something Aidan had known, even though he hadn't been bold enough to admit it.

An image of his sister's face from earlier, all lit up when Derek ran to her and climbed into her lap, was yet another reinforcement for all he was feeling himself.

For all he could feel for the right person.

Because he could picture himself holding the baby Ciara was carrying in his arms.

Making a family with her.

Building a life.

Damn Sean Colton, Aidan thought, *for seeing far more than he should have.*

And for making Aidan see the truth.

He *was* in love with Ciara.

After spending a lifetime running away from it, he'd finally realized the truth. When love did arrive, there actually wasn't anywhere to run.

Chapter Thirteen

Ciara appreciated the large group of people surrounding her, but by early afternoon she finally admitted to herself that she needed a bit of space. For all her dreams while growing up as an only child, fantasizing about having lots of brothers and sisters, she had to admit that the reality of having so many people around was a lot.

Wow, it was a lot.

All the talking and good-natured arguing and the sheer number of people filling up the space.

She'd feigned a need to check email and fled to her room, closing the door on a heavy sigh.

It wasn't a lie, she quickly realized, as she logged in to find notes from several students as well as two from the associate professor who was helping out with her class. After dealing with a scheduling mishap on one of the boats they'd chartered as well as confirming the pay rate for another boat captain she'd used for years, she was nearly ready to start in on a few of the student emails when there was a light knock on her door.

Emily was on the other side, and Ciara waved her in.

"You doing okay?" Emily took a seat on the edge of the bed, her six-months-pregnant belly settling neatly onto her lap.

"I'm good." Ciara gestured to the desk chair she was using. "Please, take this seat."

"I'm fine," Emily insisted, waving off Ciara's offer. "I've been sitting most of the morning at the courthouse, and it feels good to perch on something a bit more cushy."

"It was quite a morning."

"Our office is still reeling. The man flat out confessed, right there in front of everyone." Emily shook her head. "I've never seen anything like it, and I've been a lawyer for quite a while now."

"It's stunning. Why would someone do that?"

"It's a level of arrogance that's hard to imagine. Forget the fact that he's now been lying his ass off for months saying he was innocent, but what could he possibly have expected would happen? The moment the court officers put him in cuffs to lead him out, he was screaming about his rights." Emily's excitement was palpable. "Who does that?"

"So that means Humphrey's fake testimonial can't be used any longer?"

"It won't be. Not with that sort of confession. He said it in front of a room full of witnesses in a courthouse. He's sealed his fate, and it's not life outside a prison cell, regardless of any notes sitting in his file."

Ciara felt the sudden well of tears at the news but was no longer surprised by them. For a woman who'd cried very little as an adult, she was certainly having a moment.

Or her hormones were.

As she wiped at her eyes, she couldn't quite stem the whipping waves of emotion. "I've hated the idea that Humphrey's life's work would be so soiled by that faked psychiatric evaluation."

"I know it's bothered Cormac, too. He's understood that Humphrey did it against his will, but it didn't change the upset that someone he cared about so much was tainted with that sort of connection. We can all rest easier that your husband's memory won't be linked to that criminal."

Ciara took a tissue from the box on the corner of the desk, wiping the tears. "I'm sorry. Everything sets me off nowadays."

"My pregnancy has had me experiencing a range of powerful emotions, too." Emily's smile was kind. "But don't discount that these are also extraordinary circumstances."

"They are. I know what a good man Humphrey was. These past few months have made it clear how many important clients he had, and that's been something to adjust to. The fact that he kept secrets for some very powerful people, not all of whom are decent or moral. But I also know that he had a good heart. He did right by the Coltons, and he's done right by me. That means something."

It did mean something, but more than that, it was one more proof point that Maeve O'Leary wasn't going to win.

And wasn't that a special victory all on its own?

Ciara had spent a lot of time thinking and processing her current reality. And what she kept coming back to, over and over, was the strange feeling that they were literally doing battle, good versus evil.

There was a lot about Maeve they didn't know, but after spending time with the Coltons she had to admit that there was so much they'd uncovered in such a short time.

"It does mean something. So does the promise all the Coltons keep making to you, Ciara. They *will* keep you safe. They would all do it for you, no matter what. But their love for Humphrey is a part of this, and they'll honor him through you."

"I know that. And when I stop feeling frustrated by the fact she's still out there, I can see how far everyone's come. Here's a woman who has stayed off the radar of law enforcement for decades, and in a matter of months they've uncovered her connection to Wes Westmore, the clear evidence she murdered Micah Perry's father and the vastness of her crimes."

"That matters. Because when they do catch her, she's going into a cage for every single one of those crimes, as well as all we may still uncover."

An image of that day shimmered to life in her mind, and Ciara gave herself a moment to lean into it.

It was both goal and promise and she needed to believe it would happen. That it *would* come to pass.

The baby kicked in affirmation, and Ciara laid a hand over her stomach. "Does it ever bother you? Dealing with all this nastiness while pregnant?"

"A big part of me feels like I should be bothered. But, well—" Emily broke off on a wry smile. "Cormac and I didn't exactly have a traditional romance. We're both elated about the baby, but this wasn't exactly the expected outcome of a romantic fling we had back in December."

"It sounds like things have turned out exactly like one might hope from a romantic fling." Ciara couldn't resist the gentle tease.

Her own path to pregnancy might have been devoid of romance, but that didn't mean she didn't enjoy a good love story for someone else. Whatever obstacles Emily and Cormac had faced, they'd obviously worked through them. She saw the way the man positively doted on her, and his sweet, lopsided yet ever-present grin each time he looked at Emily was a pretty positive clue that he was very happy with the outcome, too.

"They did turn out well in the end. But I spent quite a while thinking they wouldn't." Emily laid a hand over her own belly, glancing down at that round bump before looking back up. "I am so grateful every day that things have worked out. I never expected to become a mother this late in life. I'm already in my forties."

Ciara rolled her eyes. "Which means you've no doubt read reams of articles on the web about being a geriatric mother."

"Yes!"

Ciara raised a hand. "I'm one, too. And my doctor keeps assuring me that I'm fine and that the baby is fine, despite the questions I keep peppering her with at every visit. Or what it says on my maternity charts."

"It's a lot of external feedback. And it has its place. I mean, I want to know the realities of the world. I want to understand my risks so I can do everything in my power to be as healthy as possible. But—" Emily's smile was a bit wobbly. "Sometimes it's a lot to take in."

"Please know I'm here to talk if you need a friendly ear."

"I'd like that."

Ciara glanced toward the closed door before offering up a small smile of her own. "So…confession time. I came in here to get away for a bit. I mean, I did check emails, but I could have done that later, if I'm being honest. The Colton family is amazing, but there are a lot of them."

"Confession time back?"

"Sure."

"I came to check on you for the exact same reason. I mean, I did want to make sure you're okay, but I needed a bit of a breather, too."

"You know, they say it's good for pregnant women to rest from time to time."

"So that's our story?" Emily's smile was wide, even as her eyes carried a conspiratorial glint. "You know, when everyone asks us where we got off to?"

"That's *exactly* what we're going to tell them."

AIDAN DROVE AROUND Jersey City, the journey around the city that bordered the Hudson River on the New Jersey side a bit more aimless than he'd have liked, but still somewhat useful. He and Sean had looked at the various cameras as they drove through the Holland Tunnel, the mounted units at what appeared to be evenly paced intervals.

"How the hell do you hack the tunnel cameras?" It was Aidan's turn to ask the question, but Sean had echoed the same several times, in various iterations, as they worked through all their theories on how Maeve was getting in and out of Manhattan in a vehicle.

Did Maeve hire an actual hacker? Or did she have an inside mole she was using to do her dirty work?

It was the same question he was facing with the marshals.

Dismissing the possibility of an inside man or woman was foolish in the extreme, but considering the technical aspects was essential as well. Because now that they were dealing with comparable outcomes, across two highly competent law enforcement agencies, they needed to consider that angle.

Both of her information breaches—evading the street cams and discovering a safe house—were predicated on manipulating a digital footprint. Which suggested some skill—or purchased skill—in the world of high-priced hacking.

Especially because the financial and prison-based consequences of such acts were extreme. No hacker for hire in their right mind would do any of it without a significant payoff in hand.

Since they'd followed a few routes Maeve could taken coming out of the tunnel and Sean had already gotten his team working on connecting with the Jersey City cops on reviewing traffic cams, Aidan made the last turn to head back into the tunnel from the opposite side.

"What's in this for her? That's the real question I keep

coming back to. I know I'm looking at this through a rational lens she doesn't possess, but it's still hard to see what's worth the time, expense and risk this has become."

"For my money?" Sean said. "I think what we're witnessing is a true psychotic break."

"Deirdre said the same earlier. But I was thinking about it through a different angle."

"You have a different theory?"

"Not theory yet so much as observation. There are a lot of similarities in the circumstances between her and my mother. Could this all be more personal than we think?"

It pained him to say it, yet even as he did, Aidan had to admit it felt good to say it to someone. And who better than a family member who did know him and his circumstances? There was no need to recount a messy backstory or sordid history.

Sean knew it all already.

So his cousin's response was both a surprise and oddly comforting.

"I don't see that. I've only met your mother a handful of times, but I don't see any similarity at all."

"Come on, Sean. Think about it. My father acknowledged me and gave me the Colton name, but he's never really been a father to me. My mother got pregnant and ultimately raised a child primarily on her own. Maeve's done the same."

Sean shook his head. "Look, I see it in my work all the time. There are a lot of men who aren't prepared to be fathers, for any number of reasons, most of which are just immature excuses. But regardless of reason, there are a hell of a lot of women who raise children on their own. They don't become psychotic killers."

"So you don't think there's something related to motherhood in all this?"

"To the extent it's an excuse? Yeah, I buy it. Her need to raise Wes and find a way to fund their life. That might have even been how she first excused her behavior or made herself feel better about her actions. But to extent that it's the actual reason? Nope." Sean shook his head again. "That's where I can't make the leap."

"But reason or excuse, the outcome's the same."

"That's where I don't agree. If you need money for your lifestyle so bad and you get a big, rich fish on the hook, why kill him? That money still keeps coming even if you're not in love. That's the real reason I don't see the responsibilities of being a single mother as the reason Maeve's doing this. Why she's made a life at this."

For all he'd looked at the motherhood angle, Aidan hadn't really considered the kills. And now that he did, the last piece fell into place.

It chilled him to the core, but it was also the final confirmation of what they were dealing with.

It was why Ciara wasn't safe.

It was why none of them could rest until Maeve was locked away.

"She loves the kill."

"You bet, cuz. That's why they call women like this black widows. The rich husband is the means to an end."

"And the end is the kill."

"Every damn time."

MAEVE FUMED AS she took the exit off the highway and headed toward the small neighborhood that was her destination. What the hell had Wes done?

All her work. All her efforts to get his sorry ass free of those charges was all for nothing.

Her impetuous, darling boy had ruined everything with a few misplaced words stated in arrogant rage.

I killed Lana Brinkley and there's nothing you morons can do about it!

Anger moved through her in a coiled, seething mass. She'd learned long ago how to handle it, how to manage it.

But now?

Now she was ready to let it off the chain and give that anger its due.

Hadn't she earned that right?

She'd done everything for him. Everything! And this was how he showed his gratitude? Blurting out his guilt in front of a room full of witnesses.

Ungrateful idiot!

She'd expressly hired that shark of a lawyer, Ed Morelli, to keep Wes in line. Yet even that had been a waste of time and money. She'd told him he needed to keep Wes on a short leash, and Morelli had said he understood.

Clearly he hadn't paid enough attention.

Could no one do their job any longer?

That anger burned through her in great, purifying waves as she navigated the small neighborhood. Again, memories of a different time filled her mind as she drove toward one of the few links to her son's childhood.

The lonely boy Wes had befriended and emotionally manipulated had grown into an incredibly accomplished hacker, and Maeve had stroked his ego and his wallet to monstrous proportions to get his help and unwavering support.

She'd yet to find a computer system Ansel Haggerty couldn't get into.

His work with traffic cams was inspired and had given her the final measure of cover she needed to get around unnoticed. He'd already set up the programs to glitch the moment her various license plates registered.

It was amazing.

And all so seamless.

Her added disguises for the cars went the rest of the way toward avoiding any eyes out looking for her.

But it was Ansel's little program that gave her the measure of freedom she needed.

Freedom to do her work and snip every last loose end without those damned Coltons being any wiser.

Humphrey had spoken of them—all those adult children of his old friend. Although she'd kept him well sedated and in a deeply suggestible state, it still hadn't been enough to keep him from mentioning his friend Kieran over and over. And oh, the way the man went on about his friend's children. He spoke of them lovingly and with such pride, and no matter how she'd pressed and cajoled and implemented her hypnotic suggestions, she hadn't fully erased that love and devotion.

The full proof of her failure had come when Humphrey had leaped in front of that bullet intended for Sean Colton.

It was unacceptable.

Maeve O'Leary didn't fail.

Which was why she was ending this.

Wes had already put the nails in his own coffin, and she wasn't wasting another minute on him. Hadn't she wasted enough of her own life worrying over her boy?

A boy who'd proven—endlessly—that he didn't have the maturity or intelligence to grow into a man. He was perfectly content to have Mommy clean up his messes.

Well, no more.

If she could, she'd handle all the Coltons, but that was going to take time she didn't have. Which brought her right back to the plan she'd had all along.

After she snipped all the other loose ends, Humphrey's widow was the last. She'd handle Ciara Kelly and then leave.

She pulled up to Ansel's home, the yard overgrown with weeds that were increasingly choking the broken concrete of the driveway. With a small shudder, she got out of the car and stepped carefully over the long strands of weeds and shards of concrete.

With a quick rap on the front door, she waited, only to be assaulted by the distinct scent of marijuana and an overwhelming stench of stuffy air when Ansel opened the door.

Did the man ever open a window?

"Mrs. W! Come in." His thin face broke into a broad smile across pale, pasty skin that was further proof of closed windows and a life lived almost entirely indoors.

She fought against a visible shudder and followed Ansel into the house. Each of the small rooms was cluttered by food trash, empty dishes and stacks of magazines and books everywhere she looked.

Was this a way to live?

She supposed it was the detritus of a life that had supported hers for a long time, but it still hammered at something so fundamental inside her she felt her knees buckle.

This could have been her life.

It *might* have been, if she'd allowed her squalor and circumstances to dictate who she was and who she'd become.

But she'd wanted something different.

And she'd spent her entire life ensuring she didn't just want, but she actually *had* something different.

Wasn't that the difference between those who were successful and those who weren't? She didn't simply dream about what she wanted.

She *made* what she wanted.

With that thought buoying her spirits, she followed Ansel

into his small office. The window was gray with years of outside dirt and inside smoke from the cigarette butts she saw in an ashtray.

Hell, the whole place was gray.

Dull.

Lifeless.

"I've kept an eye on the feeds. You're clean, Mrs. W. No trace of you on the traffic cams, just like you wanted."

"That's great, Ansel. It's inspired work."

His smile grew even wider. "I work hard. You're one of the few people who appreciate it."

"Oh, I do." She feigned an interest she didn't have. "How are your other clients?"

"None of 'em appreciate me like you do. They don't pay very well, either."

"It's hard to be the favorite, but I try." She smiled broadly as she made the joke and knew the real truth of it was that she paid well over market value for his services and his loyalty.

And it had worked.

He grinned back, waving her over to his desk and the wall of screens covering the surface. Images of highway were visible on the one he directed her to look at. "Right there. I knew you were coming down Route 1, but no one else did." He laughed, the chuckle rapidly turning into a wet, heavy cough.

With a sadness she didn't know she was capable of, Maeve reached for her large bag. "I brought your payment. Your work on this has been outstanding, Ansel."

She pulled the thick envelope out of her purse and laid it on top of a stack of papers on the desk.

Ansel already had the money out of the envelope when she reached back into her bag. He never saw her pull out the gun. It was only when she had it extended, aimed at his head, that the threat registered.

But the lone bullet to his forehead ensured there was nothing he could do about it.

Maeve watched the body fall to the ground, then reached over and gathered the money off the desk. A bit had scattered with the force of Ansel's fall, so she bent and picked up the few bills on the floor before plucking the last twenty out of his dead fingers.

Rising back to her full height, she faced the various screens in the office as well as the large processing unit stored on the floor. With methodical precision, she aimed her gun and fired at the thick metal, emptying her clip into the guts of Ansel's work.

She couldn't hold back a smile of her own.

Let the cops have fun with that one. If they could find anything on the machine, she'd be long gone.

Then they'd know just how badly their systems had been tampered with.

More, they'd know who was really in charge and who had played them every step of the way.

HIS CONVERSATION WITH Sean still haunted him as Aidan let himself into his apartment. The distinct scents of pizza wafted from the direction of the kitchen, along with the excited, high-pitched conversation that he always associated with his Colton cousins.

Sean went directly to Orla the moment they cleared the entrance and left Aidan to stand there and search for Ciara.

She's after the woman you love. I get it. And I get how freaking impossible it is to see straight when you're quaking in fear up to your eyeballs.

Sean's earlier statement—so simple and straightforward—lasered through his mind again.

Had it ever really gone away?

He'd replayed his cousin's comment over and over as they'd followed Maeve's path out of Manhattan and driven around Jersey City evaluating the possibilities of where the woman had gone.

Even with his focus on the work, those words had continued to tumble, over and over, in his mind.

But they became tangible and real when Ciara walked into his line of sight and everything inside him relaxed.

He'd missed her.

And it was that moment that all of it crashed inside him in a wild, raging mix of joy that he'd never felt before.

Was this love?

There'd been something about her, from the very first moment they'd met, that had captivated him. Yes, she was beautiful, with those enticing green eyes, high cheekbones and the firm line of her jaw that drew a man's eye.

But there was more to her than just that heartbreaking beauty.

In the time since, he'd discovered a woman who was fiercely protective of those she loved. Who believed deeply in her own convictions. And who was determined to bring a child into the world with love, acceptance and the deepest commitment to his or her well-being and development.

She was every single thing he wanted in his life, even if he'd never believed in those sorts of feelings or that a depth of commitment like that could possibly be meant for him.

"Aidan." Ciara came up to him, stopping a fair distance before him. The sort of distance maintained by friends or by colleagues.

It wasn't the embrace currently shared by Sean and Orla. Nor was it the casual touching he could see happening between Cormac and Emily across the room.

And he wanted that.

Without checking the impulse, he pulled her close, wrapping her in his embrace and breathing in deeply as her arms went around his waist.

"Aidan." She whispered his name, the warmest of welcomes, and he knew Sean was right.

He *was* in love with this woman.

He had no idea what to do with it, and he wasn't ready to say it—to put those words out in the universe when they were still so new to him—but he also knew he couldn't keep denying what was between them.

What had developed, without any intention on his part or, he was quite sure, on hers, either.

Yet here they were.

And if he had anything to say about it, right here was where they'd stay.

"Did you find anything?" The question drifted up to him from where Ciara's head was pressed to his chest.

"Nothing concrete, but Sean's got questions going with the Jersey City cops. The traffic cams on their side of the tunnel should have registered something, and he's working on running that down."

She raised her head and stared up at him, a knowing smile on her face. "So what you're really telling me is that you spent an hour in traffic to go two miles and turn around and come home."

"Detective work isn't all cops, robbers and high-speed chases."

"You can say that again." Carmine laughed as he came into the living room, his arm slung around Eva's shoulders. "I keep trying to tell our bright-eyed and eager rookie here that very thing."

Eva patted his chest and offered the seasoned detective an indulgent smile. "Then why do you keep dragging me into all the high-impact action, DiRico?"

"Somebody's gotta train you right. That blowhard partner they assigned you to first certainly wasn't going to."

Eva rolled her eyes before taking Carmine's hand and pulling him down next to her on the couch. "Captain Reeves knows what she's doing."

"Up until now, I'd agree with you wholeheartedly. But Mitch Mallard couldn't find his way through an investigation with both hands and a flashlight. I still don't know why the cap partnered you with that dude."

"I think she's testing my mettle."

It was Carmine's turn to roll his eyes. "Then Colleen can consider you battle tested."

Aidan waited until Sean and Orla and Cormac and Emily made their way into the room. Everyone made sure Ciara and Emily were comfortably settled before Sean filled them all in in on their afternoon.

Aidan hadn't wanted to let Ciara go, especially after such an intense personal realization, but he also recognized it was likely for the best. His cousins were watching the two of them closely, and he needed the space to figure out his feelings—*and* to feel ready to share them with Ciara—without an audience keeping tabs.

Besides, they still had a killer to catch.

Cormac had created an electronic version of the case board on his computer, and Aidan helped him set the program up on the TV screen. And as they all sat reading the latest details—Wes's confession and Maeve's disappearance out of the city—Sean filled everyone in on the theories he and Aidan had developed in the drive back and forth to New Jersey.

"It keeps coming back to the disguises, as Ciara keeps saying."

Aidan didn't miss how deliberately Sean had praised her, and it touched him that his cousin was trying so hard to repair their relationship. He'd been rightfully challenging of Ciara at the start of the investigation, but Sean had also done his very best to show that he no longer saw her as a suspect.

"So now we're extending the search to New Jersey?" Eva asked.

"I've let Deirdre know the direction of the case so she can look at this through a federal lens, assuming Maeve is crossing back and forth across state lines. The call to the Jersey City cops was both an olive branch to give them a heads-up and a way to get their cooperation before the feds start nosing around." Sean smiled before shooting Aidan a pointed look. "No offense to your sister, but the feds know how to make local jurisdictions itchy."

Aidan wasn't worried. "Deirdre knows how to handle herself. She also knows how to make nice when she needs to."

A distinct ring went off on Aidan's phone, and he glanced down to see his sister's name flash on screen.

"Speaking of Deirdre."

He answered and recognized immediately this wasn't a friendly phone call.

But it was the details she shared that had him once again acknowledging just how deeply they'd underestimated Maeve.

"You're sure?"

"Yep," Deirdre affirmed. "A guy who delivers dinner every night found the body."

"Well, hell."

Deirdre filled him on a few more pieces and promised to get them more information after she had a call with her boss. But she'd shared enough for Sean to get started on calls.

Aidan disconnected and looked up to see every set of eyes laser-focused on him.

"A victim was discovered in New Jersey, about an hour ago." Aidan thought through his sister's description. "The guy's been on the FBI's watch list for his suspected hacking skills. He's slippery but not fully invisible."

"What do you mean by discovered?" It was Ciara who asked the question, and it pained Aidan to speak the truth, even as he knew he needed to.

"The guy's computers were shot up to hell, rendering them either useless or so badly mangled they'd need quite a bit of time in the lab to be pieced back together."

"What did you mean by victim?" Ciara's voice remained strong, her chin firm with determination.

"The hacker was dead on the floor of his office. A single bullet in his head."

Chapter Fourteen

Ciara kept up a good front but couldn't deny the sigh of relief when everyone finally left Aidan's home around nine. Her conversation with Emily had gone a long way to building up her spirits, but all the talk of death and murder had finally taken its toll.

She got the sense Aidan recognized it first, because he began offering up hints that it was getting late. To everyone's credit, they caught on quickly, but it still couldn't change how dark the discussion had been.

"Do you really think Maeve killed that man?"

Aidan settled the cup of herbal tea he'd prepared for her down on the coffee table before taking a seat beside her. "It's certainly looking like that. Maeve might think she's smart, but the NYPD's electronics division aren't a bunch of slouches. They already had a solid digital fingerprint on those traffic cams and triangulated that the changes came from New Jersey."

"So she's cleaning up."

"In a matter of speaking," Aidan said, seeming to consider his words.

"Which means yes?"

"Yeah."

She reached for her tea, willing the heat from the mug

to seep into her suddenly cold skin. "Aidan, this woman is a monster."

"In every way."

"If she's basically made herself invisible in how she gets around, how will you catch her? Months of efforts and she's remained elusive this long. What's to say she can't do it indefinitely?"

"She won't remain elusive on the traffic cams. The electronics team knows about the problem and is already fixing it."

"So she'll find a new way. Hire someone else to help her."

"She can't do that quickly now, because she underestimated our resources. Our tools. It's a serious mistake and proof that she's misjudged us, which is a major miscalculation."

She wanted to believe him. She wanted that so badly. But the news of the dead man had flipped a switch inside her. She'd worked so hard to remain positive and hopeful. And while she'd faltered here and there, overall she'd managed it.

But this?

Whether Aidan wanted to verbalize it or not, killing the person who provided you anonymity meant something.

It meant Maeve was getting desperate to close out this stage of her life, destroying everything in her path.

Although her overarching focus had been marine creatures, Ciara had studied the animal kingdom for most of her life. She understood the way animals acted in packs and how they acted alone.

And Maeve was a cornered animal, desperate enough to kill whatever got in her way.

With her son's confession today, that could only make things impossibly worse. If Maeve's child had been acting as some sort of grounding force for her, Wes Westmore had effectively destroyed that along with his claims of innocence.

"These past few weeks I feel like I'm in an endless loop of terrifying ideas that, up until now, never had a place in my life. Not in my mind or in my considerations of how the world worked."

"And now?" Aidan asked gently.

"It's all I can think about. In an all-consuming way that's impossible to stop thinking about."

It was only as the words left her that Ciara had a new thought. One that had haunted her more and more over the past few days.

But did she dare give it breath and air?

"Your life has been upended in every way," Aidan said. "I can't tell you how sorry I am or how dedicated we all are to giving you that old life back."

"But don't you see? It's just like what we talked about with Guy Sands. There is no going back. There's the comfort in the moments that I allow myself to believe that the danger and the risks will be handled, but the going back? I can't do that, because my old life no longer exists."

She took a deep breath. One that was for courage and bravery.

All because she was taking a leap toward the unknown, with no net below.

"I want to do something that might give me a feeling of what my new life might hold. After this is over. After the threat has been neutralized."

"I'll help you however I can."

Aidan's expression was so earnest it nearly had Ciara laughing when she considered what she wanted to ask him. Even as she recognized this was one of the most serious moments of her life.

"I want to make love with you, Aidan. But that may be a bit more than you had in mind when you offered your help."

She saw the exact moment her request registered, his dark eyes shifting from the sincere desire to help to a different sort of desire. One laced with heat and awareness and a need that she knew matched her own.

"Ciara, are you sure?"

"Beyond sure." She reached out to take his hand. "I want you. I want to be with you. If you want the same."

"You have to know I do."

"Then let's take it, Aidan. Nothing is assured, and I don't want to lose the chance."

That need in his eyes never abated, but his voice was calm, rational when he spoke.

"I know a lot happened today, on top of some incredibly dangerous moments these past few weeks. I don't want to take advantage of you."

"It's not taking advantage when it's offered freely."

"But these are hardly normal circumstances."

She recognized his deep honor and willingness to do right by her, and she adored him for it. But damn it, what was wrong with the man? She was offering no-strings sex and he was balking?

Which meant it was time to get him to turn his brain off. He had said he wanted to, after all.

Standing, she walked the few steps to where he sat on the love seat that cornered the couch. With careful movements, she climbed onto his lap, her legs straddling his thighs.

"Aidan. I want to have sex with you. Tonight. Now, as a matter of fact. Are you in or out?"

"Ciara—" He hesitated, and for the briefest moment she was convinced he'd put an end to all of it.

And then he placed a hand on the side of her face while the

other rested at the base of her neck, his thumb tracing back and forth over her clavicle as he pulled her close for a kiss.

"I want you."

"Well, thank goodness for that." She smiled against his lips before leaning in fully. Mouths met, tongues clashed and sighs arced between them as the kiss built with mutual need and an intensity she'd never experienced.

Never in her life had she wanted to crawl inside someone's skin, becoming so entwined she had no idea where she started and he ended.

But now?

Now it was all she could *feel*.

There was even a place inside, dimly shouting at her that she should worry about what he'd think when he saw her pregnant belly, but even that couldn't quite get her to stop kissing him. Or roaming her hands over the cords of his neck and the firm play of muscles over his shoulders. Or pressing her breasts into his hands where he palmed her through her T-shirt.

Sparks shot through her at the sensitivity in her breasts. Glorious pleasure filled her, every sense heightened as he touched her and stroked her nipples to tight points. An answering tug pulled at the apex of her thighs. That aching pull throbbed with an insistent drumbeat of need for him.

Had her body ever been this sensitive?

She'd read her pregnancy books and had understood her hormones heightened her emotions, making everything more extreme. How wonderful to realize the books were spot on and those hormones also heightened other things, like pleasure during sex.

She'd assumed it was a pregnancy benefit she'd never get to experience based on her partnership of a marriage, so how amazing to find this now, with Aidan.

"Let's move to the bedroom," he whispered against her lips. "I think we'll be more comfortable there."

She answered by doubling down on the kiss, dueling with his tongue in the most delicious sort of foreplay. But in the end, he won simply by standing, his hold on her absolute as he walked them to the bedroom.

The idea of being carried under any circumstances was marvelous, but to have it happen while pregnant and moving into the stage where she felt ungainly was a tremendous gift. One that, as he gently laid her onto his bed, had tears pooling in her eyes.

"Ciara. Are you okay?" He stopped immediately, stepping away from the bed as if he'd been bitten.

"I'm fine."

"You're not fine. You're crying."

"You carried me."

"Did I hurt you?" She heard the confusion in his voice and recognized the matched emotion in the downward slash of his mouth.

A mouth that still glistened from their kisses.

"Of course you didn't hurt me. You carried me. It was sweet how you did that, and I teared up. I'm emotional, Aidan. And if the past few days haven't convinced you, I cry a lot." She dashed away the few tears that had managed to slip out. "Now would you please get in this bed and make me forget about everything except this driving need to have you?"

She extended her hands to further her point, pleased when he settled a knee on the mattress, then came down over her.

"Far be it from me to argue with a woman who knows her own mind."

"Finally," she said with a smile. "You believe me."

"Oh, I believe you. It's the pregnancy signals I'm having trouble reading."

"Welcome to the club." She pressed a quick kiss to his chin. "And for the record, any tears that might happen in this bed for the next several hours are to be construed as happy tears only."

"I'll keep that in mind."

"See that you do."

And then he pulled her up to a sitting position so they could remove their clothes. Within minutes they were both naked, pressed against each other. The indecision about what he'd think of her growing belly was proved unfounded when he laid a hand over the rounded mound and whispered reverently, "I will keep you safe. I swear on my life."

And then he followed his words with a kiss and Ciara was gone.

Mind.

Heart.

Soul.

With that simple gesture, she saw every good thing that could possibly exist in life and, for the first time in weeks, felt real hope.

Soul-deep hope that things would work out.

And until they did, she was going to take this glorious moment for both of them.

AIDAN SENSED A change in the air as he kissed his way up Ciara's body from that sweet bump of her stomach. The child she carried was between them, and there was something so profound in that.

Something that took his breath.

He'd meant his promise. He would die to keep them safe. It was his job, and he had taken on the responsibility willingly when Ciara was assigned to his protection detail. But now?

Now that responsibility had become a vow. A calling. A mission.

The beautiful woman in his arms writhed under his steady kisses, and he palmed her breasts as he kissed his way over her shoulder. She pressed insistently into his hands, and he used his thumbs against her nipples to work the tight peaks. The light moans that had only built up his own pleasure turned deeper, throatier, as he worked her flesh. But it was the pull on his shoulders, coupled with the husky demands, that reset their pace from leisurely exploration to insistent, tortured need.

"Aidan. I need you. Inside me. Now."

He was hard-pressed to deny this woman anything, but the demands matched his own need, and he reached for the end table to grab a condom.

It was only as he came back, the small foil packet in his fingers, that he caught her lopsided grin.

"I can't exactly get more pregnant."

"I thought… I mean. Well, condoms aren't just for pregnancy prevention," he finished up quietly, hating the suddenly proper notes in his voice.

"I understand that. And I do appreciate the consideration. It just struck me as funny in the moment."

"I'm healthy. I mean, I'm careful and I do make sure I get tested each year at my physical."

"I was fully tested before my pregnancy, so I'm good, too."

It was about the most unsexy conversation he'd ever had, yet it struck him as one more facet of Ciara's straightforward personality and attitude. Real life and honest conversation didn't faze her, nor did she back away from it.

Since old habits died hard, he made quick work of unwrapping the condom and slipping it on. They could talk further about if they needed to use one moving forward after the heat of the moment had passed.

But now?

Now he just wanted her.

With that sole focus spurring him on, he shifted her to her side, slipping a hand between them to stroke all that warm, welcoming heat.

She responded immediately, gentle cries spilling from her lips. And as he felt her fingers tighten against his shoulder, he positioned himself at her entrance, lifting one of her legs up over his hip. He pressed forward, the sweet sheath of her body welcoming him home.

He gave himself a moment, settling into her and giving them both time to adjust to the fit of their bodies. She moved first, shifting her hips so she could take in more of him. And in that acceptance, Aidan began to move. His thrusts were gentle at first, picking up speed as she met his every action with a matched one of her own.

He'd wanted to give her the room to set the pace, but as she spurred them on, driving his body higher and higher with pleasure, Aidan admitted the truth. He was utterly, hopelessly lost to this woman.

Her inner muscles clenched around him mere seconds before his own release overtook him, and Aidan held tight to her as he thrust one last time, his orgasm rushing over him.

This was life.

Racing heartbeats. Pumping lungs. Heavy breaths. And the deepest arcs of pleasure that spun out between them, only to wrap around them both.

Every single moment affirmed the beauty of life.

And as he gathered her close, Aidan knew a deeper truth.

There was nothing he wouldn't do to protect it.

CIARA WALKED BACK into the bedroom wrapped in nothing but a sheet, two plates held high.

"Cold pizza?" he asked as he stared up at her from where he lay stretched out on the bed.

"I can warm yours up in the microwave if you want to be a baby about it."

The sass was back, and Aidan couldn't help but smile as he sat up and took his plate, pressing a hard kiss to her lips as he took the pizza. "Saucy vixen."

"The pizza's saucy. I like to think I'm spicy." She settled herself on the bed beside him, crossing her legs underneath the mile of sheet that wrapped around her midsection.

They ate in companionable silence, the ease bringing back a memory that had him grinning.

"That's quite a smile, Aidan Colton. You look like a cat with a mouthful of canary feathers."

"I just had a funny memory."

"Of?"

"How hard you tried to ignore me the first few weeks we were in the safe house together."

"I was aloof."

"You were deliberately giving me the cold shoulder. There's a difference." He leaned forward to snag her un-eaten crust off her plate. "And you know it."

To her credit, she didn't go down easily. "I was scared and worried, and the last thing I needed was to try and make friends with my captor."

Her captor?

All semblance of teasing vanished. "Did I make you feel that way?"

"*I* made me feel that way," she said, stressing the personal. "It was all me. Trying to understand how I ended up needing to be watched. Why my home suddenly wasn't safe. Why my personal routines weren't, either."

Ciara shook her head. "The only measure of control I had was to take it out on you. I'm sorry for that."

Once again, the woman had managed to upend him with a few well-placed words.

"I didn't know. If I had—" He stopped himself. He wanted to say he'd have done something different, but would he?

If given the chance to go back and do it all over again, would he really have acted any other way?

He was used to being listened to, absolutely. In a protection situation, that acceptance on the part of the person he was watching wasn't simply needed, but it was essential to keeping them safe.

"We sure do a lot of apologizing. Maybe it's time we cut each other a break," Aidan said.

"I'd like that."

"I would, too. Especially because through all this you've helped me understand something." When she only appeared curious at his comment, he continued. "Before our time together, I never gave all that much thought to the people I was guarding. I don't mean that dismissively, but I saw the protection of someone at a difficult time in their life as my job."

"It is your job."

"Yes, but there's a person on the other side dealing with a host of emotions and anxieties that I could be a bit more considerate of."

"Like Guy?"

"Yeah, like Guy."

"I think it's a hard balance. You have to maintain a distance and an air of authority. I might have projected back my anxieties as being aloof and uncaring, but I never doubted your purpose or your work. And I'd imagine getting too close is hard, too."

As she said the words, those wonderfully expressive eyes widened. "Are you going to get in trouble for sleeping with me?"

Aidan hadn't felt this good in a long time. Maybe ever? And there was something in that sudden concern that only added to the lightness. She might be under his protection, but they were grown, unattached adults. He wasn't exactly going to run back to his management and spread the news.

Despite the danger surrounding them and his fear for Ciara and the baby, he couldn't deny there was a completeness inside him he'd never felt before. A sort of bone-deep satisfaction that he wanted to revel in for a while.

But her question, asked with such sincerity, also lightened something through the tension of what they were currently living with.

"Are you going to tell my boss?"

"I'm not telling anyone. I mean, not because I'm not happy about it, but because it's no one's business." She scrunched up her nose before settling her plate on the end table. "Though I'm not sure any Colton is going to believe we're not sleeping together any longer."

"My cousins are discreet. And no one's going to run to my boss."

"Then I guess it's all okay."

"It's all very okay."

He reached forward and tugged on the sheet, pulling her toward him. "Who knew you were such a rule follower?"

"I'm full of surprises." Her hand snaked out, whip quick, and slipped beneath the blanket Aidan had covered himself with out of modesty.

He sucked in a hard breath as she palmed his flesh, his

body already responding to her deft touch. "Maybe you should show me a few."

"Maybe I just will."

She rose up over him, a goddess of beauty and seduction, and Aidan was lost. To her.

And to that incredible magic that seemed to be the very definition of who she was.

CIARA PULLED HER hair up before focusing on the variety of things she'd laid on the counter. Orla had been kind enough to bring food with her the day before, unequivocally stating that a bachelor pad that had stood empty for several weeks wasn't going to be full of any sort of sustenance a pregnant woman needed to keep up her strength.

Which meant she had the makings of poached eggs, avocado toast and fresh fruit.

Aidan walked into the room just as she started peeling the first of two avocados she'd laid out.

"Please don't give me any of that."

"You don't like avocado?"

"Ew." He looked visibly disgusted. "No."

"No guacamole? No avocado toast? No avocado in your turkey wraps?"

"No, no and why would I ever make a turkey wrap, let alone put avocado in it?"

It dawned on her that their time together hadn't exactly revealed these sorts of personal clues.

"What do you normally eat?"

"Steak. Burgers. I have a local Chinese place on speed dial."

"That's not healthy."

He shrugged, nonplussed. "I work out."

"Yeah, but—" She shook her head, well aware she could

hardly poke at the Chinese food based on her neon-pink lunch the other day. But…well…wasn't worrying about someone's health akin to worrying about *them*?

"When all this is over, I'm going to take you out on the water." And if she only put fruit and water in the cooler, then so be it.

"I'd like that. Where do you go?"

"My work takes me all over the harbor and surrounding waterways. The entire region's an estuary, so there's endless marine life to study. But we'll definitely go around Governor's, Ellis and Liberty Islands. I love that part of the harbor for the views."

"I'd like that." He moved in, pulling her close. She set her knife down just as his arms closed around her.

"Me, too."

He bent his head for a kiss, and she raised her lips to receive him. The gesture was so simple, so natural, Ciara nearly marred his shoulders with the remnants of the avocado on her fingers before catching herself, settling her wrists on his shoulders while she kissed him back.

Goodness, she wasn't sure how he did it, but Aidan Colton had the distinct ability to make her forget herself. He was a life force—all consuming, yet not overbearing—and she wasn't sure how she was going to go back to her regular life after this.

Even as she wanted that desperately, she did understand there was a sort of cocoon around them, shielding them from the mundanities of real life. It was such a strange juxtaposition—the daily fear and worry coupled with the odd sort of vacation from life.

Making love with Aidan had only heightened that sense of separation. As if her life existed in two places.

Hovered, really, more than existed at the moment, she mentally corrected herself.

Because she might want things to be different, but until Maeve was caught, she didn't have an old life *or* a new life.

She just had a very large boulder hanging over her head and a woman desperate to cut the last thread keeping it at bay.

Chapter Fifteen

Aidan reviewed the plans for Ciara's safety, considering all angles. The safe house had been compromised, but, so far, he believed his home was functioning well in its place. He'd detected nothing out of the ordinary, and there had been enough cops and law-adjacent folks coming and going to reinforce the fact that none of them appeared to be under surveillance.

Sean had also affirmed that the traffic cameras were almost all back online, so the NYPD electronics team had doubled down on their efforts to keep track of Maeve's return to the city.

A return that could have happened already, Aidan had argued when Sean had recounted the course correction on the cameras.

"She's been able to move freely for nearly twenty-four hours that we know of. And likely days or weeks before that."

"You want to tell me what I don't already know?" Sean had barked the question, but Aidan recognized his cousin's frustration was simply a match for his own.

So he ignored it and fired one more barb. "Any luck finding property with her name or her aliases?"

"Still working on that, too."

The near growl had Aidan ending his line of questions and then the call shortly after.

He'd switched gears to managing Ciara's protection and movements to his own satisfaction and hadn't realized how much time had passed until she came into the kitchen, fully dressed and ready to go.

"My appointment is in less than an hour."

"I know."

"So we need to get going. Operation Baby Doctor needs to kick into high gear."

He'd been pleased to see the marked lightness in her that morning and knew he should have felt the same. Making love had been a revelation, one that still had his body keyed up and relaxed, all at the same time. It was a feeling he would have leaned into under other circumstances, but which was at odds with the somber need to keep her safe.

Especially since he had to take her outside the bubble of his apartment.

"We'll get there on time."

"We will if we leave. Traffic this time of day is totally nuts, and we have to get from nearly one end of the island to the other. We've got to go."

He'd received her list of scheduled appointments as part of the intake process for the marshals but had completely put out of his mind that she had an appointment with her obstetrician. He'd tried getting her to move it, but she'd pressed hard on wanting to keep to her schedule, muttering something about being a geriatric mother that he didn't understand.

"Do you have the phone I issued to you?"

"Of course. I've had it on me since you gave it to me. Thankfully I haven't needed to use it, but I've kept it charged."

The phone had a direct line to the marshals and carried extra layers of tracking and protection should something unexpected happen to her.

"Good. What about the pepper spray I gave you?"

"I've got it. Aidan, come on. Today's an ultrasound day, and I get to find out if I'm having a boy or a girl. Let's please go. I've had to delay the appointment once already because it was the same day as my intake to the safe house, but I'm not missing it again."

Since arguing was not only futile but unfair in the extreme—she had made sacrifices, and she also needed to have proper medical care—they headed out. He'd prearranged with building security to have the elevator avoid stopping on any other floors, and they took the car down to his building's underground parking garage.

"Excellent work, Marshal Colton." She gave him a jaunty salute he caught out of the corner of his eye as he turned onto West Street.

He couldn't hold back the smile. "Your support is appreciated, Ms. Kelly."

They talked casually on their way to her appointment, the traffic she'd predicted keeping them moving at a sedate pace as they worked their way steadily uptown.

"Does it hurt?"

"The ultrasound? Not at all. The gel they use is cold when they first apply it to the skin, but it's not painful."

She explained a bit more about the images she'd seen to date.

"You're supposed to be able to see the sex at twenty weeks. A lot of people say even earlier, but nineteen to twenty weeks is supposed to be definite. And I'm two weeks after that because we had to reschedule my appointment."

"Do you have a preference?"

"Not at all, but I am so curious. I know there are people who want to wait, and more power to them, but I'm all about finding out so I can get going on the shopping and the nursery and all that fun stuff."

After the bleakness of the past few days, it was special to see how excited she was about the baby and all that was to come. Whether she recognized it or not, talking about decorating the nursery and buying baby clothes carried the distinct notes of hope.

A focus on the future.

And a belief that there was a wonderful one waiting for her and her child.

Unable to hold back the impulse, he reached out and linked his hand with hers. The past few hours, since they'd gotten out of bed, had given him a lot of time to think.

Last night with Ciara had been amazing, and while he'd initially worried he was taking advantage of her, it was hard to look at the night they'd shared and see it as anything but the right decision. Yes, they were attracted to each other. And they had chemistry.

Even as he knew he wouldn't go back and change it if he could, he'd committed to doubling down once more on the work this morning. She was in his professional care, and the risks if he lost his focus were extreme.

Yet when she tightened her fingers around his, that simple connection conveying all the things they hadn't said to each other, he savored her touch and all it meant.

Comfort.

Support.

Care.

"I know our circumstances are pretty terrible right now. But I need to say something before I don't have the courage to any longer."

He glanced over, taking advantage of the fact that the light they were stopped at was still red. "You don't need courage to talk to me. You can tell me anything, Ciara."

"I know, but—" She took a heavy breath. "Our circumstances aren't normal. Having to basically have an armed check of my surroundings before going to a doctor's appointment isn't normal."

"No, it's not."

"But I want you to know, no matter how not normal it is, I wouldn't change a single moment of what brought us to last night."

Something soft and warm unfurled in the depths of his chest at her confession. It was only the sudden honking from the car behind him that shifted his attention to the green light. Even with the interruption, Aidan felt her words like a bomb had exploded in his chest.

Whatever he'd expected when he'd taken on the job to guard Ciara, never had it crossed his mind that he'd experience something so life altering *and* life affirming.

Although the very real danger in their lives still existed outside the car windows, he took a moment to lift her hand to his lips, pressing a kiss to smooth skin.

"I wouldn't change anything, either."

CIARA'S DOCTOR HAD moved from a small suite of offices near the American Museum of Natural History to a bigger practice on one of the large hospital campuses that dotted the Upper West Side. She appreciated the number of services available all in one place, but it never failed to amaze her just how large the city's hospital complexes were.

This one spanned more than three blocks and seemed like a small city unto itself. With the number of people moving around, coming and going through a variety of exits marked with various instructions—check in, check out, emergency— as well as additional signs for radiology, labor and delivery, and intensive care, it was a hive of activity.

Oddly, she felt safe here. The volume of people was a strange sort of comfort in the midst of a decidedly unsafe time.

Aidan found parking and, per their usual routine, she waited until he came around to help her out of the car. Although she could still move relatively freely, she mentally thought about the coming days when getting in and out of the car was going to prove more challenging as her pregnancy continued.

"What's that smile for?"

"I was thinking how concerned you are for me now, but I can still move fairly well and I can get myself in and out of a car. In a few more months, when I'm at whale-size proportions, I'm going to need a lot of assistance."

"Then I'll still help you. In the meantime, stay between me and the cars as we head to the door."

Ciara did as he asked, sort of gobsmacked at his inference he'd still be around in a few months. Especially because he seemed oblivious to what he'd just said.

Or rather, the suggestion beneath what he just said.

Would he be helping her because Maeve wasn't caught? Or because he'd be there, helping her even *after* Maeve was caught?

And why did that thought—especially one that came with a Maeve-free future—ignite such a sharp longing inside her?

Yes, they'd made love. And while she had the fondest wish to do it again, she was a grown woman. She wasn't about to make the mistake that sex between two single, consenting adults suddenly meant forever.

But oh, to have him in her life. Especially after all the pain and sadness of Maeve's continued crimes had become a thing of the past.

The thought filled her with a lightness and a sense of hope that had been sorely lacking for some time now.

"You will never be a whale," Aidan said as he helped her from the car. "But you will always be beautiful."

"Dude, way to make it hard for the rest of us, saying gooey crap like that."

Aidan turned quickly to the young couple currently passing by the parked car, his attention on high alert at the sudden intrusion. But the young man helping his very pregnant partner through the parking lot wasn't a threat.

Not even close, Ciara thought, smiling at the young man's clearly bewildered look.

"I think we're safe. No danger lurking about."

Ciara's sentiment was reinforced when the very pregnant half of the couple quickly admonished her partner in return with a "you could take a lesson or two."

"Ah, young love," Ciara whispered for only Aidan to hear, pleased when the joke was enough to chase the last bit of tension from his gaze.

They followed the same winding path through the parking lot toward the bank of elevators. The young couple had already gotten into one of the other cars, and it gave them the continued privacy Aidan sought in public places.

"Do you think I say gooey crap?"

Ciara batted her eyelashes as the elevator doors swished closed. "I think you say lovely crap. There's a big difference in my book."

He just grinned at that, reaching for her hand once more. "I'm a world champion sweet talker, what can I say."

They rode the rest of the way in silence, a calm quiet settling over them, and she was pleased to see Aidan seemed to have relaxed with the banter. Oh, his gaze remained alert and his body held a ready sort of stiffness, but there was also a calmer, more focused feeling to him.

He was ready for action while also settling into his surroundings.

They'd made it through the drive and the parking and they had the last few floors to get to her doctor's office. As the numbers on the elevator escalated, one by one, Ciara felt herself calming with the ride.

With Aidan's large hand holding hers.

And with the mounting excitement that she'd soon see her child on the ultrasound.

These were good moments. Happy ones she wanted to breathe in deeply.

The elevator doors swung open, and Aidan stepped through first, scanning the lobby before gesturing her out. They walked the long corridor from the parking garage lobby toward the bay of elevators that went to the doctors' offices. Bright June sunlight filled the corridor, and Ciara reveled in the warmth of the hallway under the sun.

It felt like this when she was out with her students, their boat moving through the water and the sun beating down to warm all of them on deck. She could even smell the salt water, the sense memory a vivid reminder of how much she missed teaching her summer class.

Ciara turned toward Aidan to tell him about the memory, further reinforcement for why she wanted to take him out on the boat, when she caught movement outside the wall of glass windows.

And screamed when she saw a woman lift a gun, the windows shattering as three bullets punctured the glass.

AIDAN GATHERED CIARA CLOSE, rushing her to the ground and covering her with his body. Screams erupted through the halls as more bullets hit the glass, and Aidan was torn between the desperate need to keep her covered and protected and the raging urgency to chase after the shooter.

Maeve.

Every fiber of his being screamed with certainty that the woman was standing on the other side of the glass with a gun.

Since he refused to leave Ciara, Aidan could only hope she'd arrogantly miscalculated the sheer number of officers surrounding the hospital complex who'd ensure she was captured.

But he'd worry about that later.

With Ciara his sole focus, he shifted so that she could take full, deep breaths without his heavy weight on her.

"We need to get out of here, Aidan. You're wide-open. You're—" The rising tone of her voice suggested a certain level of shock, and he tightened his hold on her, willing as much warmth and comfort into her body as he could.

"The shooting has stopped. We're okay."

"We're not okay. She's out there. She knew. How did she know where we were?"

The words spilled out in a frantic litany, and Aidan did his best to just let her talk it out. To let that racing adrenaline pump through her system and burn itself out.

Wasn't he feeling much of the same?

He'd had a long time to learn to deal with it in his line of work, but he understood that hard jangle of nerves and the rushing energy that coursed through the body, unabated.

But Ciara was right.

How did Maeve know?

He'd kept close watch on the drive from his home, and they hadn't had a tail. He'd scanned the parking garage on every level as well as once they walked to the elevators and, once again, the space had been free of threats.

Yet right there, through the large decorative windows that made up the hospital hallway, the woman had been waiting.

She hadn't even concerned herself with the number of people around or the significant presence of security guards and cops. A city hospital was the epicenter of a lot of activity, often stressed, and the NYPD always kept officers stationed there.

Would this miscalculation finally be the end of her?

The volume of police presence had to be enough to stop the threat that was Maeve O'Leary.

He was banking on that as he helped Ciara to her feet and then rapidly out of the windowed hallway. The cops had quickly set up a makeshift intake area near the front entrance, and Aidan brought her there, settling her in a chair with her back against the wall.

His phone rang before he could even turn to talk to any of the assembled cops and introduce himself. He quickly answered, finding Sean on the other end of the line.

"The call came into the precinct a few minutes ago. I figured there was no way a shooting at Ciara's hospital wasn't tied to Maeve."

"You figured right." Aidan heard the grim notes in his own voice, a match for the anger and frustration still rattling through him. "The windowed tunnel between the parking garage and the main hospital elevators. Bitch was standing outside the windows and took shots at Ciara the moment she came into view."

"Damn it. This isn't just escalation, it's damn near suicide."

"I don't know that she cares any longer, Sean. Any methodical thinking she may have been known for in the past is gone. These are the actions of a cornered animal."

Hadn't that been his real concern as he'd worked on Ciara's security duty this morning? The risks weren't just about mapping out safe routes and prevetting safety protocols. The problem they now faced was a determined adversary who wasn't following any sort of plan.

Sean asked a few more questions before promising to come straight to the hospital and then disconnected the call. Aidan dropped his phone into his pocket and took the seat next to Ciara.

"That was Sean?" Her voice was dull, and those wonderful green eyes were dimmed with the impact of all that had happened.

"The news was all over the precinct, and he quickly made the connection. He's on his way."

"Good. That's good."

It *was* good, but the flat way she said it had Aidan thinking of those moments in the car. Her excitement about decorating the nursery and buying baby clothes had vanished, ruined once more by the actions of a madwoman.

He'd been angry up to now. It was hard not to be when a threat remained so crafty and so elusive. But in that dull haze that had settled over Ciara, muting the sheer life that spilled out of her on a regular basis, Aidan's anger turned to a sort of raw fury he'd never felt before.

How was it possible Maeve had taken so much?

He'd seen it with his sister, the reality of Micah's father's death no longer a suspicion but fact. Maeve had killed the man in cold blood to get his money.

Along with that, he had the stories Carmine and Eva had shared after they'd gone undercover about Orrin Westmore's late brother, also killed at Maeve's hand.

And then there was her son, Wes, and his disregard for the life of his girlfriend.

These people were cold, soulless killers, and they had little care for anyone who got in their way.

All of it was awful, but somewhere in it he'd also recognized something of a means to an end. They were soulless, yes, but these were also selfish acts designed to advance their own wealth, power and position.

But with Ciara something was different.

She wasn't a wealthy husband to steal from or a sexy girlfriend who'd outlived her usefulness.

Ciara was a target.

And object of anger and crazed frustration who had no real role in this other than her quiet marriage.

Humphrey had been targeted for his profession and his wealth, but Ciara was outside all that.

Until she wasn't.

Not in Maeve's eyes.

It burned in Aidan's gut as he desperately tried to channel his anger.

Fury had no place in this if it tripped him up and caused him to lose focus. But it had plenty of place if he could work it to his advantage.

A pair of cops came back through the hospital doors, and he confirmed with Ciara he was going to go speak with them. The volume of police presence inside the cordoned-off lobby ensured she'd be safe, and he needed to know what had happened.

Had they caught Maeve?

Was she, even now, on the ground with a horde of cops surrounding her?

He pulled out his badge and introduced himself while quickly bringing the officers up to speed. He also dropped Sean's name, letting them know the well-known detective was on his way.

"Do you have her in custody?"

"No." The larger of the two men shook his head. "One

of the rooks chased her for several blocks, but she'd clearly mapped out a plan. He lost her around the back of the hospital. He thought he might have seen someone zigzagging through the intersection another block down but realized it was just a runner keeping pace with the traffic lights."

"Where was this?"

Aidan listened as they shared what they knew, and once again, the ongoing discussion of disguise struck him.

He'd run it by Sean, but he suspected when they looked at the security cams around the hospital just before the shooting, they'd see a heavier woman, likely due to several layers of clothing.

Clothing that she no doubt stripped off as she made her getaway.

Costume changes that would give just enough alteration to her appearance to anyone chasing her to catch them off guard.

He pointed to where Ciara sat huddled on a chair. The bleak expression that had covered her face hadn't changed since he'd helped her into the chair, and he was increasingly afraid there was no way to erase it.

Especially if Maeve was still on the loose.

"That woman is the target of the shooter. We need to get her to a more secure location."

"We'll find you one."

True to their word, the cops were back in a matter of moments, gesturing Aidan from across the lobby to follow them.

He helped Ciara to her feet, his hold on her secure as they made their way to the two officers.

"We're going to settle into a safer place until Sean gets here. Then we'll call your doctor and see if they can come take a look at you."

"I'm fine, Aidan."

"Humor me."

They followed the cops to a small office off the main security room, and he was pleased to see there were no exterior windows in the small conference room. Was even more pleased to see they had to walk past five security specialists to get in the room.

He settled her into one of the chairs, and before he could even ask, one of the security specialists was bringing in bottled water and a few prepackaged snacks.

"Sean will be here soon."

"It doesn't matter."

"Why do you say that? Of course it matters."

Ciara stared at the wall across the office, never meeting his eyes. It was that empty gaze that finally pushed him to take a seat beside her, laying a hand over hers. "Come on, Ciara. What do you mean?"

"She's out there. In the wind, yet again. She had this planned. Methodically. Purposefully. And, clearly," Ciara said on a hard laugh, "Perfectly."

"We'll get her. She didn't do this perfectly. She got caught on camera and she put herself out in the open."

The hand beneath his was cold, nearly lifeless, but it was that unseeing stare that frightened Aidan the most. "She's not going to stop, Aidan."

"That's why we're going to take care of her and put her away."

"She won't stop until I'm dead."

Chapter Sixteen

A tight fist wrapped around Aidan's gut, an ever-tightening vise. "How the hell did she get past what had to be at least thirty cops?"

Sean had joined Aidan in front of the wall of cameras in the main security area. Eva and Orla had arrived along with him, and both were now sitting with Ciara inside the small, windowless conference room.

Aidan hoped the presence of the women would be a calming force, but the few times he'd peeked through the open door, all he saw was that continued bleak stare. Which only made that vise grip stronger.

"I don't know." Sean shook his head, the man's frustration and anger evident in the tight set of his shoulders. "We've got good cops all over the city, but the ones on duty here train for special circumstances. Hospitals bring out challenging behavior in people, and the officers on medical assignment are equipped to handle out-of-the ordinary situations."

"Isn't that police work in a nutshell?"

"Maybe," Sean acknowledged, "but consider this place a special brand of extra when it comes to human behavior."

They'd spent the better part of an hour running through video from various camera angles around the hospital. They'd zeroed in on Maeve quickly before the gunshots, both in her strange unwillingness to hide herself from the cameras as well as the fact that Aidan had gotten eyes on her and the disguise she was using when she made the shots.

They'd then followed her around the hospital grounds, across several cameras.

And then the images went cold as they just lost her. From one camera where they could see her to the very next one where she was gone, it was once again like the woman had vanished.

Sean had requested—and gotten—the agreement to bring in a team of electronics experts, and even now the small group was setting up. Conversation ran fast and hot between the hospital's existing security unit and the e-squad, with words like *algorithm*, *facial recognition* and a host of AI references batted back and forth by both teams.

Aidan caught about every third word and figured that was a positive note in their favor. Anyone who could not just decipher but engage in what they were talking about had to be good at their job.

Or at least he hoped so.

With their attention occupied on reviewing the abundance of detail captured on the hundreds of cameras positioned around the hospital, Aidan walked back into the conference room. Eva and Orla made quiet goodbyes and excused themselves, leaving him and Ciara alone.

"How are you doing?"

Her doctor had come down earlier and sat with her for a while, determining after a cursory examination that Ciara and the baby were fine. The woman also rescheduled Ciara's appointment for two days later and pronounced mother and baby in good health.

"I can't live like this, Aidan."

The words were quiet, barely audible, yet Aidan heard her as easily as if she'd used a bullhorn.

"It'll only be a little while longer. I just need you to hang on a few more days."

"I can't."

"You can and you will."

It was harsh truth, but there was nothing to be done about it. And while he felt for her and her situation, he'd be damned if they'd come this far to suddenly shut down when Maeve was nearly in their grasp.

"I saw her face. I saw the sheer hatred she has for me. It's twisted her into something monstrous. She stared right at me and aimed shots at me with something like glee in her eyes. I can't—" She crumpled in the chair. "I just can't."

Up to now, each time the stress had gotten overwhelming for her, he'd seen the tears form, falling readily. He'd felt helpless in those moments, yet he'd also understood the tears had provided her the relief of stress, tension and the sometimes overwhelming changes currently happening in her body.

But just like that bleak, aimless stare, the lack of emotion or tears right now had Aidan far more worried than a good crying session ever could.

So he did his best and tried to find the words that would break through that overwhelming sense of emptiness.

"You've come so far, Ciara. All you've worked for up to now. Your job. Your care for your mother in her darkest days. Your willingness to help and do right by Humphrey, even in the face of scrutiny and judgment."

He reached out and gently stroked her cheek.

"And now the baby. Your excitement in bringing life into the world. In being a mother. You've done all that all by yourself. You're so strong. Don't give her one single moment of doubt or let her take that away from you."

"But don't you see? She's taken it all from me already."

"No, she hasn't. Don't say that. Don't think it. She's on the run with an entire city's vast police force looking for her, and you're alive. You've got a team of people around you who will stop at nothing to keep you and the baby safe. She hasn't won, Ciara. You have. You're the one who is on to her. Who's understood her use of disguise. Who's helped find the answers that will put her away."

"With all those resources, she's still managed to vanish."

"For the moment. Because she's planned this and created a temporary getaway for herself. But she can't run forever. The team's found the street camera problem and fixed it. We understand her use of disguise and are looking at her whereabouts with more precision and a better understanding of how to track her."

He had no idea if he was getting through, but he had to believe some way, somehow, she understood what he was saying.

What he truly believed.

They'd come so far, and failing simply wasn't an option. They were much too close to give up now.

A flurry of excitement echoed outside the door, and Eva peeked her head into the conference room. "Come here. You guys need to see this."

He glanced at Ciara, and she nodded, bracing her hands on the arms of her chair to stand. He quickly reached for her and helped her up, wrapping his arm around her as he did. Although he hadn't cared all that much up to now, he no longer had any concern what his family thought. No one seemed to think anything of the budding relationship with Ciara, anyway, and he wasn't going to keep some facade of distance between them when what she really needed was his support and care.

So he kept his arm tight around her as the two of them walked to the outer office. The wall of screens had paused images all over them, time stamps evident in the corners.

"We have her latest disguise," Sean said, triumphant.

Aidan followed the screens, one by one, from the twisted woman with a gun aimed at the corridor windows to the way she transformed as she raced around the perimeter of the hospital. The shedding of the outer track suit she wore, followed by a wig, followed by what looked to be a chin prosthetic. Each camera image provided a new view to Maeve O'Leary.

But it was the last image, of a different hairstyle, a filmy blouse and slacks, that matched what the electronics team had pulled up on their computers. One of the electronics guys pointed to his screen. "That's a street camera three blocks from the hospital."

And, there on Maeve's shoulder, just as Cormac had predicted, was an oversize bag.

They weren't going to find any elements of the disguise she'd shed on the move in trash cans or tossed off into street corners. She was methodically shoving each costume change into her bag, holding it all close to avoid one more bit of detection.

One more place where her DNA might be discovered.

But now they knew what they were looking for.

And there was no way she could run much longer.

CIARA STARED AT the wall of screens and quietly marveled at the exhaustive technology. That overwhelming sense of hopelessness she hadn't been able to fully shed since the shooting still filled her, but she couldn't deny the incredible detail of what she was looking at.

The sheer power of the work and the technological infrastructure that made it possible.

She lived in a major world city and understood her movements were always being captured somewhere. From street cameras to ones in stores to the constant image capture they'd all become somewhat ignorant of, she abstractly knew she was always on camera somewhere.

But this?

The volume and magnitude of a person's movements—of what could be pieced together—was incredible.

"Cops are already dispatched uptown," Sean said. Even with the precise focus and grave demeanor she'd always sensed in him, Ciara could sense the excitement in him, too.

They were close.

And they all wanted this done.

Could she believe in that promise? She didn't doubt the commitment—of Aidan or any of his Colton cousins or the other police, for that matter—but she also didn't doubt Maeve's equally deep commitment.

The woman had a goal, and she'd proven that she was nothing if not goal oriented. When she set her sights and focus on something, she played to win.

And when the game was killing, it was an all-or-nothing sort of outcome.

She'd succeeded this long. Years' worth of plots and plans, disguises and dead husbands.

Did they really have the means to stop her now?

Humphrey hadn't. For all his skill and talent and understanding of the human mind, he'd been as much a victim of her as all the men who'd come before.

Aidan's phone rang, and she saw his face brighten before he answered. "Deirdre."

She abstractly heard him bring his sister up to speed on the day's events before genuine surprise lightened his voice. "You're here?"

He spoke with her for a few more minutes before they all moved back into the conference room for a family discussion.

"Your sister's in town?" Sean asked the moment they were seated.

"The FBI called her back in. She's agreed to stay on for a while supporting the field office up in Wyoming, but they wanted her back to close out this case. She's spent a lot of time studying Maeve, and they want her support."

"Bureau's still really pissed about those traffic cameras," Sean affirmed before adding a smile. "Our tech team's not real happy about it, either. But it's got a lot of cross-jurisdictional infighting flaring up."

"And here I thought everyone knew how to play nice," Orla said with a wicked smile.

Despite herself and the events of the day, Ciara was reluctantly fascinated by the discussion.

"I'm not sure if *nice* is quite the right word," Aidan added, "but tensions do flare high and hot when things go wrong across jurisdictional lines. I've been on that firing squad a few times myself."

"Deirdre will handle it," Eva said. "She's got the mettle to manage her own work and the sweetness to smooth the way."

"Sweet?" Aidan asked.

Other than the videoconference with Derek, Ciara didn't know Aidan's sister. But she heard the clear skepticism in his tone. For some reason, it was enough to have her defending the woman. "Your sister seemed lovely on our video call. And she's in love with that baby in every way."

"My sister *is* lovely. For a highly trained federal agent. She's sort of like a shark."

"Your sister?" Ciara clarified.

"The same," Aidan affirmed. "She always looks like she's smiling—until you see the teeth."

CIARA THOUGHT THE shark reference was highly misplaced as she, Aidan and Deirdre sat around the living room several hours later. Deirdre had spent the better part of the evening at Bureau headquarters working on the feds' approach to taking down Maeve and had arrived a short while before.

"Can I get you anything else?" Aidan asked.

"Aidan, would you please sit down?" Deirdre asked, waving at her brother.

He finally did as she asked, and Ciara couldn't quite hide her enjoyment at the byplay between the siblings. Where she'd observed high energy and a lot of shouting between Sean, Liam, Cormac and Eva, Deirdre and Aidan had a more subtle sort of chemistry.

One that, if she'd pieced together Aidan's comments up to now correctly, had only recently blossomed.

Because of it, she sensed deep care yet an underlying veneer of reticence in their interactions.

What she'd also gotten—quite clearly—was that Maeve O'Leary was public enemy number one.

"That hospital stunt today was a miscalculation," Deirdre started in. "I understand your life was on the line, Ciara, so I don't say that to be clinical or heartless, but as far as the woman's tactical warfare, it was a bad approach. And it reinforces our continued belief that she's had a full psychotic break."

Although she understood the magnitude, it was hard to reconcile this behavior with Maeve's past actions. From Humphrey's kidnapping nearly six months ago to Micah's father's murder fifteen years ago, none of it seemed very rational. Or *not* psychotic, as it were.

"Up to now all her behavior was considered stable?"

"I'm focused on the clinical definition. While society wouldn't look at all she's done as stable, her personality remained in equilibrium. She set goals, and she accomplished those goals. So her own sense of self and personal satisfaction remained in place."

"Now she's been thwarted."

"Exactly. She's not used to making mistakes or failing at anything. So when you layer on the loss of Humphrey because he took the bullet for Sean, her failure to remove you as a threat and the added failure of her son's trial, you've got an extremely dangerous shift taking place."

"Something foundational," Ciara murmured.

"Exactly."

"And you're playing nice with Sean's team?" Aidan pressed.

"I always play nice."

At the flash of teeth Ciara couldn't help but think of the shark comment earlier. And she found that there was a measure of truth to it all.

Deirdre cut an impressive figure. She was highly competent, and Ciara didn't doubt that the woman avoided failure as stridently as Maeve did.

Which added one more facet to the equation.

"So if the FBI's got a plan in place and Sean's got the cops working on a plan and all the cameras are now in sync for everyone to follow her, who gets to take her down?"

That grin flashed once more. "Whoever gets there first."

SEAN TAPPED LIGHTLY on Ciara's door. He'd given his sister his bedroom and had every intention of sleeping on the couch, but he did want to check on Ciara before he bedded down for the night.

For all his concern about Ciara's ability to comfortably take in what was happening, Deirdre's straightforward discussion and recounting of the approach to capturing Maeve had seemed to lighten her concerns. That dullness that had bothered him all afternoon hadn't fully faded, but he had seen sparks of interest and moments of ease while his sister had shared her work.

"Come in!"

He opened the door to find her propped up in bed, her laptop open and positioned on her thighs. Her pregnancy was obvious through her nightgown, and Aidan wondered how he'd managed to live with the woman for twelve days and not know.

It was hard to see her as anything *but* pregnant now.

"I wanted to make sure you were okay. See if I can get you anything."

"Deirdre looks exhausted." She waved him in. "Close the door so we don't disturb her."

His sister *was* tired, her 6:00 a.m. flight on the FBI jet coming after an extensive briefing session the night before. By Deirdre's recounting, those meetings were all tied to the embarrassment of the traffic cameras and the Bureau's intention to build an op to take Maeve down. And all those plans were before the incident at the hospital, which had only added to this afternoon's exhaustive planning session.

"She's doing her best, but there's always an additional layer of pressure when the top brass has egg on their face."

"That's a backward-looking reaction."

"It doesn't make it any less true. Besides," Aidan added, taking a seat on the edge of the bed, "they were already reeling from the amount of time it took to find Humphrey at all. Prominent people get real twitchy when other prominent people disappear and the law enforcement community can't find them."

"I can see where that would be hard."

"And the cross-jurisdictional thing I mentioned isn't easy, either. New York has a lot of politics already, both with being such a large city as well as how tied it is to another state right across a narrow body of water. So there's a lot of city, state and federal overlap here anyway."

"That's a lot to navigate in your day-to-day work."

"It is. But it also means a level of focus and, by extension, safety here for residents. There are a lot of highly qualified eyes all looking at the same information. All working toward the same outcomes."

"Catching Maeve."

"Maeve and a whole host of bad people who should be locked up."

"I do get that. I know my reaction earlier suggested otherwise, but I do get how much work and effort and sheer determination is happening around me."

"But that doesn't make any of it easy."

"No." She shook her head before she snapped the laptop closed, settling the slim device on the bedside table.

Extending her hand, she reached for his, fitting their palms together.

"I can't change how I feel, but I can tell you that I believe you when you say you'll catch her. That she's facing a cage any day now. It's an outcome I'll relish."

"Me, too."

"In the meantime, please stay. Tonight. Hold me and don't let me go."

He nodded, a tight lump forming in his throat.

This woman had given him everything. Her trust, her belief, her body—every bit of it was his, and he had never held anything more precious.

Climbing fully onto the bed, he nestled his body against hers, curving around her. He wrapped an arm just below her baby bump and then laid a large hand over that growing swell.

This might be for her—for her emotional well-being and

sense of safety—but as her breathing evened out and her body grew slack beneath his touch, Aidan knew there was more to it.

This moment was for him, too.

He needed to hold her just as much as she needed to be held.

He had a desperate, aching need to feel—way down deep inside—that she was safe.

CIARA HADN'T FULLY regained her equilibrium, but as she hovered over the kitchen counter making her avocado toast, she smiled. At the easy comfort of the meal and at the funny memory of Aidan's recounting of his food preferences, avocado most certainly not on that list.

It had been two days since the attempt on her life. Deirdre had stayed with them that first night and then had transferred to a Bureau location as they finalized their plans for the op. With the facial recognition software reprogrammed to account for Maeve's variety of disguises, the NYPD had found a lot more evidence of her movements.

They'd nearly captured her the prior afternoon but had missed her by what had to be less than two minutes.

But it was the triangulation of Eva's work searching for her potential homes, the patterns pulled off the street cameras and the FBI's digging into the hacker's life's work that ultimately pulled it all together.

Deirdre had been part of a raid just before 8:00 a.m. on what they believed was Maeve's New York address.

Ciara wouldn't fully breathe easy until this was all over, but for the first time since the shooting in the hospital, she felt those glimmers of hope shimmering back to life.

They'd found Maeve O'Leary, and they were taking her down.

In the meantime, Aidan had been hard at work building out

the plans for her second trip to the doctor. She still needed her full prenatal exam, and the doctor had provided a different location in the city, much closer to Aidan's apartment, to do the appointment and ultrasound. The practice had bent over backward to comfort her and accommodate her, and Ciara was beyond grateful.

Even with the upset at the hospital a few days ago, she couldn't fully tamp down her excitement. The quiet time she'd spent with Aidan had helped, as had nesting in the apartment for a few days recentering herself.

And now today had finally come.

She'd learn if she was having a girl or a boy. Even more exciting, she'd see her child on the ultrasound, safe and warm inside her yet growing and changing every day.

Wasn't that the true miracle?

For all that was happening in the world around her, her child remained safe inside.

The temptation to stay in Aidan's apartment was strong, but her commitment to the baby's health was absolute. And it bothered her that she was nearly three weeks late having this appointment. Ultrasound images aside, she wanted the reassurance her pregnancy was progressing as it should.

Aidan had remained concerned about having her go out in the open, but with the change in her doctor's office location from uptown to an address about seven blocks from his home, he'd calmed down. He'd also ensured two officers were posted on the building to further support their departure to the appointment through to their arrival back home.

He came into the kitchen just as his phone went off, Deirdre's special ringtone echoing from his pocket.

"You get her?"

Ciara didn't miss the excitement or the bright light in his eyes, only to see both dim immediately.

"What? Who is this? What happened?"

Ciara watched him closely, the color leaching from his face as he took in a few more details. "But she's okay?"

The voice on the other side was too low for her to hear all the words, but she got enough to know that Deirdre had been injured.

"I'll be there."

Aidan hung up, his dark gaze filled with pain.

"What happened?"

"It's about Deirdre. That was one of her colleagues. She took a nasty hit to the head. She's in observation and—"

He broke off, and Ciara moved to pull him close, her arms wrapping around his waist. "Go see her."

"I need to take you to the doctor."

"There are two police officers downstairs who are going to take me the seven blocks to the doctor's office."

"But I can go after."

"You can go now, especially since Micah isn't here. And I'm going seven blocks, Aidan. With officers you've briefed personally."

She pulled back and looked up at him. "Seven blocks, Aidan. I could run it in three minutes, even in my current condition. But I have an armed police escort there and back. Go. Your sister needs you."

"She's receiving care. But…"

That last bit of hesitation filled his voice, but Ciara pressed on. "You need her, too. Go."

Aidan called down to the cops positioned downstairs and seemed pleased with the report they shared, even if Ciara figured they were rolling their eyes at his overzealous planning for seven blocks.

But it was worth it to see Aidan calm a bit. "They've been

down there all morning. Nothing out of the ordinary, and they're ready and waiting for your call."

"Please go, then. I'll call them when I'm done cleaning up, and I won't make any moves to leave the apartment until one of them arrives as planned. I'll be careful, Aidan."

He leaned in and pressed a hard kiss to her mouth. She opened under that firm press of lips, their kiss as much about comfort as attraction. And then she stepped back, smiling up at him. "Go take care of your sister. Tell her I'm thinking of her."

In just a few moments he was gone, and she finished her breakfast, then cleaned up the kitchen and got herself ready. The tenderness that had only grown between them over the past few days filled her with that pervasive sense of calm, and she floated through getting ready before calling the cops downstairs.

At the confirmation the one named Tom would come get her, she settled in to wait by the door, double-checking she had remembered everything in her bag. Her cell phone and the one issued by the marshals were tucked in the front pocket of her purse, and she had her insurance card in her wallet.

She was ready.

And in a matter of minutes, she'd be seeing her child.

The knock on the door pulled her from the happy thought, and she followed the protocol Aidan had taught her. "Name and badge number?"

When Tom rattled off the exact numbers Aidan had written on a notepad *and* looked through the peephole exactly like the man she'd met the day before, she exited the apartment.

"Ms. Kelly?" He smiled at her. "You ready?"

"Absolutely."

Tom managed their movement through the building and, just like Aidan, shielded her body as they walked. They had the elevator to themselves and then were moving through the lobby and out to the car. She saw the black SUV at the corner, and Tom pointed it out as their destination. He helped her up into the back seat before closing the door. It was only as the door snicked closed that everything changed.

A heavy "ooof" echoed from the other side of the door, and as she looked through the window, she saw Tom fall to the ground.

Reaching for her door handle, she was determined to help him when she heard and felt the resistance, the door locked firm. And then looked up to find a gun pointed at her face over the driver's seat.

A woman, dressed in a cop's uniform, stared at her through the space between the two front bucket seats.

Maeve.

"Hello, Mrs. Kelly. You and I are going to take a little drive."

Chapter Seventeen

Panic rose up in her chest, a hard swell of adrenaline racing through her body. Maeve had found her. Not just found her, but also managed to outwit two highly trained officers.

"Where's Jason?"

"I left his body around the corner." The words were flat and cold and much too matter-of-fact as the woman extended her hand. "Cell phone. Now."

Ciara simply sat and stared at the woman, the sheer disbelief of the moment washing over her.

All the planning and preparation to keep her safe. All the various branches of law enforcement working to bring her down.

It had all been for nothing.

"Now!"

Maeve's face twisted into something dark and oh so disturbed, and Ciara fumbled for her purse. Her hand dug into the front of her purse, only to come in contact with two phones.

Two?

Of course!

With careful movements, she kept her face blank as she pulled her own phone out and handed it over, keeping the one issued by the marshals inside her bag. Her mind already whirled with what Aidan had told her about the special device issued to her.

She could record. The marshals tracked her with it. And there was a stealth device mode she could activate that could record and alert the team. It was that feature she wanted to use to send the distress signal and also keep them informed of what Maeve was up to.

Maeve was smug as she took the phone and turned off the tracking signal before turning back in the seat and putting the car into Drive. Ciara saw several people start running down the sidewalk toward Tom's prone body, but Maeve was off and down the street before anyone could stop them.

Ciara quietly tapped the various buttons on the screen, mindful to keep her gaze focused forward on Maeve. Although the woman was concentrating on driving, her eyes kept darting to Ciara in the rearview mirror.

"I knew I'd get you alone sooner or later."

Ciara glanced down, making a show of wiping at her eyes so she could tap a few of the apps on the phone. It was funny, she had to admit as she first hit the distress icon and then the icon to record—everything had set her off these past months, tears flowing freely from all she was going to straight through to a touching commercial.

But now, faced with the enemy she'd worried over for months?

All she felt was a keen sort of anger that began to bubble hotter and hotter.

They'd come so far, and in the next several minutes she could get the law enforcement community the information they needed to put this woman away for a very long time.

No, Ciara thought as she added her own heated stare into that mirror.

This wasn't a time for tears.

Nor was she going down without a fight.

"AIDAN, I'M FINE. Seriously," Deirdre groused from where she sat propped up in a hospital bed. "You're like a mother hen."

Although he appreciated his sister had enough of a bad mood to complain, he wasn't buying her dismissal of her symptoms for a minute. He'd seen the concern in the doctor's eyes as Deirdre's condition was relayed.

She was lucky.

Damn lucky.

"You took a major hit to the head from a rigged apartment door."

"I ducked," his sister muttered, even as a light blush suffused her cheeks.

She might have ducked—and he was glad of it, because the damage could have been far worse if she hadn't—but it didn't mean she'd gotten off scot-free.

Far from it.

Stitches on the top of her head and a serious concussion were the souvineers she'd walked out of Maeve O'Leary's place with.

Her phone went off, and he saw Micah's picture fill the face. "Go ahead and answer that. He must be out of his mind by now."

Aidan had left a message for Micah earlier, aware he was probably already out doing early-morning chores around the ranch. He'd left enough details that Micah would at least know what had happened if she didn't answer immediately, but Aidan headed out into the hall to provide some privacy as he heard his sister begin describing how she'd been injured.

Was this ever going to end?

The thought had haunted him on the rush over to the hospital. It had dogged him while he'd waited for Deirdre's doctor to come back to the waiting room to brief him. And it lingered with a harsh malaise now as he considered all they knew after the FBI raid.

Maeve was gone.

Again.

The woman was shockingly elusive, and none of them quite knew what to do with it. Obviously she'd had a long time to plot and plan, but this was an escape the likes of which he'd never experienced before in his career.

Various law enforcement teams, city, state and federal, were working this. And she was one woman. A person acting alone on each and every step.

Perhaps that was why she'd been successful, Aidan considered. She didn't have to take anyone else into consideration. Her personal safety and her own whims were the only things spurring her on.

Her madness was all that drove her any longer.

He knew Ciara was at her appointment, but he considered texting her when his phone began vibrating and lighting up, the app specific to his job blinking.

It could be Guy Sands or an incoming assignment, but the immediate transformation of his communication device suggested otherwise.

This was an emergency.

He opened the app with his fingerprint, shocked when he saw various alerts tied to Ciara.

Confirmation the tracking on her issued device was pinging.

And the stealth-mode activation that was recording her even now.

Clicking in, his blood ran cold with the details.

"I knew I'd get you alone sooner or later."

He'd heard minimal recordings of Maeve, but there was no one else it could be.

And then Ciara's voice registered through the recording app.

"You're not going to get away with this."

"Of course I am. Your precious guards are dead, your boyfriend doesn't know where you are and I'm not taking you that far. I'll be in the wind before anyone even realizes you're gone."

"You're mad."

"No, darling, I'm just very, very determined."

Aidan was already in motion, racing back into Deirdre's room. Even with the hazed look still filling her gaze, she was already waving him on, well aware his urgency had a purpose. "Go!"

He didn't wait any longer but ran, already dialing for backup from Sean. In moments he was in his car and heading determinedly in the direction of Maeve and Ciara.

He had to get there in time.

Missing them simply wasn't an option.

CIARA AVOIDED LOOKING at the phone, but she made sure she had the front pocket of her purse as open as possible to avoid any garbling of her conversation with Maeve.

"Where are you taking me?"

"Due time, darling. Due time."

"Then tell me something else. Why'd you kidnap my husband?"

"You mean your sugar daddy?" Maeve laughed, and regardless of her protests that she wasn't gripped by madness, Ciara knew better. The unsteadiness in her voice and the odd, rambling quality suggested otherwise.

"He was my husband and my friend."

"Come now, darling, you're talking to a woman who knows the real score. We need to take care of ourselves as we come up in the world. Humphrey Kelly was a means to an end for you, nothing more."

It pained her to hear it—Humphrey had been so dear to her—but as Ciara listened to the conviction in Maeve's voice, she recognized there was something there she could work with.

Aidan *would* come.

He had to.

That's why she had the phone and why they'd taught her how to use it for her protection. She had to keep that in the forefront of her mind or she'd go mad herself with worry.

In the meantime, perhaps she could use some of that madness to her advantage.

"You are right about that. A woman has to protect herself. Always."

The steely-eyed gaze that kept pinning her from the rearview mirror narrowed. "Yes, she does."

"Humphrey was my friend. He'd been in my life since I was small. Which made it all so easy there at the end to get his help." She added a light sniff to her voice. "You were the one who went and messed it all up for me. I was barely married."

"You, my dear, are the one who ruined my plans."

"Hardly."

Ciara hated what she was about to say, but all she could hope was she could explain it away later to the people who really mattered. Aidan. Deirdre. The rest of the Coltons.

They might not have been in love, but she did love Humphrey Kelly. She'd never disrespect him or ruin the reputation of such a good man.

But her child had to come first.

"I had just gotten him in my trap, and you went and ruined it all by kidnapping him. *I'm* the one who is the injured party here."

"You're a pathetic little problem and nothing more. You're the one who got in my way. He wasn't married when I first set my sights on him. It was only after I hatched the plan to get my son off on his charges that I realized Humphrey would do nicely as my next husband." That gaze returned to the mirror as Maeve came to a stop at the light. "You're the one who ruined all that."

Ciara wasn't quite sure how hard to push—especially since the words spilling from the woman's mouth were hardly rational or calm—but since she was being recorded, Ciara opted to go for broke.

"Why'd you bother helping your kid at all? He's a grown man, but instead he seems like an awful big dead weight."

"He's my baby!"

Something odd echoed beneath Maeve's tone, part longing and anguish, part frustrated dismissal, that had Ciara wanting desperately to lay her hand over her own stomach. Only she didn't dare—she didn't want to do anything to draw attention to her pregnancy. Even as the thought of how dark that mother-child relationship had become was perhaps the worst part of all of this.

Maeve had raised a child through the lens of her own twisted view of the world. Was it any surprise Wes Westmore had thought he could take whatever he wanted, regardless of the cost to anyone else?

"He's done nothing to act as if he's grateful for all you've done for him."

"Men and their impulses."

Ciara saw the lights down the stretch of the West Side Highway turning green and knew she needed to ramp this up. The faster Maeve got to the tunnel to New Jersey, the sooner they'd get to a destination.

The place that had to be her hidey-hole the cops hadn't found yet.

She was about to launch into a new line of questioning when the distinct peals of police sirens lit the air.

Ciara turned to look out the back window and saw several cars making their way up the highway behind them. Hope spilled through her even as terror began low in her gut.

Maeve wasn't going to lose. Which meant there was nothing to do but brace for whatever came next.

A reality that flooded her veins when Maeve put the SUV in Park, right there in the middle of the intersection, and turned from the front seat, that gun once again aimed for Ciara's heart.

AIDAN DROVE ALONGSIDE Maeve and Ciara, his lack of siren deliberate as he kept watch on the black SUV. He'd woven his way from the hospital, his eyes on the small dot on his phone that was Ciara, determined to cut them off if he could time it just right.

He'd put his siren light on as he navigated through the warren of streets, bulldozing his way through any cars that got in his way, but pulled it down once he turned onto the highway to track them up the west side of the city.

There was no way he could tip Maeve off to his presence.

But there was equally no way he could let them get to the tunnel entrance.

He ran scenarios in his head as he drove. How well strapped in Ciara was in the back seat in the event he needed to ram the vehicle. What side she was sitting on so he could minimize impact of a possible side collision. Even the risks if he hit at an angle that put the SUV in a tip-over situation.

One after the other, he ran them through his head, visualizing the impact and the risks, all while admitting time was running out and he'd have to make the choice if it was a matter of keeping them on the island.

"Aidan. You have eyes on them?" Sean barked out from the car's speakers, on Bluetooth the entire time Aidan had made the trip from the hospital.

"I'm next to them."

"We're behind you, and the copter's four blocks down. We're not letting them in the tunnel, but we have to minimize the risk to civilians. On-duty officers are stopping the traffic behind us, but we can't account for those near you."

Aidan recognized the risk. Ciara's life was infinitely precious to him, but there were hundreds of people in surrounding vehicles, equally precious to their loved ones.

"Got it." Aidan considered his moves, Maeve pacing a car length in front of him. "I can do a side impact, cut her off from the front driver's side."

"Do what you need. We'll be right behind you."

Aidan assessed the car, considering speed and angle. He desperately hoped he had it right, but as soon as the light changed, he moved.

And realized Maeve hadn't progressed through the intersection. He was already in motion, his actions decided, when he pulled hard right on the steering wheel, crashing into the front of the SUV.

CIARA STARED AT the gun, cradling her stomach and using her purse as a further shield. She had no idea what would happen to her, but the cops were coming. If she could keep the baby safe, they could save him or her.

They had to.

She had to have faith in the cops.

And then the car skidded and went sideways, Maeve's arm flying as she was jarred from her twisted position in the front seat.

The gun fired, the sound impossibly loud in the small space.

Was she hit? If so, why didn't anything hurt beyond that impossible ringing in her ears?

The thoughts were abstract and quickly dismissed as Ciara saw the large char mark spread into the ceiling where the shot had gone wild.

Still struggling with the noise and assimilating her senses, everything was suddenly in motion as the car was rocking, slamming on all sides before she distantly heard Aidan's voice—that sweet, precious voice—hollering through the front door as he dragged Maeve from the car.

The woman's screams echoed as she was bodily dragged out, but Ciara couldn't do anything but stare out her own window, the child locks in place keeping her inside.

And then Eva was there, helping her from the car and quickly shuttling her across the highway, the distant honking of horns spilling into the air.

Ciara abstractly saw Sean as well as about eight cops helping Aidan, but Eva was determinedly moving her across the highway.

And then Aidan's sweet cousin had her wrapped up tight in her arms. "You're okay. You're okay now."

Ciara leaned into the comfort and warmth and hugged that small frame back for all she was worth.

AIDAN WATCHED THE screaming banshee of a woman as she was escorted by two cops to the back of a police vehicle. The near-constant honking hadn't stopped, and the air was filled with it, along with the steady whirl of helicopter blades, both from the NYPD as well as the various news outlets hoping to get visuals of the action going down.

They got her.

Maeve O'Leary was in custody, and she was never getting out.

Aidan saw Eva across the highway, settled with Ciara on the sidewalk, before Sean came up and slapped him on the back. "We'll debrief later. Go to her."

Aidan didn't need to be told twice as he jogged his way through the traffic that would be moving shortly. Several uniforms were already setting up to get cars moving slowly around the wreckage.

"Aidan!" Ciara ran to him, and he wrapped her up in his arms, desperate just to feel her, safe and whole.

It chilled him to the bone, what she'd been through, and he couldn't stop the gushing waves of gratitude that kept swelling over him that she was safe.

That he'd gotten there in time.

That Maeve O'Leary was captured for good.

They stood there for long minutes, huddled together on the side of the road as the sounds of the city surrounded them, and Aidan fought the deep trembles that threatened to pull him under.

He'd left her.

After all he'd sworn to protect her and keep her safe, when it had really mattered, he'd left her.

That thought haunted him as they were given a police escort to Sean's precinct, the Ninety-Eighth.

It continued to beat in his breast after statements were taken and reports were written up and cross-jurisdictional teams ran through all that had happened.

But it was as he brought her to the Upper West Side apartment she'd shared with Humphrey that Aidan acknowledged the truth.

He'd failed her.

Chapter Eighteen

"Aidan?" Ciara stirred in the passenger seat, waking up out of the deep sleep that had claimed her the moment they'd begun moving after leaving Sean's precinct. "Where are we?"

"I brought you home."

"Home?" She heard the thick question in her sleep-infused voice before quickly recognizing the street. "You mean Humphrey's apartment."

"I mean your home."

Whatever she'd been expecting after this entire nightmare with Maeve was over, this wasn't it. But as she sensed what he was doing—the distance she'd already begun to feel while they were at the precinct—Ciara knew the truth.

"So this is it, then? Job's done and you're dropping me home?"

"I have to. The job is done, and you deserve to sleep in your own bed. I can see that your things are delivered first thing tomorrow. I can even have them run over tonight if you'd like."

"Aidan." When he continued to stare out the front windshield, she pressed harder. "Aidan!"

"Ciara. This is for the best. Come on, wait for me to come around and I'll walk you in."

She already had the SUV door open, her purse slung over her arm. "Don't bother. Threat's gone—I can get inside myself."

Even with her clothing and personal items still downtown in his house, she was happy to have her purse and her keys. She'd worry about the rest later.

The cops on scene had even retrieved her cell phone for her, and it was that memory that had her picking up the last piece. Dragging the marshals' phone from her bag, she tossed it toward him across the expanse between their seats. "Don't forget that."

"Ciara, wait. Can we talk? Can I explain?"

She stared down at the hand he'd laid on her arm to still her movements before meeting his gaze. She took the slightest satisfaction at the sheer misery stamped in his dark gaze, but she refused to give in to it too much.

"There's nothing to say. Not until you realize that you didn't fail me. You aren't at fault. And my life is better for having you in it."

"I didn't say anything."

"I know you, Aidan. The past week has ensured we know each other. And what I know is you decided a long time ago that a life, a real one with all the things your heart desires, can't be yours."

"Now you're a mind reader?"

"When it comes to you? Yeah. It's a skill a woman develops pretty quickly for the man she's in love with."

The sheer shock lining his features was enough to give her the time she needed.

To get out of the car.

To escape the embarrassment of her unrequited confession.

To get inside her building and up to her apartment so she could fall apart.

IT'S A SKILL a woman develops pretty quickly for the man she's in love with.

Those words had haunted him, in every single waking moment, for a week. Since he'd barely slept, that was a lot of moments, Aidan thought with no small measure of disgust.

"I'm ready to do this."

Guy's steady voice pulled Aidan out of his dismal thoughts as he turned to his witness.

"No more backing out?"

"Nope." Guy smiled. "I just needed to find my reason to do this. Now I have it."

He'd spent the time since Ciara's rescue focused on Guy Sands.

The first few days he'd focused on doing everything he could to convincet the man to come forward, only to find the real surprise was how ready the man was to commit to WitSec.

They'd spent the past three days prepping for the case. And, now, most important of all, Guy was ready to testify.

"I thought you had a reason when you made the whistle-blower call?" Aidan asked.

"No, man." Guy shook his head. "I needed a reason. And now I have it."

"What changed your mind?"

"I've spent the last five years missing the one woman who'd ever made me feel whole. I fouled things up badly when I ended it, and it's haunted me. But I decided, I owed it to her to apologize. To tell her that I regretted what I did. You know, so I'd said the words in the event I didn't make it out of this."

For all his unsteadiness up to now, it was a genuine surprise to see how calm and level Guy was with the decision.

"I'm glad you got that closure."

Guy grinned. "Hell, I got her back. Honesty and a whole lot of groveling did the trick. She's with me. Through it all, she's going to stand by me. She's even willing to go into Wit-Sec. Turns out that's all I needed.

"What about you? How are things going with that psychiatrist's widow? I heard about the chase downtown and that black widow woman getting put away."

"She was in my custody. Now she's safe from a threat and at home."

"But—" Guy's eyes narrowed as his mouth thinned into a straight line. "You messed it up."

"I told you. Job was done. She's safe."

Guy shook his head. "You're a piece of work, Colton. You're totally gone for the woman. That's obvious getting within twenty feet of you. Why are you being such an ass?"

"I'm not. I mean, it's better this—"

Guy nodded, his gaze softening. "Seriously, man, take it from someone who's been a serious ass for more than half a decade. Fix this. Make it right. You love her."

"Yeah, I do."

"Make it right."

HE AND GUY had spent the rest of the day working out his protection detail as well as getting his upcoming sessions with the DA's office set up. Through it all, he'd considered Guy's words, even though the man had avoided saying anything more on the subject of Ciara.

Make it right.

Those instructions kept him company as he drove uptown, as he nodded to the doorman in Ciara's lobby and as he took the elevator up to her.

He figured the doorman would have announced him, but it

was a surprise to see the door open when he got to her apartment. Peeking in the door, he called out her name. "Ciara!"

At the lack of an answer, he raced in, suddenly desperate to make sure she was okay. "Ciara!" He hollered her name as he progressed through the large apartment, dodging and weaving around packing boxes as he went.

Was she okay?

Was there something with the baby? Or worse, had Maeve somehow gotten to her from prison?

An endless litany of scenarios flew through his mind before he ran back to the living room after coming up empty-handed on his search. He already had his phone out, ready to call in support, when she walked back in the door, her hair pulled up in a messy topknot, an old T-shirt and sweatpants framing her small figure, even as they were a bit tight over her bump.

She'd never looked more beautiful.

"Ciara!"

Her eyes widened in startled surprise that someone was in her place, but she recovered quickly. "What are you doing here?"

He thought about Guy's advice and realized they were the exact words.

"I've come to be honest and to grovel. A whole lot."

He was heartened by the slight twitch he saw at the edge of her lips before her face set into firm lines. "Oh?"

"Yes." He moved closer, shoving his phone into his pocket. "But first, what's going on here?"

"I'm packing. I've put the place on the market, and I'm moving."

"Where?"

"Not entirely sure yet. I don't want to leave the city, but I can get a temporary place on campus in professors' quarters until I find something." She glanced around. "I don't have a whole lot to move. Much of this is going to charity or to support various organizations Humphrey favored. It's what he'd want."

"What about what you want?"

Her gaze stayed firm on his. "I know what I want, but it was suggested to me that I was never going to get it."

"Even if the person suggesting that was a total, unmitigated ass?"

"You don't say?"

"Please, Ciara. I was wrong. So incredibly wrong. And misguided. And stupid." He shook his head, sighing. "So unbearably stupid."

"That's all you've got?"

A small, lopsided smile was the last piece of encouragement he needed. He moved in close, thrilled by the baby bump between them. "I love you. I love your unborn child. And if you'll give me the chance, I will spend my life proving that to you both."

"What changed your mind?"

"You mean besides the whole 'being an ass' part?"

"Yeah."

"Our friend Guy Sands had a bit to do with it."

"Guy?"

"Turns out he's way more knowledgeable about matters of the heart them I gave him credit for. And he reminded me of something very important."

"What's that?" She stared up at him, wrapping her arms around his neck when she did.

"He told me to find my reason. And as soon as he said it, everything fell into place."

"Your reason?"

"My reason to be brave." He pressed a kiss to her forehead. "To get up in the morning." Then he pressed another to her jaw. "To share my life."

With that, he pressed his lips to hers, gratified when her arms tightened around his neck and her mouth opened beneath his. Long moments spun out between them, along with deep sighs and the warmest welcome home.

"I love you, Ciara. I want to make a life with you."

"I love you, too, Aidan. You're my reason, too. You and this baby. She's a girl, by the way."

A girl?

Images of small, perfect features filled his mind, and he couldn't deny the sheer, life-affirming power of the image.

"A baby girl?"

"Yes. And we're going to call her Marina, after my mother's love of the sea."

"Please, Ciara. Let's go make a life. You, me and, if you'll allow it, *our* daughter."

"Yes, Aidan. That's all I want. Let's go make a life." She nodded. "Together."

And as their lips met in another kiss, Aidan knew that's exactly what they would do.

Epilogue

"Club soda or milk, take your pick, sweetheart."

"Milk in a bar?" Ciara wrinkled her nose. "Club soda, please."

She watched Aidan cross through the throng of people in the cop bar near the Ninety-Eighth and couldn't help but smile at his broad shoulders and well-cut form, misguided drink questions aside.

Goodness, she loved this man.

"He's a little besotted." Orla's broad smile flashed brightly beside her before she leaned close, her voice dropping to a conspiratorial whisper. "And since I've got a very fine Colton also besotted with me, I know the look."

"I'm still getting used to it, but it's—" She stopped, searching for the exact right word. Because *mind-blowing, heart-pounding* or *swoon-inducing* didn't quite hit the mark. "It's incredible."

"And it gets better every day."

Aidan returned with her club soda and his beer, and Sean followed, two drafts in hand for him and Orla. As the men took their seats, Sean raised his glass high.

"To catching Maeve and putting her black widow ass behind bars forever."

"Hear, hear!" They all raised their glasses to that, clinking happily.

"And to Humphrey," Ciara said, lifting her glass once more. "He paid the biggest price but in the process gave all of us gifts beyond measure. I will be forever grateful."

"To Humphrey!" Aidan, Sean and Orla said in unison, their glasses going up once more.

Their happy cries were enough to draw attention, and Carmine and Eva wandered over, with Liam and Ellie and Cormac and Emily not far behind.

Ciara missed having Deirdre and Micah with them but was already looking forward to the trip she and Aidan would take in a few weeks to visit them. And she couldn't wait to spend time with little Derek. She was even more anxious to see Aidan with the boy and watch what she knew would be the same gentle calm and deep love he'd give to their own child.

Because whatever else her future held, she knew that Aidan was a part of it. They'd already spoken of marriage, and when she'd first suggested they wait until the baby arrived, he'd pushed to get married even sooner.

She glanced down at the small band of diamonds on her left hand, smiling inwardly at how impossible it was to deny the man anything. And even happier that she'd suggested they make it official with a small ceremony in Wyoming when they went out to see his sister. His and Deirdre's relationship had come so far, and it would mean everything to have her with them as she and Aidan started their life together.

They celebrated through a few more rounds of drinks and several highly delicious plates of fried appetizers before Carmine's attention shifted to the front door of the bar. "What's Captain Reeves doing here?"

Eva gave her fiancé a light smack on the shoulder. "This is a cop bar. The woman has more than proven herself worthy of a drink or two from time to time."

"She has in every way." Carmine snagged the same hand

Eva had used for the swat and lifted it to his lips for a kiss. "But she looks really serious. And definitely *not* in the mood for a relaxing drink."

Sean was already on his feet as Captain Reeves came up to their table. "I had a feeling I'd find you all here."

Greetings of "Captain" and "Hello" rose up around the table before the woman directed her attention at Sean.

"I'm not a woman who goes back on my word, but I have some bad news." Before anyone could ask, she barreled on, her no-nonsense attitude proof of why she held her esteemed position. "As I told you when it wrapped, you all did an outstanding job with the O'Leary case, but perhaps you did it a bit too well."

"Too well?" Sean moved next to her. "Maeve O'Leary's behind bars. Wes Westmore confessed on the stand that he killed Lana Brinkley. We even know how they smuggled Humphrey out of the courthouse."

"Yes, but all that press coverage has landed the black widow an admirer."

Aidan reached out and took Ciara's hand in his own. She took comfort from the warm feel of his fingers around hers, even as chills skittered up and down her spine.

A copycat?

Hadn't the city been through enough? Hadn't they all been through enough?

"What does that mean, exactly?" Ciara asked the captain. "I know the media has run with the story of a black widow killer, but so many of her deeds were known only to you. To the police. How could someone copy that?"

Reeves's face remained set in implacable lines. "As with most copycats, lack of information doesn't stop them from filling in the blanks."

"What happened?" Sean asked.

"A man was found shot to death in the Ramble in Central Park this morning. In reviewing the body and the crime scene, the officers on-site found a note in his pocket."

Those chills amped up, and Ciara tightened her hold on Aidan's hand. She loved the Ramble, the wooded area in Central Park one of her favorite places to walk on a pretty day.

Reeves handed Sean, Carmine and Eva photocopies, which Ciara could easily see were reprints of the note. But it was Sean's quiet reading that had their merriment fading away.

"'Until the brilliant and beautiful Maeve O'Leary is freed, I will continue to kill in her name. M down, A up next.'"

Aidan reached out and pulled her close, his arm firm around her shoulders. But despite the immediate comfort she took in having him close, Ciara couldn't help but react to the note's cryptic clues. "Aidan's name starts with an *A*. Is he up next? Is that what this threat all means?"

Captain Reeves remained stoic, but her face did soften as she acknowledged the immediate concern and leap of fear that had settled over their group. "The killer is currently suspected as male and going after men. That's the only connection to Maeve's MO, especially as it doesn't appear the victim has any connection to your family. But you all need to be careful. Hell, the whole damn city needs to be careful."

"And what about the precinct?" Sean asked. "We put Maeve in prison."

Colleen shook her head. "We have no sense that this is directed toward the Ninety-Eighth."

"Do we need to handle it, though? Is that why you're here?" Sean pressed his captain.

"Another precinct has the case, and the FBI's Behavioral Analysis team has already been called in." Reeves's command was evident, along with her compassion. "You all need to watch out for yourselves, but don't lose unnecessary sleep. I've already let both teams know we're here to help, but I also trust they've got the matter well in hand."

Although Ciara respected the woman's authority and experience, she was thrilled she and Aidan would get out of town for a bit with the trip to Wyoming.

A up next.

The mere thought had her stomach turning over on itself, and she wanted to be as far away from a potential threat as possible.

The captain made her farewells, and after she was gone, the photocopies were passed around before Sean sensed the mood of the table and requested them put away.

"Sean, you can't bury your head in the sand about this," Liam argued.

"I'm not burying anything." Sean's gaze roamed around the table to each of them before settling firmly on Ciara and Aidan. "But the Coltons take care of their own. We might not be on this case, but we'll be watching it and taking every precaution we need to. In the meantime, we have a closed case, and two criminals are spending a lifetime in jail. That's still something worth celebrating."

"To justice." Cormac raised his glass.

But it was Aidan who brought them all full circle. With their cheers still ringing in the air, he lifted his glass once more, his gaze following a similar path as his cousin's before coming to fully settle on Ciara.

"To family. Always!"

And when he sealed the toast with a deep, soul-searing kiss, Ciara knew that they'd face whatever came their way.

With family.

With each other.

With love.

Always.

* * * * *

COMING SOON!

We really hope you enjoyed reading this
book. If you're looking for more romance
be sure to head to the shops when
new books are available on

Thursday 6th
July

LET'S TALK

Romance

For exclusive extracts, competitions and special offers, find us online:

- **f** MillsandBoon
- **🐦** @MillsandBoon
- **📷** @MillsandBoonUK
- **♪** @MillsandBoonUK

Get in touch on 01413 063 232